# ABOUT THE AUTHOR

David Chadwick is an author, historian and award-winning journalist whose novels include *Tin Soldiers*, *Headload of Napalm*, and *Hot Metal Hobo* in his Nixon's America Trilogy. This was preceded by his debut novel *Liberty Bazaar* and *High Seas to Home*, an historical account of the Battle of the Atlantic. David has spent a forty-year career in the Media and uses his experiences reporting crime, politics and business to inform his fiction. He divides his time between homes in Greater Manchester and southern Spain.

# ALSO BY DAVID CHADWICK

**Novels**

*Liberty Bazaar*

The Nixon's America Trilogy:
*Tin Soldiers*
*Headload of Napalm*
*Hot Metal Hobo*

**Non-fiction**

*High Seas to Home – Daily Despatches from a Frigate at War*
(with Shirley Morgan and Allan Seabridge)

**Short stories**

*Panopticon* (edited with Nicky Harlow)
*Weird Love* (edited with Nicky Harlow)

# HOT
# METAL
# HOBO

DAVID CHADWICK

The manufacturer's authorised representative in the EU for product safety is
Authorised Rep Compliance Ltd, 71 Lower Baggot Street, Dublin D02 P593 Ireland
(www.arccompliance.com)

Matador
Unit E2 Airfield Business Park,
Harrison Road, Market Harborough,
Leicestershire. LE16 7UL
Tel: 0116 2792299
Email: books@troubador.co.uk
Web: www.troubador.co.uk/matador
Twitter: @matadorbooks

ISBN 978 1836281 597

British Library Cataloguing in Publication Data.
A catalogue record for this book is available from the British Library.

Printed and bound in Great Britain by 4edge Limited
Typeset in 11pt Minion Pro by Troubador Publishing Ltd, Leicester, UK

Matador is an imprint of Troubador Publishing Ltd

*For Chris Walder, my old friend, former boss and sometime hot metal hobo, who took a risk on me at a point in my career when most editors wouldn't have.*

# ONE

If Johnny Tedstone hadn't been so messed up that night, I might have paid attention sooner.

'My dad's gonna put a bullet through Keith Zetchik's brain,' he told me. But he was so juiced that it sounded like small talk. As if he'd said, 'My dad's gonna put a fishpond in the backyard.'

He chugged more beer. His face was slack and droopy, like it was sliding off his head. Yet his hand movements were manic and he couldn't stand still. Not for the first time, he'd gotten the balance of uppers and downers badly wrong.

'You hear me, Wat?'

I said, 'Yeah, Johnny, I hear you.'

I was a newspaper reporter and my crap-ometer was a finely tuned instrument. It had to be. I'd written off outrageous claims before, only to see them make the opposition's front page. Right now, though, my crap-ometer was showing batshit crazy with extreme prejudice. The fact that Johnny's dad and Keith Zetchik were Pentagon big-shots pushed it right off the scale. I liked Johnny. He was a colleague on my paper and a buddy of sorts. But, man, he was fucked up. And right now, he was really pissing me off.

'He's gonna do it tonight. Zetchik's a dead man already.' Johnny leaned forward, shouting in my ear as Joey Ramone grabbed the stage mike and belted out the lyrics to *Blitzkrieg Bop*. My buddy's slender frame was wrapped in a tight black T-shirt and leather pants, hitched at the waist with a belt made of bullet cartridges. Short bleached hair and wraparound shades completed the deal. Punk was starting to get hot in the summer of 1976, and Johnny was at the front end of it. When sober, he was a righteous rock critic, hip to the punk scene in New York, even London.

We were standing near one of the balcony bars at the Bayou in Georgetown. The place was jumping. It was one of the coolest music venues in DC and Johnny turning up with this junk-fuelled jive was the last thing I wanted. I must have been mad when I agreed to score tickets for the pair of us.

A guy with long feather-cut hair moved into a space near Johnny. He waited for a break between songs, then cupped his hands to his mouth and shouted, 'Play some Kiss!'

Johnny looked at the guy like he was a piece of shit.

But he ignored Johnny, waited out the next song, then repeated his demand.

Something in Johnny's head went spang and he turned on Feather-cut. 'The Ramones are a punk band, man. They write their own stuff. Why should they play someone else's?'

'Ain't as good as Kiss.' Feather-cut was as out of it as Johnny. 'I wanna hear some Kiss.'

Johnny poked his forefinger into Feather-cut's chest. 'Why don't you *Kiss* my ass?'

Feather-cut shoved Johnny away.

There was a drunken stand-off as the two guys weighed each other up. Then Johnny threw a punch. It was so slow and wide that Feather-cut hardly needed to move to avoid it. He retaliated with a half-assed jab that came nearer to me than Johnny. These two could have gone all night without laying a finger on one another.

But a bouncer across the room clocked the situation and start moving toward us.

Time to go. I grabbed Johnny by the arm and tugged him away from Feather-cut, then downstairs and out the front door.

The Bayou was at 3135 K Street NW, which ran under the riveted steel supports of Whitehurst Freeway. At night this gave the place a far-out subterranean vibe. A quarter moon hung over the Potomac River like a pale-bellied fish in a net of ragged cloud. On the opposite bank, lights still burned in the shiny new office blocks in Rosslyn, Virginia – spillover from the cramped corridors of downtown DC.

The late-June air was hot and humid, but at least it was fresh and that would help Johnny sober up some. He staggered to the kerb, puked into the gutter. And that, I hoped, would sober him up some more.

We wandered along the street.

I opened a pack of Camel cigarettes, took a smoke for myself and handed one to Johnny.

'My dad has one hell of a good reason for wanting Zetchik dead.' His speech was a little less slurred, a little less blasé.

This didn't mean I was any less angry with him. He'd totally wrecked the Ramones gig I'd been looking forward to for weeks. But I had nothing else to do, so I agreed to hear him out. 'What reason?'

He dipped the tip of his cigarette in the flame of my lighter. 'Zetchik is planning to wreck Dad's career.'

'How's that gonna work?'

'They're both one-star generals angling for the same two-star job. If Zetchik gets it, the first thing he'll do is fire my dad.'

I nodded. The Pentagon was much more of a shark tank for ambitious officers than the combat zone ever was. Operational command was about leadership qualities; staff work at the DoD, that was politics and statecraft.

'Killing someone to get ahead of them for a job is one hell of a drastic measure.'

Johnny looked out across the river, sucking in lungfuls of air and breathing out real slow. When he turned to back to me he seemed to have regained control of his face muscles and the out-of-place flippancy had vanished. Maybe the night air and the throwing up were doing him some good. 'My dad's a drastic guy. And he and Zetchik have history. Big buddies at West Point, then served as battalion commanders in the same brigade in Vietnam. Had a massive bust up some time after Little Tet in '68.'

'Your dad say why?'

'Refused to talk about it.'

'Vietnam wrecked a lot of friendships.' I knew it did. I saw it happen.

Johnny seemed to sense my reluctance to take him seriously. Next time he spoke his manner was more animated. 'When he's done with Zetchik, my dad's gonna come for *me*.'

I walked a few yards along K Street. 'Why would your old man do that?'

Johnny followed at my elbow. I detected an undercurrent of anxiety. 'Isn't that obvious?'

'Not really.'

'I'm gay.' He said this as if I was obtuse. 'I'm a disgrace to the dynasty. A stain on the family honour. But more than anything, I'm another obstacle standing between Dad and that promotion he's so desperate for.'

Johnny's dad, Joseph Tedstone, had gotten nicknamed Holy Joe in Vietnam on account of his outspoken conservative Christian opinions. I tried to imagine how he'd react to finding out his only son was gay. He might throw Johnny out of the family home. He might cut him out of the will. He might even see Johnny as a threat to his chances of copping that second star. Gay rights had made big strides in recent years, but not in the military. Some of the Pentagon's movers and shakers might look on a gay son as a black mark against the father. Some might go further and blame the father for the way the boy turned out. But, as with Johnny's claim about Keith Zetchik, homicide seemed a stretch and then some.

'You're way off beam, man,' I said. 'Your dad might be a lot of things, but he's not a murderer.'

He sucked on his cigarette and jetted the smoke through his nostrils. Now he was visibly agitated. 'The twisted old bastard hates me. Hated me since I was in junior high.'

We paused near the smokestack of Georgetown garbage incinerator, left to decay after they shut it down five years back. 'What makes you say that?'

'Made me take electroshock treatment. Said I had behaviour problems. Just because I was gay and didn't wanna play sports or join the fucking army.'

This wasn't as alarming as it might have sounded. When Johnny was a teenager in the sixties, a lot of middle class parents sent their kids for electroshock therapy – especially because shrinks were pushing it. Parents saw ECT as a cure, not a punishment. I knew something about psychiatry because I'd had shit of my own to deal with. Still did. And I knew something about being gay because my adoptive mom was a sister.

So I asked, 'How could your dad have known you were gay? Back then, I mean.'

'I didn't chase girls.'

I shrugged. 'Some teenagers develop later than others. It doesn't mean their parents think they're gay.'

'He knew, man.' Johnny was getting more and more worked up. 'He fucking knew.'

But I wasn't so sure Holy Joe *could* have known. Mainly because I wasn't so sure Johnny knew, even now. Sure, he liked people to think he was gay. He liked to dress in eye-catching gear, wear mascara, paint his fingernails. He liked to give out on gay rights. But that was as far as it went – and it could have gone much farther. The gay scene in DC was easy enough to get into. Take a walk around Dupont Circle, along 9th and 14th streets NW, you'd find gay bars and porno stores, bathhouses and hustlers. A new gay district was coming up in the area between South Capitol and 1st streets SE. Nightclubs, X-rated movie theatres, strip joints, the works. Yet Johnny hung out in the same places I did. He talked a lot about gay clubs but didn't seem to spend much time in them.

I wondered if he wanted to get his own back, shocking his dad, but not with electricity.

'I don't wanna go home tonight.' Now Johnny's voice was flat-out fraught. And he looked scared. 'Could I stay at your place?'

'Listen, pal, I think you need to get this into perspective and – '

My sentence got cut short by a voice from somewhere behind me. 'Ain't this cute!'

I looked over my shoulder. Three heavy guys were heading our way from the direction of 31st Street.

'Look what we got here: Pair of fags making out.'

Johnny's attention-grabbing garb had grabbed attention all right.

'Stay cool, fellas.' I held up the flat of my hand in a placatory gesture. 'No need for trouble.'

They came closer. The one doing the talking was a swarthy individual, six-three and maybe 220 pounds. He was wearing a plaid shirt with the sleeves rolled up, Alice Cooper tattoo on his forearm. The other two were fair haired with pale complexions, a little shorter and less stocky. They were decked out in wide-lapel jackets and bellbottom pants. They might have been brothers. One had a droopy moustache, the other was clean shaved. I put all three in their late twenties.

Blue Stratos aftershave and stale sweat invaded the space between us – maybe six feet.

I made a let's-be-sensible shrug. 'Why don't we save ourselves a whole lot of grief and just move on?'

'Fuck that.' Johnny pushed ahead of me and spoke directly to Alice Cooper. 'What if we are gay? What you gonna do about it, huh?'

'There's this place we like to put faggots.' Alice spit a gob of phlegm. It slapped on the sidewalk. 'It's called intensive care.'

Johnny wasn't cowed. Just the reverse. He leaned forward, poking a finger at Alice. 'You better back off, man. My pal here, he was Special Forces in Nam. He'll fuck you up real bad.'

I made a weary sigh. Tell that to a bunch like this, it's not a deterrent, it's an incentive.

They circled us, fists clenching and unclenching in the way of wild west gunfighters.

I made a quick assessment of the odds. These boys had been drinking, but they weren't drunk. They weren't in great shape, but looked solid and mean. And if serving in Vietnam taught me one thing, it was underestimating your opponent is the surest way to get beat.

Johnny tucked in behind me. I was pissed off with him for provoking these guys, but glad he was out of the way.

'Green Berets, red butts, that how it works?' Alice grinned. 'I don't think you're tough. I think you're a bunch of pansies.'

My tone stayed even. 'You really wanna find out?'

'I sure do.'

Alice came at me with a wild roundhouse punch. I tilted clear and let his big torso roll in front of me. I half-turned, jabbed my elbow into his kidney. He yowled, went down hard.

The fair-skinned brothers fanned out. The one with the droopy moustache took a quick look at what just happened to Alice and pulled a switchblade.

Kept my eyes on the knife. He wouldn't think twice about cutting me. He wouldn't think once. He didn't look like the thinking type. Which meant this could go bad in a whole lotta ways.

Droopy feinted left, slashed right. I blocked his knife-arm with my left forearm and slammed the heel of my right hand into his jaw. Head snapped sideways, legs buckled and he was out cold before he joined Alice on the sidewalk.

I wheeled round, expecting the third guy to attack. But he was backing off already, palms raised slightly to indicate that he was no longer a threat.

'You better get your buddies outta here.' I picked up the switchblade, retracted the business end, and tossed it in a garbage can. 'And don't come back.'

Over my shoulder, I said, 'We should check out too, Johnny.'

But Johnny had vanished.

# TWO

Next morning, I finished writing a six-inch short on a spate of muggings in Anacostia, ratcheted the copy paper from my typewriter and dropped it in the city desk basket.

This was my last story for the first edition so I went to the vending machine for a cup of coffee.

The package was on my desk when I returned. It was addressed in typed capital letters to WAT TYLER, CRIME REPORTER, WASHINGTON TRIBUNE.

Setting down my plastic coffee cup, I lifted the package a few inches to get some idea what might be inside. I gave it a gentle shake. Seemed to contain a solid, heavy object.

My curiosity escalated. I ripped open the brown paper wrapping and found myself looking at a regular cardboard shoebox. The lid was Scotch-taped down in four places. I used my pocket knife to cut it free. Inside the box were layers of old newspaper, balled up to form padding. The smell hit me first. Those years in Vietnam gave me a sharp nose for small arms lubricant. Cautious and focused now, I lifted away the balls of newsprint like an archaeologist removing rocks from a precious find. Slowly, barrel first, the Mauser C96 'broomhandle' pistol revealed itself.

My eyes were drawn to a note, about the size of a postcard. Like the address label, it had been typed in fuzzy-edged capital letters. It said: FIREARM USED IN THE HOMICIDE OF GENERAL KEITH ZETCHIK. Strange wording, I thought. It wouldn't have been out of place next to a museum exhibit.

Yammering typewriters and ringing phones faded to a murmur.

I thought about what Johnny told me last night. Seemed he'd extended his drunken rambling into a full-blown hoax.

I looked over at the features department where Johnny normally worked. But his desk was deserted. I talked to Terry Siebert, the features editor, who told me Johnny was on a day off.

I thought *Fuck you Johnny* and snatched up my phone. I dialled his home number. I expected to hear his smug voice, saying *Gotcha!* or something similar.

But the phone kept on ringing out and out and out.

I replaced the receiver. The package had been hand-delivered, which meant Johnny had brought it in personally or had a pal do the dirty work for him. Probably the latter.

I thought some more. I thought the unthinkable: What if Johnny really had been trying to tell me about a murder conspiracy? He'd been on a trip to outer space when he made those claims. But that didn't necessarily mean everything he said was bullshit. Maybe I should have listened better.

But I'd made a round of calls at the cop shops less than half an hour ago and nobody mentioned a homicide on the overnight sheets.

I took a closer look at the Mauser. The 1896 date stamp on the steel frame told me it was an 80-year-old relic. But it was clean and shiny, as if it had come straight from the factory. Like most German firearms, it combined elegant design with efficient engineering. Did it belong in a museum? Maybe. Could it blow a lethal hole in somebody? Damn straight it could.

I called the front desk and asked if anyone saw the person who left the package. Nobody did and I wasn't surprized.

My next task was to check out the claim on the note.

I picked up my phone and called Rhyme Dillard, head of the Metropolitan Police Department's Homicide Branch. He'd gotten the nickname because his first name was Willard. He was a tough black cop from South Philadelphia who didn't have a lot of time for me, or the *Tribune*, or reporters in general.

'This is my direct line.' He sounded indignant. 'How the hell did you get hold of it?'

I ignored his question. 'You know anything about a Pentagon bigshot named Keith Zetchik getting shot to death last night?'

I heard him catch his breath. In that surreal second I realized this was no hoax. Dillard said, 'How did you know about it? We're not ready to go public.'

Information on homicides was usually given to the press straight away – not least because the cops wanted the media to put out an appeal for witnesses. Clearly this wasn't a run-of-the-mill homicide.

'Why the delay? You think Zetchik's killing might be related to his work at the Defense Intelligence Agency?'

'No comment.'

'In that case, I guess it's no comment from me on how I know about Zetchik getting hit.'

The homicide chief made a raspy sigh. 'Don't mess with me Tyler.'

'Tell me what happened and I'll tell you what I know.'

I waited out another slow silence. I'd put Dillard on the spot and could imagine the Ping-Pong thoughts in his head. Should he take a risk and trust me? Or play safe and tell me to get lost? There was no bad blood between us, but I'd only been on the paper six months so there was no good blood either. He knew about my reputation, sure. But that could cut both ways.

At last he said, 'Zetchik took a bullet to the brain. Wee small hours. My people just got there. I was on my way over when I got your call. I thought it might have been … '

I almost heard him bite his tongue. I finished his sentence, 'Important?'

He came back at me fast. 'It better be, Tyler.'

I pressed my questions, 'Where did this happen?'

'His apartment. California and Phelps in Kalorama.'

'Any signs of a forced entry, a struggle?'

'Not that we know of.'

'So it was a professional hit, or he knew the killer.'

'You know I can't speculate.' He cleared his throat. 'Now, tell me what you got.'

'Have you recovered the bullet?'

'I'm losing my patience here, Tyler.'

'Was it a 7.63mm Mauser round?'

Dillard sounded pissed and astonished at the same time. 'How the fuck do you know that?'

I said, 'I think I'm looking at the gun that fired it.'

# THREE

I hung up with Dillard and hurried from the *Tribune* office at H Street and New York Avenue NW. Fifteen minutes later I parked my '68 Ford Maverick rustbucket outside the Tedstone place on Wyoming Avenue – less than 300 yards from the crime scene at Keith Zetchik's apartment.

All the way over the same question kept coming back at me: *Why hadn't I taken Johnny seriously?*

The house was a red brick mansion in the colonial style, shawled in ivy, with shuttered windows and a Doric-columned portico over the front door. On one side was the embassy of a mid-sized African nation; on the other, an international scientific institute. Kalorama was one of DC's most affluent neighbourhoods and absolutely not the type of place that kept Rhyme Dillard and his Homicide Branch boys busy.

I'd left the Mauser with Maggie Call, my city editor, and asked her to hand it over to Dillard. Maggie was unhappy because she wanted me to file a story, then give the gun to Dillard myself. Yet she wasn't half as unhappy as Dillard was gonna be because I'd ignored his instruction to wait for him at the *Tribune* office.

But I was worried about Johnny.

Zetchik's murder was exactly what he said would happen – and exactly what I ignored.

What was eating into my brain was Johnny's other prediction: *When he's done Zetchik, my dad's gonna come for me.*

I hadn't mentioned this to Maggie or Dillard. First I wanted to talk to Johnny, face to face – and sober.

A driveway ran along one side of the Tedstone house and I walked along it, looking for a discreet entrance.

A side door was unlocked. I went inside and found myself in a kitchen and dining area that could have functioned as a modest restaurant. I opened a door at the far end and entered a circular lobby. There was a parquet floor and double stairway curving up to a balustraded landing. Embassy-grade real estate, no argument there.

I shouted, 'Hello? Anybody home?'

My words echoed in the vaulted ceiling. No one answered.

I shouted again, louder.

Still no response.

I looked around the lobby.

To my right, a door had been left ajar. I looked inside a realized this was the living room. It was extensive and expensively decorated. Furniture looked old enough to have come from an antique store, yet so new it might have arrived fresh from the craftsman's workshop. Walls were lined with book cases and gilt-framed paintings. A pair of civil war-era cavalry sabres were hung, blades crossed, over the Victorian hearth.

Yet it was Johnny who grabbed my attention.

He was sitting in a wing-backed leather armchair, facing

away from the door at an angle. He was wearing the same trendy gear he had on at the Bayou. A heavy glass tumbler sat on the armrest. It contained two fingers of amber liquid. Looked a lot like whiskey. I went around the front of the chair. Johnny's gaze was glassy, his skin waxy. He wore an expression of complete indifference. He might have been a fashion store manikin.

You didn't need to be as familiar with death as I was to realize this was one trip Johnny was never coming back from.

# FOUR

Rhyme Dillard clicked his spring-loaded ball pen in a series of short bursts that sounded like a kid's toy machine-gun. He'd quit smoking and it seemed the pen clicking was some sort of replacement activity. He'd been doing it every few minutes for the last two hours. Right then, I wished he'd go back to cigarettes.

He said, 'Let's go through it again.'

First thing I did after I found Johnny was call Maggie on the city desk and tell her everything. Then I called Dillard and told him the same. And again after he brought me to Homicide Branch at MPD headquarters on Indiana Avenue NW. I wasn't under arrest, but it sure felt that way sitting in this interview room with its bolted down furniture and breathed-already air.

There was no use arguing with the homicide chief so I told him again.

He watched across the metal table, still making up his mind about me and my account of events.

I watched him back. They say black don't crack, but Rhyme Dillard did. His face was rutted and crumpled and saggy in a way that made him look fifty-five when he was probably forty-five. Eyes were hooded and miry. Broad mouth was downturned at the sides, like a catfish's, and his hair was ragged grey. The polyester blend suit clung to his overweight frame like he never took it off – not to sleep, shower, shave or screw. That last notion made me cringe. I stopped my train of thought right there.

When I was done talking, he loosened his tie even more and carried on making notes in a pocket book.

After a while I said, 'Look, Captain, I get that you have your questions, but I do too. I got a story to write.'

Dillard looked up from his notes. I sensed fast calculations behind those seen-it-all eyes.

'Okay, Tyler, this is how it's gonna work. I finish up with my questions. Then – if I'm satisfied you're not shitting me – I'll do what I can to answer yours.'

It was as good a deal as I was gonna get, so I nodded okay.

He said, 'I wouldn't have put you and Johnny Tedstone together as buddies.'

I took out a Camel from the pack of the table but didn't light it. 'What's your point, Captain?'

He shrugged. 'The kid was 24, old-money rich, Peace Movement activist, outspoken on gay rights. You're more than ten years older, you talk with a hillbilly accent, and – unlikely as it seems – you were a Special Forces captain in Vietnam. Medal of Honor winner to boot. You're opposites every which way.'

He was right about Johnny and me, but his reasoning was way off. I didn't stay in country all those years because I was a big patriot, or because I got off on industrial-scale slaughter. I stayed because doing dangerous work made me feel normal – or leastways what I imagined normal felt like.

And I left when I realized this whole idea was the diametric opposite of normal. But, of course, I couldn't say this to Dillard.

Instead I smiled and said, 'I get along with most folks. Johnny was no different.'

'He didn't get along with most folks though, did he? You said you had to leave the Bayou because he got into a fight over the music that was being played. Then he provoked those guys outside – and left you to deal with them. Word is, he'd start a scrap in a phone booth. Why was that?'

I made a what-do-I-know? expression. 'It's no secret that Johnny liked to be provocative. We weren't close friends, but I understand his mom died when he was in high school and he didn't get along so well with his dad. He told me more than once that he had an unhappy adolescence. He blamed his dad first and foremost, but also the establishment his old man represented.'

Dillard didn't look up from his note-taking. 'Can you expand on that?'

I placed the cigarette between my lips. 'A lot of the things Johnny got into were motivated by a compulsion to antagonize his dad and the older generation in general. Like the gay stuff and the peace movement. But I'm not anti-gay or anti-peace so that was never a problem for me.'

'You and Johnny go out on the town often?'

I lit my cigarette. 'The *Tribune's* staff is small, so as well as crime reporting I help out with music reviews. Johnny was already a critic when I arrived so, yeah, sometimes we went for a beer after work, and occasionally to rock concerts like the Ramones gig last night.'

'So why weren't either of you reviewing it?'

19

'It was my night off and Johnny had a fight with Terry Siebert, the features editor.'

Dillard's frown put a few extra furrows on his brow. 'Could that have affected Johnny's career prospects?'

'I doubt it. He and Terry never agreed on anything to do with music. And since that was all they ever talked about, they pretty much disagreed all the time. See, Johnny was a punk and Terry's into the progressive scene.'

Dillard looked at me like I said this in a foreign language.

'They're different types of rock music.'

He made a dismissive shrug. 'All sounds the same to me.'

I tried to help him out. 'Kinda like the difference between bebop and trad jazz.'

Dillard seemed just as baffled and I twigged that he didn't like jazz either, which was unusual for a brother of his generation living in the home town of Duke Ellington. Maybe Dillard was a classical type. Maybe he didn't like any kind of music.

He sniffed my cigarette smoke, clicked his pen some more. 'Those guys who attacked you outside the Bayou, you think they were locals?'

I thought about it. 'I'd say so.'

'Could they have been out to get Johnny Tedstone?'

I took a pull on my cigarette. 'It's possible he pissed them off in some bar on a previous occasion and they saw an opportunity to get their own back. But they didn't know him by name and they were in no fit state to go after him afterward. I can't imagine they had anything to do with what went down in Kalorama.'

He gave me a dubious look, but didn't press the point. 'And you have no clue where Johnny Tedstone might have gone to after the Bayou? He hadn't said anything earlier about going someplace else?'

'Nope. He was there one minute, gone the next.' I shrugged. 'It was strange behaviour, even by Johnny's standards, but I can't explain it.'

'Apart from him being under the influence of alcohol and narcotics?'

'Possibly. But he seemed to sober up a lot after we left the Bayou.'

Dillard opened a manila file folder and slid a passport-sized headshot across the table. It showed a good-looking young woman, probably late-twenties, with wide-spaced baby-blues, a rounded jawline and unruly tawny hair that spilled to her shoulders. A slightly flat nose made her look goofy, but in a cool sort of way.

'You know this girl?'

I shook my head no. 'Wish I did. Who is she?'

'We found this photo in Tedstone Junior's wallet. It was in his pocket when he died.'

'Johnny never talked about any girlfriends.'

He returned the picture to the file and I took the opportunity to start asking my own questions. 'You think Johnny died of a drink and drugs overdose?'

'Probably. We're still waiting on the autopsy report.'

I started making my own notes. 'How close are you to establishing whether the Mauser was used to kill Zetchik?'

'Close. Test results are expected soon.'

'Was the gun registered to Tedstone Senior?'

'Yes it was.'

'Is he a suspect?'

'Right now, he's a person of interest.'

'What about Johnny's allegations?'

'We're looking into the kid's claims. As you say, though, he was inebriated.'

'Does the general have an alibi?'

'Says he was at his sister's house in Lincoln Park at the material times. We're checking it out.'

'So the deaths of Zetchik and Johnny could be connected?'

'Too early to say.'

'But you're keeping an open mind?'

'Always.'

I smiled. That was good enough for my lead: DC's homicide chief was not ruling out a link.

Dillard leaned forward on his elbow. 'You know you can't publish anything about the kid's allegations? Tedstone Senior would shut down your paper.'

I stubbed out my cigarette. 'He couldn't stop us running the story. He could sue for libel afterward, but he wouldn't get a bean if what we printed was true.'

Dillard leaned closer still. 'Okay, Tyler, I'll square with you. Tedstone Senior is our prime suspect. But if you print his son's allegations, you show him our hand. You could enable the guy to get away with murdering your buddy. You wanna be responsible for that?'

I waggled my head from side to side as if I was considering the options – even though I'd already made up my mind. 'Okay, Captain, I'll play ball.'

'Good man.'

'But I want something in return. I wanna stay ahead of the *Post* and the *Star*.'

He shook his head. 'Sorry, no can do. MPD can't favour one paper over others.'

'I dig that. And it's fair enough. But what you can give me is direct access to you as the ranking homicide detective.'

He clicked his pen. Then he clicked it again. Then he said, 'Okay, deal.'

# FIVE

I filed my copy from a pay phone outside the cop shop. The piece wasn't as strong as I'd have liked, but my agreement with Dillard meant there'd soon be more. And in any case, Maggie wouldn't have exposed the *Tribune* to a libel action based on the highly defamatory and unsubstantiated claims of a dead son against his powerful pop.

I looked again at the opening paragraphs scribbled in my notebook and decided the piece would pass muster, leastways as a gambit:

> *A Pentagon general was slain at his DC apartment early today and the son of another senior DoD officer found dead at the family home 300 yards away.*
>
> *Homicide detectives are not ruling out a link between the deaths of Brig Gen Keith Zetchik, aged 50, and John Tedstone, 24, only son of Brig Gen Joseph Tedstone.*

I was sure there was a link. But without evidence, the story Johnny tried to give me was going nowhere. Maybe I could get something from Keith Zetchik's widow, Christine. Luckily for her, she wasn't at the apartment when he got shot.

Back at the *Tribune*, the archive clips told me she was a 39-year-old State Department diplomat who had been in Vietnam at the same time as her husband. There was a picture of the Zetchiks together at some lavish function. He was a tall man, barrel-chested, with a craggy face and high and tight haircut. The expression on his face suggested he'd be more at home in olive drabs than the dress blues he was wearing for the event. His wife was 11 years his junior, but could have passed as his daughter. Blonde hair was pinned up with wispy strands falling across a suntanned brow. Her features were even and her smile engaging. She looked chic in a black taffeta evening gown.

I called her at State but her secretary told me she was on leave. That wasn't surprising in the circumstances. I drove to the Kalorama apartment, but found it deserted. So I tried the phone book and got an address for the family home in Earlstown, a small community in rural Maryland. I took US-50 deep into the fertile heartland of the Old Line State. The drive took over an hour and I guessed the Zetchiks used the Washington apartment to avoid the weekday commute.

Earlstown was a picturesque place on Chesapeake Bay, comprising 650 souls, three churches, and a colonial courthouse. Vibe was privilege and old money. A sign near the courthouse stated that the local militia stopped the advance of the redcoats here during the Revolutionary War. Seemed they'd also stopped the advance of time. This could be 1940; with a little imagination, 1840. Houses were large timber frame bungalows with pale grey or burgundy walls. Lawns were smooth, driveways long. The most downmarket car I saw was a late-model Mercury. In the centre of the town was the Old Line Bank of Earlstown, an imposing brick and mortar building with fluted marble columns and a big old clock. Town of this size having its own bank said a lot more about it than its three churches and Seventeenth Century heritage. I guessed the population would be one hundred per cent Anglo Saxon. I was wrong there, though.

The Zetchik house was a grand two storey affair with pointy gable roof dormers and a porch with elaborate wrought iron stanchions. A mint green Porsche 911 was parked on the driveway next to a chocolate brown Cadillac Eldorado. I guessed Mrs Zetchik drove the Porsche and the big Caddy belonged to her late husband.

I pressed the bell push but there was no response. I went around the side of the house and found the back door open a few inches. Poking my head inside, I saw a kitchen that was comfortably as big as the Tedstones'. The place was immaculate – it might have been set up for a lifestyle magazine photo shoot. Except for the far corner. Porcelain shards were scattered on the floor, along with the shattered remains of a cafetière jug. Spilled coffee spattered the white cupboard doors.

Logic pointed to a domestic accident.

But the world wasn't always a logical place.

So I entered the place cautiously.

I paused near the sink, listened.

Nothing.

Something wasn't right though.

I saw the woman as I drew level with the breakfast counter. She was lying on her back, feet in the doorway, the rest of her in the hallway.

I went to red alert.

Maybe she had some medical condition. Maybe she'd passed out.

But all my instincts told me otherwise.

If there was an attacker, he was likely still in the house or very close.

Yet I couldn't hang back. If the woman was still alive, every second would be critical.

So I moved toward her.

She was wearing a floral pattern skirt and white blouse – very different from the taffeta ball gown, but I recognized Christine Zetchik instantly.

Except I didn't. The glowing, smiling face I recalled from the archive photo was now twisted in a dire rictus. Eyes were bulging and marbled red where capillaries had burst. A purple tongue thrust between bared teeth. I knelt down to get a closer look and saw a red ligature mark running horizontally around her neck. She'd been strangled from behind.

What to do? I'd stumbled across the scene of a very recent homicide and technically I was trespassing. That meant I'd be a suspect. Yet I couldn't walk away. Not with a killer at large. Calling the cops was my only option.

As I came to my feet, I sensed someone close behind.

Had to be the killer.

I didn't look around, didn't give any indication I knew he was there. I inhaled real slow, real deep. Then I pivoted from my hip, driving my elbow in a hard horizontal blow.

The attacker reacted fast. My elbow struck the back of his forearm. Sensing an incoming counter to the back of my neck, I ducked and swivelled and saw a karate chop skim over my head.

I completed my turn, raising one hand behind the other and –

Froze.

The Asian woman facing me had adopted a similar offensive/defensive stance.

For a few long seconds we pinned one another, locked in a weird stasis.

I looked into her face and in that tripped-out instant I saw someone I couldn't possibly be seeing.

'Who the hell are you?' Her accent was American.

I struggled for words. Not often you could say that about me. But the resemblance between her and the girl I'd known freaked me out. You could say that about me even less. Fuck, you could *never* say that about me. That was part of my problem.

I got my shit together though. I said, 'Who the hell are *you*?'

I was looking at a woman in her mid or late thirties. She pinned me through brown eyes that had a translucent, liquid quality. Her face was long, elegant, with smooth cheekbones and a broad mouth. Black hair was centre-parted and tied behind her ears. Looking at her pitched me back to the spring of 1971, to poppy fields in Vietnam's Central Highlands and girlie bars in Saigon's To Do Street. Quan Giang Linh had been just sixteen, but she was a precocious kid with astonishing street smarts.

Now, five years later, I might have been looking at her older sister.

She took a step backward and said, 'I asked first.'

I lowered my hands, pulled out my press card and held it out.

She came a little closer so she could read it. She was wearing tight jeans and a fitted shirt. This told me she wasn't packing heat or wearing a badge. Not a cop then. But something about her manner suggested she was hardened to this sort of scene.

I made a tight smile. 'Your turn.'

She opened her mouth to speak, but the guy came into the room before she could say anything. He had a Browning .45 automatic levelled at our chests.

# SIX

'This is a federal crime scene,' he said. 'And you just put yourselves in the frame.'

He was a fraction taller than me, maybe six-two, but much skinnier – less than 150 pounds. Long, thin legs joined forces with sandy hair and a pale complexion to give him a giraffe-like appearance. A corduroy jacket with a knitted tie and plaid shirt made me think college tutor rather than law enforcement.

The woman asked, 'You with the Bureau?'

Keeping the gun in his right hand, he flashed a Drug Enforcement Administration shield.

The woman nodded toward me. 'This guy didn't do it.'

The giraffe guy raised a ginger eyebrow. 'How do *you* know that?'

'I saw him arrive. Mrs Zetchik was already dead. Besides, he's a reporter.'

The eyebrow stayed raised. 'And how do I know *you* didn't kill her?'

'I need to talk to you in private.' There was quiet authority in her tone.

Dollars to dimes she was CIA.

Seemed the DEA guy thought so too. He motioned for her to approach him. 'Over here. Hands where I can see them.'

She moved across the kitchen until she was six feet from him. There was a whispered interchange. Then, with the gun still in his right hand, he used his left to pick up the phone on the counter. Cradling the receiver under his chin, he dialled a number.

The call got picked up fast and the DEA guy started talking quietly. I didn't catch all of it, but I got his name, Bobby Delacroix, and hers, Kim Lamb, before he hung up.

Lowering the gun, he turned to her. 'Okay, what you told me checks out. You can go.'

She glanced at the door, then at me. Something in that look provoked a feeling I didn't recognize. Someplace between regret and guilt and loss. Most of the time I welcomed new feelings because they made me feel more normal. I wasn't sure about this feeling, though. Not sure at all.

There was an edge of concern in her voice. 'What are you going to do about him?'

'That's not your concern. Now beat it.'

She gave me the briefest nod and left.

When the door closed DEA Agent Bobby Delacroix turned to me. He asked for my press card and I showed him. He asked me what I was doing here and I told him that too. Then he told me I was free to leave. He spoke in a laid-back way, like he really was a college tutor who just graded my paper and gave me a pass.

'You don't want a statement?'

He shrugged his sloping shoulders. 'What can you tell me that I don't already know?'

'Don't you people have procedures?'

'Sure we do. But we already had this house under surveillance. I saw you arrive, then I saw the girl arrive, so I knew all along you weren't the killers.'

I frowned. 'If you've been watching the place, how come *you* didn't see the killer?'

'Our stake-out team reported a disturbance. They weren't authorized to enter the property so they called me. I came as fast as I could.' He might have been explaining a math problem, or a rule of grammar.

'What interest does the DEA have in a State Department diplomat?'

'I can't tell you.'

'Are you aware that Christine Zetchik's husband was shot to death last night?'

'Of course I am.'

'And do you believe there could be a connection?'

'You know I can't comment on that either.'

Only angle this conversation was gonna get me was as another 'not ruling out a link'. I considered asking him about the Asian woman, but decided to keep quiet. No way he was gonna tell me if she was with the CIA.

So I accepted his invitation and split.

When I opened the front door I saw a middle-aged Hispanic woman in a maid outfit heading up the driveway toward me. House that big, husband and wife both working, it made sense to get help. She made a courteous nod and walked past me into the hallway.

It occurred to me that the maid would be a good source of information on both Keith and Christine Zetchik. Then I heard a wail go up from inside the house and I realized the maid just found out what had happened. Now was not a good time to approach her, but maybe I could come back later.

I found a payphone near the courthouse and filed my copy. Maggie was impressed. Sure the *Star* and the *Post* would find out soon enough about Christine Zetchik's murder. But they wouldn't get the inside story that we had.

Maggie made a bleak joke about me developing a knack for turning up at people's homes and finding them dead. She asked me to do her a favour and not call at her house any time soon. We laughed, but we both knew this was serious shit. A Pentagon general and his State Department wife had been murdered in less than 24 hours. A quarter mile from the first homicide, and within a few hours, the son of a second Pentagon general died in suspicious circumstances. There had to be a link. But with the DEA and CIA involved, my gut told me nothing about this was gonna be straightforward.

*

MACV-SOG sounded like a McDonald's experiment gone bad. It stood for Military Assistance Command, Vietnam – Studies and Observations Group. The second part had the ring of some stuffy academic undertaking. That was even farther from the truth. See, MACV-SOG was the Man's black ops outfit. And it was behind all sorts of shit, ranging from questionable to what most folks would consider out of the question. I knew this because I'd been on detached duty with SOG on a number of occasions. None of the stuff I did was gratifying, but the last was worst.

The look I got from Kim Lamb at the Zetchik house hauled it out of a dark hole in the back of my mind.

I thought of nothing else all the way back to DC. Part of me was cruising along US50 toward Chesapeake Bay.

*Another part is back in Saigon five years ago.*

*I'm walking into the girlie bar in To Do Street, where you can score a bottle of 33 Beer for 250 piasters or a shitload of maryjane for 2,000 or a number one fuck for not much more. I'm meeting my CIA liaison officer, Chuck Shaughnessy. Two days earlier, my Green Beret A Team and Bru strikers covertly photographed an ARVN colonel named Truc Van Thanh sealing a cash deal with poppy farmers in the highlands of Quang Nam Province. Most Green Berets get a security clearance of 'Secret', but SOG guys are allowed to work at 'Top Secret' level. This is why I was assigned to detached duty and packed off to Saigon the moment we returned to base.*

*My orders are to hook up with Shaughnessy as soon as I hit town. He's sitting in a smoky room at the back of the bar, a good-looking cat with a smart haircut and expensive suit. He explains that Colonel Thanh sources his raw material from the Central Highlands and ships it to a big refinery in Saigon. From there, he moves enormous quantities of 'weight' to the USA – in collusion with a number of unidentified senior Americans. My job is to recruit a female asset, infiltrate her into the colonel's household, extract intel on his activities, and bring them to an end. The name of my asset is Quan Quy Linh. Shaughnessy tells me her parents were tortured and killed on Thanh's orders the previous day, allegedly for collaborating with the Viet Cong. Linh has just completed her studies at a Roman Catholic boarding school in Saigon. She doesn't know about her mom and dad yet. I know the drill: Tell her the colonel was behind their murder, show her some gruesome photos Shaughnessy has no doubt taken, and explain how Uncle Sam can help her even the score.*

*The spook produces a newspaper clip of a want ad for a nanny. I presume it was for the colonel's kids. Shaughnessy tells me Thanh is a lecherous bastard who can't keep his dick in his pants. Getting hired will be a shoo-in for Linh.*

*Then he shows me a picture of her and I see why.*

*She looks into that camera lens with easy grace and a defiant gaze that totally nails me.*

It was the exact same look I saw on the face of Kim Lamb at the Zetchik house.

# SEVEN

It was late afternoon when I got back to the *Tribune* newsroom. I figured I'd make a round of calls, then finish up and grab a beer.

Maggie had something else planned. She usually sat at the city desk in the middle of the newsroom and I knew something was up when she asked me to step into her office along the hall.

She took a seat at her desk. I sat in a chair opposite.

Maggie was a solid sister and leading figure in the gay rights movement, though her attire was somewhat conservative – usually a dark pantsuit. She was aged 55, but her fine features and smooth skin made her look much younger. Short dark hair and a slim build gave her the look of a runner.

At last she said, 'You served with Hector Weschler in Vietnam, didn't you? What can you tell me about him?'

I gave her a puzzled look. Wasn't sure what I'd been expecting, but this wasn't it. Heck Weschler was a former three-star general who was running for president as an independent candidate against Gerald Ford, the Republican incumbent, and his Democratic challenger Jimmy Carter.

Weschler's campaign slogan was *Heck Yes!* Cheeseburger City, sure. Effective? Well, Heck Yes! The man from Kansas City was polling so strongly that both Ford and Carter were reportedly courting him with offers of a senior cabinet post – Secretary of State, Defense or National Security Advisor – if he pulled out of the presidential race and backed them.

I gathered my thoughts and told Maggie what I knew. 'He was a two-star in the fall of '69 when he hitched a ride with my A team on a recon mission. Said he wanted to eyeball Charlie up close, get first hand insight into what we were up against.'

Maggie smiled. 'You admired him for that?'

'I admired him for a lot of things. He was a different kind of brass.'

'How so?'

'He had salt, no argument there. But a heart too. And he was thoughtful. Out in the boonies, he ate and slept with my guys – officers and enlisteds, blacks, Hispanics – even our Bru strikers. One time we got caught up in a close-quarter firefight and he was right there in the thick of it. Like he was one of us. He gave a wounded Bru a morphine shot, stayed with him until our medic arrived.'

She tapped her pencil on some agency copy. 'Says here he's polling strongly among non-white voters. That seems to tie in with your experience.'

I nodded. 'He took the time to learn about the racial make-up of Vietnam. He was hip to the particular issues faced by the Bru and other minorities like the Nung and the Tay. He understood how these hill folk got persecuted by the South and Charlie just the same. To most brass, those guys were just dispensable CIDG fighters – that's Army-ese for

Civilian Irregular Defense Groups. To him, they were brave and reliable comrades with some godawful problems.'

'Sounds like he's going to get your vote.'

I shook my head. 'You know I don't vote. But you wanna know what was most righteous of all about Heck Weschler? He read poetry. Knew TS Eliot and Hart Crane better than me.'

Maggie smiled. She knew I was a soft touch for poetic types because poetry, like rock and roll, helped me to reconnect with my AWOL emotions.

Then she went and sprung the trap I just walked into. 'So how'd you like to work with him again?'

'As a reporter?'

'What else?'

'But I'm not a political correspondent. I'm not political at all.'

'That's what makes you ideal. Besides, you know the score on the *Ob*: We all muck in.'

'Does Neil Dickinson know about this?'

Neil Dickinson was the *Tribune's* chief White House correspondent. He covered election stories and he wouldn't be best pleased having me treading on his turf.

Maggie leaned forward, resting her elbows on the desk. 'Weschler specifically asked for you. He doesn't trust reporters, but he trusts you because you served together. If he doesn't get you, the deal's off. He'll go to the *Star* or the *Post*.'

She softened her tone and injected a note of reasonableness. 'Look, I'm not asking you to do Neil's job, or even cover the whole of Weschler's campaign. We're simply looking at a series of one-on-one interviews with the guy.

We're not going to endorse him and this isn't puff. Just the opposite – we want a warts-and-all picture of the man; what drives him; how Vietnam shaped his views; why he entered the political arena. He has a high-profile wife, too, who is heavily involved in his campaign. You could do a joint-interview with the man-and-wife team.'

She seemed to grow weary with the hard-sell and her voice went flat. 'Bottom line, Wat, we need this. *Really* need it.'

I couldn't argue there. The *Washington Star* was trying to compete with the *Post* by going down market. The owners of the *Tribune* planned to go lower still. But a tiny budget and limited staff meant we were pushing a big rock up a steep hill. We had cramped office space in the old *Washington Times* and *Herald* building at 13th and New York. The *Times* and *Herald* closed in 1949 after being bought out by the *Post* and the *Tribune's* owners thought this was a smart move – a newcomer preserving the journalistic ethos of the place. I thought it was like claiming squatter rights in someone else's grave. They got Maggie on the cheap because she wanted out of New York City, and they got me on the cheap because Maggie needed me and, well, I had no better offers.

'Truth be told, Wat, *you* need this too.'

She caught me off guard.

'Come again?'

'You could make a career here in DC, put down roots.'

'What makes you think I want to?'

'You know people are saying you can't stay the course in any one place? That you move on before you get found out? They're even calling you the hot metal hobo?'

I made a so-what? shrug. Those were the days of hot metal printing presses and I guess I was considered a hobo because I'd had five jobs in as many years on papers across the country. It wasn't about commitment, though, it was about stimulation, staying engaged. I liked the challenge of developing new sources, discovering new places. Sooner or later, though, I got bored and had to move on. It was the same with women.

'You need to show you can stay the course, Wat. For the sake of your career.'

I didn't agree. I'd broken some big national stories in those five years and anyone calling me a quitter or a hobo was probably jealous. But I didn't want a fight with Maggie. So I said, 'Okay, I'll do the Weschler job – but only on the condition that I keep the Tedstone/Zetchik story.'

'You're still our crime reporter. I wouldn't expect anything different.'

She gave me the tender-tough look that made me feel fifteen again. 'Look, Wat, I know Vietnam didn't affect you like a lot of people ... '

What she meant was that the Nasty never traumatized me because my mind was damaged long before I got there. I'd lived in the combat zone of domestic violence since before I could talk. Even so, Maggie had something to tell me and I knew from her manner that I probably didn't want to hear it.

'But?'

'But I think seven years over there has changed you in other ways. I think that's why you can't settle down. Maybe you should think about seeing the shrink again.'

'Not gonna happen, Maggie.'

'At least give it some thought. I'm only saying this because I'm concerned – '

'Don't be. I'm not a kid anymore, Maggie.'

'Then stop acting like one!' Her normally cool eyes flashed with anger.

She was the only person on the planet who could speak to me like this.

As my boss, I respected her more than any journalist I ever worked with. As my adoptive mom, I loved her deep, even if we fought sometimes. It was like this: My natural mom took me to New York City to escape my dad, a West Virginia coal miner who regarded wife-beating as rest and relaxation. But New York wasn't a good deal either. First place my mom went was Skid Alley.

I shrugged. 'I'm sorry, Maggie, but I really don't need help.'

She'd helped me when it really mattered though and I could never repay her. I'd been ducking school and running wild and Maggie couldn't have come into my life soon enough. She hauled me off the streets of Brooklyn when I was a sixteen-year-old delinquent with very little education and still less hope. She gave me a schooling of sorts, trained me as a reporter and eventually helped me get a staff job on the *New York Examiner*. She was the first person in my life I really mattered to – my first and only safe haven.

She fixed me with the skewering gaze I knew so well.

'I'm doing fine,' I said. 'Really.'

It wasn't a lie, but neither was it the whole truth.

*

When I got back to my desk I saw a note on my typewriter. Rhyme Dillard had called.

I dialled his direct line.

He didn't waste time on pleasantries. 'Ballistics results came back. The Mauser that came into your possession *was* used to kill Zetchik. We already knew it was registered to Joseph Tedstone. Only prints on the gun are his.'

I scribbled this down in shorthand.

Dillard wasn't done. 'Also, the medical examiner's report says Johnny Tedstone died of cyanide poisoning. We just executed a search warrant and found ampules of soluble cyanide kill pills in a locked drawer in Joseph Tedstone's desk. A lethal concentration was found in Tedstone Junior's body as well as the glass of whiskey he had with him.'

'Has Tedstone Senior been arrested?'

'We brought him in earlier this afternoon.'

'Did his alibi check out?'

'He spent the night at his sister's house in Lincoln Park, as he claimed. But he arrived after the Zetchik killing and the death of his son. We're treating this as a double homicide.'

'What about a triple homicide? You heard about Christine Zetchik?'

'Sure I did.'

'They gotta be connected.'

I could hear the plastic clicking of his ballpoint. 'We're talking to DEA and Anne Arundel County Sheriff's. I can't tell you any more than that – and you already have a damn sight more than the *Star* and the *Post*.'

I forgot about the after-work beer. I went back to my desk and wrote the lead story for tomorrow's front page. Some folks said journalism was literature in a hurry; others that it was a first rough draft of history. As far as I was concerned, getting the written word into print this fast, this sharp, gave me a jolt like no other. It put me in touch with myself, made me feel alive in a way that I imagined normal folks felt most days. But only for as long as it took me to write the piece, which was never long enough.

# EIGHT

I decided to walk to my place in Columbia Heights. It was a warm summer evening – around 70 degrees – and I needed the air. Whether I needed the hassle was another question. Back then DC's main red-light district was located in the blocks around 14th, H, and I streets NW. You'd see 25-cent peepshows and Jell-O wrestling joints; hookers on street corners; 'model studios' turning $120 tricks. There were strip shows, blue comedy clubs and X-rated movie theatres. It all went down in a neon microcosm on the *Tribune's* doorstep.

I hurried along H Street to 14th and went north.

I suspected I had a tail before I reached L Street. By the time I crossed Thomas Circle, I was sure of it.

My follower was a slender guy in a grey baseball cap, dark windbreaker and jeans. Seemed to be alone.

I stopped at a newsstand where a pack of Camels freed my wallet of 60 cents. Subtle glance over my shoulder told me my tail had also stopped and was browsing a window display. Fact that the store was closed and the display in darkness said it all.

Should I have been worried? I really wasn't sure.

Whoever was following me was obviously not making a

good job of disguising it. But that didn't mean he couldn't pull a gun or put a knife through my ribs. Come to think of it, making me aware of his presence could have been deliberate. Wanna intimidate somebody in these paranoid times, what better way?

I stayed at the newsstand, browsing a magazine rack by the counter and took a minute to put the situation into context. In the space of 24 hours I'd somehow gotten involved in three homicides, almost certainly linked. Ruthless and desperate people someplace not far from here would be making life-or-death decisions for reasons I couldn't even guess at. Maybe I knew stuff I didn't know I knew. Maybe some of these people wanted to get to me before I joined up the dots. Also, you need to understand that in 1976 DC was an angry, edgy place. The city hadn't recovered from the '68 riots following the assassination of Martin Luther King Jr and 14th Street had gotten hit harder than most. Vacant lots resembled punched-out teeth among the buildings left standing. Most were run-down, many burned-out. Muggers watched for victims and junkies mainlined heroine in dark abandoned spaces.

Maybe I could flip this to my advantage.

I saw my opportunity in a derelict drug store in the 1800 block. The windows were boarded up, but the door had been jimmied off its hinges and was left propped against the frame.

I ducked into the gloomy interior. It smelled of piss and damp concrete and maryjane. Sodium light from 14th Street revealed tangled steel rebar poking from shattered chunks of concrete, like blood vessels from severed limbs. Busted display shelves were covered in vermin shit and trash. Above the sales counter, I could just make out the slogan: *We're not happy if you're not happy.*

I looked around. I had the place to myself.

Pressing my back against the wall, I waited.

Soft footsteps on the sidewalk told me my tail was approaching. Then I heard sneakers crunching on broken glass as the guy stepped inside.

Slim frame moved slow, head craned forward as he tried to see where I'd gone.

I was standing right behind him, close enough to touch.

Whoever this dude was, his tradecraft was someplace between grossly incompetent and suicidal.

I tapped him lightly on the shoulder. He spun round and I grabbed his collar, shoving him hard against a boarded up window.

'Don't hurt me. Please!' The voice was shrill but I didn't immediately dig why.

I pulled the baseball cap off his head and long tawny hair spilled over narrow shoulders. The features were smooth, boy-like. The penny dropped. My tail was a girl.

Something familiar, too, about the wide-spaced eyes, the slightly flat nose, the rounded jaw.

This was the girl in the picture Dillard showed me. The girl whose picture he found on Johnny's body.

I injected a edge of menace into my voice. 'Who are you?'

'Reggie,' she said. 'Reggie Acheson.'

I frowned. 'You putting me on?'

She shook her head no. 'My name's Regina, but nobody calls me that.'

'Okay, Reggie, why are you tailing me?'

'I'm not.'

I strengthened my grip. I was in no mood for bullshit. 'I clocked you back at L Street.'

'I don't mean you any harm, really I don't.' Her well-to-do accent said she wasn't off the streets.

'So what's this about?'

Blank face.

'How do you know Johnny Tedstone?'

The mention of Johnny's name registered a hit. She sucked in a sharp breath.

'We were friends.'

'Was he your boyfriend?'

'Just my friend.'

'When was the last time you talked to Johnny?'

'Can't remember.'

Slowly at first, I started to piece this together.

'It was last night, wasn't it? Not long before he died.'

Reggie Acheson said nothing. She looked away and that told me a lot.

I said, 'You sent me the gun, didn't you?'

'What gun?'

'The one you left in a shoebox at the *Tribune* office.'

'I don't know what you're talking about.'

'Sure you don't.'

The silence played weird but I was cool with that. It suited my purposes better than hers.

Deep in the shadows of the wrecked store, something stirred the carpet of trash. Maybe it was the wind, maybe a rat. Didn't matter to me, though she was clearly spooked.

'Please let me go.' The tension in her voice scaled up.

I tightened my grip on her collar. 'When the cops found Johnny he had a picture of you in his wallet. Wanna tell me why he was carrying it?'

She shook her head no.

'Okay, you can tell it to the Homicide chief at MPD.'

'I don't wanna get involved with the cops.'

'Why not?'

She appeared to become aware of the dead-end she'd backed herself into and made an okay-you-win shrug. 'Johnny and I, we were close friends – soulmates you might say. We met at a smoke-in a few years back. We had a lot of stuff in common – army officer dads in particular. We talked things through. If I had a problem, I'd go to Johnny. If something, was bugging him, he'd come to me.'

'Like he did last night?'

She nodded yes. 'He called me at home, told me he'd just heard his dad on the phone with a guy called Zetchik – General Zetchik. Johnny said his dad left the house soon afterward, cursing and saying he was going to fix Zetchik once and for good.'

I frowned. 'Did Johnny say how his pop was planning to do this?'

She nodded. 'He said he heard his dad slamming around in his study. After he'd left the house, Johnny took a look and realized a handgun was missing from the display case.'

'What time was this?'

She took a few seconds to think. 'Around 11pm I guess.'

I let go of her collar but stayed close enough to catch her if she made a run for it.

'I tried to get Johnny to calm down. We talked about this and that and it seemed to be working. Johnny had a butterfly brain – it was never difficult to distract him. But then he cut across me. Told me he was looking through his bedroom window and could see his dad parking up on the driveway at the back of the house.'

'So when would that have been?'

'Dunno. We'd have been on the phone for about 15 minutes, so around 11.15, give or take.'

I studied her features. Hippie girl was twitchy. She was clearly in this way over her head. 'Then what happened?'

'Johnny said his dad was going into the garden with a flashlight and a bundle. Johnny was convinced this was the gun taken from the display case. He thought his dad was gonna hide it in the garden. Apparently his dad quit smoking years ago because of his mom's nagging. But he kept a secret stash of cigarettes in an old tree stump. Johnny knew about this because he stole those cigarettes when he was a teenager. He knew his dad could never nail him without blowing the deception.'

I made a one-sided smile. 'That sounds like Johnny.'

She appeared not to hear me. Now her words were coming in a torrent. 'He said his dad was heading for the house. He shared a lot of bad shit with me over the years, but I never heard him sound as scared as he did last night. He was freaked. I mean really, really freaked. Suddenly, he said he had to go. But he made me promise something first.'

She looked at me direct. 'He asked me to get the gun from that tree stump and give it to you. He said, 'Wat Tyler at the *Tribune* will know what to do.' Then he hung up. Those were the last words I heard from him.'

I gave her a moment. 'That what you did?'

She nodded. 'I went straight to the house. I live on 19th Street, a ten-minute walk away. Suppose I got there around 11.30. First thing I saw was General Tedstone driving away from the place in a hurry. He almost ran me down when he pulled out of the driveway. But he didn't even see me. I went to the side door, which was unlocked. I found Johnny in the living room. He was dead. I was certain of it. Dunno how I could be so certain, I just was. No signs of violence. Just sitting there with a glass of whiskey at his side. I didn't know what to do. I wasn't scared or panicky, but I remember thinking I should've been. It was as if it was happening to somebody else.'

What she said rang true. I'd known grunts in Vietnam go beyond fear. The more desperate the situation, the more detached they became.

I tried to encourage her. 'You did well – a lot of people would have totally lost it.'

She gave me a searching look. 'Part of me said call 911, another part told me to do what I promised Johnny. I knew nothing would bring him back, and I knew General Tedstone might return any minute and maybe dispose of the gun for good. So I got a flashlight from the kitchen, went into the garden and found the tree stump. There was a hollow right where Johnny described. Inside it, I found the gun wrapped in soft leather cloth.'

At that point she ran out of words.

'You took the gun home, parcelled it up, and brought it into the *Tribune* first thing this morning?'

She didn't need to answer.

'Why the secrecy? You're a witness to Johnny's murder. You gotta give a statement to the cops. When you've explained what happened, they'll understand.'

She looked at me like I was crazy. 'So Johnny's dad can come after *me*?'

'He's been arrested. And anyways, the cops will protect you.'

'He'll get bail. Then he'll get the charges dropped. Then

he'll kill me.' Her tone was calm, but in a worryingly flat sort of way. 'You have no idea what sort of power the guy wields, what he's prepared to do. Johnny told me all about Holy Joe. Some of it I didn't believe. I do now.'

She looked over my shoulder, as if she'd seen something. Without thinking I followed her gaze, peering into the gloom.

Realized I'd gotten suckered way too late.

She dodged past me and headed for the doorway.

'Wait, just a minute – '

But she shot through the empty doorframe and was out on the street.

I could have chased her, but something held me back. An upper class radical like Reggie Acheson would be easy enough to find in DC. Besides, my gut said she'd have a whole lot more to say about Holy Joe Tedstone when she got her head right. I made a bet with myself that she'd come looking for me before I needed to look for her.

# NINE

I never knew anyone who looked more like Hollywood's idea of a soldier than Heck Weschler. Entrenched eyes, blade-thin nose and breech block jaw were mounted on a neck of dense-weave muscle. You got the impression that if you cut him he'd bleed camouflage pattern blood. The flat-top buzz cut was still there, although his fair hair had turned grey around the temples.

He met me on his doorstep and extended a hand. 'Been too long, Wat. Good to see you.'

'And you, General. Gotta say, you're looking good.'

I wasn't being glib. Weschler was 55 but looked ten years younger. His six foot two frame was honed without being pumped. He seemed at ease in a dark business suit, white shirt and maroon tie. For a veteran of World War II, Korea and Vietnam, he was one cool cat – JFK with a bench press and Kansas accent.

The parallel extended to his wife, Paula, whose old-money background and righteous good looks had drawn comparisons with Jacqueline Kennedy. Like the former first lady, Paula Weschler was a significant crowd-puller and a major asset for TV ads. She was waiting in the hall, laid back yet elegant with auburn hair and a willowy figure. At 46, she didn't look much older than me at 33.

She welcomed me to the family home and explained that she was on her way out, but hoped to see me later. I got the impression this brief introduction had been planned – after all, she was a crucial part of Weschler's presidential pitch. Even so, she handled the situation without a hint of awkwardness.

He showed me to his private office, a modest room at the back of the house with a desk, file cabinets and walls covered in maps, graphs and tables. A bookcase contained works by poets from John Milton to Sylvia Plath. One shelf was reserved for three framed photos. They showed Weschler with Paula and their two young daughters; Weschler with Creighton Abrams, the US military commander in Vietnam from '68 to '72; and Weschler with Len Dawson, Kansas City Chiefs quarterback and hero of their historic Super Bowl victory over Minnesota Vikings in 1970.

We sat in two armchairs separated by a coffee table.

'Drink?' He picked up a bottle of Scotch and poured generous measures into two glass tumblers.

This was a little early for me, but saying no didn't seem to be an option.

'Old Orcadian single malt.' He sipped the whiskey and smiled. 'Distilled in the Orkney islands in Scotland, where my mom's family is from.'

I swallowed a mouthful. 'Nice stuff.'

He sat back, nestling his Scotch, looking me in the eyes. 'What do you think of this place?'

He was referring to his mock-Tudor house overlooking Mark Twain Park in Alexandria, a couple of miles outside the

Old Town and a half mile south of the Beltway. It was hardly a hovel, but neither was it an Embassy Row mansion like the Tedstone place.

'Impressive,' I said. 'But not too impressive. And I bet my boots you didn't end up here by accident. You don't do anything by accident.'

He chuckled. 'You know me too well, Wat. But yes, it was a tactical choice. Not just the house, but also the location.'

I took out my Camels and lit one. 'How so?'

He shrugged. 'It's making a statement. Like: *I'm close to the Establishment and I understand it, but I'm sure as hell not owned by it.* Folks know my real home is in Kansas City and that I'm here because I need a presence in DC. But they get that I'm not here to cosy up to the Beltway barons. Interstate 495 marks the edge of their fiefdom. That's why I live outside it.'

'Can I quote you on that?'

'That's why I said it.'

This was smart politicking. He'd played me, but respectfully, and in a way that gave me something solid in return. No doubt it was qualities like this that made Gerald Ford and Jimmy Carter want this dude on their teams.

We drained our Scotch glasses and got stuck into the interview proper. We discussed why he went into politics, the changes he wanted to see, his chances of winning the presidential race. He gave me a lot of good stuff. Vibe I got was a man who had gone on a journey and learned from it all the way from Monte Cassino to the Tet Offensive. He gave out like a firm Republican, strong on defence and the economy, yet with clear liberal sympathies for big issues, especially equality and welfare. *No one left behind* was a phrase he repeated. It was a motto more associated with the

Marines than the Army, but there was no hint of hokeyness. Without doubt, though, his strongest appeal was being an outsider. I started to see why living outside the Beltway was so important to him.

When we were done I accepted Weschler's offer of another Scotch. 'Mind if I ask you about something completely unrelated, General?'

He sipped his whiskey. 'Sure you can ask. Whether I can answer is another matter.'

'You saw the newspaper stories about Joseph Tedstone getting arrested for the murder of his son and Keith Zetchik?'

'I could hardly have missed them. Mostly with your name at the top.' There was a wariness in his tone.

'I understand Tedstone and Zetchik were light colonels under your command from '63 to '69.'

He looked at me hard, said nothing. He could guess where this was leading.

'I'm looking for background. What sort of guys they were, back in the day. Also, Johnny Tedstone told me there was a bust-up between them after Little Tet. I'd be very interested in any light you could shed on what happened.'

He leaned forward and slowly placed his whiskey glass on the table.

'I'm running for president, Wat. I can't afford to get involved in an ongoing homicide investigation.'

I set my glass on the table beside his. 'Anything you say would be strictly off the record, absolutely non-attributable. You'd have my word that nothing would or could be traced back to you.'

He made a give-me-a-break expression. 'Gotta say you put me in a difficult position.'

'Sorry about that, General. But I wouldn't ask if this wasn't important.'

'Okay, tell me what you know. Then I'll tell you if I can help.'

I gave him the nub of events on Thursday night and yesterday morning.

He pursed his lips. 'What's *your* assessment of Joe Tedstone's position?'

'Precarious. The evidence suggests he killed his son and Keith Zetchik. And he has no alibi.'

Weschler made a pained expression. 'I find it hard to believe that Joe could do those things. He wasn't the fire-and-brimstone bible-basher that a lot of people made out. He was a deeply moral man. He considered all human life to be God-given, despite – and even because of – the fact that thousands of folks were getting killed every day. Also, Joe wasn't ambitious. He wanted to get ahead, sure, but not in the Machiavellian way this version of events indicates.'

'So the evidence is misleading – or the cops aren't seeing something?'

He spread his hands, palms upward. 'It beggars belief that a general officer with Joe's religious convictions would get his hands dirty blatantly murdering a promotion rival, then poison his own son in the family home, all on the same night.'

'Unless beggaring belief was the whole idea.' I wanted to say more, but I left it at that.

What bothered me was that if Joseph Tedstone wasn't ambitious, why had he gone up against Zetchik for the same high level job at the Pentagon? As for being capable of killing, until five years ago Joseph Tedstone commanded a combat unit in one of the most savage and long-running wars in human history. That meant he could easily have killed Zetchik, his near-neighbour and friend-turned-foe. Besides, if Joseph Tedstone *had* hired a hit man to avoid getting his hands dirty, that would potentially expose him to blackmail, or the killer getting caught and turning state's evidence. As for Johnny, he foretold his own death – and I hadn't taken him seriously.

But I decided to take a different tack. 'Then there's the murder of Christine Zetchik. I can't believe that's unconnected. And nobody can explain the appearance of the DEA guy Bobby Delacroix or this woman Kim Lamb, who I'm sure is from Vietnam.'

Weschler made a deep sigh. He said he'd known Christine Zetchik and was saddened by her death, but couldn't imagine how her murder could be linked to her husband's, or Johnny Tedstone's. And he'd never heard of either Bobby Delacroix or Kim Lamb.

I said, 'I'm pretty certain she's CIA.'

He ran his fingers real slow through his stiff silver hair, as if he was combing out stubborn thoughts. 'Very well, Wat, here's a proposition for you. Dig a little deeper into the possibility that Joe got framed – and make sure he gets fair and balanced coverage. In return, I'll tell you what I know about him and Keith Zetchik. I'll also make some calls and find out what I can about this guy Delacroix and the woman you think may be a spook.'

I considered the deal I was being offered: Extra, and possibly classified information in exchange for doing my job in the way I would have done it anyway. Taking a closer look at Joseph Tedstone's story was part of a thoroughly researched story. And writing fair and balanced copy was nothing more or less than a professional obligation. Besides, if Tedstone was the patsy in some high level conspiracy, my story would be even stronger.

This made me wonder why Weschler was offering a deal that wasn't a deal. Maybe he wasn't as media-savvy as a contender for the country's top job needed to be. Or maybe it was me who was missing something.

But I had nothing to lose and a lot to gain, so I said, 'You got a deal, General.'

He came to his feet and walked to his desk, standing with his back to me. For a few stretched-out seconds, he said nothing. It seemed whatever he had to say wasn't gonna come easy.

# TEN

At last he turned to face me and started talking. 'Okay, here's what I know about Joe and Zet. They came from similar old money backgrounds and became firm friends at West Point, then served together as lieutenants in the same infantry company in Korea. Zet went to it like a Pitbull; Joe was more considered but equally effective. Both made captain in short order and were majors in '53 when the Korean War ended.'

Weschler parked his ass on the corner of his desk. He seemed more relaxed now that he'd gotten into his stride. 'Ten years on, both were light colonels commanding infantry battalions in the same brigade, which happened to be mine. In those early years everything was hunky-dory. The three of us were solid friends. We socialized. Went to dinner parties, social functions, family events, and it helped that our wives got along too.'

He went to a sideboard and brought out a leather-bound photo album, which he handed to me. 'Take a look for yourself.'

I flipped through the opening pages and saw images of Weschler, Tedstone and Zetchik and their wives on sunny days by the pool, and on sparkling evenings at upmarket restaurants. They all looked happy, carefree, full of zest.

'You guys knew how to have a good time,' I said. 'But I'm guessing something happened.'

He made a sober expression. 'Vietnam happened. At first, everything was fine. We continued to work well together. Same team, different location.'

I turned a few pages of the photo album and Fort Stewart morphed into Saigon. The most noticeable difference was the absence of the wives, and I wondered if this had something to do with the deterioration of relations between Tedstone and Zetchik. They seemed pally enough though – there was even a shot of them horsing around in the ocean, with Zetchik giving Tedstone a piggyback ride in the surf while Weschler looked on, slightly abashed.

'But it didn't last.' Weschler's voice sounded heavy with sour memories. 'As the war went on, Joe's and Zet's views on how it should be fought went in opposite directions Zet's unit took heavy casualties in the fall of '66 after bad intel led them into an ambush. He caught a chunk of shrapnel in his shoulder during the worst of the fighting and was never quite the same after that. Joe was talking to God more than ever. Few weeks after Zet got wounded, Joe had a religious experience after a bullet missed him by inches and killed his radio operator. He was never quite the same either.'

Weschler returned to the armchair and picked up his whiskey tumbler. 'There'd always been differences of opinion between them, but this turned to friction, then downright animosity. It all came to a head after Little Tet when Zet's battalion went in hard and racked up the body count. Joe did the opposite. He put the emphasis on engaging with hamlet chiefs, winning hearts and minds. By getting support from local communities, he restricted Charlie's room for manoeuvre and forced a VC withdrawal with minimum American casualties. Joe's tactics were sound, but Zet didn't see it that way. He accused Joe of going soft on Charlie, of failing to support Zet's boys when they were getting mauled. After that it was tit-for-tat. Joe hit back, calling Zet a dangerous hothead and worse.'

I turned more pages of the album and both Tedstone and Zetchik seemed to have been leeched of their earlier exuberance. Their expressions seemed wooden, smiles phoney, postures stiff. Toward the end of the album, the pictures were formal and ceremonial shots only. And Weschler was always jammed between the other two, as if they couldn't bear to stand next to one another.

I looked up from the photos. 'Must have been tough managing that sort of situation.'

He made a rueful expression. 'It was the most shit ever. Worse still was the officers and men from both battalions were getting sucked in. As you know, a little rivalry between units can be healthy, but this was nasty. Early in '69 I came to the conclusion that it was intolerable. One way or another, I needed to stop it.'

He knocked back the rest of his whiskey. 'I tried to play peacemaker. I got them over to dinner at brigade HQ, just the three of us. But it didn't work. We sat there for two hours, barely said a word. And the biggest irony of all was that both their methods succeeded. A few weeks after that dreadful dinner, their battalions received Presidential Unit Citations. I got my second star and they were boosted to bird colonels. By '71, they were brigadier generals and when the war ended they both ended up at the Pentagon.'

I placed the album on the table in front of me. 'And despite all that bad blood, you still can't imagine Tedstone offing Zetchik?'

He made a wan smile. 'No I can't. I *could* imagine Zet offing Joe, but of course that isn't what happened.'

We wrapped it up at that and I arranged for a photographer to call round later that afternoon to get some shots of Weschler at home. We'd meet again for another interview the following week.

As I was headed through the front door he said, 'See much of Leaping Larry?'

He was referring to Laurence Westerby, a general my unit rescued after his plane went down deep in Charlie territory. Westerby liked the way I worked and got me my field commission – plus a whole lot of black ops, grey ops and crazy-as-a-loon ops. He got called Leaping Larry on account of his enthusiasm for engaging Charlie to the max at every opportunity. He wasn't doing much leaping from behind his Pentagon desk these days, but he was three-star brass and widely tipped for the next vice chief of staff.

I said, 'We live less than a mile apart, but I saw more of him before I came to DC.'

This wasn't a lie, although when I did see Westerby it was often in secret and usually involved off-the-books work. Like reporting for a daily newspaper, it helped me connect with feelings stifled since infancy. Problem was I'd gotten addicted to life in Charlie's crosshairs and doing ad hoc jobs for Westerby was my way of avoiding cold turkey. Whichever way you looked at it, though, putting yourself in harm's way as therapy was just not rational. But this was a truth I wasn't ready for – and why I rejected Maggie's advice to see the shrink.

Weschler walked me down his driveway to the street where I was parked. 'Well, give him my regards if you do meet up any time soon.'

We shook hands and I climbed into my car. As I drove away I watched him in my rearview mirror standing at the end of his driveway. Something in the way he asked me about Westerby made me think he knew more than he should.

I took the Beltway then US-1 back into town.

I thought about Westerby and MACV-SOG. And Weschler's offer to make some calls regarding Kim Lamb. I thought about Quan Quy Linh, my sixteen-year-old agent, who might have been her younger sister.

On one level I was driving through Alexandria.

*On another I'm back in Saigon in 1971. I'm meeting Linh in the little presbytery on Cong Ly. The French priest who lives here allows the CIA to use it as a safe house and my liaison guy Chuck Shaughnessy assures me it isn't on Charlie's radar.*

*Linh comes into the room wearing a blue silk ao dai and white baggy pants. Her slender frame makes her seem even younger than sixteen.*

*I ask her if she's sure she's okay about this? I'm damn well not.*

*She sits opposite me on a wicker couch. 'Of course I am,' she says.*

*I don't share her confidence. After a crash course in tradecraft I'm about to send her to be interviewed by Colonel Truc Van Thanh and his wife for the position of live-in nanny that Shaughnessy spotted in a want ad.*

*'You read the brief?'*

*'Thoroughly. I know Thanh inside out and back to front.' She speaks good English with a French accent.*

'Knowing that stuff is one thing. Passing yourself off as somebody you're not is something else.'

'I'm completely familiar with my cover story.' She makes an assured expression. 'Test me if you want. Again.'

It's too late for that. It's also too late for me to develop qualms about deploying a juvenile asset in a high risk operation. I remind myself that I'd gotten involved in equally serious shit in Brooklyn when I was sixteen. But that was a whole other scene. And thinking about it makes me more concerned, not less. Truth is I'm sending a naïve kid up against one of the most ruthless power-brokers in Vietnam. I want to protect her in the way somebody should have protected me when I was her age. But I can't.

I keep my tone stern. 'Just be careful. Don't take any unnecessary risks. You need to get the colonel to like you, but you also need Madame to like you.'

As Shaughnessy predicted, Linh had been easy to recruit. When I told her what happened to her parents on Thanh's orders, she showed zero emotion. As if she hadn't heard me, or was refusing to listen. Then I produced the photos Shaughnessy took of their bodies and she freaked. Couldn't blame her, but I sure blamed myself. She went away and came back the next day. By then she was totally together – disturbingly together. She already knew about Thanh's racketeering activities so wasn't surprised to hear about his heroin exporting enterprise. She said there was nothing she wouldn't do to nail the bastard. And despite her lack of proper training, I had to admit she was a natural, even at her age.

So I watch her go off to her interview at Thanh's mansion on Hong Thap Tu and wait in the presbytery with a pack of Camels and a quarter pint of bourbon.

*I'm ten smokes into the Camels and half way through the whiskey when she comes back.*

*'I got it.' She's clearly elated, as if she's gotten a real job – one that won't put her life at risk.*

*'That's great,' I say. 'You did well.'*

*But I can't look at her. I can't show her I'm not pleased.*

# ELEVEN

Reggie Acheson was right about one thing: Joseph Tedstone did not spend a whole lot of time behind bars. Sure, the judge set bail at $250,000, took the general's passport and ordered him not to return to the family home, which was still a crime scene. Even so, Holy Joe was a free man forty-eight hours after being arrested on two counts of first degree murder. I'd covered more bail hearings than I cared to recall, but I never saw anything like this.

Rhyme Dillard and the district attorney were visibly pissed off and I got why. Maybe somebody high up had a word in the judge's ear. Maybe there was some truth in Reggie's fears that Tedstone would get the charges dropped, then go looking for the folks who helped bring them. Sounds far out, but you gotta remember this was 1976 – just two years after Richard Nixon resigned the presidency on the brink of impeachment, only to get pardoned by his buddy and successor, Gerald Ford. I understood Ford's argument that a long and bitter prosecution would prolong the country's suffering after defeat in Vietnam and the Watergate scandal. But to a lot of people, Tricky Dick's Get Out of Jail Free card was a betrayal. It provoked yet more conspiracy theories, fuelled the mood of national paranoia.

One good thing, though: I got to interview Holy Joe in the comfort of his sister's home – a big brownstone on Independence Avenue SE – rather than DC Jail.

He was waiting for me in the living room – a large, white-walled space with a lofty ceiling and broad bay windows overlooking the leafy street. Very little furniture and still less decoration made the place seem more like the waiting room of a private clinic than the living room of somebody's home.

Tedstone was standing by a portrait of his great grandfather, a Union Army colonel in the Civil War, and this told me a lot about the importance of military tradition to the Tedstone dynasty. It also made me reassess just how angry Holy Joe might have been when Johnny rejected an army career and got hip to the counterculture.

Yet despite his West Point pedigree, I'd never have nailed Joseph Tedstone as a serving army officer. If Heck Weschler was the archetypal soldier, Tedstone was the opposite. With delicate features and a sparse comb-over, he looked more like a family doctor. He inspected me through pale, almost colourless eyes, like I was a grunt on an insubordination rap. The stiff tweed suit seemed too big for his sloping shoulders and slim frame.

He raised a short, dark eyebrow and held out his hand. 'I wish I could say I was glad to meet you, Mr Tyler. Perhaps in happier circumstances … '

He showed me to a studded leather couch and two armchairs. I took a seat on a chair while he sat on the couch.

I'd requested the interview to keep my side of the deal with Weschler and was surprised when Tedstone agreed to it. When we talked on the phone I'd mentioned that Johnny had been my friend and colleague. Perhaps this had swung it.

For a few slow seconds he sat still, staring at his shoes.

I said nothing. Hadn't imagined how tough this was gonna be because I never imagined it would happen. Very probably, I was talking to the guy who murdered Johnny and Keith Zetchik. And possibly Christine Zetchik. Then again, what if Joseph Tedstone was the victim of a put-up job? In that case I was sitting with a grieving father at the centre of some vicious conspiracy. I'd promised Weschler I'd look into this in a fair and balance manner. Yet I couldn't bring myself to tell this egg-headed dude that I was sorry for his loss.

Then he looked me in the eye. 'So you've come to get my side of the story?'

'That's the idea, General.'

'Will you print what I tell you?'

'Depends what you say.'

'Can I trust you? As a brother officer?'

'You can trust me as a journalist.'

'I never trusted correspondents in Vietnam.'

'I'm your best hope.'

He made a harsh, hacking laugh. 'Apart from the Lord above, You may well be my *only* hope.'

'One thing I can promise you: I want justice for Johnny.'

'That's good enough for me.'

Was it though? I decided to toss him a frag grenade, see what effect it had. 'I'll be straight with you, General. Your son told me you were going to kill him. This was on Thursday night – four or five hours before he died.'

The detonation I was expecting didn't come. Instead, Tedstone gave me a bleak smile. 'Johnny had been saying that for years.'

I had another grenade ready. 'He also said you were planning to murder Zetchik.'

That *did* shock him. I clocked an alloy of confusion and anger in his small features.

I pushed on. 'Johnny said you were gonna hit Zetchik first, then come looking for him.'

Holy Joe got his shit together real fast. 'I have absolutely no idea where Johnny got that information about Keith Zetchik.'

This might have been true, and it might not. But I was clear about one thing: Joseph Tedstone was deeply concerned when he discovered that Johnny knew about the plan to murder Zetchik. It didn't fit right with his laid back admission that Johnny had been telling people for some time that his dad was gonna kill him. What this meant, I couldn't tell. At least not then.

# TWELVE

I tried a different approach. 'Johnny told me you forced him to have electroshock therapy when you found out he was gay.'

'I would never do anything contrary to my son's best interests.' He said this with the dispassion of a public service Tannoy announcement.

'Forgive my frankness, General, but I can only go off what your son told me. He said you never forgave him for being gay; that you saw his homosexuality as a stain on the family honour; and an obstacle to your career.'

He shook his head. 'Johnny wasn't homosexual.'

'I know it's difficult to accept, sir, but – '

'I know – *knew* – my own son.' He cut across me with a sharp glance. 'This sodomite business was an act. Mainly because he wanted to hurt me, but also because he'd always liked to dress up and fantasize, and because it was a good way to grab attention. If there was one thing Johnny liked, it was attention.'

Harsh judgments from a father who was meant to be mourning the loss of his only son. And yet, much of what he said chimed with my own take on Johnny's personality. And if Johnny wasn't gay, how could he be a stain on the family honour? Or a barrier to his dad's career? Yet it was all about perception. If the Pentagon brass perceived Johnny as gay, that could damage Holy Joe's promotion prospects just as much as if he *was* gay. Same went for the family's honour, whatever that meant.

I kept my tone formal. 'But you did induce him to have ECT as a result of him displaying homosexual tendencies?'

'Personal matters are difficult for me to talk about, Mr Tyler.' He ran his fingers through the thin strands of his comb-over. 'It feels like a betrayal. Not just of Johnny, but also of his mother.'

'Off the record, not for publication,' I said. 'Not even for deep background.'

'I still don't know … '

'That's up to you, General. But I do understand family stuff – and why folks want to keep it private. My dad was a wife-beater. My mom became an alcoholic. Domestic violence left me with serious psychological issues. And I know from personal experience about shrinks – how their methods work, and how sometimes they don't.'

He made a drawn-out sigh, as if he was about to have a tooth pulled and needed to get it over with as quickly as possible. 'Shortly after Johnny went to junior high school, he started behaving in disturbing ways. As he grew older, this got worse. Of course, I was in Vietnam and that put his mother under even greater pressure.'

He seemed to run out of words.

I said, 'When you say disturbing ways, sir, do you mean gay ways?'

He threw me a look of poorly disguised contempt. 'No one ever talked about Johnny being homosexual, not back then. Back then, my son was depressed, weird, anxious, and withdrawn. His one outlet was rock and roll music. He joined a band at high school and they played small venues. I never liked rock music, but it did bring Johnny out of his shell, gave him some self-belief. The problem was that it also introduced him to drugs. When he was 17 he crashed my car into a tree and suffered concussion. While he was in the hospital we found cocaine, amphetamines and cannabis in his room.'

Again he went quiet. The silence played awkward. I tried to prompt him. 'That must have been a terrible shock for any parent. Whatever his psychological condition, taking that stuff would've complicated everything.'

He nodded. 'He got into a downward spiral. He was increasingly out of control. We prayed, we beseeched the Lord, of course we did, but we were at our wit's end. When Johnny was eighteen we brought him to a psychiatrist. The shrink recommended electroshock therapy and we agreed.'

'I gotta ask this, General, but was Johnny pressured into taking this treatment?'

Tedstone looked miserable. 'We told him he needed it. We said if his condition got any worse, we'd be forced to think about having him committed to a psychiatric hospital. He was terrified of that idea. So, yes, I guess you could say we pressured him.'

I gave him another nudge. 'This psychiatrist, he didn't mention homosexuality?'

He made a dreary expression. 'The only person who mentioned *that* was Johnny – six years later when he started to tell people like you he was homosexual. He backdated this 'awareness', as he called it, to his teens. And accused me of forcing him to take the ECT as a punishment.'

I kept my voice even. I didn't want to provoke the guy but needed to mention what I'd found in the *Tribune's* library clips. 'You were quoted in my paper last year as saying that gay people are morally corrupt and tolerating them is contrary to the Christian faith. Is that correct?'

'That's what the scriptures tell us, Mr Tyler. That's a matter of fact, not opinion. But if you're asking if I would have punished Johnny if he *had* been homosexual, let me tell you this.' He leaned forward, resting his elbows on his knees. 'One time in the fall of '69, when I was back here on leave, I brought him home after one of those horrible treatment sessions. I had to help him in and out of the car because he was in a semi-stupor and could barely stand up. No father worthy of the name would inflict that sort of suffering on his child. In retrospect, the electroshock therapy was a mistake. But at the time we were desperate. We just took the shrink's advice.'

He sounded convincing, gotta say.

Time to switch to another topic. 'What can you tell me about your relationship with Keith Zetchik?'

He made a longsuffering expression and told me what Weschler told me. Only difference was that Tedstone had nothing good to say about Zetchik, leastways not after they went to Vietnam together. I asked about the Pentagon job they were both in the running for – assistant chief of staff for intelligence. Tedstone confirmed what I heard from Johnny: If the job had gone to Zetchik, Tedstone would have either resigned from his current position as number two in that department, or been fired. Despite the bust-up, despite the competition for the high-stakes job, Tedstone said he didn't kill Zetchik.

But what else was he gonna say?

I moved on. 'How about your Mauser broomhandle? The cops say they ran ballistics tests that show it was the same gun that was used to murder Zetchik. That correct?'

He nodded yes. 'It looks bad, I know. But I simply can't explain how that gun came to be in the possession of the killer.'

'When did you become aware it was missing?'

'When the police came.'

'What about the cyanide pills? Did Johnny know you kept them in your desk drawer? And where you kept the key?'

The guy looked wretched. 'I have no idea what my son knew and what he didn't know. I'd kept them there for years. I should've trashed them when I came back from Vietnam. I don't know why didn't. But to answer your question, it's entirely possible that Johnny knew they were there, and where I kept the key.'

Long hush.

Then he said, 'I didn't poison Johnny.'

He said it like he meant it.

But what else was he gonna say?

I pressed on. 'Why did you leave your house so late at night?'

He gazed at the Wedgwood vase on the mantelpiece, but his eyes looked opaque, as if he wasn't really looking at anything at all. Then he made another frustrated sigh. 'I needed to clear my head. I'd had words with Johnny after he got back from his night out. He was clearly under the influence. We both said some hurtful things. I thought we needed time apart, to cool off. And in his case, sober up. So I took the car for a drive.'

'Where did you go?'

'Just around the neighbourhood. After some time, I decided to come over to my sister's, so I took Massachusetts Avenue through downtown.'

'Did this neighbourhood drive take you near Zetchik's house?'

'I may have driven past his place. I didn't stop and I certainly didn't see him.'

'You must admit, General, that the gun, the kill pills, and not having an alibi are serious problems.'

'Don't I know it.'

I asked if he could think of anyone who had reason to frame him.

His pale eyes locked on mine. I got the impression he was trying to see into my head. Then he made a rueful smile and said, 'Yes – Keith Zetchik.'

I returned the smile. 'Anybody else?'

He looked away and didn't reply right away. Maybe he was running some names in his head. At last he said, 'No. But I didn't kill my son and I didn't kill Zetchik. I've committed many sins that will count against me when I stand before the Lord, but those tragic deaths are not among them.'

Gotta say, I felt some sympathy for the guy. If this it was an act, he was a damn good actor.

Yet what else was he gonna tell me?

And I couldn't ignore the evidence. First, I was sure Johnny had been poisoned by someone who wanted to make his death look like suicide – probably by inducing him to drink the cyanide-laced whiskey.

Second, Keith Zetchik was assassinated with Joseph Tedstone's Mauser. Tedstone had means, motive and opportunity. The one thing he didn't have was an alibi. And although it was possible he had powerful enemies, it was probable he had powerful friends. How else had he gotten bail for two raps of murder-one?

'Ever heard of a friend of Johnny's called Regina Acheson? Also known as Reggie?'

'No I haven't. Who is she?'

'I'm not sure,' I said. 'But I need to find out.'

# THIRTEEN

First thing next morning I called Rhyme Dillard, but he didn't have anything further on the Tedstone/Zetchik investigation. Not unless you counted the three guys who attacked me and Johnny outside the Bayou – which I didn't. For what it was worth, though, Dillard gave me the skinny. He'd used the Alice Cooper tattoo on the swarthy guy's forearm to identify him as Duane Henry, aged twenty-eight, a Southeast DC bruiser who had pulled time for assault and battery and other violent offences. As I'd suspected, the other two were brothers – Arty and Drake McDonagh, aged twenty-seven and twenty-five. They were from the same neighbourhood as Henry, but didn't have any felony convictions. Not yet, anyways. I wasn't surprised that none of them wanted to press charges. They'd have learned at an early age not to play ball with the cops. Besides, they insisted none of them had been hurt in the incident. Henry claimed I never landed a blow to his ribcage or anywhere else, while Arty McDonagh said his swollen jaw was the result of an automobile accident. For his part, Drake McDonagh denied backing out of the fight before he could get hurt: He said Johnny and I ran back into the Bayou, shouting for help.

'Got another homicide that might interest you.' The sound of Dillard clicking his ballpoint filled the short pause. 'Remember that TV show in the 60s – *Man in a Suitcase*? Well, DC's version turned up in Georgetown yesterday. Only this suitcase was floating in the Chesapeake & Ohio Canal and the man was literally in it – minus his head and limbs.'

This was of interest – no argument there. 'The killer must've gotten a shock when the case floated.'

'It *didn't* float. Not at first. It was weighted down with building rubble. The medical examiner tells me it must have resurfaced seven to ten days later, due to the process of putrefaction. As the torso began to decay it released methane gas into the chest cavity, creating buoyancy.'

I scribbled shorthand outlines in my notebook. 'How about identification?'

'No head, no arms or legs, it's gonna be difficult. There are some old scars on the chest that could mean something. I need to check them out.'

I hung up with Dillard and wrote the piece as a six-inch short for the front page, then dropped it in the city desk copy tray.

With the first edition put to bed, I set off on foot to the US Botanic Garden on the south west corner of the Capitol. I was meeting Heck Weschler. We weren't due another interview for my series of features, so I wondered why he wanted to see me.

I suspected I'd picked up a tail soon after leaving the office. But unlike Reggie Acheson, this wasn't a straightforward stop and spot job. I tried a couple of old tricks – tying my shoelace to get a glance over my shoulder; and crossing the street then crossing back again. But I still couldn't be sure. Whoever was following me knew their shit.

I stopped at Ford's Theatre and scanned the street behind me. Nothing of interest. Next, I veered left into E Street, along the back of the FBI Building, left onto 9th Street, up to F, and left again down 10th to bring me back to the theatre. Anyone still behind me after the 360 degree manoeuvre would certainly have been suspicious. But no one was there. Or no one that I could pin.

So I pressed on, walking so fast that anyone following would have to run to stay with me. I continued along 10th between the Internal Revenue and Justice Department buildings and started out across the National Mall. To my left the marble of the US Capitol shimmered blinding white, as if radiating its own internal light. Then a slab of overcast moved across the sun and the great building dimmed to sullen grey.

I carried on moving, crossed Jefferson Drive, and paused again at Independence Avenue. No sign of anyone hustling to keep up. Or anyone remotely suspicious.

I looked again at the sightseers milling around a coach from Pawhuska, Oklahoma. I scanned the office workers entering and exiting the Federal Aviation building. I even glanced at the gaggle of bums sucking booze from paper bags opposite the Hirshhorn Museum. No sign of a tail, but that wasn't to say he – or she – wasn't there.

I went straight to the Botanic Garden and found Weschler sitting on a wooden bench in the Tropics section of the conservatory.

I sat on the opposite end.

Without looking at me, he said, 'This place remind you of anywhere?'

'If you're talking about in country, kinda.' I took a closer look around me and clocked some familiar sights. 'Dig those da quy blooms and foxtail grasses. Saw a lot of those in the Central Highlands.'

'You used to eat some of that stuff, as I recall.'

'Noshing edible vegetation preserved C-rations. Provided, of course, you knew what you were eating. Otherwise you were doing Charlie's job for him.'

He chuckled. 'When I hooked up with you snake-eaters, I never guessed you actually ate the damn things.'

'Whatever it took to keep body and soul together.' I looked up to watch the sunlight play on the canopy of royal palm fronds high above. 'But you didn't ask me here to talk about Special Forces dietary arrangements or the flora of Indochina.'

'True enough.' He gave me a quick glance. 'I wanted to know how you got on with Joe Tedstone?'

I gave him a résumé of what Tedstone told me.

'So you think he could've been set up?' Weschler sounded encouraged.

'These days, this town, anything's possible.'

'That's good. Or at least it's preferable to you telling me he's guilty dead to rights.'

'I still think the evidence against him is compelling.'

'And yet by all accounts his boy Johnny was a mixed-up young man with a psychoactive drugs habit and a history of mental illness.'

'What are you suggesting?'

'He truly hated his old man, right?'

'He said he did. But Johnny said a lot of stuff he didn't really mean.'

'Nonetheless, might it be possible that Johnny staged this whole thing? Steals his dad's Mauser from the display case, uses it to shoot Zetchik, then swallows the kill pills to frame his dad for a double homicide?'

I gave him a sideways look. The idea was ludicrous.

Wasn't it?

I took a few beats to process the theory. I'd known grunts in Vietnam who fantasized about their own death to the extent that they willed it to happen. They'd write down their funeral plans in detail, talk about watching the service from above. A common theme was witnessing the hurt and regret for things done or not done by wives, girlfriends, pals, family members. Sometimes these guys fielded a big one and left me wondering if they'd deliberately exposed themselves to enemy fire. Maybe Johnny's state of mind wasn't so different.

And Weschler was right. As well as professing to despise his pop, Johnny was using all sorts of shit that messed with his brain chemistry. The night he died, he started a fight in the Bayou, then another with those three guys outside the club – mysteriously vanishing and leaving me to handle the situation alone. On top of this, he had a record of mental health problems. And if my buddy wasn't gay, he sure was a drama queen. The pure theatre of directing and starring in a production like this would have flipped his on switch. It was the ending that bothered me because Johnny never hinted at suicide. But then a lot of suicides didn't.

I said, 'You know it sounds crazy.'

He smiled. 'You know it doesn't.'

We went quiet as an elderly couple approached and stopped to examine the coils of a strangler fig.

When they moved on, he said, 'I got some intel on that DEA agent and the Asian woman you came across at the scene of Christine Zetchik's murder.'

'That was quick work,' I said. 'I'm impressed.'

He kept is voice low but audible. 'The DEA guy is Bobby Delacroix. Seems he's a straight-up operator, though I couldn't get anything on the investigation he's working on out at Earlstown. And you were right about the woman. She *is* CIA. She's from a Vietnamese family and using an anglicized version of her real name – Lam Thu Kim.'

'Any idea what she's up to Stateside?'

He glanced quickly along the pathway to make sure no one was coming our way. 'After Saigon fell last year, a number of former South Vietnamese generals living in the States have been lobbying Congress for funds to carry on the fight using guerrilla warfare. Keith Zetchik had been outspoken in his support for these guys, including a fellow named Pham Tan Giang. Until last April he was an ARVN three-star. Now he works at a grocery store on the 1100 block of U Street NW, here in DC.'

This was useful information, though it raised as many questions as it answered.

'So Lam Thu Kim, aka Kim Lamb, could be investigating Keith Zetchik's links with General Giang?'

He said, 'She could be doing a damn sight more than that.'

He had a point. The agency could have sent her to recover something from Keith Zetchik's Kalorama apartment, maybe connecting him to the ARVN generals and their no-surrender lobbying. She could have zapped Zetchik when he came home unexpectedly and disturbed her search. And if she didn't find what she went for at Kalorama, she could have gone looking for it at the Earlstown house. Christine Zetchik may have been strangled because she got in the way.

Weschler stood up to leave. 'As you say, these days, this town …'

# FOURTEEN

The retail outlet where Pham Tan Giang worked was a shabby mom and pop store with an adult magazine outlet on one side and a vacant lot on the other.

An Asian guy, late forties/early fifties, was at the counter, unpacking stock from a pile of cardboard boxes.

'General Giang?'

He looked up.

I told him who I was and that I was investigating the murders of Keith and Christine Zetchik.

'I was terribly sad to learn of General and Mrs Zetchik's untimely demises.' He spoke good English with a French accent. This wasn't uncommon as Vietnam was a French colony long before America established a presence there. 'The general was a generous friend to us back here in the USA, although I never had the pleasure of Madame's acquaintance.'

He was a short, slender guy with a sloping forehead and receded hair. Large brown eyes were engaging and his broad mouth made an expansive smile. In a green plaid shirt and tan slacks, it was tough to imagine him in the uniform of a lieutenant general, though his manner was quietly authoritative.

'May I enquire, Mr Tyler, did you serve in Vietnam?'

I returned his smile. 'Went over in the fall of '65 with the 101st Airborne and joined 5th Special Forces Group in '67. I was a captain when I mustered out in '72.' I gave him the works on my military credentials because I figured he'd be more likely to cooperate with someone who'd fought on the same side.

He placed four boxes on a small trolley cart and pushed it to the nearest aisle of shelves. 'Clearly my country is in your debt, Captain.'

'I prefer Mr these days.'

'Of course.' He opened one of the boxes on his cart and started transferring cans of Big John's Beans 'n' Fixins to a shelf. 'Tell me, how may I be of assistance?'

I took out my notebook. 'How would you describe your relationship with General Zetchik?'

He carried on stacking the shelf. 'Cordial. Productive. Helpful. But the relationship was more with my group of expatriates than with me as an individual.'

I followed as he moved the cart to the next shelf. Next out were packs of Bubble Yum Bananaberry gum. 'What can you tell me about your expatriate group?'

Giang hesitated, just for a beat, then continued to fill the shelf. 'We meet once a week in a local church hall for companionship and mutual support. Sometimes we bring our wives, but I'm sure you will know that old soldiers like nothing better than to relive old battles, so we often attend alone. We started getting together in May last year after the Communists took Saigon. Our church sponsors were very good at putting us in touch. Currently we have about thirty members and we are also affiliated to other groups, for example in Baltimore and Philadelphia.'

Another trolley stop brought us to the baking products shelf and Giang began loading it with boxes of Bisquick Buttermilk Baking Mix.

'It must be tough for you, General,' I said. 'Starting a new life in a foreign land.'

He made a resigned expression. 'Certainly it's difficult. But by the same token, I'm lucky to be here. I'm lucky to be alive.'

I didn't entirely buy the stoicism act. Not so long ago this fellow had real power and status. He was deploying brigades and divisions. Now he had a minimum wage job in a little grocery store and was deploying Big John's Beans 'n' Fixins and Bubble Yum Bananaberry gum. His world had been turned on its head and that would be devastating, regardless of the brave face he was putting on.

I probed a little more. I was looking for reactions as much as answers. 'Did you serve with General Zetchik, or know him in Vietnam?'

Giang's response gave away nothing. 'I did not have that honour. None of us here in Washington did.'

'So how did you hook up? Did he hear about your group and make contact?'

He finished unloading the baking mix and nodded yes. 'He came to some of our meetings, listened to our concerns, and helped where he could. If he knew of a job vacancy, he would put in a good word. He arranged events for us – a meeting with our local council representative and a tour of Congress. He was a faithful friend to us lost and lonely souls.'

Part of me felt some sympathy for Giang and his group. Yet I had to keep in mind that they had been locked in a pitiless struggle for their homeland that went back way beyond

US involvement. When those guys got together, they must have talked about more than filling in benefits claim forms and enrolling at community college. Especially if a hawkish intelligence chief like Zetchik was spurring them on.

'When was the last time you saw General Zetchik?'

'Last Monday.'

'Did you at any point discuss lobbying the US government for funds to continue a guerrilla war against the North?'

'If it was your country, Mr Tyler, would you walk away?'

I picked up a hint of anger in his voice. This was worth pushing. 'We had a civil war too. The Union defeated the Confederacy. And walking away was what most people did.'

His undertone of resentment remained. 'The Communists now occupying Saigon are not as accommodating as Lincoln and his successors. There are no olive branches for us. Only exile, extermination, or that sinister euphemism, re-education. General Zetchik understood this.'

He finished adjusting the boxes of baking mix and turned to me with a placid smile. The vexation of a few moments ago was gone. 'You should understand, though, that all my group talks about is writing a few letters to congressmen and senators. We are realists, Mr Tyler. We know there is no appetite in the US to continue the conflict in Vietnam. We write our letters out of duty, not expectation.'

I thanked him for his time and walked toward the door.

I was halfway there when he called to me.

'Mr Tyler, you surely don't think General Zetchik's murder was in some way connected to my group?'

I looked back. 'No I don't. I just wanted to find out a little more about the general's relations with Vietnamese folks here in DC. Now I know.'

But the truth was, I didn't know. A guy like Keith Zetchik gets together with a bunch of exiled ARVN brass, their agenda is gonna be a whole lot more ambitious than promoting community relations from a drafty church hall.

# FIFTEEN

I got home late thanks to a story that broke just before I left the office.

Mother of three barricaded herself and her kids in their Southeast Washington apartment, threatening to kill them all. Social services wanted to take the kids into care because they'd been turning up at school with unexplained bruises. Mom's response sort of underlined the social workers' worries. I'd suffered as a small child from domestic violence. Even now my emotional scale was a few notes short of an octave. So I dug the need to protect the children above all else. After two hours of anguished discussion with a police negotiator, Mom let her kids go. Then she blew her brains out.

Siege ends in tragedy, that's a strong front page lead – although I'd rather have written a piece for the bottom strip on page two in which Mom didn't die.

I arrived at my place at 7.30pm in urgent need of beer and food.

Half my wish list was sitting by the front door in the shape of two six-packs of Narragansett Beer.

I didn't think to question who might have sent it, or why. I'd been out of that frame of mind way too long.

So I picked up the beer and

Bang!

I threw myself behind an azalea bush. Someplace down the road a dark barked. A neighbour across the street looked at me strange. I went through the instinctive routine of checking my body for signs of injury.

But I wasn't hurt.

I looked where the bullet hit the soft earth near my doorstep.

But there was no bullet.

The ground under the beer had been scooped out and an anti-personnel mine was nestling in the hollow. It had the circumference of a small dinner plate and was about three inches deep.

But why hadn't it exploded?

One of my Special Forces guys stepped on a mine like this. Smoke was all over the place. When it cleared, so was the guy.

So why was I still in one piece?

I forced my scattergun thinking to slow right down, analysed the situation.

Could be the fuse or detonator were defective. Something could have been wrong with the TNT. There were other possibilities.

Perhaps the most obvious was the most likely: The mine didn't explode because it wasn't meant to explode.

That loud bang had been caused by a pressure-release mechanism triggered when I lifted the beer off the ground. It was a classic booby trap ruse. But anti-personnel mines weren't booby traps. They didn't use pressure release detonators either. Tread on one and bam! The thing exploded instantly. Not like in the movies, where a guy steps on a mine, hears a tell-tale click and then has to figure out how to escape the blast when he takes his foot off the detonator. In the real world, that never happens.

So my next question was: What the fuck was going on?

Dusting off my pants, I picked up the mine and the beer and went into my kitchen.

I popped a can of Narragansett and drained it in a few large swallows. It was warm after standing in the sun, but right then the alcohol was more important than the taste. Then I got my toolbox, placed the mine on the table and set about dismantling it. I'd handled a lot of these babies in Vietnam and knew my way around them with my eyes shut. But that didn't mean I took anything for granted – especially because the one I had in front of me was a customized number. After removing the pressure plate assembly, I opened up the plastic casing and looked at the inner-workings. Only there weren't any. The casing had been stripped out: No fuse, no detonator, no spring, no charge. The compartment that would normally have been filled with TNT had been used to accommodate a crude pressure release mechanism that fired a blank 12 gauge cartridge when I lifted the beer. The bang that sent me scurrying for cover sounded like a gunshot because it *was* a gunshot.

I stood back, opened another Narragansett. Someone had obviously gone to a great deal of trouble gutting a land mine and using it for a sinister prank. Whoever they were, they'd be laughing their socks off at the way I fell for it. Having said that, this wasn't Pleiku or Kontum, it was a respectable residential street in DC. So maybe I should cut myself a little slack for my lack of combat zone awareness.

I drank some more beer, more slowly this time, and tried to figure out who could be behind this. The fact that this type of mine was widely used in Vietnam wasn't lost on me. It seemed the people who set me up wanted me to know that they were bringing the Nasty to DC. They were making a fairly unambiguous threat: Back off on the Tedstone/Zetchik story, or next time we won't fool around.

A number of candidates came to mind.

First up was General Giang. The guy may have come over as unassuming, but unassuming didn't get you three stars in the South Vietnamese Army. ARVN generals had to be ruthless, but they also had to be cunning. I'd talked to Giang less than six hours ago. Time enough to pull off this stunt, but only in a way that made him the obvious perpetrator. Unless that was the idea.

Then there was Holy Joe Tedstone. Perhaps he was sending me a message. I had no doubt he had the resources. And if he'd killed Johnny and Zetchik, it would be in his interest to stop me poking around.

I thought, too, about Kim Lamb. I knew very little about her, although if she was a spook, she'd know all about dirty tricks. My gut said she wasn't responsible. But my judgment was clouded. I couldn't look at Kim's face without seeing Linh, my teenage agent in Saigon. And I couldn't imagine Linh on any side but mine.

And what about the DEA agent Bobby Delacroix? Again, he'd be hip to all sorts of nasty capers. I wasn't aware that he had any Vietnam connections. Yet after what just happened, I had to admit there was a lotta stuff I wasn't aware of.

I drained the beer can and tossed it in the trash. The reality was that anyone connected to the killings of Keith and

Zetchik and Johnny was likely behind the fake mine. That could mean the people I'd thought about, or it could mean people I didn't even know existed.

I thought about reporting the incident to Rhyme Dillard. I thought about confiding in Maggie. I even wondered whether to run it by Heck Weschler.

In the end though I decided to keep it to myself.

# SIXTEEN

Lam Thu Kim – alias Kim Lamb – was waiting for me at a table in Jr Hot Shoppes at 13th and New York NW – a thirty second walk from the *Tribune* office.

She didn't seem best pleased to see me. I couldn't blame her.

I slid into the seat opposite and ordered an espresso from the waitress.

'You're a real piece of work, aren't you?' Her misty brown eyes drilled into mine.

'Just doing my job.' I made a teasing smile. 'But you were a reporter not so long ago. So you must understand that as well as anyone.'

She set down her tea cup and spoke without looking up. 'How did you know where to find me?'

'I don't reveal my sources. I bet you never did either.'

I couldn't have told her, even if I wanted to. A foolscap envelope had been delivered to me at the *Tribune* office earlier that morning. Inside were photocopies of a typewritten report. The heading and several paragraphs were redacted, but it didn't take a genius to figure out it was a CIA document. And although I genuinely wasn't sure who sent it, the fact that

Heck Weschler knew I was asking questions about Kim's CIA activities suggested he was involved in one way or another.

The file told me everything I needed to know about Kim – and a whole lot more. She was aged 36 – same as me – and had spied for North Vietnam before she got burned and turned in '68. Since then, she worked for the CIA as a double agent. The file also told me she was the daughter of a wealthy Vietnamese family, educated at Vassar, one of the exclusive Seven Sisters colleges for women, where she read the great socialist thinkers. She was recruited by Hanoi in October '63 and worked as a journalist here in DC while gathering intel for Uncle Ho up until March '67. She returned to the Circus later that year as a war correspondent and was immediately put to work by Charlie. But she got compromized the following year and agreed to switch sides rather than face a firing squad. Couldn't blame her for that.

Armed with this information I'd called a contact at Langley and asked him to pass a message to Kim's section chief, requesting this meeting. I didn't make any demands. Didn't need to. Just knowing what I clearly knew was enough to get me what I wanted.

She sipped her tea and said, 'So what can I do for you?'

I made a friendly smile. 'Answer some questions I would have asked out at Earlstown if I'd been given the chance.'

'Such as?'

'Such as what were you doing there?'

'You know I can't answer that.'

'Okay, what's your interest in Keith Zetchik?'

'Who said I had an interest?'

'My source.'

'If I *did* have an interest, it would be classified.'

'Then tell me about Christine Zetchik.'

'Honestly, there's nothing I can tell you that you won't already know.'

'What about Bobby Delacroix, the DEA guy?'

'Never saw him before you did.'

'Any idea why DEA is staking out the Zetchik house?'

She shrugged. 'They wouldn't tell us about their operational activities any more than we would them.'

I eased off on the questions, let the cafeteria noises fill the silence – gabbling voices, chinking crockery, a hissing coffee machine. A little girl dropped her fork on the floor and it jangled harsh.

She looked out the window. Weather was humid – ninety degrees of heat trapped under a heavy thermal seal of overcast. It released thin drizzle that smeared the sidewalk, creating dim mirror images of shop fronts and passers-by. Days in DC like this, you were never sure if it was rain or sweat trickling under your shirt collar.

I looked at her. She was real gone elegant, no argument there. But more subtle than head-turning. And more challenging than alluring. I thought again how much she reminded me of my teenage agent Quan Quy Linh.

I broke the short silence. 'I spoke to a guy named Pham Tan Giang yesterday. Former ARVN three-star. He and other émigré generals are lobbying for funds to carry on fighting a guerrilla war in Vietnam. Keith Zetchik was a big supporter. If they got their way, that would stoke fears of the USA getting dragged back into the Nasty by the rear entrance.'

'Of course you're free to speculate, but that's not something I'm at liberty to discuss.'

'How about if I told you I'm gonna dig deeper into the activities of General Giang and his associates?'

She hesitated. I glimpsed a gap in her wall of intransigence.

'They're dangerous people. You should stay away.'

'I can take care of myself.'

'I know perfectly well what you can do, *Captain* Tyler.' There was frustration in her voice now. 'But you're not Special Forces anymore. And this isn't your fight.'

I looked at her hard. 'Was it ever?'

Her flinty gaze softened. This surprised me. 'You did your best. You did what you thought was right.'

She stood up to leave. 'Take my advice. Don't go sniffing around Giang.'

As she headed for the door I called after her. 'Why were you tailing me yesterday?'

She turned and gave me a don't-be-ridiculous look that confirmed the exact opposite.

Then she walked out and left me with a whole bunch of questions I didn't have when I walked in.

The main one was why did she want me to steer clear of Giang?

If I had to guess, I'd say Giang was in her crosshairs and I'd walked into her line of fire. Guys like him, they'd be an embarrassment to a US government that wanted to leave Vietnam in the past. It was easy to imagine why the CIA would want to keep tabs on them – as well as any high-profile supporters like Keith Zetchik. But someone had put a damn sight more than tabs on Zetchik, probably his wife too. Were the homicides sanctioned by the CIA? The spooks had done worse. I'd done worse at their behest.

Maybe she tailed me because she thought I might lead

her to other members of Giang's group. If so, she'd have been disappointed – and no doubt surprised – when I went to see Weschler. That also got me thinking what she might have read into my secretive meeting with a presidential candidate.

All that thinking was tiring so I hung around for another expresso and a smoke.

Through a haze of cigarette fumes I saw Kim returning.

Only it wasn't Kim, it was Linh.

And I wasn't at 13th and New York.

*I'm at the presbytery on Cong Ly in Saigon. There are scents of herbal tea, incense and floor polish.*

*Linh has finished her first week as a live-in nanny at the home of Colonel Truc Van Thanh. Today is her day off and she's reporting back.*

*She sits facing me on one of the wicker couches.*

*I've been worried about her in a way that's unprofessional. When all your emotions are dialled right down, it comes as a shock when one of them flips up to maximum. Maybe it's about using a kid in this brutal business – even though, in the context of Vietnam, sixteen-year-olds aren't really kids. In the context of Vietnam, nobody is a kid.*

*I ask, 'You okay?'*

*She nods vigorously. She's upbeat, flush with excitement. She looks lovely with her hair pinned up, decked out in a white linen dress and heels. This is Chuck Shaughnessy's idea: The more Thanh likes Linh, the more likely he is to trust her. And that would give her greater freedom to move about his mansion on Hong Thap Tu. But I know men like Thanh go a lot farther than simply liking girls.*

*Linh takes one of my cigarettes without asking and lights it. I say nothing. Technically, she's a minor and I'm not allowed* to let her smoke, but fuck technically. And besides, she's doing a job I wouldn't entrust to most service personnel.

She makes an impish grin. 'I got something for you.'

She overheard a conversation between Thanh and one his staff. They talked about arranging a meeting with somebody at MACV called Bootstrap – clearly a codename – and another person, a US State Department official, who wasn't named but referred to as 'she'.

I give her an encouraging smile. 'That's great. I never expected so much so soon.'

'That's not all.' She takes a long pull on her cigarette. 'This meeting is scheduled for next Tuesday. In the summer house in Thanh's garden. I can easily get out of my room undetected. I can sneak down to the summer house and listen in.'

I shake my head. 'That would be difficult. If they catch you snooping around the grounds at night … '

'They won't. It's a big garden with lots of cover.' She shrugs. 'More like a well-tended jungle.'

Her flippancy bothers me. 'We're not playing a game here, Linh.'

She goes stony serious. 'I know that. This is my way of dealing with what Thanh did to my family. It's a focus, a distraction.'

I give her a dubious look. 'I still think it's too risky. You've barely gotten your feet under the table with the Thanhs.'

She leans forward, filling my eyes with hers. 'This could be a big opportunity. I can do it. I'm going to do it.'

'Be careful,' I say. 'Be very, very careful.'

# SEVENTEEN

That evening I walked over to the Keg, a hard rock dive in Glover Park, to hear an upcoming punk band named Overkill. They played edgy versions of songs by the Velvet Underground, Roxy Music and unheard-of garage rock outfits from the sixties. I arrived to hear them cranking up an interesting take on Lou Reed's *Vicious*. The lead singer, Barney Jones, sported short hair and wraparound sunglasses along with tight-fitting clothes. Reminded me of Johnny's look, which wasn't surprising since it was Johnny who told me about these guys. He'd been badgering me to go see Overkill for weeks and I felt I owed him that much, even if it was somewhat late in the day.

Gotta say I wasn't disappointed. Their stuff was spiky, energetic, different. I dug punk because it drew on influences like those garage bands that never really made it and never really cared. You could see too the where the Velvets and Roxy elements came from – not just in the music, but also the stage set, with stacks of TVs, tuned to random channels.

Trouble was the long-haired rockers who came to the Keg wanted to hear covers of Led Zeppelin and Van Halen.

It was the same culture clash I saw at the Ramones gig at the Bayou when Johnny locked horns with the Kiss fan. I bought a beer, found a table, and consoled myself with the thought that I was on my own, so staying out of trouble wouldn't be a problem.

'I know where you got your name.'

Reggie Acheson slid into the seat right next to me.

I tried to disguise my surprise.

She studied me with her wide-set eyes. Thick tawny hair spilled over her shoulders. She looked svelte in faded jeans and a torn T-shirt. It depicted a grim-faced prophetic dude with a mane of white hair and full bush beard. Moses or Marx. Wild guess, the latter.

I squinted at her. 'Come again?'

'Your name – Wat Tyler. I thought it was far-out, so I looked it up. He was the leader of the English Peasant's Revolt, aka Wat Tyler's Rebellion, 1381.'

She seemed much more relaxed than a week ago. She'd certainly had a drink or two, maybe washed down with a goofball or two.

'That old revolution didn't work out so well for your namesake, did it?' She swigged from a beer bottle and shuffled a little closer so her knee brushed mine. 'He got suckered into talks with the king, whose goons promptly did the dirty. But Wat was a stand-up guy. A medieval democrat, you might say.'

I explained how I copped the name after a copy-editing error left the l out of Walt, resulting in my byline appearing as Wat Tyler.

'That's a cool story,' she said.

I grinned. 'Maybe the first thousand times I told it.'

'I guess.' She looked around the bar as if she was looking for somebody.

When she'd bolted from the burned-out store on 14th Street five days ago, I figured she'd be easy enough to find. Never counted on *her* finding *me* though.

I asked how she did it.

She leaned toward me and whispered in my ear, 'I didn't. I come to this place a lot.'

'Me too, but I never saw you here before.'

She indicated the crowded room and pushed herself closer so her thigh was touching mine. 'Not easy to spot people when it's jumping – and if it isn't, I don't come.'

I let my shoulder rub hers. If she was after sex, maybe I could oblige. 'You ever come with Johnny?'

'A few times.'

She looked over her shoulder, then back at me. There was an odd edginess in her manner. 'Johnny's dad got out just like I said, didn't he?'

'Yes he did.'

Again, the nervy twist, the backward glance. 'He's one mean motherfucker.'

'You all right? You seem a little antsy.'

'Sure I'm all right.'

She clearly wasn't. 'Is somebody spooking you?'

'No. I don't think so. Sometimes your mind plays tricks.'

'Goofballs play tricks. So does nose candy.'

'I'm clean. Just a few drinks is all.' She grabbed her things. 'But I gotta go.'

'Go where?'

'Anywhere.'

'Where do you live?'

'Adams Morgan.'

Figured. Back then Adams Morgan was still a countercultural magnet for bohemians and radicals.

'I'll take you.'

She didn't protest. I led her out. This was the second gig in a week I'd left midway through. But what could I do?

The night air was damp and sticky, well into the seventies. We walked south along the 2300 block of Wisconsin Avenue NW. I tried to hail a cab. Two went by but they already had a fare.

A pale coloured Buick Regal peeled off from a stream of traffic and moved across the street, slowing right down.

Clearly this wasn't a taxi, but it came rolling along the kerbside as if the driver was gonna pick us up anyway.

My first thought was that the dude behind the wheel figured I was trying to hitch a ride.

The Buick drew level.

The passenger window began rolling down.

Something weird was going down here. Were these the people who spooked Reggie in the Keg?

A stubby black object appeared in the Buick's rolled down window.

My second thought was that we were gonna get shot.

I grabbed Reggie and shoved her to the ground behind a pile of trash.

We hit the sidewalk. A bullet fizzed overhead, shattering a store window.

I rolled sideways on top of Reggie, searching for better cover.

Tried to tell her to keep low, but my words were submerged by the screech of tyre rubber on tarmac. I glanced across the street. The Buick was accelerating away fast. It swerved right into W Place NW and was gone.

'What the fuck did I tell you?' Reggie continued looking at the street corner. Her voice was quiet, but in an edge-of-hysteria sort of way. 'What the fuck did I tell you?'

'Okay, Reggie.' I gripped her shoulders and turned her to face me. 'We gotta call the cops.'

'No cops no cops no cops – '

'Okay, okay.' I tightened my hold on her shoulders. 'Then we need to get away from here.'

'No more taxis. No more taxis. Please take me home.'

'All right, we can walk.'

We set off, hand-in-hand, skirting the south-east edge of the US Naval Observatory grounds, then cut through Rock Creek Park, heading for Massachusetts Avenue. From there we hustled through Kalorama to Connecticut Avenue and on to Adams Morgan.

Reggie's apartment was on the second floor of a rundown rowhouse on Columbia Road NW. I drew the living room curtains, turned on a soft light and poured us both a decent measure of bourbon from a bottle on the sideboard.

The place was a mess – more like a guy's than a girl's. A mismatched assortment of rugs were tossed on the wood flooring. Coffee table was littered with takeout wrappers and empty cigarette packs. The hi-fi system was righteous, but a half dozen LPs hadn't been returned to their sleeves and that was downright unforgivable. The walls were covered in posters of Guevara, Lenin and Mao. Books by the likes of C Wright Mills and Jean-Paul Sartre were scattered about the place. And, of course, there was the pervasive scent of maryjane that seemed to be ingrained in the fibre of places like this.

I sat beside her on the couch.

She swallowed a mouthful of whiskey and winced as if it was volcano larva.

I took a sip of mine. 'You okay?'

For a few moments she stared into her whiskey. I thought she may have been fighting back tears, but when she looked up she was dry-eyed.

'Kinda tough to be okay when someone just tried to kill you.'

I lit two Camels and handed one to her.

We took long pulls on our cigarettes and drank a little more whiskey.

After some time I said, 'The cops can protect you, Reggie. I know the head of MPD Homicide Branch. He's a solid guy.'

She went back to staring at her whiskey. 'There's a reason I can't go to the cops.'

I'd guessed as much. But I kept quiet. Whatever she was gonna tell me, she needed to do it in her own time.

At last she set her glass down and looked at me direct. 'I didn't meet Johnny at a smoke-in. We met two years back when we were patients in a private psychiatric hospital in Bethesda.'

Another pause. Again, I waited it out.

'Truth is, I'm schizophrenic. And I got a cocaine habit.'

I placed my glass beside hers and leaned closer to her. Kept my voice gentle. 'That doesn't alter the fact that someone took a shot at you.'

She looked wretched. 'The cops won't see it like that. There's nothing to link what just went down with Joseph Tedstone. They'll say it was some dealer I owe money to. Believe me, there are lots of them. And I have no evidence at all to support anything Johnny told me. They'll see me as a basket-case junkie. Fuck, I wouldn't blame them.'

I kept my tone upbeat. 'But you knew where Joseph Tedstone hid the murder weapon. You went to retrieve it from that tree hollow.'

'But I can't prove any of that.'

'I can vouch for the fact that you sent me the Mauser.'

'You can't, though, can you, Wat? I made sure you couldn't. I thought anonymity would protect me. But it did just the opposite.'

It was difficult to argue with her logic.

'Listen, Rhyme Dillard is a good cop. At least talk to him off the record.'

She shook her head, again and again. She shook it so hard her hair became a fuzzy halo.

Then she seemed to get her shit together. 'You don't get it, do you Wat? I guess you can't get it.'

'I get that you're scared. Justifiably paranoid. Sure I do.'

'No. What you don't get is that I'm terrified of getting put back in the secure unit of some psych hospital. Tedstone could make that happen. He could easily make that happen. And there's nothing your guy Dillard could do to stop him.'

Whether this was true, I couldn't say. What I could say was that no way Reggie was gonna talk to Dillard or any other cop.

All I could do was tell her to do nothing and go nowhere until I worked something out.

She leaned her head against my shoulder. 'You're more than I deserve, Wat.'

'I'm your friend, Reggie. Just like Johnny was. This is what friends do for one another.'

'Will you spend the night with me?' Her face loomed in mine. Her hand smoothed the inside of my thigh. My dick went to stand-by.

I took her hand and held it firm.

Reggie was one hot babe and casual sex was all right as far as I was concerned. Hell, two hours ago I thought that was exactly what was gonna happen. Now I wasn't so sure. Screwing a woman as mixed up and messed up as she was just didn't seem right.

'I'll spend the night here,' I said. 'But I'll sleep on the couch.'

She gave me a hurt look.

I pulled her against me and held her close. 'It's not that I don't want you, Reggie. But right now, you need to rest.'

I thought again about Joseph Tedstone, the power and influence he wielded. I wondered too about the fake landmine left outside my place yesterday. Was that Holy Joe's doing? If he was the killer, he'd clearly benefit from eliminating Reggie and frustrating my investigation.

And I felt a stab of guilt. *I* gave Reggie's name to Tedstone when I asked him if he knew her.

I told her this.

I expected an angry reaction, but she just snuggled closer. 'He already knew. He already knows everything.'

'I'll protect you.'

'Nobody can protect me, Wat. But you're a sweet guy.'

There was a mellowness in her voice, a laid-back stoicism, that made me want to hug her and shake her at the same time. One thing I was clear about though: We were caught up in a lethal crapshoot, with no direction out.

# EIGHTEEN

Both Kim Lamb and Bobby Delacroix could have had a reason to tail me to my meeting with Heck Weschler. But if I was 95 per cent certain my shadow was Kim, I was 100 per cent certain it wasn't the DEA guy. You got the general appearance of a giraffe, there's no place outside the National Zoo you won't look conspicuous.

This came to mind as I watched Delacroix come loping on those long thin legs across the polished wood flooring of the National Gallery of Art. Sandy hair and pale skin completed the giraffe-esque appearance. He was wearing the same clothes as last time: Corduroy jacket with leather sleeve patches, tan canvas pants, plaid shirt and knitted neck tie.

He stood beside me in front of Titian's *Venus With a Mirror* painting. This was the location he gave me when he called the newsroom two hours earlier to request this meeting.

He started talking, but didn't look at me. 'Good of you to come, Wat. May I call you Wat?'

I followed his lead and kept my gaze on the painting. 'Sure – if I can call you Bobby.'

'That's how I like it.'

'So why did you want to see me, Bobby?'

In my peripheral vision I saw him take a small item from his pocket and place something in his mouth. 'Isn't it a wonderful work of art? Titian painted it in, or around, 1555. That's more than 400 years ago, and yet the colours and textures seems so fresh, so vivid, so rich.'

His manner, like his clothing, was exactly like a college tutor's and nothing like a federal agent's. Maybe that was his trick.

The smell of peppermint freighted the air between us. He must have been feeding himself mint candy. I said, 'It's a righteous painting.'

'Some experts say it idealizes the beauty of the female form. Others believe it to be a critique of vanity. Others still suggest it's both.'

'What do you think?'

He ignored my question as if I was a disruptive student. 'Its journey here to DC is mind-blowing in itself. It was acquired by a syndicate of art dealers in a secret deal with Joseph Stalin because he needed shekels for the Soviet Union's first Five-Year Plan. The syndicate then sold it to the American collector Andrew Mellon. His dream was the creation of a national art museum in the USA and he donated his Titian to our government in 1937. It was one of the first masterpieces to go on display when the gallery opened four years later.'

His art history lecture might have been interesting in another context. Right now, it seemed irrelevant. 'What's your point, Bobby?'

He sounded irritated – like I should have let him get to this in his own time. 'My point, Wat, is that works of art, like people, take unexpected journeys – sometimes starting in the turmoil of revolutionary change – before finding their way to our national capital.'

Was he putting me on? I wanted to turn my head and talk to him direct. But that would really piss him off. So I waited.

Finally, he said, 'Take, for example, our mutual acquaintance, Kim Lamb. She started out on her travels to Washington in similarly tumultuous circumstances.'

'Okay, Bobby, now I'm interested.'

'You see, Wat? Good things come to him who waits.' He sounded pleased with his cleverness. 'Kim is a legit CIA operative, but what's bothering me – and which may also concern you – is that she has another agenda. Maybe there's no conflict with her official agency work. Then again, maybe there is and the agency is covering it up. The spooks always, *always* close ranks when there's a fuck-up involving one of their own.'

'What sort of other agenda we talking about here, Bobby?'

'A whole other, other agenda, Wat.'

He went quiet. I got the impression he was enjoying the suspense.

Then he said, 'Kim's mom and pop were killed by US soldiers during the Phoenix Program in the spring of 1969, along with most of her community. The village where she grew up was wiped out in a particularly aggressive search and destroy op. Guess whose unit was responsible.'

I had no need to guess. 'Keith Zetchik's.'

'Smart boy, Wat. Go to the top of the class.'

It wasn't smartness, it was background information that gave me the answer. I knew Zetchik and Tedstone had a big bust up when they were lieutenant colonels during Phoenix. According to Weschler – their commanding officer at the time – the falling out was caused by Zetchik's hard-hitting tactics. Tedstone went farther. He'd called Zetchik a butcher.

I asked, 'Was Zetchik there – I mean physically present in the village when this was going down?'

He put another mint in his mouth. 'According to my information, yes he was. There are various accounts of Zetchik strutting around the place chomping on a cigar like he was George Patton. He even used his own nickel-plated sidearm to shoot down any poor bastard who ran in his general direction.'

This stacked up in some ways, not in others.

There was no mention of the incident in the classified document I'd received – the stuff detailing how Kim was recruited by the CIA. Some paragraphs had been redacted. Quite possibly they related to this alleged atrocity. If Weschler sent me the file, why didn't he want me to know about the killing of Kim's family? Having said that, it was equally possible that Weschler received the same sanitized version that arrived on my desk, so he may not have known either. I even wondered if the information had been kept from Kim.

Something else troubled me: Kim got turned by the CIA in 1968 – nearly a year before this alleged atrocity. How must it have felt, spying for the side that slaughtered your parents and neighbours?

The DEA guy cleared his throat. 'Food for thought, wouldn't you say, Wat?'

'Sure would, Bobby.'

There was another inconsistency. I said, 'It might explain why Kim would go after Zetchik. But why the wife?'

'You got me there, buddy.' I pictured Bobby making a what-can-I-tell-you? shrug.

'I mean, where's the sense in it?'

I got the impression he was thinking about this. After a time, he said, 'Kim's mom and pop were her only family. Maybe she went after Christine Zetchik because Keith Zetchik killed all her kin and she wanted to do the same to him. The Zetchiks never had kids. So killing the husband and wife would wipe out them out completely.'

There was another pause. Again, I sensed him thinking. Eventually he said, 'Also, you gotta remember Kim's a Catholic. Aren't they into that eye for an eye stuff? Or it could have been an honour thing. I heard the Vietnamese are that way inclined too.'

'Do *you* think that's what happened, Bobby?'

Another mint went the way of the previous two. 'Dunno, Wat.'

I didn't know either. But Kim's folks had been well-to-do and enlightened – wealthy enough to send her to the States for a top college education. They may have been Catholics, like a lot of folks in the former French colony of Vietnam. But I couldn't imagine them bringing up their only daughter with that sort of Old Testament mentality, still less a feuding one. Truth be told, both were much more common in the West Virginia hill country where I came from. Back then, though, there was a lot I couldn't imagine about the story I was chasing.

I heard Bobby crunching his mint. 'Another possibility is that Zetchik took something of value from Kim's family home when his grunts turned the place over. I mean, they were rich people, right? Could've been jewellery or something else you could carry away. Kim couldn't find it at Zetchik's apartment so she went looking in Earlstown, but found his wife instead.'

'Plausible, I guess.'

Something else was worrying me. I put it to him straight, 'Why are you telling me this, Bobby?'

He chuckled. 'What is it with you reporters? This is a gilt-edged gift horse and you're giving it a full dental exam.'

'I need to know.'

He sighed. 'Okay, to put it bluntly, I want you outta my hair. I got a lot at stake out over in Earlstown and I don't want you poking around, asking questions. It's the wrong direction for you, so I just pointed you in the right one.'

'What about Kim? Won't she go back there and cause problems?'

'If my first hypotheses is correct, she's already killed Keith and Christine Zetchik so it's mission accomplished and she has no reason to go back.'

'What about your second hypothesis?'

'My guess is she found whatever she was looking for. But either way, now that she knows DEA has the place under surveillance, she'll stay away. End result is the same.'

'Presumably you shared this information with Rhyme Dillard at MPD and Anne Arundel County Sheriff's?'

'I told them what they needed to know, without jeopardising my operation.'

I held back my next question while a school party moved past. Then I asked, 'What *is* your operation, Bobby?'

Another mint went into his mouth. Man, that dude liked his mints. 'Sorry, Wat, can't tell you.'

'Come on, Bobby. Just give me some idea what's going on out there, and I promise to stay away.'

I sensed more deep thinking. Eventually he said, 'Off the record? And strictly not for publication? *And* you'll never go back there?'

'You got my word.'

'Any of this gets out and you'll fuck up a two-year investigation.'

'I get it, Bobby.'

Another brief silence, then he said, 'My subject is the Zetchiks' maid.'

This was not what I was expecting to hear.

I thought back, recalled the Hispanic woman arriving at the house as I was leaving.

He said, 'She's a Columbian national who manages the US end of a cocaine trafficking operation. It involves big quantities of bump being brought in container ships from Cartagena to Baltimore. As you know, the port is just a short drive from Earlstown and you can observe the big ships steaming into Chesapeake Bay.'

'I saw the maid on my way out of the house. She didn't look much like a narcotics kingpin.'

Bobby made another short laugh. 'Do they ever? She's a dumpy middle aged Latina: The perfect invisible woman.'

He was right there.

But was he right about Kim?

The woman was a puzzle. And the deeper I dug, the more I realized she was the key to my story.

Bobby's lean figure vanished from the corner of my eye and I heard his footsteps receding on the polished wood flooring.

When I looked around, he was gone. The only signs of his presence were the fast-dissolving scent of peppermint and an empty pack of Pez candy mints in a nearby trash can.

# NINETEEN

Rhyme Dillard had stopped clicking his spring-operated ballpoint and started chewing the plastic top of a BIC pen. He had it wedged between his uneven incisors as he watched me sit in the visitor chair opposite his desk.

The office was spacious and airy, a pleasant change from the stuffy interview room where we last saw one another. He called me over because he had some news on Joseph Tedstone, and another unspecified matter he said needed to be handled face to face.

Dillard went straight to it, 'Joseph Tedstone has been cleared of Christine Zetchik's murder.'

He looked down at a typewritten report on his desk. 'Medical examiner puts Mrs Zetchik's time of death between 10.00am and 2.00pm on Friday. Joseph Tedstone's sister confirmed that he was with her between those times.'

I looked up from my notebook. 'You took her at her word?'

He made a slow shrug. 'She already demonstrated her bona fides by admitting she couldn't give him an alibi for the two other homicides. No reason I can think of why she wouldn't lie about those, but would about this.'

He nibbled the BIC some more. 'But no, I didn't take her word for it. I was talking to Joseph Tedstone at 10.15am on Friday. No way he could have gotten back from Earlstown in under 15 minutes – even assuming the earliest possible time of death.'

I scribbled shorthand in my notebook. This wouldn't sit well with Reggie. She was still holed up in her grubby apartment in Adams Morgan and her mental state was not encouraging. I'd seen her the previous evening and she'd clearly been snorting bump. Which meant she'd put herself at risk by going out on the street to score it. Again, I urged her to speak to Dillard. Again, she refused. And I was no nearer finding out if Holy Joe was behind the attempted hit.

Even so, the news about Christine Zetchik was helpful. If anything, it strengthened Bobby Delacroix's theory that Kim Lamb could have eliminated Keith Zetchik, then gone to Earlstown and killed Christine. But how did any of this relate to Johnny? I was almost certain his and Keith Zetchik's deaths were related; and I was equally convinced the homicides of Keith and Christine Zetchik were linked. Yet I couldn't imagine how the two sets of murders were connected.

Dillard's bass voice broke into my thoughts. 'I got something else might interest you. And maybe you can help me.'

This was why he asked me to drop by in person. 'I'm all ears, Captain.'

'It's concerning our man in a suitcase. Lab reports say the torso is that of a man in his late 20s or early 30s, of south east Asian origin. In itself, that doesn't narrow things down to any meaningful degree. But, as I said on the phone, there are some old scars on his chest. At first I thought they were symbols, but then one of my guys who served in Vietnam saw them, and thought they were Vietnamese letters. He can't read the lingo, but then I remembered you can.'

He slid a set of one foot by two foot colour prints across his desk and went back to chomping the top of his pen.

I picked it up and saw the image of a naked male torso crammed inside an old fashioned suitcase – the kind with protective brass covers on the corners. I looked closer. The head and limbs had been cleanly severed and the smooth skin turned pale grey, giving a plastic appearance. Scars on the chest were old, deep and ragged, gouged into the flesh with a sharp instrument, possibly the point of a knife. I squinted and tilted the picture to the light.

I read out the three Vietnamese words carved into the flesh, '*Kẻ phản bội.*'

Dillard frowned. 'What's that mean?'

I looked across at him. 'It means traitor.'

'My guy says he never saw anything like it. I thought you might have, though, in your line of work.'

I nodded yes. 'I sometimes saw this cut into the bodies of people denounced by the Viet Cong as collaborators.'

'So this guy could've been working for us?'

I thought about it. 'That would add up. See, compared with the other things Charlie did to his victims, scars like these were usually the very least of their worries.'

I pushed the photo back across the desk. 'So this guy was lucky to escape much worse?'

I thought about it again. 'Either that, or he got turned.'

'So he could've been working for the North Vietnamese?'

'It's possible. We need to find out more about him.'

Dillard made a dour expression. 'Guy with no head and no hands, that's gonna be all kinds of difficult.'

*

I knew a way to make the *Man in a Suitcase* investigation a little less difficult, though I doubted Dillard would appreciate it. If I told him what I was planning, he'd think I was trying to hijack his investigation. So I didn't tell him.

Instead I called Steve O'Hara, area manager at the C&O National Historical Park. I'd interviewed Steve a couple of months back for a story about a spike in vandalism along the canal's towpath in Georgetown.

Like most folks in Washington, Steve had already read about the body in the suitcase.

I asked his opinion on the most likely spot to ditch the suitcase in the canal, assuming it was transferred from the trunk of a car, or the back of a van, probably at night and in a hurry.

Steve said, 'The suitcase came to the surface near Lock 4, right?'

I checked my notes. 'Right.'

He paused a few seconds, then he said, 'My guess is that it was put into the water someplace close by. It would have drifted downstream, but very slowly, and only when the suitcase started to float. Hang on a second. Let me go check the map.'

He came back a couple of minutes later, sounding excited. 'There's a section of the towpath with a concrete surface at the south end of 33rd Street NW. Access is off of Water Street and you drive a car or a van to within ten yards of the canal bank. That would be my best guess.'

# TWENTY

An hour later I was smoking a Camel at 33rd and Water NW, looking west toward the Key Bridge.

Halfway through my smoke, I pinned Kim walking along the street.

She agreed to meet me after I contacted her at Langley and laid my cards on the table: The Vietnamese words cut into the victim's chest pointed to a link with Giang. There could also be a connection with the murders of Keith and Christine Zetchik. Given that Kim and I had direct knowledge of black ops in Vietnam, I suggested joining forces for a closer look at the location Steve O'Hara suggested.

I'd approached her partly to make a peace offering, and partly because I realized she could be useful to me. We were coming at the same thing from different angles and sooner or later our paths were bound to cross. When that happened, I wanted her onside. Also, as a CIA operative she could access resources I'd need to nail this story.

Gotta say I was pleasantly surprised at her willingness to co-operate.

Sure, I kept in mind what Bobby Delacroix told me about Kim having a score to settle after Keith Zetchik wiped out her family in '69. I was also aware that Kim could have been behind the fake landmine left outside my place. But one way or another, I was certain she was at the heart of this story. And keeping her close was the best way of finding out exactly what she was after.

We walked up the narrow section of 33$^{rd}$ Street to the canal bank and the area of the towpath Steve described.

She surveyed the glassy surface of the canal and the tree-lined towpath. A jogger and a woman walking her dog were headed in the direction of the Commercial Traction Company tower a quarter mile upstream. 'You got any idea what we might be looking for?'

I shook my head.

She gave me a doubtful glance. 'You weren't kidding when you said this was a longshot.'

'Better than a no-shot.' I tried to sound upbeat. 'Look, these people would've been in a rush, almost certainly working in the dark, and anxious not to be seen. Maybe they made a mistake. Maybe they dropped something.'

The area we were looking at wasn't extensive, but it was covered in every kind of trash you could think of: Beer bottles, take-out cartons, candy wrappers, dog turds. Plenty of dog turds.

After half an hour of poking in the garbage, Kim made a frustrated sigh. 'Look, this was worth a try, and I'm grateful for your sharing the information about the torso scars. Also, for what it's worth, I agree the John Doe is probably linked to Giang, maybe the Zetchiks too. But we could be here all day … '

She was right. I was about to agree when a couple of ideas slotted together.

I grabbed a fallen tree branch and used it as a broom to sweep away some of the garbage.

I sensed her eyes on me, and her unspoken question: *What are you doing?*

I kept on sweeping, clearing a yard-wide path from the where the road ended, across the concrete surface, to the canal.

I found nothing.

I repeated the process, this time working back from the canal to the road.

Still nothing.

I felt her rising impatience.

I said, 'Let me take one last shot at this.'

'One last shot at what?' She sounded exasperated and I didn't blame her.

But I was determined. I started brushing another channel through the trash. I'd reached the half way point back to the canal when I saw what I was looking for: Two parallel yellow lines, about three feet apart, on the cracked concrete surface.

'Bingo.'

She looked at me like I was crazy.

I pointed at the ground. 'The suitcase was one of those old-fashioned ones, with brass alloy covers to protect the corners. If you drag a case like that by hauling one end, the other will leave marks on any hard surface. Marks like these.'

I went back to sweeping with fresh energy and quickly uncovered tracks leading all the way from the end of the road to the canal, where they vanished.

'What's this?'

Kim was indicating a third line on the concrete. It was the same colour as the tracks I'd found and ran alongside them for three or four feet, then veered away, under the carpet of crap. I went to work with my improvised broom and cleared the trash around the third mark. This quickly revealed a fourth.

The penny dropped in Kim's head a fraction before mine.

She said, 'There are two sets of tracks.'

I said, 'You thinking what I am?'

She nodded. 'There could have been two suitcases.'

'But why?' I tried to force my brain to figure out what this might mean.

Again, she got there first. 'Your pal Dillard logically assumed the head and limbs were severed to prevent identification. But what if the killer chopped up the body simply because it wouldn't fit in one suitcase? If he had two cases, he could remove the head and limbs and put them in the second case. Then fill both cases with building rubble and sink them in the canal at the same spot. Hence, two sets of tracks.'

I glanced along the canal toward Lock 4 where the floating suitcase was found. 'The case with the torso floated to the surface 10 days later when the chest cavity filled with methane and created buoyancy. But there are no cavities in the head or limbs. So, if they were in the second case, it would have gone to the bottom and stayed there.'

We looked at one another.

I said, 'We need divers.'

# TWENTY-ONE

Rhyme Dillard wasn't best pleased to have a spook and a reporter poking around his investigation. But he'd take help any way he could get it and wasted no time requesting a team of divers from MPD Harbour Patrol.

They soon found the second suitcase at the bottom of the canal, close to where the two sets of tracks ended.

No one was surprised that it contained a head, two arms and two legs, or that the features indicated Vietnamese origin.

This was a big stride forward. Even so, there were major problems with identification. Ten days' immersion in the canal meant the guy's face would be tough to match with any photos held by the federal agencies – assuming there were any. In the same way, using his teeth for ID would hinge on whether he had dental records.

I couldn't fault Dillard for trying, though. He also had a fingerprint specialist working on the shrivelled fingertips, and an artist drawing a sketch of what the victim would have looked like.

Sitting in his office alongside Kim, I watched him gnawing the plastic top of his BIC ballpoint while he read a memorandum that had just been delivered. His crumpled polyester suit and fuzz of grey stubble made him look more like a drunk who'd spent the night in the tank rather than a homicide chief. Overburdened and under-resourced, Dillard was a man under all sorts of pressure.

Even so, he'd spared us the time to go through the medical examiner's preliminary report in as much detail as he was allowed, explaining technicalities and answering questions – in my case, off the record.

When he finished reading, he looked up through mournful eyes. 'Memo says the DA wants to put Joseph Tedstone in front of a grand jury next week and I'm nowhere near ready. So if you two wouldn't mind, I got work to do.'

'One last thing,' Kim said. 'Could we take a gander at the rubble in the second case?'

Dillard gave her a dubious look. 'It was filled with broken brick and stone, same as the other case. Could have come from dozens of places across the city.'

She persisted. 'Mind if we look anyway?'

'Yes I do.' His tone hardened. He was near the end of his rope. 'All the stuff we pulled from the canal is down at the medical examiner's office. I don't have the time to go with you and I can't spare anyone to take you.'

I leaned forward with a help-us-out-here smile. 'C'mon, Rhyme, we just did you a big favour.'

He eyed the pair of us, as if weighing up the quickest way to get rid. With a begrudging sigh, he opened his desk drawer, riffled through a file, and produced a large colour photograph.

'This shows what was left inside the second suitcase after the body parts were removed. You can take it away, but I want it back first thing tomorrow morning.'

Kim picked up the picture and we headed for the door.

'Hey, Tyler.'

I looked over my shoulder at the world-weary cop.

'That picture better not appear in print.'

'Never happen, Rhyme.'

I set off again.

'Oh, and Tyler.'

I turned back from the doorframe.

'It's Captain Dillard to you.'

Outside the cop shop Kim walked toward her AMC Hornet parked on the street.

I followed. 'What's your interest in the stuff in the second case?'

She dipped in her purse for her car keys. 'I just wondered if the killers left anything behind that might help us. Maybe this is a waste of time, maybe not. But your buddy Dillard has a lot on his plate and I got the impression this wasn't top of his agenda.'

'He's not my buddy. I thought he made that plain when we walked out the door.'

'He's a grumpy old bastard for sure, but he likes you.'

'He tolerates me.'

She smiled. 'For a guy like him, it's the same thing.'

I got into the passenger seat beside her. She'd picked me up at the *Tribune* office and we came down to MPD HQ together. 'Where we gonna examine that picture?'

She started the engine. 'Who said anything about we?'

I ignored the jibe. 'Your place or mine? We could use the conference room at the *Tribune*.'

Quick glance in her side mirror and she pulled onto the street. 'Well you sure as hell won't get into Langley.'

I'd been inside Langley often enough, but I took her point.

So we went to the *Tribune* conference room and sat with the photo between us on the long glass-surfaced table.

Gotta say, it seemed that Dillard was right: We were scrutinising a bunch of random rubble that could have come from any derelict lot in DC.

But I forced myself to concentrate because Kim was also right: People in stressful situations make mistakes. They could have left something we could use.

I couldn't see anything helpful though. After 15 minutes the back of my neck started to ache from craning over the photo.

I pushed my chair back from the table. 'I could use a cup of coffee. Want one?'

She shook her head.

When I returned from the vending machine two minutes later her gaze was still fixed on the picture.

I said, 'Could be we're missing something because the picture only shows one side of that stuff. Why don't we go back to Dillard when he's in a better mood and ask to see the actual case?'

Her brow furrowed. 'Maybe one side is enough.'

I went back to my seat.

'Look at this.' She pointed to a piece of round-rimmed stone with a hammer-like shape carved at the centre.

'And this.' She indicated a smaller chunk of stone on the opposite side of the suitcase. This featured a similar engraving, but it looked more like a machinist's set square.

She looked up at me. 'Put these together, what do you get?'

I looked again. And again. I frowned and squinted. The jagged edges of the two pieces of stone fit together perfectly.

And the combination of the two carvings was so familiar that I couldn't get how I didn't see it from the get-go. I said, 'It's a Christian cross.'

She nodded. 'Odds on it's from some part of a church. But which part?'

I leaned out of my chair forward to examine the picture more closely. Both pieces of stone were mottled by a mustard-coloured substance that I guessed was lichen. There were also small pale flecks. Hard to be sure but it looked a lot like bird shit.

I told her what I thought and she agreed: The stone was from the outside of the building.

She said, 'Outside is good. Easier to identify the place. All the same, it's not gonna be easy.'

I said, 'I know a shortcut.'

# TWENTY-TWO

Late that afternoon we arrived at the Church of St Aloysius off Lincoln Road NE in Eckington. It was a handsome building with white rendered concrete walls and tall stained glass windows. There was a newness about the place that corresponded with the remains of the old church, piled in a vacant lot on the opposite side of the street. The site was fenced off, but kids were playing on the pyramid of rubble, so access wouldn't have been a problem for the people who murdered the man in the suitcases.

My shortcut had involved basic newspaper work. We swung by the DC Office of Planning and asked if any raze permits had been issued recently for the demolition of deconsecrated churches. A helpful clerk told us there were three, but two had been timber structures and only St Aloysius was built of stone and brick. Just as importantly, the two wooden churches were protestant, while St Aloysius was Roman Catholic. This stacked up because a lot of Vietnamese folks became Catholics during the French colonial period. The clerk also produced a pre-war photo of St Aloysius that clearly showed the engraved stone cross we'd spotted in the suitcase. In the photo it was mounted on a pediment above the church entrance.

Our next stop had been MPD Homicide. Dillard wasn't in his office but one of his sergeants let me have the artist's sketch of what the dismembered guy would have looked like. It showed a thin, fine-boned man, early to mid-thirties, with a broad brow and receding hairline. It was difficult to associate him with the butchered body parts crammed into the two suitcases. Whatever he did, he didn't deserve that. I felt a jolt of anger and that was good because it showed the emotional circuits in my head were sparking on some level.

Kim parked outside the new church as a middle-aged dude in a dog collar and black cassock appeared from the main doors and headed toward us. He was a tall, sturdy fellow with blue eyes and broad features. Ragged white hair was pushed behind fleshy ears, giving the impression that his appearance took second place to whatever else he had to do. I placed him in his mid-fifties.

'Mr Tyler and Miss Lamb?' He spoke with a Boston accent. 'I'm Father Collins. We talked on the telephone.'

He showed us into his office at the rear of the church and we sat in two visitor chairs facing his desk. On the wall behind him was a framed portrait of Pope Paul, beside one of Boston Red Sox batter, Dwight Evans. Size and positioning of the photos suggested Father Collins held the pontiff and the ballplayer in equal esteem.

He took out a pack of non-filtered Chesterfield cigarettes and a book of matches. 'You said you were trying to identify a young Vietnamese man who may have been a member of my congregation.'

I produced the sketch and pushed it across the desk.

The look of recognition on priest's face was immediate. 'His name is Le Nguyen Chau. Came over from Vietnam last year. One of my regulars.' He made a warm smile. 'Why is the *Tribune* writing about Chau? He won one of your reader competitions, did he?'

Short silence played awkward.

I said, 'I'm sorry, Father, but he was the victim of a brutal murder. That's why we're writing about him.'

Collins put down his unlit cigarette. 'You better tell me what happened.'

I told him. Of course he knew about the man in the suitcase. Everyone in DC knew about that. Homicide victim turns out to be someone you know, that's a whole other deal.

He ran his fingers through his hair. 'And what? You think he was murdered by members of the Vietnamese community here in DC?'

Kim said, 'There's a strong possibility.'

The priest blew a lungful of air through an O-shaped mouth and leaned back in his seat.

I asked, 'What can you tell us about him?'

Collins lit his Chesterfield. 'Came to DC last April after the fall of Saigon. Attended mass once, sometimes twice a week. He also helped out with running the church wherever and whenever he could. He had a small apartment at Elm and 3rd, so was close by.'

I made some notes. 'What did he do for a job?'

'Worked as a clerk at the Department of Agriculture.'

I looked up from my notepad. 'Do you know anything about his background in Vietnam? Family, where he came from?'

'Never spoke about family. He was an accountant in Saigon before enlisting in the South Vietnamese Army. His American dream was to study for his accountancy exams in the US. He was doing well, too.' Collins made a sorrowful expression. 'And look where it got him.'

Kim asked, 'Did he have any enemies here in Washington?'

Collins shook his head. 'Not that I was aware of. He was an all-round nice guy. No edge. Never knew anyone who met him and didn't like him.'

I said, 'Can I quote you on that?'

'Sure you can.' He stubbed out his cigarette in a series of angry stabs. 'And I hope whoever did this to poor Chau gets to burn in hell.' He looked at me with a stony expression. 'That's *not* for publication.'

Outside the church, Kim threw me a quizzical look.

I knew what her question was. Hang around spooks as long as I had, you get to anticipate what's coming next.

I said, 'You wanna take a look at Chau's place?'

'Makes sense.'

'Dillard won't be happy.'

'If he finds out.' She unlocked her car and got into the driving seat.

'Okay.' I swung in beside her. 'But if we do find anything, we share it with Dillard.'

This seemed to amuse her. 'Admirable loyalty from a reporter.'

'Not really. I piss him off, he'll never give me anything useful again. But then you only ever worked for the nationals, so I guess that logic never bothered you. No doorstep to shit on, where's the problem?'

She released the parking brake and pulled away from the church. 'You should learn to take a compliment, Wat. And come down off that high horse.'

I guessed maybe she had a point.

We arrived at Chau's second floor apartment five minutes later. Kim made short work of the lock with a set of picks. But we found nothing of any use. The place was small, tidy and furnished like a monk's cell. Anything that wasn't strictly necessary wasn't there. No TV, no phone, nothing hung on the walls, save a carved wood crucifix. And not one ornament or personal affect. It was the same bare-essentials story in the kitchen, bedroom and bathroom.

I said, 'You think somebody's already cleaned the place out?'

She closed the door of an empty kitchen cupboard and turned to look at me. 'Doubtful. I think the guy was hardly ever here. Maybe he just used the address for appearances, or to collect mail. Whatever he did to get himself killed, he did it someplace else.'

She moved toward the door. 'Let's go, we're wasting our time here.'

Before following, I looked out the front window across LeDroit Park.

She called from the landing 'You coming?'

Her tone of voice, the grass and trees threw me right back to Saigon in '71.

Different park, different voice.

But some powerful force connected then and now.

*The park where I'm meeting Linh is off To Do Street. A warm breeze lifts off the Saigon River, swaying palm crowns and rustling scarlet poinciana blooms. Underfed kids play soccer on parched grass. A pair of nannies push strollers along the shaded pathway.*

*We sit on a stone bench. She opens a paperback, I face the opposite direction.*

*This is the first time I've seen her since the meeting at the summer house in Colonel Thanh's garden – the one involving a MACV staff officer codenamed Bootstrap.*

*More than anything I'm happy to see her in one piece. If she got compromised …*

*I ask, 'Any problems?'*

*'None that I couldn't handle.'*

*She's headstrong. So was I at her age. I try to reassure myself with the notion that it never did me any harm. But I'd gotten lucky. And Saigon in 1971 is not a lucky place.*

*I say, 'Please tell me nobody saw you.'*

*'Nobody saw me.'*

*I lean back on the bench. 'Did you get anything?'*

*'Not much, but something.' She turns the page of her paperback. 'Bootstrap was there. Problem was he didn't say very much. He left that to Colonel Thanh. But Thanh talked only in general terms. From what he said, they could have been producing automobile parts. And I was listening through a wooden wall so their voices were kind of muffled.'*

*'This Bootstrap. Did you get any kind of look at him?'*

*'Afraid not. I was limited to quick peeks through a window and he was sitting with his back to me the whole time. All I can tell you is that he has dark brown hair.'*

*In the soccer game on the grass opposite, a big kid puts in a heavy tackle on a much smaller boy. He's left on the ground clutching his shin while the game continues. No referee, no foul.*

*'Did you learn anything at all from what Thanh said?'*

*She turns another page. 'I'm pretty sure they're processing the heroin somewhere on Pasteur Street. The colonel made several references to product coming out of Pasteur, and increasing capacity at Pasteur, and security at Pasteur.'*

'That's good,' I say.

But Pasteur Street is nearly three miles long. Chuck Shaughnessy at CIA will know where to focus his surveillance efforts, but even so it's going to be a huge challenge.

'There's something else,' she says. 'Not much, but you said not to overlook detail.'

'Go on.'

'I know which cigarette brand Bootstrap smokes. Thanh offered him one of his own – Thanh smokes Rubis – but Bootstrap must have declined because Thanh then said something like, 'Of course, you like Pall Mall. I'll remember that for next time.''

I say, 'You did well, Linh, really well.' And I mean it. Because picking up precise nuggets of information like that tell me she had an aptitude for this type of work. Yet knowing that Bootstrap smokes one of the most popular cigarette brands in the United States isn't tremendously helpful.

She closes her book and rests it on her lap. 'I'll get more about Bootstrap.'

# TWENTY-THREE

I was sitting in my living room after breakfast with a coffee, a cigarette and thirty minutes to kill before work. The radio was tuned to a local station phone-in and I was listening without really concentrating. I glanced out the window. It was gonna be another very hot day – in fact it was warming up already. I loosened my collar, rolled up my shirtsleeves.

The mail slot opened and I heard stuff drop onto the doormat. I wasn't expecting anything more interesting than the daily dollop of bills and junk mail. So I sipped more coffee and went back to the radio.

Folks were calling in to give their ten cents' worth on the topic of whether children these days were coddled. It made me think about those three kids with unexplained bruises who faced a future in care after their mom shot herself in the head. They'd never been coddled, that was damn certain.

I took another pull on my cigarette.

One guy called to say he used to get wupped regular by his poppy and it never did him no harm. I wondered how he could possibly know that, and about his dumb presumption that he'd somehow grown up to represent the apogee of human aspiration.

I drained my coffee cup, sat back and thought about the day ahead. I had nothing in my diary so it was really a matter of calling round the cop shops for anything on the overnight sheets. There'd been nothing of note on the radio news 20 minutes ago, so I was probably looking at writing up a few short news items.

My thoughts were derailed by a faint tickle on my wrist. Then I felt the hairs on the back of my arm being pushed aside and dozens of pinpricks tracking across my skin. Turning my head real slow, I pinned a six-inch centipede moving toward my elbow. His square head controlled a pair of venomous claws at the end of two long forcipules. Behind these, a segmented brown body was propelled by 80 orange legs.

There were two reasons why I didn't freak out: First, I learned that it did no good before I learned to walk; and second, I was already acquainted with this fella. He'd come a hell of a way to see me – 8,000 miles across the Pacific. He had a bunch of names – Chinese red-head, jungle centipede, orange-legged centipede and more. But the one I knew was the best: Vietnamese giant.

As if sensing that I was watching him, he froze. This was fine by me because it gave me time to think.

I recalled the short pep talk I used to give to guys going into the boonies for the first time: The Vietnamese giant is a highly aggressive critter that preys on anything that isn't significantly bigger than itself – spiders and scorpions, even mice and small reptiles fall into its prey range. Its fast-acting venom isn't lethal to an adult human, though it will leave you with a nasty wound, and in some cases cell-death around the area you got bit. So you really, really don't wanna get bit.

Right now I had three choices: Wait until my visitor decided to move off my arm; brush him off with my free hand; or persuade him to go. Experience told me I could be waiting a long time – hours maybe – for him to move on. Also, these guys were quick on the draw and any attempt to knock him off with my hand would very probably result in a painful bite. Option three seemed the most promising, especially when I pegged last night's leftovers – a slice of pepperoni pizza and an empty beer glass on the coffee table. I wasn't sure if Vietnamese giants were partial to pizza, but if I could lure him onto the dough base, I could capture him by placing the upturned beer glass on top of him.

I reached for the pizza. It was only three feet away, but I couldn't get to it without twisting my body and risking moving my other arm. But I had to try. The manoeuvre went well at first. I shuffled sideways on my butt, swivelled at the hip and grabbed the pizza. But as I lifted it, the couch cushion slipped. I lurched forward, my forearm tilted upward and the centipede skittered. I felt the pointy feet gripping my flesh.

I waited for the bite.

But it never came.

My buddy stopped a couple of inches short of my elbow.

I went back to my task. Placing the pizza slice inside the beer glass, I managed to slide back to my original position. Then I put the beer glass on the couch near my thigh and lifted out the pizza, laying it on the crook of my arm with the tip of the dough an inch from the centipede's head. He didn't move, but then I didn't expect him to. These guys snapped into feeding mode when they detected vibrations made by the movements of their prey. Otherwise they weren't especially dynamic.

So I waited and watched and hoped my visitor would go for a bite of pizza rather than a bite of me. There was a juicy slice of pepperoni right in the middle of the slice. If he went for that, he'd be exactly where I wanted him.

I gave it five minutes, ten.

I'd been in a lot of weird situations, but I couldn't think of anything weirder than sitting in my living room with a venomous centipede and a slice of pizza on my forearm.

Fifteen minutes had ticked by and I was thinking about trying to knock him off my arm when his head inclined slightly, then his forcipules started to twitch. Slow and cautious, he moved forward, scoping out the meal on offer. He shifted half his body length onto the dough base and began nibbling at some mozzarella three or four inches from the pepperoni. In my free hand, my fingers tensed around the upturned beer glass. Finally he appeared to tire of the cheese starter and headed for the main course of meat. I watched his tiny gnashers bite into the pepperoni. I moved the beer glass over the top of him, lowering it a few inches at a time, no sudden movements.

With the glass four inches above the pizza, I brought it down fast, digging the rim into the dough near his head. His tail snaked around, which was a good deal for him because his body was coiled rather than straight. That meant I could press the whole glass down without slicing him in two. His reaction was violent. I saw him claw at the glass, tiny traces of venom tracking down the side. After a few seconds, though, he seemed to realize there was no threat and returned to his meal.

This gave me the opportunity to slide the pizza-and-beer glass arrangement off my arm and onto the coffee table.

With the immediate problem dealt with, I turned my attention to the question of how the fuck he got into my living room.

Recalling the arrival the mail, I went into the hall. There was no post on the doormat, just a small clear plastic bottle with the screw-top missing. Didn't take a great mind to figure out that the centipede had been lured into the plastic bottle, which had then been pushed through my mail slot, minus the top. And *voila*, he'd gotten the freedom of my house. Whoever put him there didn't much care where or when I encountered him, though it was a reasonably safe bet that this would happen sooner or later. And it was a nail-on certainty that the person behind this was also behind the fake landmine. Both incidents were Vietnam-related and that was no coincidence.

The same list of suspects came to mind, but this time Pham Tan Giang was the clear favourite. The former ARVN general had almost certainly discovered the role Kim and I played in identifying the dismembered body of his former aide Le Nguyen Chau. If anyone had a direct interest in deterring further investigation, it was Giang.

Having said that, I couldn't rule out Joseph Tedstone. If he'd killed Johnny and Zetchik – and the evidence said he did – he'd want to stop my investigation, or at least throw me off the scent. Also, like Giang, Holy Joe had been in Vietnam and he knew that I'd been there too.

The same went for Kim. I liked her, sure. But I still wasn't sure if I could trust her. Was she manipulating me? Wouldn't be the first time I'd gotten played by an attractive woman. I couldn't figure out why she might be responsible for the landmine or the centipede, but there was no shortage of stuff I couldn't figure out.

I thought too about Bobby Delacroix. The DEA guy had gone to great lengths to give me Kim's background story, which included a powerful motive for murdering Keith Zetchik and possibly Christine. And that story was also rooted in Vietnam. But Delacroix's thing was the stake-out of the Columbian narcotics operation at Earlstown. As far as he knew I had no reason to go back there. And even if I did, the landmine and centipede would hardly deter me. There wasn't any logical connection. Then again, there weren't a lot of logical connections between many elements of the whole situation.

As well as my list of potential antagonists, I detected a disturbing trend. The landmine had been purely psychological – intended to worry me without doing physical harm. The centipede, that represented psychological *and* physical intimidation. Okay, it was non-lethal and somewhat hit-and-miss. I might have come across the centipede, I might not. It might have gotten its claws into me, it might not. All the same, this was a definite move toward a more concrete threat.

So I had to ask myself: What next?

# TWENTY-FOUR

By mid-afternoon a fug of blue-grey tobacco fumes had settled at chest height in the *Tribune* newsroom. We only did one edition and knocked off early on Saturdays. Most of the reporters had left and a handful of copy editors were working on layout sheets for Monday's features pages.

I was getting ready to head out when Maggie appeared at my shoulder.

'Got a minute, Wat?'

That tone of voice, it wasn't a minute and it wasn't a question.

She led me into her glass-walled office, not the desk she normally occupied in the middle of the newsroom. I took a seat.

Maggie perched on the corner of the big mahogany desk and made a teasing smile. 'I got a call from Heck Weschler this morning. He was very pleased with your first piece.'

I shrugged, took a pull on my cigarette. 'That's good, I guess.'

'You guess?'

'You know what I think about that sort of feedback.'

Like a lot of reporters, I was always ambivalent about

compliments from people I wrote about. On the one hand, it was a damn sight better than them saying I'd come up with a bunch of crap and they were suing for libel. On the other, it sounded like I'd produced a piece of puff that stroked their ego and ruffled no feathers. But I dug where Maggie was coming from. She was an editor, not a reporter. She had different perspectives, extra responsibilities. 'I get what you mean,' I said. 'It's good for the paper that Weschler likes what we're doing.'

She nodded. 'Gotta say the guy oozes charisma – even down the phone. And he's incredibly photogenic. So is his wife. I get why they're getting talked about as the new Jack and Jackie Kennedy. They'll sell papers for us. And God knows we need to sell papers.'

She went to sit at her desk. 'Your next interview's on Monday, right?'

I nodded.

She reached forward and took a Camel from the pack I'd placed on her desk. 'Word from the campaign trail is Weschler's been offered senior cabinet positions by both the Ford and Carter camps. Be good if you could find out which way he's leaning and what's on the table.'

'We both know he won't tell us. But I'll ask the question anyways.'

Weschler wouldn't tell because he couldn't tell. Any offer had to be conditional on him keeping schtum. But you didn't need to be a genius to figure out that he was in the running for secretary of state, national security adviser and secretary of defense. As for endorsing Gerry Ford or Jimmy Carter, he'd want a much clearer idea of who was most likely to win before committing.

Maggie tapped a stack of ash into a trash can. 'At some point there'll be a Mr and Mrs interview with Heck and Paula. Word is she's using a big chunk of her family wealth to bankroll hubby's presidential campaign, but also contributes to his strategic planning in a way that no prospective first lady ever did.'

I lit a cigarette. 'You want me to ask about that too?'

She could tell by the tone of my voice that I wasn't happy about receiving all this direction. 'It's your story, Wat. But I think it's a good thing, don't you? A woman playing such a senior role in presidential campaign?'

I could see why she was interested in the feminist angle and made an accommodating smile. 'I guess one day we might have a woman running for president. Maybe even Paula Weschler.'

'Maybe.'

She stood up and walked to the window. 'I also wanted to tell you that was good work on the *Man in a Suitcase* story. Our owners were impressed.'

The *Tribune's* lead story in yesterday's final edition revealed the name of dismembered murder victim Le Nguyen Chau. Dillard agreed to give us a four-hour start before he made an official statement, which effectively meant we had the piece the day before the *Post* and the *Star*. It was his grudging acknowledgment of the assistance I'd given him.

I shrugged. 'It's what you pay me for.'

'So how's the broader investigation shaping up?'

I made a resigned sigh. No point holding back with Maggie so I told her all I knew.

When I was done, she asked, 'Could we be looking at a quadruple homicide?'

'We could be. Or two doubles, or a triple and a single. Even four singles. So far there's nothing to tie Johnny Tedstone to Christine Zetchik. And Le Nguyen Chau may or may not be linked.'

She skewered me with her gaze. 'You think they're all connected, though, don't you?'

'That's what my gut says. But we're a long way from a hard news story. We don't even have enough to make a coherent conspiracy piece.'

'How does this attempted shooting of your friend Reggie Acheson tie in? Or doesn't it?

I ran my fingers through my hair. 'Reggie is absolutely convinced Joseph Tedstone killed Keith Zetchik and Johnny, and is now going after her.'

'You don't sound entirely convinced.'

'She's fragile, vulnerable and confused. Also, she scores drugs from dangerous people. By her own admission, she owes a great deal of money. They could be trying to scare her into paying up. Or they could just have run out of patience.'

She picked up my hesitation. 'Go on.'

I made a can't-believe-I'm-saying-this expression and told her Weschler's theory that Johnny may have killed Zetchik and then committed suicide in order to frame his dad.

'I know it sounds far-fetched. But if it's true, Johnny would also have played Reggie. He'd have convinced her that his dad was guilty, which wouldn't have been difficult because Johnny knew perfectly well that Reggie was mixed-up and highly suggestible.'

I wanted Maggie to disagree, but she did the opposite. 'I covered an inquest in Brooklyn a few years back after a teenage boy hanged himself in a public park and left a note blaming the girl who just dumped him. Admittedly the Johnny Tedstone hypothesis goes way beyond that. But it's on the same spectrum of disturbed thinking. It's a difference of degree, not a difference of kind.'

I conceded that I'd known soldiers in Vietnam talk about getting killed in action to punish folks back home, then step into Charlie's crosshairs.

Her gaze didn't waver. 'There's something else bothering you about this Johnny-did-it idea, isn't there?'

# TWENTY-FIVE

I nodded. 'Heck Weschler wants it to be true. He wants Joseph Tedstone to be innocent. I think Weschler feels protective of his own. I get why, but I think he's wrong.'

She gave one of her tender but unyielding looks. 'Whoever was responsible for that shooting on Wisconsin Avenue, Wat, you should have reported it to the cops.'

I shook my head. 'If I did that, Reggie wouldn't trust me ever again. She'd very probably leave town, end up God knows where.'

There was a tense silence. I knew she didn't approve of my keeping schtum to protect Reggie, but she seemed to realise we were at a dead-end.

She said, 'Okay, and what do you make of this DEA guy Bobby Delacroix's information about Kim's revenge mission.'

'It's plausible. I got it from Weschler – Keith Zetchik's commanding officer during the Phoenix program – that Zetchik had a reputation for going in hard, maybe too hard.'

'Could we be looking at a war crime?'

I couldn't hold back a bitter laugh. 'Technically, yes. But the normal rules of war didn't apply in the Nasty. Proving an atrocity happened is one problem. Holding somebody accountable, that's something else.'

'Like the massacre at My Lai?'

'Exactly. Broadly speaking, the facts aren't disputed – hundreds of unarmed civilians killed, including small children and pregnant women. But where do you pin the blame? The platoon leader? Company commander? Battalion level? Fuck, you could go right up to the president. And My Lai only entered the national consciousness because those guys got caught. Countless other atrocities went unreported or were just ignored.'

Maggie looked angry. 'So Zetchik's okay because he was just following orders like the rest?'

'I didn't say that. If it's right that he killed Kim's family and slaughtered her community just for the hell of it, I sure wouldn't blame her for going after him. I'd do the same in her place.'

She gave me a baffled look. 'I thought you'd give the guy a medal if he got rid of *your* family.'

I made a weak smile. 'I was being flippant, and I was referring to my mom and dad. When I said I'd do the same in Kim's place, I meant if anybody did anything to *you*.'

There was an awkward moment. We knew what we meant to one another, but we rarely if ever said it out loud.

She said, 'Let's hope it never comes to that.'

Then she changed the subject. 'You like Kim don't you?'

'Sure I like her. But I don't trust her.'

'What about Bobby Delacroix. You trust him?'

I thought about it. 'He's an odd bird, no argument there. But he checks out.'

'What about Giang, the dime store general?'

I jetted cigarette smoke through my nostrils. 'Most or all this shit, it's either on him, through him, or with his knowledge. And I think its starts with his relationship with Keith Zetchik.'

'Did their paths cross in Vietnam?'

'I'd be surprised if they didn't. But my best guess is that Zetchik did something to piss Giang off much more recently. Could be he reneged on a funding commitment, or promised something he couldn't deliver.'

'Then what? Christine Zetchik knew about this and Giang's people killed her to keep her quiet?'

'Quite possibly.'

'And our *Man in a Suitcase*, Chau, was a go-between of some sort who was silenced for similar reasons?'

'Again, entirely plausible.' I rested my cigarette in the ashtray on her desk. 'Johnny Tedstone is the real mystery. He has no connections to any of them.'

'Except through his dad.' She gave me a thoughtful look. 'Could Joseph Tedstone have known Giang, either in Vietnam, or after Giang came to DC?'

'Unlikely.'

I thought about it, though, and started thinking aloud. 'Having said that, Holy Joe could have gotten wind of some shady deal Zetchik was working on with Giang. Maybe he went round to Zetchik's apartment that night and threatened to expose whatever it was unless Zetchik put a stop to it.'

'At gunpoint?' She sounded dubious.

'Holy Joe isn't stupid. He wouldn't have taken the Mauser with any intention of using it. More likely for insurance if things with Zetchik turned ugly. Or if Giang's goons showed up.'

She leaned forward, resting her elbow on her desk and cupping her chin in her palm. 'Go on.'

'According to Reggie, Joseph Tedstone had a heated discussion with Keith Zetchik on the phone and drove around to his apartment soon afterwards. Reggie says Holy Joe returned to the family house about 45 minutes later, hid the gun, then confronted Johnny. We don't know what happened after that. But maybe Johnny threatened to tell the cops what he knew. Johnny had caused his dad a lot of grief over many years. According to Joseph Tedstone, Johnny's whole gay thing was fabricated to hurt and embarrass his dad. Could be this was the moment the old man's patience ran out. He got the kill pills, slipped one into Johnny's whiskey, and watched him drink it.'

Maggie wrinkled her brow. 'So how come Johnny knew what was going to happen before it actually did – when he met you at the Bayou?'

I sucked in cigarette smoke, exhaled slowly. 'God knows where Johnny's head was at –Johnny certainly didn't. He could have overheard his dad on the phone with Zetchik on a previous occasion. Or, overheard his dad telling someone else that he was gonna pull the plug on whatever it was Zetchik was up to. I can't explain how he could have known about the threat to his own life.'

Maggie leaned back in her chair. 'Assuming somehow he did, how would Christine Zetchik tie in with any of that?'

'Dunno.' I extinguished my cigarette. 'But if Joseph Tedstone had the resources to order the hit on Reggie, he could have used the same people to kill Christine Zetchik.'

'Then why get his hands dirty killing Keith Zetchik? Why not get these third party people to do that?'

I pulled a give-me-a-break face. 'I never said I had all the answers, Maggie. I never even said I had any. But how about this for a situation: Joseph Tedstone goes to talk to Keith Zetchik. He takes his gun, but doesn't plan to use it. Something goes wrong, things get out of hand, Zetchik ends up dead. Holy Joe goes back home and silences Johnny because Johnny knows exactly where his pop's been. But then Tedstone Senior realizes he doesn't have the time to take care of Christine Zetchik and Reggie, so he calls in these third party dudes.'

She said, 'It's just about credible, I suppose.'

'Maybe it is.' I gave her a tired look. 'To be honest, Maggie, my brain's hurting with all this thinking.'

'I'm not surprised. You've been at this night and day. You look like the walking dead.'

'You always did know how to make me feel good.'

She made a maternal smile. 'Why don't you go to New York? Recharge your batteries in the Batcave? You could drive up there right now, come back tomorrow evening.'

The idea was tempting. The Batcave was Maggie's nickname for my sound-proof apartment in the East Village where I kept my entire record collection and sound system. Every song that shaped my life was there, starting with Burl Ives' 1949 recording of *Big Rock Candy Mountain*. That was the song I listened to on the radio, and more often in my head, when my dad came home drunk and beat the shit out of my mom while I lay in bed. The song didn't remind me of the violence, it reminded me of how I survived it, how music took me someplace else. I didn't use music to tune out and hide, I used it to come alive, plug into the sort of emotions most folks took for granted. In my New York apartment I had bootlegs, live albums and studio LPs. I had hard rock and catchy pop, folk and country, soul, reggae, arthouse and – best of all – stuff you couldn't pigeonhole. And recently, the punk sounds coming out of New York and London and other places – including DC.

'I'd love to,' I said. 'But I gotta see Reggie.'

'You really think it was Joseph Tedstone's people who tried to kill her?'

'Honestly? I don't know. What I *do* know is she's absolutely certain that's what happened.'

That should have been the end of the conversation. I should have closed it off and left her office. Instead I hesitated.

'What?' She leaned forward, looking worried.

I ran my fingers through my hair. When I came in here I was unsure whether to tell her about the hoax landmine and the giant centipede. On the one hand I didn't want to worry her; on the other, what if those guys really upped the ante and I ended up dead without having told anyone?

So I shot her the works.

'You should go to Dillard.'

'I already thought of that and I don't think it's a good idea. Not just yet. Ditto, running a news story.'

'But you're being intimidated.'

'Am I?' I gave her a hard look. 'Or am I being pranked?'

She returned my stony stare. 'It not that simple, Wat. It's very likely linked to the Tedstone/Zetchik story and it's certainly linked to Vietnam. This is all about context.'

'But a lotta folks wouldn't see it that way. If we ran a story, they'd see an ex-Special Forces guy bleating about a hoax landmine containing nothing more dangerous than a shotgun shell, and a creepy-crawly pushed through his mail slot.'

'All right, we hold back on the story – use it for background later. But you could still alert Dillard.'

'I'd rather not, Maggie. I need to handle it myself.'

She seemed irritated. 'So when your friend Reggie refuses to go to the cops, she's a knucklehead. But when *you* refuse, you're, what? A tough Green Beret who's above asking for help?'

'I didn't say that. And I didn't rule out calling Dillard altogether. I just wanna see how this plays out.'

'And what if it continues to escalate? What if you get seriously wounded, or worse?'

'I'll be more careful. I'm used to handling this shit. They're trying to get into my head. That's what booby traps are all about. I saw how they worked in Vietnam – punji pits, bamboo whips, snake pits, flag bombs, grenade-in-a-can traps, lots more. I set plenty myself. They're designed to put you off your game, stop you functioning. They make you doubt yourself and your buddies, hesitate and hold back. With all due respect, Rhyme Dillard didn't serve in the Nasty, so he'd come at this like a cop and that wouldn't be the best approach.'

She sat back and gave me an unimpressed frown. 'So what did you do with the centipede?'

'I took him to the Museum of Natural History. They have a new a live insect section and were happy to have him. Far as I know, he's still munching my pizza leftovers.'

'It's not funny, Wat.' Maggie gave me an imploring look. 'Do me a big favour and mind how you go.'

# TWENTY-SIX

The door to Reggie's apartment in Adams Morgan opened two inches and she peeped through the narrow aperture.

'Did anyone follow you?' She sounded freaked. Her eyes had an opaque glaze, yet they were red-rimmed and nervy, scanning me up and down, over and over.

I couldn't even guess what sort of shit she was on. Booze, certainly; coke, probably; maryjane, amphetamines, barbiturates, possibly. Put enough drugs in your veins, it's tough to tell which one is jerking which trigger.

'Nobody tailed me, Reggie,' I said. 'Trust me.'

She slid the door chain open and let me in.

The place was in the same sort of mess as last time I was here. Takeout cartons and candy wrappers told me her diet wasn't the healthiest, but I guessed it was better than eating nothing at all.

She combed her fingers through her hair but just made it more dishevelled. She wasn't wearing a bra under her Che Guevara T-shirt, but not in a feminist way or a sexy way. More in the way of someone who couldn't be assed putting one on. Or had the shakes so bad she couldn't fasten the strap.

I sat beside her on the couch. 'How have you been?'

'You should have come sooner, Wat. I'm scared, real scared.'

I took her hand a squeezed it. 'Sorry, Reggie. I've been busy. But you're fine. And I'm here now.'

It would have helped to check up on her if she had a phone. But the company disconnected the line because she didn't pay her bill. It would have helped even more if she went to Rhyme Dillard, but she remained determined not to involve the cops.

'Wanna beer?' She sounded abruptly upbeat.

I said yes.

She went into the kitchen and I browsed the dog-eared cardboard box containing her record collection. Everything was in there from the Jimi Hendrix to Donny Osmond. And while I figured a wide-ranging taste in music was a good thing, this collection was all over the place, like she'd gone to a thrift store and bought a boxful of stuff before it had been sorted.

She came back with two beers and seemed much less agitated. Maybe it was my calming presence. Maybe she'd just taken something.

She walked over to the sound system. 'I got a new record. Righteous DC band called the Slickee Boys. Wanna listen?'

I nodded and sipped some beer as she played the Slickee Boys' *Hot and Cool* EP.

It wasn't the best rock music I ever heard, but it sure wasn't the worst. And I dug the rough energy, the we-don't-give-a-shit brass.

'The Slickee Boys are the most,' she said when the last song ended. 'They formed their own label and did everything themselves – even glued the cover. That's what punk's all about, isn't it? You just put your shit out there and anyone who doesn't like it can fuck off.'

She was right there. What puzzled me was how she'd gone from a bag of nerves to an punk rock evangelist in the time it took to grab a couple of beers and play five short songs.

'I went to see the Slickee Boys with Johnny,' she said. 'They played a gig with Overkill at My Friend's House. That's a crab and beer joint in the Maryland suburbs. You and I should go there some time. I like little concerts and I like big concerts. I saw Led Zeppelin play at Oakland Coliseum last year and that was outasight. You into Zep?'

'Sure I'm into Zep.'

So much so that I bought tickets for the second of Led Zeppelin's two dates at Oakland Coliseum but got a refund because the tour was cancelled. The band had toured the US earlier in the year, though, and I figured Reggie went to one of those gigs. State her mind was in, I could easily understand how she'd gotten confused.

But her spirits were up right now, and I was glad of that. We ordered pizza and drunk more beer and listened to more music. When she rested her head on my chest I knew she only wanted a little comfort, and that was cool too.

Later I went to the bathroom. I was washing my hands when I pinned a small plastic bag of white powder on the window sill.

Hardly a shock to find nose candy lying around in an addict's apartment.

I opened the bag and smelled the contents. But the odour was neutral, not the slightly medicinal whiff I'd come to recognize.

I dipped my index finger into the powder and tasted some.

That did give me a shock. This wasn't cocaine, it was baking soda. Some hustler must have seen Reggie coming. In a way, this was more worrying than if the bag had contained pure coke. Put random domestic products into your body, the results can sometimes be more harmful than street drugs.

I opened the wall-mounted cabinet. It was stacked with the usual stuff – toothpaste, toothbrush, Alka-Seltzer, Aspirin, mouth wash. There was also a small bottle of pills with no label. I unscrewed the top and poured a few into my hand. The small pink tablets could have been anything but I doubted they were anything legal.

Back in the living room I showed her the bag of baking soda. I told her where I found it. I explained my concerns.

Seemed to take a while for the penny to drop. Then she said, 'My usual dealer wasn't around so I went this guy Lenny. Bastard must have ripped me off. But I haven't taken any.' She made a sarcastic laugh. 'Guess I can use it in the kitchen.'

Then I showed her the bottle of pills. I said I didn't like prying, but she was scaring me and I wanted to know what was in the bottle.

I expected a show of anger but her voice stayed even. 'Just a little D.'

'As in Dilaudid?'

She chuckled. 'Well, not as in Doritos.'

'You took one when I came in, didn't you?'

She looked at me with an amused expression, like a kid accused of doing something just a little bit mischievous.

'That's not funny, Reggie.' Dilaudid was a morphine-based analgesic, a lot closer to heroin than coke.

I said, 'This is heavy shit. Very easy to OD. You should be real careful.'

That *did* rile her. She threw a paperback at me, and not in a playful way. 'Don't fucking patronize me, Wat.'

'I'm trying to help.'

'You *are* helping. Just by being here. But please don't tell me what to do.'

'Okay.' My mom had been an alcoholic and I knew better than to use conventional reason against the inverted logic of addiction. 'No more advice.'

Her anger dissolved in a fast second. She reached out and pulled me back onto the couch and clung to my arm as if her life depended on it.

\*

I stayed at Reggie's that night but I didn't get much sleep. Not because I was getting it on with Reggie, but because her couch was hard and cramped and reeked of spilled booze and stale maryjane.

The upside was that I did a lot of thinking that I wouldn't have done if I'd gotten a good night's sleep. I thought mostly about Keith Zetchik. I thought about him and Kim. Him and Giang. Him and Holy Joe. And him and his wife.

First thing next morning I went back to the *Tribune* clippings archive and took the Zetchik file back to my desk. It was a Sunday, so the newsroom was empty save for a duty reporter and the copy chief. The quietness suited me. I'd gone through the file already but I figured another look was worth a shot.

Keith and Christine Zetchik were an odd couple: He was US Army through and through, a clenched fist of a guy with pumped-up muscles and prize-fighter features to match; she was a blonde glamour puss, more than 10 years younger, with the education and independence to pursue her own career at the State Department. If she wasn't pictured in a ball gown, she was decked out in a sharp business suit.

As I dug deeper into the clips, the separateness of their relationship became more apparent. And although the file was labelled 'Zetchik, Keith', most of the stories it contained were about 'Zetchik, Christine'. She'd served in various inter-departmental organisations, both in DC and Saigon and had been an active charity campaigner.

I'd been at this for more than two hours and gotten nowhere when I pinned a picture of Christine attending some government function with a bunch of guys. But it wasn't Christine who grabbed my attention. It was the tall teacherly dude at the back of the shot. The reproduction was a little fuzzy, but he looked a lot like Bobby Delacroix.

I read the cutline:

*Mrs Christine Zetchik, chairwoman of the State Department Narcotics Liaison Committee presented a long service certificate on Wednesday to Mr Ted Kirby in recognition of his 20 years of service. The ceremony took place in the Harry S Truman Building in Washington, DC, and was attended by Mr Kirby's colleagues.*

Bobby Delacroix – if it *was* Bobby – was among the dozen or so colleagues who weren't identified. Unless they were celebrities or big shots, a punchy paper like the *Tribune* wouldn't name all those people in a presentation pic.

What bothered me was that I'd seen this picture last time

and hadn't nailed Delacroix. Then I realized why: I'd never seen him before the encounter at Earlstown, which was *after* I first looked through the Zetchik archive.

I read the dateline: September 19, 1970.

The picture had a lot of implications, none of them positive. It seemed Bobby Delacroix served on the same inter-departmental committee as Christine Zetchik going back at least six years. So why didn't he tell me he knew her? Maybe he had sound operational reasons for withholding that information. But some weird shit must have gone down for a DEA agent to end up staking out the home of someone he'd worked with.

Had Bobby strangled Christine Zetchik?

Had Bobby shot Keith Zetchik?

And had Bobby played some role in the deaths of Johnny Tedstone and Le Nguyen Chau?

These were legitimate questions, but I was getting way ahead of what I actually knew.

I forced my brain to slow down. Bobby told me he was staking out the Zetchiks' Hispanic maid. I'd seen her arrive for work at Chez Zetchik and my gut said she didn't kill Christine. But one of her drug trafficking associates may well have. What if Christine realized the maid was involved in suspicious activity and confronted her about it? Was Christine eliminated for that reason?

Too many questions, not enough answers. One place I might find some was the last place Bobby's and Christine's paths crossed. I needed to take a closer look at the house at Earlstown.

# TWENTY-SEVEN

My problem wasn't getting into the house, it was getting in without being pinned by Bobby Delacroix's stakeout team.

Maybe the maid had been arrested. Even if she hadn't, she'd probably been laid off due to the deaths of her employers, and that would probably have shut down the drug traffickers' activities in Earlstown. But one maybe and two probablys didn't add up to a certainly and I couldn't take the risk.

So I parked on the edge of town and went in over the back yard wall. This bordered a belt of trees on the shoreline of Chesapeake Bay. I was fairly confident I hadn't been detected.

The french windows overlooking the lawn at the rear of the property were secured by a single mortice lock that gave me no problems.

I searched the house methodically, room by room, floor by floor, found zip.

I repeated the exercise, with the same result.

This wasn't altogether unexpected because the sheriff's detectives had already completed their investigation here – and I had no doubt the DEA had taken a very thorough look too. Could well be that Kim had been back here as well.

So I was counting on seeing something that at least two sets of professionals hadn't spotted. I didn't think I was better than them, but I was coming at this from a different angle, with different information. I was hoping this would make a difference.

I sat awhile in the living room and thought again about what the Zetchiks might want to hide and where they might hide it. I knew the kinds of places to look and I'd already checked the property from top to bottom, twice. I was clean out of ideas. After a half hour of futile contemplation, I decided to call it quits.

Closing the french windows behind me, I went over the back wall and headed through the trees toward the shoreline.

The sea was lumpy and leaden under saggy sacks of cloud and a sharp wind loaded with sand scraped my face. Farther along the shoreline, pleasure craft were moored at jetties or in colourful boathouses. The land around the coves and inlets was covered in dense woodland that looked like a big sponge put in place to mop up the spilled water of the bay. In the middle of the channel a sailboat heeled right over as if it was going to capsize, then tacked and sailed away on an even keel. A powerful motorboat cut across its stern, churning a ruler-line of foam. And far out in the bay, a maroon-hulled tanker butted north toward Baltimore. I wondered if its holds were full of Columbian narcotics.

As I moved through a little grassy clearing I stepped on something that crunched under my foot. I looked down and saw that I'd crushed a half-eaten pack of Pez candy.

I thought immediately of Bobby Delacroix popping those little mints into his mouth at the National Gallery of Art.

Maybe Bobby had come here the same way I did.

But why would Bobby have come in at the back?

Again, though, I had to rein myself in. A lot of people ate a lot of Pez mints and I had no evidence whatsoever linking Bobby to this half-eaten pack.

I continued back towards the shoreline. This was when that I noticed an old fishing hut 15 yards from the water. I hadn't seen it when I arrived because it was half hidden in the trees and would have been behind me as I approached the house. It was a rickety wooden structure with peeling grey paint and a tarpaper roof. There was a small jetty on the shore nearby where Keith Zetchik could have cast a line and maybe reeled in striped bass or seatrout for dinner.

The hut was an unlikely place to conceal anything valuable. But that was exactly why some people picked unlikely places. Why would anybody think to look in a beat-up old cabin? Also, it wasn't on the Zetchiks' land and that meant it wouldn't be covered by a search warrant.

So I decided to take a look.

The door was secured by two padlocks but they were there mainly for show and I made short work of them.

Inside I found a selection of fishing poles and some perished rubber wading boots. A work bench was stacked with Tupperware boxes containing floats, hooks, lead sinkers and other pieces of angling kit. There was also a plastic tub of live-bait that had been dead some time, plus a pair of fold-up canvas chairs.

The wood flooring was loose. It shifted and creaked as I walked on it. Then I stepped onto a section that didn't shift and didn't creak. I looked down. The board under my feet was old and dry like the rest, but this one was screwed down securely. Down on my hands and knees, I saw that the screw heads were new. I unscrewed them with my multi-use pocketknife and lifted the board from the timber frame.

A waterproof plastic wallet lay on the gravel under the hut. Placing it flat on the workbench I unzipped it. Inside were three foolscap manila envelopes.

I opened the first and found a half dozen pictures of Le Nguyen Chau. I recognized him right away from artist's sketch of the man in the suitcases. The first photo was a portrait shot of Chau in the uniform of a South Vietnamese Army captain. The rest showed him in black bondage gear with a whip-wielding dominatrix doing her thing on his bare butt.

Pieces of the puzzle started coming together.

The second envelope contained another set of pictures. These were much less saucy but a lot more mind-blowing.

One showed Chau with Bobby Delacroix. They were walking together toward the door of a business premises. I squinted at the picture. It had been taken in a hurry, at an awkward angle. This meant part of the shot was taken up by a delivery van that must have driven across the photographer's line of sight. Even so, I clocked the firm's name in scarlet capital letters on a pale blue fascia board: THORNE ACCOUNTING SERVICES.

More puzzle pieces coming together.

In the third envelope I found a dozen sheets of bank statements. The name of the account holder was Robert W Delacroix. My eyes scanned the columns of numbers and dates. And I soon nailed a pattern. On the last day of every month exactly $19,871 was paid into the account by an organisation called Meridian Pacific. These contrasted sharply with DEA salary payments of $9,231. The statements covered a six month period, at the end of which Jimmy Delacroix had netted nearly $120,000 on top of his DEA pay checks.

I stood there a long minute, processing this latest information.

Deduction # 1: Christine Zetchik was a shakedown artist.

Deduction #2: Her victims included Le Nguyen Chau *and* Bobby Delacroix.

Deduction #3: Chau and Bobby were involved together in some kind of racket – probably drugs-related.

Deduction #4: Bobby killed Christine and probably Chau.

Pieces of the puzzle were coming together all right.

Back in the *Tribune* newsroom I called a DEA contact who confirmed Deduction #5: There was no DEA operation in Earlstown.

*

I met Kim at Jimmy's Café at 209½ Penn Street SE. I gave her what I had and she gave me another piece of the puzzle – Chau had been an aide on General Giang's staff from 1969 to last April, when they came to DC after the fall of Saigon.

She stirred some creamer into her coffee. 'So what do you think happened? Bobby killed Christine because she was blackmailing him?'

'It's a strong possibility. He was already in the house when you and I arrived. And we know his story about staking out a drug trafficking operation is bullshit.'

She nodded. 'We can assume from the photo you found in your archive that they've known one another at least six years. Odds are they were working together on some narcotics number back then. That would explain those six big payments that went into Jimmy's account in '68 – which are just the ones we know about. Did you discover anything about who made the payments?'

'All I got is the name: Meridian Pacific. I tried all sorts of directories and spoke to a lotta people and came up with zip. My money is on some front organisation in Vietnam that doesn't exist anymore.'

She nodded. 'Christine spent a lot of time in Saigon during the war. Maybe she hooked up with Chau – and Giang – over there and cut a deal with Bobby stateside. But we need to know more before bracing Bobby.'

I drank some of my coffee. 'That's what Rhyme Dillard thought.'

She didn't look pleased. 'You told the cops?'

I made a what-can-I-say? shrug. 'I can't afford to piss Dillard off. Besides, the DA's putting Joseph Tedstone in front of a grand jury next week and Dillard has his hands full. He's cool with me carrying on with my investigation as long as I don't fuck with his – and keep him in the picture.'

'Then I suggest we look into Chau's background,' she said. 'Given his background in accounting, my guess is that he was Giang's money man. We need to find out what he's been up to since he got here last year – apart from getting his rocks off with Madame Whiplash.'

I gave her a hard look. 'That sadomasochism stuff doesn't make him a bad person.'

She gave me one back. 'I never said it did. But it clearly made him a vulnerable one. That's how Christine got her hooks into him, and ultimately why he ended up in two suitcases in the C&O Canal.'

Had to admit she was right. As an accountant, Chau had the professional skills to handle Giang's finances. As an S&M fetishist, he'd be regarded as a loathsome deviant by the staunchly Catholic Giang. And as a blackmail victim he was a major security risk, which made him a dead man.

I said, 'We should check out the firm in the photo – THORNE ACCOUNTING. It could tie a lot of stuff together.'

She agreed. We went to the *Tribune* where I looked through the library clips and a bunch of phone and business directories. I found nothing close in DC or the neighbouring states. Kim called Langley from the conference room and got the same result for the whole country and Canada too. Maybe the firm had stopped trading after the picture was taken. Maybe it had been taken on some English-speaking Caribbean island, or in Britain or Australia. But at least for now, the lead was dead.

She made a frustrated sigh. 'There must be someplace else can we look.'

'We could try the red light district. See if anyone knew him.'

'Not on a Sunday lunchtime.' She got up and headed for the door. 'I have another idea. Come on.'

I followed her out of the building. Her Hornet was parked on the street. She got into the driving seat and I climbed in next to her.

I said, 'Where we going?'

She started the engine. 'There are some people you need to see.'

# TWENTY-EIGHT

She drove to R Street and Florida Avenue NW in Shaw and we went into George's Quality Eats, a big cafeteria with Formica-top tables decked with vases of faded plastic flowers. It was mainly patronized by African Americans who ate cheap but tasty fare served up by the black proprietor.

Back then, the population of DC was 70 per cent black. The 'Chocolate City' tag sounded progressive. And in some ways it was. DC had a black mayor, Walter Washington, and a black delegate to the House of Representatives, Walter Fauntroy. This wasn't to mention senior black police officers such as Rhyme Dillard. But it didn't seem so progressive when you considered that the black majority was largely due to white civil servants and professional types decamping to affluent suburbs like Bethesda and Arlington. This left less well-off black folks in run-down inner city neighbourhoods like Shaw, where pimps and pushers prospered around the burned out blocks of the '68 riots.

I took a seat opposite Kim. 'Why are we here?'

She picked up the menu. 'Take a look around.'

'I already did when we came in.'

'What did you see?'

'Lotta black folks eating lunch after church.'

'Take a closer look.'

I did what she asked. And I saw what she wanted me to see: dotted among the black folks were some white families and small parties of Asians.

'What do you think?'

I pulled a you-tell-me face. 'The place reflects the neighbourhood, which is not wealthy and mainly black. There are a few white faces and fewer still yellow ones. And the fact that you brought me here suggests some of the yellow faces are Vietnamese.'

A waitress arrived at our table and Kim ordered an omelette with fries and a side of green salad. I was hungry and didn't want to waste time looking at the menu, so I asked for the same.

As the waitress moved away, Kim nodded to her left. 'See those guys over the by main doors?'

I saw four middle aged Asian guys, presumably Vietnamese.

'Fifteen months ago they were all ARVN colonels with high social status and no material needs. Now, two are construction workers, one is a truck driver, the other a delivery man.'

She indicated another table where a man and woman in their late-thirties or early forties were eating with a teenage boy.

Kim filled me in. 'The guy was a senior official at the South Vietnamese Department of Defence, his wife a popular socialite. Now their son is giving them backchat in English, which he speaks much better than mom and pop.'

I waited while the waitress served our food, then said, 'What's your point?'

'Last year 130,000 people – just like these – came to the US. Many more will come this year and next year and in the years after that. Back in Vietnam, they were the elite; here they're just another group of immigrants marked out for discrimination by their skin colour.'

I loaded my fork with omelette and fries. 'I can see why that's depressing. But I still don't get what you're driving at.'

She pushed the food she was chewing to one side of her mouth. 'Latest government figures show 30 per cent of the Vietnamese who came to the US last year were doctors, lawyers, teachers and other professional sorts. Another 15 per cent were managers. After more than a year in America, just seven per cent are in professional jobs and under two per cent have found managerial positions. What I'm driving at is that there's no future here for a great many Vietnamese folk. Some will integrate, sure. But a substantial proportion aren't here to build a fresh life; they want their old one back.'

I put some pepper on my omelette. 'You didn't bring me here to talk about official stats over a low-cost lunch.'

She set down her knife and fork and glanced around the room. 'These people are General Giang's natural constituents. I wanted you to see them in their new habitat – and there are places like this in every major American city.' She paused and took a mouthful of table water. 'Giang is harnessing this disillusion, frustration and the general wretchedness of life in exile as a recruiting drum. These people might not represent much of a problem now, but, like I said, their numbers are rising fast.'

I swallowed more omelette. 'And the CIA wants any notion that the war can be rekindled nipping in the bud?'

She made a no-comment smile. 'When you're done eating, I'll drive you home.'

Back in the Hornet, she turned into Florida Avenue and headed toward Rhode Island Avenue.

We were crossing the intersection when she said the stuff she was about to tell me was not for publication.

I said I was cool with that.

'You better be.' She threw me an armour-piercing stare. 'Any of this finds its way into the *Tribune* and that's the end of my career.'

'I know the score, Kim. You can trust me.'

She stopped at the 6th Street traffic lights and looked at me again, as if still deciding whether this was true.

As the lights went to green, she said, 'You already know Keith Zetchik has been supporting the cadre of former South Vietnamese generals led by Giang. A lot of people in the DC intelligence community also know that. What very few people know is that those generals shifted huge amounts of wealth from Vietnam to the USA when it became clear the North was going to take Saigon. As a result, Giang's paramilitary group has enough assets to fund a sustained guerrilla war.'

'What type of funding are we talking about?'

'Every type you can think of, some you can't. You know what the corruption was like in Vietnam. Giang and his associates were running every type of operation from narcotics and vice to importing black market goods and exporting looted art. I heard of one general using combat troops to harvest cinnamon and control the market.'

She turned right into 9th Street.

'We made a breakthrough when an asset close to Zetchik

discovered that he possessed documents detailing how and where this wealth has been deployed.'

She glanced in her rearview. It was a habit you never lost.

I said, 'Let me guess. Your mission is to find these documents.'

'Give the gentleman a prize.' She spoke with mild sarcasm, then became more serious. 'First place I looked was Zetchik's apartment in Kalorama. I was there the night he died.'

I blinked. Did Kim just put herself in the frame for Zetchik's murder?

Then again, if she was the killer, why tell me? And why tell me now?

She seemed to pick up on my thoughts. 'I'd been gone for over an hour when he got hit.'

I kept my tone level. 'Did you find anything?'

'Not a scrap.'

She turned onto Sherman Avenue NW. 'Next morning I heard about the shooting and went straight to the house in Earlstown. I figured that if the documents weren't at the apartment, they may well be at the family home. That was when I found the body of Christine Zetchik. Then you arrived and Delacroix appeared a few seconds later.'

Again, I got blown away.

I couldn't help but wonder if she went to the house looking for these documents and was confronted by Christine Zetchik. Maybe Christine came home early and Kim strangled her before I got there – and before Bobby arrived. True, it was more likely that Bobby killed Christine to shut her up because she was shaking him down. But what if he really went there to make a payment, or to discuss whatever it was she wanted from him? I'd assumed this was money, but it could have been something else.

Once more, I had to ask myself why Kim would tell me this if she *had* killed Christine.

Once more, I had no satisfactory answer.

# TWENTY-NINE

She parked outside my place on Kenyon Street NW. It was mid-afternoon. I didn't have much else to do so I asked her in for a coffee.

She took a moment to think about it then said sure, why not.

I lived in a modest row house at the end of a block. Not the best place I ever lived in, but a way off the worst. Kim walked round the sparsely furnished living room with amused curiosity, as if she'd tracked a peculiar critter to its lair. If she was expecting to find out more about me through my domestic scene, though, she'd be disappointed. The only thing that said anything about me was my portable record collection. This was two cardboard boxfuls of LPs I was listening to at the time. It was tiny compared with the full collection at my New York City pad. But, like the rest of my possessions, it could be packed into the trunk of a car.

I went into the kitchen to make the coffee and suggested she put some music on. She picked out Bob Dylan's *Desire* album, which I considered to be a righteous choice.

A few minutes into *Hurricane*, the opening track, she came into the kitchen and leaned against the counter.

As the coffee started to percolate, I said, 'I have a question.'

'Shoot.'

'It's not an easy question to ask, but I need to ask anyways.'

She placed her hands on the counter and looked at me straight. 'I said shoot, didn't I?'

I returned her frank stare. 'I heard your folks – and the hamlet where you grew up – got wiped out by Keith Zetchik's unit back in '69. Is that true?'

'You know it is. But that's not what you really wanna know, is it? What you're really asking is, did I kill Keith Zetchik?'

Her directness caught be off balance and I decided to be upfront. 'You got a powerful motive for killing him. And you just told me you were at the scene of his murder an hour before he died.'

The space between us went tense and fragile.

'You think I killed Keith Zetchik?'

I shrugged. 'In your shoes, I wouldn't have hesitated.'

More tension. She let it hang and I felt compelled to say something. 'But no, I don't think you killed him.'

Even as the words left my mouth, I wondered if I was saying them because I believed them, or because I wanted to.

She looked straight at me, but through me, to someplace distant.

The extended silence was filled by *Isis*.

At last she said, 'You asked about what happened to my parents and my community. Very well, I'll tell you.'

She hesitated and I sensed she was struggling to summon up the words.

Then she took the plunge. 'Zetchik's soldiers arrived on the morning of Tuesday, May 6th, 1969, at our village – An Bai in Quang Duc province. They killed 247 people in six hours of improvised slaughter. I knew each one of the victims by name. Two were my parents. Many were relatives and close friends. The soldiers went to work soon after dawn and didn't finish until noon. They claimed to be hunting Viet Cong, but there were none anywhere near. My dad spoke good English so he went to explain this. A grunt spontaneously clubbed him to death with his rifle butt. While this was going on, my mom tried to intervene. Another grunt put a bayonet between her shoulder blades. It was reported that my parents approached Zetchik's soldiers with 'an aggressive demeanour that justified swift and assertive action'. But they were found to be unarmed.'

Kim's manner was conversational, even throwaway. Like 'Oh yeah, this happened, then that happened'. Chilled my blood. Don't know how many times my blood had gotten chilled like that, but it was not a lot of times and might have been never. I'd seen horror, sure. I lived with it, cheek by jowl, for seven years. But I never heard about 247 unarmed people I knew by name, who I grew up with, getting butchered in a few hours.

She started talking again. 'In another part of the hamlet, a heavily pregnant woman called My Thi Hoa was killed along with her unborn baby by multiple gunshots to her abdomen. Apparently they thought she was hiding a rucksack of grenades, though nothing of the sort was found. Twelve children were placed in front of a heavy machine-gun and executed. You ever see what a three-second burst of .50 calibre ammunition does to the body of a ten-year-old? Wow. I mean, wow.'

Her voice had become fractured. She stopped talking, put her fist to her mouth, cleared her throat.

I waited for the wave of emotion to swell and subside.

Then she pressed on. 'Next, a group of 26 elderly people were shoved into a hooch and a grenade tossed in after them. The killing of the kids and the old folks was to prevent them staging a counter-attack, though not one was of military service age and no weapons were ever discovered.'

Again, she paused. Again, her fist went to her mouth and she made another dry cough. 'By noon, ditches around the paddies were brimming with bodies. Seems they represented a 'credible threat', but not one of them possessed anything more threatening than a rice bowl. And, of course, there was the report of Keith Zetchik strutting back and forth with a cigar in one hand and a nickel-plated .45 automatic in the other, shooting any villagers who came his way.'

She poured two cups of coffee and handed one to me.

'I got the news shortly after the massacre. The detail came later in a classified report based on the accounts of three survivors – villagers who'd been left for dead. The report never went anywhere, but I tracked down the three survivors and they told me everything.'

I said, 'I can't imagine what that must have been like for you.'

She shook her head. 'Yes, you can. You can imagine better than anyone.'

'It was never so personal for me.'

She raise an eyebrow, as if she knew I was lying. 'Wasn't it?'

I lifted my coffee cup, realized I didn't want coffee, and put it down again. I needed to switch the subject.

'It must have been difficult for you. I mean, working for the side responsible for killing your mom and dad. For what happened to My Thi Hoa, to those little kids and the old folks and all the others.'

Her X-ray gaze didn't shift. 'You were in Vietnam. After Tet everybody was killing everybody and nobody was asking questions.'

I couldn't argue with that.

She looked away. 'As a correspondent, I was embedded with a number of combat units. I saw atrocities by both sides. Sure, I hated Zetchik and his kind. Sure I wanted him dead. Sure I would have killed him if I'd gotten the chance. But I never did. The assignment I'm working on now would have ruined him. That would have been far better revenge than a bullet to the brain.'

I nodded. 'Even so, there must have been times when you wondered why you were working for Uncle Sam.'

She sipped her coffee. 'Not all Americans were like him.'

'There were a lot like him.'

She pinned me with that look. '*You* weren't.'

'I killed a lot of people.'

'You saved a lot.'

'Not in any way special.'

'Yes you did. You got the Medal of Honor for saving people.'

'I can't even remember that action. I can remember going in and coming out but nothing in between.'

She finished her coffee. 'I read your citation. You 'displayed extraordinary heroism in the face of extreme personal danger'. You charged a fortified NVA position and forced them to withdraw. Then – under heavy fire – you carried seven wounded grunts back to the chopper. I know what you did, Wat. You can't deny it.'

'I'm not a hero. I'm not a patriot. I stayed in country for my own reasons.'

She came closer. 'I spoke to a Bru Striker nicknamed Sonny who served with you. You treated the Bru as equals. Better than they ever got treated by the North or the South. You respected their traditions. You took part in their rituals. You gave them a cause to fight for.'

'I got a lot of them killed.'

She came closer still, nailed me again with that look. 'First in; last out; nobody left behind. That's what Sonny said.'

'Sonny likes to spin a yarn.'

She entered my body-space real slow. I caught scents of jasmine and musk, then her face filled my vision and her lips were pressing on mine. I kissed her back, pulling her tight against me. She felt lithe and electric and I was starting to think about switching this to the bedroom when –

She pushed me back.

It wasn't a rejecting push but there was an urgency about it that baffled me.

'We gotta go back to Sherman Avenue.' Her voice was insistent. 'Right now.'

'Why?'

'That accounting firm in the photo of Chau and Delacroix.'

'What about it?'

'We just drove past it.'

# THIRTY

Sherman and Harvard was less than a mile from my place and we got there in less than five minutes.

Kim pulled over and pointed to a ground floor business premises with a glass frontage and scarlet capital letters on a pale blue fascia board.

I squinted at the name: HAWTHORNE & ZEISS ACCOUNTING SERVICES.

I looked again at the photo. The van being driven across the shot had blocked out the HAW part of the name and we hadn't realized any letters were missing because it was all in capitals.

I said, 'You did well. That was seriously impressive recall and deduction.'

She made a faint smile. 'I don't even recall noticing it when we drove by. It just came into my head an hour later.'

I grinned back. 'Gotta say, your timing sucked.'

She got out of the car. 'We can fix that later.'

I went after her across the sidewalk toward the premises of Hawthorne & Zeiss. 'What are you doing?'

'Going in.' She glanced over her shoulder. 'You coming?'

'What about Dillard?'

But she was gonna search the place whether I went with her or not. Also, we'd gotten lucky because today was a Sunday so nobody was at work and the street was deserted. I thought about the wisdom of looking a gift horse in the mouth and decided to go in with her.

She produced a set of lock picks and we went in through a door at the rear. A burglar alarm went off and she quickly silenced it. Then we had the place to ourselves. There was just the one office with a half dozen desks and as many file cabinets.

We started at opposite ends and worked toward each other. It was laborious work because the steel cabinets were locked and each one contained scores of client files.

I asked, 'Any idea what we're looking for?'

'We'll know it when we see it.'

I thought: *More like* if *we see it*. But I kept quiet and pulled out a file, then another and another. Hawthorne & Zeiss' clients were small businesses and there were all sorts of documents you wouldn't understand if you weren't an accountant.

We'd been at it for a good hour when an elderly black woman with horn-rimmed glasses and a heavy floral pattern frock appeared at the glass front of the office. She peered in with a scowl that did not look encouraging.

Kim moved to my side. 'What do you think?'

I made a friendly wave at the woman. She didn't respond. Even less encouraging. I said, 'There's a payphone half a block along the street. She could have the cops here real quick.'

Kim said what I was thinking, 'We get arrested, we're fucked.'

I considered the likely sequence of events. Dillard would go ape. He might prevent us copping a breaking and entering rap in order to keep a lid on his investigation into Chau's murder. But that would be the end of any cooperation I'd ever get from MPD Homicide.

Kim said, 'You gotta do something.'

'Like what?'

'Talk to her. Use your charm.'

There was no time to argue the toss so I went over to the front door, opened it and gave her my most engaging smile. Gotta say, though, she didn't seem especially receptive. Just the opposite.

She skewered me with a suspicious look. 'What you doing in there on a Sunday?'

'Extra work.' I pulled a browbeaten expression. 'Boss says we gotta finish a bunch of audits or we'll be in big trouble.'

She made tutting sound and wagged an index finger at me. 'Your boss, he got a reckoning with the Lord coming his way. Working on the Sabbath ain't right. I got a good mind to complain. I know the mayor, you know. Mr Washington, he's a friend of mine.'

I sniffed an opportunity. 'If you *were* to make a formal complaint, ma'am, it could help us.'

She frowned. 'How you mean?'

I hammed up the downtrodden worker look. 'Boss might think twice before bring us in on the Lord's Day again.'

She looked at me like I was somewhat soft in the head. 'You a church-goer?'

'Why, yes ma'am.'

She squinted. 'Where you go?'

My brain was spinning like a hamster wheel. Then I recalled our visit to the church where Chau worshipped. 'St

Aloysius, over in Eckington. We're in Father Collins' flock. You know him?'

'I'm Lutheran.' She spoke as if I should have known this. 'But I know Father Collins. Good man. For a Catholic.'

I said, 'We're all God's children, ma'am. That's what Father Collins says.'

This seemed to satisfy her and she turned away, muttering something about how I should make sure my boss knew the Lord was watching from on high.

I turned back to Kim.

'That was well handled,' she said. 'You sounded convincing.'

I made a small grin. 'It wasn't an act. If I didn't feel browbeaten before she turned up, I sure do now.'

We went back to looking through the files.

Another hour went by. I was starting to get word-blind when I saw the name: Pham Tan Giang. I rubbed my eyes and did a double take. I half expected to see some other, similar name when I looked again. But it was still there. He was listed as an 'incorporator' on a document entitled Articles of Incorporation.

I said, 'You better take a look at this.'

She dropped the file she was examining and hustled across the office.

I handed her the Articles of Incorporation certificate.

The file it came from also contained a set of audited accounts along with tax returns and a stockholder agreement. All of them named Giang as the principal stockholder. The company was called Fairmount Investments.

She studied the accounts and looked up. 'This isn't a small business. Last year's turnover was $2.3 million. We hit the jackpot.'

There were half a dozen other businesses with Giang's name on them: A laundromat, boat repair outfit, electrical products importer, steel components manufacturer and two convenience stores. I realized Giang wasn't employed by the grocery store on U Street – he owned it.

She flicked through more of the sales ledgers. 'Cash flow is exceptionally strong.'

I peered over her shoulder. 'You think these are money laundering operations?'

'That and more. This portfolio includes a financial management firm, an import company and a bunch of cash-rich businesses, all of them growing massively in the last 12 months.'

She arranged the ledgers on a desk, took out a Minox camera and started taking photos. 'This is how Giang brings wealth into the USA, how he invests it – and, yeah, how he cleans it.'

# THIRTY-ONE

Next day I needed to check on Reggie. First, though, I had a couple of important jobs to do.

Rhyme Dillard had to be kept sweet – or leastways less sour – so I paid him a personal visit. He'd ditched pens in favour of pencils and had taken to chewing the wood around the lead. His ashtray was littered with chunks of soggy pulp. Better than cigarette butts, I guessed. He listened po-faced as I told him what Kim and I found at Hawthorne & Zeiss. Then he made a show of being pissed and said he could arrest us for breaking and entering. But we both knew this wasn't gonna happen. Instead, he accepted the intel I gave him on Giang's business activities. I also told him my theory that Chau did the creative accounting before passing the books to somebody at the firm who looked after the regulatory side. On my way out I asked how Holy Joe's grand jury hearing was coming along. He rolled his eyes and told me it had been put back a week due to a hitch at the DA's office. This explained why he looked even more stressed than usual, and why he was so eager to see the back of me.

Next I went to do my second interview with Heck Weschler down in Alexandria.

I did what Maggie wanted and asked if he was going to pull out of the presidential race and throw his weight behind Gerald Ford or Jimmy Carter. I'd told Maggie he wasn't gonna tell me and I was right. He laughed and said he was still aiming for the White House himself, which was his only priority. I pointed out that he'd been spotted talking to both his rivals and he said maybe he'd been sounding *them* out for membership of *his* cabinet. It was a nice tongue-in-cheek quote that would make the lead for a sidebar.

The interview itself was productive. This time we discussed Vietnam, the Cold War and the West's policy of détente in relation to the Soviet Union. I also asked about his views on the nation's 200th birthday party next Sunday. He wouldn't be drawn, though, and I got why. After Vietnam and Watergate, and with the current economic difficulties, the celebratory mood was muted. Nobody chasing public office would advocate staging lavish events on the taxpayer dollar; and on the flipside, nobody was gonna say we shouldn't mark the occasion in some special way.

I was on my way out as his wife returned from a visit to a neighbour's house – though I suspected very little happened by chance where the Weschlers were concerned.

She asked how the interview went and I said good.

Then she said, 'I gather you want to include me in your next one?'

'Yes I would. Do you mind?'

She brushed a strand of auburn hair from her brow, gave me a porcelain smile. 'I'd be delighted, Wat – may I call you that?'

I returned the smile. 'Sure.'

'It's just that … ' She held my gaze. 'There was a story in

the *New York Examiner* yesterday insinuating that I'm using my family's wealth to buy the presidency for Hector, that I'm 'the power behind the throne', as they put it.'

I recalled what Maggie told me about Paula Weschler playing a much bigger role in her husband's campaign strategy than any other prospective first lady had. 'And you're asking me not to repeat that stuff?'

'I wouldn't presume to tell you your job, Wat.' She was still smiling, still looking right at me. I sensed this was really important to her. And something else – vulnerability, or something close to it. 'All I'm asking is that – unlike the *New York Examiner* – you give me the opportunity to give my side of the story.'

'You'll get it,' I said. 'I won't do a puff piece, but I will do a fair one.'

She held out her hand and gripped mine. 'Then we have a deal.'

# THIRTY-TWO

It was late morning when I got to Reggie's apartment.

She was stir crazy and looked as if she was going into withdrawal. After letting me in she paced back and forth across the living room – something I figured she'd been doing for some time before I arrived. Candy wrappers and takeout cartons crunched under her bare feet.

She shot me a fraught look. 'I've been cooped up in this hole all weekend. I gotta get out.'

I made a dubious expression. 'I'm not sure if that's such a good idea.'

'I'm going anyway.' She grabbed her coat and headed for the door. 'You can stay here if you want.'

Looking around the place, it was easy to see why she was so desperate to get out. Empty booze bottles and cans crammed every horizontal surface. Pyramids of cigarette butts and roaches were piled in the ashtrays. The air was stagnant and reeked of booze and maryjane.

A walk outside and something to eat would do her good. She'd also need to score a fix, but if it got her head together I was cool with that.

We went onto Columbia Road and set off toward 18th

Street NW. It was a hot day and the sun brought folks on their lunch break out onto the street. I wasn't wearing shades and the brightness was dazzling. People appeared as silhouettes, jostling and dodging this way and that. I used my hand to shield my eyes, scanning the oncoming crowds for any hint of danger. But all I saw was lunchbreak workers enjoying the fine weather.

I forced myself to unwind. Reggie's paranoia was rubbing off and I needed to get a grip. We were in the middle of a busy DC street in the middle of the day. Nobody was gonna try anything here.

Reggie hustled along the sidewalk, bumping and shoving people with the fuck-you focus of a true addict. She homed in on a street-corner dealer and went straight to business. I watched her hand over some folding green, pocket her stuff, and head back in my direction.

She was a couple of yards away when I nailed the young guy in a black cap-sleeve T-shirt and tan pants.

He went at Reggie fast.

I closed the distance.

The knife came out, arm lunged forward.

I shouted a warning, but Reggie didn't have time to react.

The blade blurred as he stabbed at her gut.

I grabbed his forearm with a half-second to spare. He howled as I rolled his arm behind his back, jamming his wrist between his shoulder blades. I slammed him face first against the wall. The knife tinkled on the sidewalk.

I said, 'Who sent you?'

'Lemme go you crazy bastard!'

'It was Joseph Tedstone, wasn't it? How much he pay you?'

'What's going on here?'

The police uniform appeared in my peripheral sight.

I relaxed my grip a little but didn't let go.

The cop was a middle-aged beat officer with a jowly jaw and too much gut weight. I knew the type: He'd seen it all too many times to be shocked or surprised by whatever he saw next.

'He attacked my friend.' I nodded at the switchblade on the pavement. 'Tried to stab her with that.'

Black T-shirt wriggled. 'This guy's a maniac. I got no idea what he's talking about. Lemme go. Officer, please tell him to lemme go.'

The cop turned to Reggie. She was standing at my shoulder, shaking. 'Miss, did this man assault you?'

She gripped my arm, refusing to eyeball the cop. 'Dunno dunno dunno.'

The cop was being patient, but there were limits. 'Miss, I need you to tell me what just happened.'

Reggie wasn't on the edge of panic, she was way beyond it. 'Wanna go home. Wat, please take me home. Please take me home.'

'He tried to kill you, Reggie.' I tried to sound calm. 'You can't just let him walk away.'

'Miss?' The cop sounded insistent. 'Miss, did this man attack you?'

'Dunno dunno dunno.' Reggie was too freaked to say anything sensible. 'Wanna go home. Please, Wat, you gotta get me home. You gotta … '

The cop raised his voice, addressing the street generally, 'Anyone saw what happened here?'

Nobody did. No surprise.

He gave me a wish-I-could-help look. 'You gotta let this man go, sir.'

I couldn't mask my exasperation. 'He went at her with that knife, officer. I saw it.'

Cop wasn't gonna budge. 'He's flat out denying it. The lady here won't confirm what you say and there were no other witnesses. Sorry, sir, my hands are tied.'

I turned to Reggie but she refused to look at me.

So I let the guy go and watched him vanish into the crowd.

Back in Reggie's apartment, she swallowed the goofballs she just scored.

Then she sat beside me on the couch and threw her arms around me, hugging me tight. We stayed there until the barbiturates did their thing.

'They'll try again, won't they?' She sounded spaced-out and detached, like she was talking about somebody else's problem. 'They won't stop now.'

'It would have helped if you told that cop what happened.' I couldn't hide my frustration. 'Then at least we'd have a lead on whoever is behind this.'

'Don't be angry, Wat.' She looked at me with sad eyes. 'I know this is fubar. I know it's all my fault.'

I gave her a curious look. Fubar was army slang that stood for *fucked up beyond all recognition*. It was World War II vintage and not a word you'd expect to hear from a hippie. Then again, she was raised in an army family – and I reminded myself that it was problems with overbearing military fathers that brought her and Johnny together in the first place.

I said, 'None of this is your fault Reggie. You were in shock back there on the street. If you could have helped that cop, you would. But those people *are* gonna stop, because I'm gonna stop them.'

Was I though? Reggie had nearly died twice in five days and both times I'd done barely enough to save her. Next time I might not be so lucky. Worse still, I might not be there at all.

I thought about Holy Joe Tedstone. I could get why he might kill Keith Zetchik. After what Kim told me the guy, he had it coming. But why would Holy Joe murder his own son? And then go after a fragile girl like Reggie, who was no threat whatsoever? What sort of asshole would do that?

I wondered, too, if Holy Hoe was also behind the landmine hoax and giant centipede that came through my mail slot. Unlike General Giang, he had links to both Reggie and me. Sure, there was a whole world of difference between two attempted hits and a couple of Vietnam-related pranks. Yet they served a similar purpose – to shut up or drive off anyone Holy Joe perceived as a threat.

Unless.

I thought again about Weschler's suggestion that Johnny could have used Holy Joe's Mauser to shoot Keith Zetchik, then swallowed the kill pills to frame his dad for a double homicide rap. Weschler had also raised a valid question about Johnny's state of mind that night. Johnny almost started a fight at the Bayou and *did* start one with those three guys on the street outside. My buddy was clearly agitated and spoiling for confrontation. When I ran the hypothesis by Maggie she hadn't ruled it out, which said a lot. And if Johnny *was* behind Zetchik's murder and his own suicide, it followed that he would also have manipulated Reggie. After all, she delivered the Mauser to me because Johnny asked her to. The two attempts on her life may have been entirely unrelated to Joseph Tedstone, but directly related to Reggie owing a good deal of money to a bunch of bad people.

Reggie was spot on about one thing, though: Whoever was behind the attacks on her wouldn't stop now.

She hugged me close. 'You're a good guy, Wat. Better than I deserve.'

We spent the rest of the evening watching TV. We flicked back and forth between *Monday Night Baseball*, *Monday Night at the Movies* and *The Sonny and Cher Show*. None of it was interesting, but it passed the time.

I couldn't leave Reggie in the condition she was in, so I spent another uncomfortable night on her couch.

Someplace between sleep and consciousness, I found a route back to Saigon five years ago.

*I'm meeting Chuck Shaughnessy at Givral's Café. Late afternoon and swarms of To Do Street cowboys are congregating on their Hondas, ready to roll hard on Americans and anyone else who falls into their prey-range. They ride along the streets snatching cameras, transistor radios, wallets, stuff you wouldn't imagine possible. Vietnamese cops in their 'white mice' uniforms look on without concern, sometimes with open amusement. The greasy sidewalks of To Do and Le Loi are thickening with R&R grunts, saffron-robed monks and platform-heeled bargirls. The air is a layered mush of camphor smoke and incense, rotting garbage and raw sewage, diesel and gasoline fumes. The muggy wind coming off the Saigon River switches the odours around but never cleans them out.*

*The CIA guy drops two sugar cubes into his coffee. 'How's the asset performing?'*

*I don't like the way he calls Linh 'the asset', even though I understand the anonymity is for her protection.*

I drink some coffee. 'She's integrated well, but information is thin on the ground. These people are cautious.'

Shaughnessy places his elbow on his knee and leans forward. 'We need results now, Wat. Maybe she should take a more direct approach.'

'You mean take more risks?'

'If necessary, yes.'

From some place across the way I hear Buddhist peace chimes jingle in the breeze.

I say, 'She did get some new information.'

It isn't much, but I want to show him that Linh is getting results. I want to shield her from being pressured into to raising the ante. So I explain how she overheard Bootstrap chatting to Colonel Thanh about his love of old accordion music. Bootstrap also mentioned his family roots, but Linh couldn't hear this so well. She caught the first word: Northern, but not the second. She thought it might have been Ireland or Iceland.

Shaughnessy shakes his head. 'Nobody comes from northern Iceland except seals and seabirds. And the stuff about Northern Ireland isn't helpful either – even assuming it's accurate. Any idea how many Americans have Scots-Irish ancestry?'

I say I don't and he says he doesn't either but it's gotta be a lot.

He gives me a condescending smile. 'So what does this give us? A guy who likes traditional squeeze-box tunes and therefore just might have a fondness for, what? Country music? Folk? And who may have family links with Ulster?'

I don't appreciate his tone so I repay him in kind. 'Maybe we should be talking to Van Morrison.'

'Fuck you, Wat.'

'No, fuck you, Chuck.'

We sit silent awhile like sulking schoolkids.

At last he says, 'Look, I get that you want to protect your asset. And I dig why. But we have a duty to stop these bastards. They're getting people killed – here and back home.'

I can't argue. I understood the risks from the start and so did Linh – notwithstanding her lack of maturity. 'All right,' I say. 'I'll ask her to step it up.'

# THIRTY-THREE

Next morning I went to see Joseph Tedstone.

I wasn't sure what I was gonna say, though I was aware of the risks involved in jiving with a guy in the frame for a double homicide. But after the second attempted hit on Reggie I couldn't stay away. If nothing else, I wanted to gauge his demeanour, see how he reacted to the stuff I had to say. Only problem was I didn't know what that was gonna be.

Since I last saw Tedstone at his sister's house, his bail conditions had been changed and he'd returned to the family home on Wyoming Avenue NW.

As I walked up the driveway, a guy wearing a dog collar and dark suit left through the front door. He walked past me with a stony expression. Tedstone was a bigshot in the Episcopal Church and I guessed the Jesus jockey had been administering pastoral care.

My host was waiting by the door. He didn't seem especially uplifted as he watched the priest depart and saw me arrive.

He showed me into the living room and offered me a cup of coffee or some tea, which I declined.

Last time I was here I found Johnny's body. And although I was no stranger to dead folks, there was a deep wrongness about being at the crime scene with the man who was very probably the killer.

There was a stretched-out silence. I asked how he was doing, and he said he was fine, even though he didn't look fine. His complexion was leeched and he hadn't fixed his comb-over so that matted strands fell loose on one side of his head. His small features were pinched, the pale eyes watery. He was on the unhealthy side of thin when I last saw him and he must have lost seven or eight pounds since then.

He said, 'You mentioned on the telephone that you had some fresh information about Johnny.'

I took out a picture of Reggie that I'd boosted from a photo album in her apartment. She'd have flipped out if I told her what I was planning, but I needed to see Holy Joe's reaction when I showed it to him.

'Ever seen this woman before, sir?' I handed him the photo, watched his face real close.

He studied the picture. His expression didn't change. If he had people chasing Reggie, he was damn good at concealing his emotions. Then again, if you can murder your own son in cold blood, you gotta be capable of a concealing a whole lotta stuff.

He looked up at me. 'I don't know her. Who is she?'

'She's called Regina Acheson, also known as Reggie.'

His brow furrowed. 'You asked me if I'd heard that name last time we met.'

'She was one of Johnny's friends.'

'What has she got to do with anything?'

'Two attempts have been made to kill her. The first on Wednesday, the second yesterday. I was with her both times.'

He thought about what I just said, as if assessing the implications. Then he threw back his head and laughed. It was a long, braying snort, someplace between hysteria and contempt.

'And you think *I* was involved?' He sounded incredulous.

But then he *would* laugh it off. He *would* make a show of incredulity.

'I didn't say that.'

'You didn't need to say it, son.' He went to a drinks cabinet and poured a large measure of Bourbon. It was 9.30am and I guessed he wouldn't normally have taken a drink much before 9.30pm. Looked like he was going downhill fast. But I couldn't take anything at face value.

'So who is she, this Reggie Acheson?' He stood opposite me, breathing whiskey fumes on my face, and made a crooked smile. 'I know it's a tough ask, but try to frame your answer on the assumption that I'm not the guy trying to kill her.'

I had to be careful what I revealed. I didn't want him to know Reggie talked to Johnny on the night Johnny died, or that she sent me the Mauser, or that she met Johnny in a psychiatric clinic. Of course he may well have known all this already – hence the two attempted hits. But I didn't want him to hear it from me.

Even so, I'd asked for this meeting. I owed him something of an explanation.

'She and Johnny were friends,' I said. 'They had a lot in common – narcotics abuse in particular. They used to help one another by talking about their issues. She's also from a wealthy background, but estranged from her family. She's a fragile, vulnerable girl.'

Tedstone drained his whiskey glass. 'Indulge me again, Mr Tyler. Continue with the notion that I'm innocent and explain what exactly happened to this unfortunate young lady.'

I told him what went down after the gig at the Keg on Wednesday, and at Columbia and 18th yesterday.

And I wondered again if the landmine hoax and centipede caper had been done on Tedstone's say-so. He certainly had the Vietnam connection. And if Reggie was right, it would be in his interest to shut her up and disrupt my investigation.

He turned away, then back again. And in those two swift seconds I was looking at a different man. Like he'd snapped out of a hypnotic trance. The sneering contempt had vanished, the self-assured general was back.

He said, 'You know, of course, that I'm appearing before a grand jury in two weeks?'

I nodded.

'Why would I jeopardize that? By your own account, this Reggie Acheson is a drug addict with mental health issues. If I *was* guilty, why would I see her as the sort of threat that would justify setting a bunch of goons on her, with all the risks that would entail? Surely her allegations could be discredited in court, or even before it got that far.'

I had to concede his point.

He elevated one of his dark bushy eyebrows. 'She hasn't been to the police, has she?'

'No.'

'Let me guess: She's convinced they won't believe her for the same reasons a jury wouldn't. And she's also convinced the cops are in cahoots with me and would either turn her over to my hoods or make sure she suffered some sort of fatal accident?'

'She's terrified, sir. She's alone and in danger. I'm extremely worried for her.'

'May I keep the photo? It could be that I met her briefly some time ago. The picture could jog my memory.'

It was a surprising request, but if he was behind the attempts on Reggie's life, he already knew what she looked like. If not, if their paths *had* crossed sometime in the past, he might be able to give me helpful information. So I said sure, he could keep the picture.

He held my gaze. 'I checked you out, Mr Tyler. You're supposed to be a rebel and a peasant, but you're actually a straight-up officer and gentleman, Hillbilly accent and all.'

I scanned his face for a suggestion of sarcasm, but he seemed to mean what he said.

'You sure you won't join me?' He went for more whiskey.

'Is that a good idea, sir?'

He ignored me, concentrated on pouring the booze. When he looked back up the sneering guy was back in the room.

'You saw the rector leaving as you arrived.' He stood in front of me with a grin that was anything but pleasant. 'He had a message from his Christian congregation regarding the church's bicentennial service.' The smile disappeared, the bitterness stayed. 'I'd been asked to deliver the sermon. Now they don't want me in the building. I've been excluded from the house of the Lord on our nation's 200th birthday. So I'll celebrate Sunday the Fourth of July here, alone.'

What to say? I had no idea. I said nothing.

I'd been dead wrong, though, about the priest who was on his way out as I arrived. He hadn't come to give Holy Joe spiritual support; he'd come to crucify him.

Tedstone walked across the living room to a burr walnut bureau and took a leather-bound King James Bible from the top drawer. 'Behold, the foundation, justification and inspiration of my life to date.'

He held the heavy book above his head and slammed it down on the bureau. Then he took a ballpoint pen from his pocket and started riffling through the thin pages. Having found the one he was looking for, he began scrawling on it with heavy, jerky movements.

'You know they called me Holy Joe in Vietnam, don't you Mr Tyler?'

I nodded.

'They thought I was some sort of crusader monk because I never blasphemed, never cussed and rarely drank. It played well for the good folks back here at the Episcopal Church of All Saints and the Incarnation. They loved it. They loved me. Not so much now.'

Tearing out the page, he came stamping back toward me and thrust it into my hand.

It was from the Book of Exodus and contained the Ten Commandments. He'd added an eleventh: *Fuck you all!* It was scribbled in big angry letters that filled the page.

'Sir, you should – '

'Don't tell me what I should do!'

He balled his fists and punched me on the chest. I rocked back on my heels, surprised by the power such a puny guy could pack. But I didn't retaliate. He wasn't attacking me, he was attacking the whole world.

'I can Goddamn blaspheme. I can fucking cuss. And I get pissed out of my tree better than anyone. Don't think I can't.'

He swung away from me and sauntered, a little drunk, across to the bay windows overlooking the lawn.

His narrow shoulders rose and fell as he fought for breath. I let the silence carry.

After some while, he said, 'Please forgive my outburst, Mr Tyler.'

It was like being in that room with two different guys. Whatever I'd been expecting when I got here, this was not it.

I kept my voice neutral. 'Of course, sir. You're under a lot of pressure.'

I joined him by the window. A red setter was basking in a sunny spot on the patio.

'When you're gone I'll say goodbye to my good and loyal friend Sherman. I can't look after him any longer and I can't trust anyone else to. My sister hates dogs and as for my friends, well, as I'm sure you understand, they're not exactly in abundance … '

'Surely, sir, you can find another home for him?'

'*This* is his home. This is where he'll stay. The police took away my guns and those cyanide pills, so I'll have to drown him. But it will be kinder that way. I'll fill the bath tub with warm water and he'll be soon be at peace. I'll bury him under the big yew tree. My late wife would have approved of that. Johnny would too. Johnny got on with Sherman a good deal better than he ever got on with me.'

His tone was casual, like he was telling me about his social arrangements for the evening. Now I really wasn't sure who was doing the talking: The edge-of-crazy neurotic or the stoical military commander.

'Let me take him, sir.' The words were out before I could stop them. Partly, I guess, because I'd always liked dogs; and partly because Holy Joe was right about Johnny's relationship with the red setter. Johnny used to talk about Sherman as if he was Johnny's best buddy. Maybe that was true. I added, 'I can look after him until you're feeling better.'

He shook his head. 'They'll put me away. They'll throw away the key.'

'They might not. And even if they do, I'll make sure Sherman is properly cared for.'

'Would you do that?' He stared at me misty-eyed.

'It's what Johnny would have wanted.' I made sure my manner was blunt. I didn't want to give the impression I was doing Tedstone a favour.

I left the his place five minutes later with the red setter and some cans of dog food but without any answers.

Joseph Tedstone was unbalanced and unpredictable – a guy at war with himself. But whether this made him innocent or guilty, or neither or both, was much less clear to me as I drove away than when I arrived.

# THIRTY-FOUR

Maggie had been less than pleased when I showed up at the office with Sherman. After I explained the circumstances, though, she softened somewhat and he was allowed to stay. In fact, he was a big hit among the editorial staff and I had no shortage of volunteers offering to take him for walks.

The mutt seemed happy enough, though obviously he'd never know how close to death he'd come that morning. After work, I took him home and let him loose in my back yard. There was a decent-sized lawn for him to gambol around in, as well as some trees and shrubs where he went hunting for scents.

I was looking for a stick to throw when I noticed some fallen branches in the middle of the lawn. This was odd because there'd been no stormy weather recently. Odder still in that the leaves on the branches were sycamore and I didn't have any sycamore trees. I wondered if one of my neighbours had hired a gardener to trim overgrown foliage and some offcuts came down on my side of the fence.

I saw a stick suitable for throwing on the other side of the branches.

Sherman was crunching around undergrowth at the end of the yard. I called his name and he came loping across the lawn.

I moved towards the stick.

I stopped.

Maybe I was being paranoid. But after the landmine and the giant centipede I had a right.

On the opposite side of the branches, Sherman went down on his front legs and barked for me to play.

I walked around the branches and grabbed the stick I'd intended to throw.

He barked again, tail thrashing.

I didn't throw the stick though. I held one end and used the other to push away the branches.

Caught my breath.

One more step and I could have lost my foot.

The toe-popper trap that had been dug in my lawn was another old acquaintance from Vietnam. It comprised a shallow hole containing a single round of ammunition, held upright in a bamboo tube. The tube was attached to a flat wood base, with a nail pointing upward. Tread on the cartridge and you'd exert downward pressure that would turn the nail into a firing pin, shooting the bullet up through your foot. I'd seen guys permanently crippled and sometimes losing a foot.

I cleared away the rest of the branches and carefully lifted the cartridge from the hole. It was a live round. The nail poking through the board was solid. The trap was for real. I had no doubt that I'd have had a 5.56mm hole in my foot if I'd stepped on it. I wondered too what might have happened if Sherman had run over it. Maybe he'd have detonated the bullet, maybe not. At any rate, he may well have had two brushes with death that day.

Whoever planted the toe-popper was certainly behind the fake landmine and the giant centipede. And the pattern of escalating threat had continued. The landmine was purely psychological; the centipede could have given me a nasty dose of neurotoxin; the bullet would probably have disabled me for life.

So what was next?

There was another pattern of escalation, equally ominous. I recalled the saying that an Englishman's home was his castle. But that didn't just apply to the English. For folk everywhere, home was a safe place, a refuge. Violate that sense of security and you really will start to mess with somebody's head. The hoax landmine had been left outside my house, near my front doorstep. The centipede incident went a stage further when the critter was inserted through the mail slot into my hall. And the toe-popper trap went further still. That involved direct trespass on my property.

Again, what was next?

All the indications pointed to something potentially lethal, probably involving breaking into my house.

I took the dog indoors and made a call.

I spoke to old buddy from 5th Special Forces Group who had gone into the surveillance business. He agreed to drive down from Philadelphia and install some motion-activated cameras. If the bastards behind these dirty tricks tried to set one up in my home, I'd find out who they were and make damn certain they regretted it.

Yet again, I ran the list of suspects in my head.

Giang was still at the top. He had a great deal to lose and when it came to an MO, the toe-popper was right on the money. Then again, I wondered if I was being manipulated into thinking in this way. Was pinning this on Giang a little too straightforward?

That lead me back to Holy Joe. It was eight hours since I visited him so he'd had lots of time to get someone round here. And whether or not he was a killer, he was on the brink of batshit crazy.

What about Kim? Surely not. But which part of me was doing the thinking? My head or my dick?

Bobby Delacroix was another possibility. Not the most likely, but he was linked via Chau to Giang. And to Christine Zetchik. And all of them had Vietnam connections.

There was another option – and in a way it was worse than any of the others: This was the work of someone not even on my radar.

# THIRTY-FIVE

Rhyme Dillard seemed to have quit nibbling pencils and taken up smoking maryjane.

His office reeked of the stuff. He even had a joint burning in his ashtray.

Then I realized it was a regular cigarette and then I realized it was neither. The pack on his desk told me he was smoking Honeybee Herbal Cigarettes.

Without taking his eyes off the document on his desk, he said, 'Before you ask, Tyler, they taste like shit.'

'They don't smell like shit, Captain, they smell like – '

'Yeah, I know what they smell like.' He looked up and rolled his blood-marbled eyes. 'I been getting grief about that all day. Even the deputy chief swung by to chip in with a wisecrack.'

He tapped the document with his index finger. 'We got Joseph Tedstone in front of the grand jury a week next Wednesday. But you must know that already. I got nothing else for you, so I'm afraid you've had a wasted trip.'

I leaned back in the visitor chair. 'Did you talk to Bobby Delacroix yet?'

He shook his head. 'Guy's a federal law enforcement officer. That means I gotta go through official channels. But every time I call, his supervisor is busy.'

'You figure you're getting the run-around so DEA can take care of this internally?'

He shot me a give-me-break look.

'This isn't for publication,' I said. 'Background only.'

'If you screw me on this Tyler ... '

'I haven't screwed you yet, Captain. Why start now?'

He picked up the herbal cigarette, decided against taking another pull, and stubbed it out. 'Very well, for background only, you're more or less correct. DEA wants to look into its man in its own way and in its own time. Meanwhile, I can't arrest him on the strength of a few illegally obtained snaps of him walking across a street with our man in the suitcase.' He held up his hands, pre-empting my protest. 'I agree, the whole things stinks. But right now I got no evidence. My hands are tied and DEA wants to keep it that way.'

I started to leave but my butt had barely left the seat when he gestured for me to stay put.

'You thinking about confronting Delacroix yourself?'

'He's a legitimate source.'

'I'd strongly advice against it.'

'Advice noted, Captain.'

He gave me a baleful look. 'Tread carefully, Tyler.'

After the toe-popper trap, I thought this was particularly solid advice.

*

With my police calls done, I drove down to Alexandria for my third interview with Heck Weschler. This time I was also talking to his wife Paula and I suspected the conversation was gonna be tricky.

Maggie – and the *Tribune's* owners – wanted a nicely crafted piece about the power-couple being compared with Jack and Jackie Kennedy. They wanted me to talk about the hero-at-home, the great woman behind the great man. On top of that, Maggie wanted me to discuss Paula Weschler's role in campaign strategy because she thought this would add a strong feminist angle. And Paula Weschler already told me that she wanted to downplay claims that she was using her family's wealth to buy the presidency for her husband. So tricky was probably an understatement.

That said, I always preferred tricky to predictable. And I wasn't gonna be told by anyone – even Maggie – how I should write this piece.

Heck and Paula – this was how they wanted me to address them – greeted me at the front door and showed me into their living room. The vibe was tasteful understatement: twin colonial-style tan leather couches, teak coffee table and matching book cases, plenty of yucca plants. She was wearing a white jersey-knit dress; he casual pants and a black turtle-neck sweater.

A pot of coffee and some cups had been arranged on the table.

We started off with straightforward approach play: I asked about the Kennedy parallel and they said that was a media invention. I pointed out that they were a relatively young, handsome couple, he a war hero, she a socialite. They reluctantly agreed that there were certain similarities and they played it just about right.

I asked whether being on the campaign trail together put pressure on their marriage.

They started to answer at the same time, then each gave way to the other.

In the end it was Paula who replied. 'We have our ups and downs like any married couple. But you must remember that Heck spent four years in Vietnam, then three in various parts of Europe, so our marriage has never really been what you might call the conventional type.'

Weschler nodded. 'If a marriage can survive an army career, it can survive anything, right Paula?'

She smiled but didn't say anything. This surprised me because I was expecting a cliché comment confirming how he right he was. Then again, maybe that was why she said nothing – because she didn't want to sound cheesy or predictable.

I helped myself to some coffee and looked directly at her. 'How do you find the campaigning? The travel, the pressure, the scrutiny?'

'I love it.' She poured herself a cup. 'Gives me a buzz like no other.'

I wrote this down. 'All the places you gotta visit, don't you ever get to the point where one blurs into the next?'

She creamed her coffee, shook her head. 'Just the opposite. Everyplace is unique. I like visiting big cities, sure, but I like rural areas just as much. Every small town has its own personality. I like to do a little local research and work it into Hector's speeches. People like it when you show you know something about their community.'

I sipped my coffee and braced myself for the next topic. Question like this, it's how you pitch it. 'It's been widely reported that a lotta folks – men in particular – come to campaign events just to see you, Paula. How do you feel about that?'

'You mean because I'm *easy on the eye*, as one correspondent put it?' She shrugged and pushed her smooth red hair back from her brow. 'Well, I guess you must make the most of your assets and I don't mind being looked at – so long my husband gets listened to.'

That was a righteous line and I underscored my shorthand note.

I asked Weschler how he felt about his wife in the role of a crowd-puller and he gave her an appreciative glance. 'Paula's an inspiration to me. I don't know what I'd do without her. She's great at stump politics, she's great at TV ads, and she's great at helping me with my speeches. There's nothing she isn't great at.'

This was a convenient lead into my next question – the one Maggie wanted to me to ask. I looked back at Paula. 'It's no secret that you're one of your husband's most influential advisers on policy issues as well as presentation – much more so than any previous prospective first lady. Some on the Republican right might ask if that's a woman's place? Or a wife's?'

'Why wouldn't it be?' She sounded mildly amused. 'I have a degree in economics and I worked at an investment bank before I met Hector. And I was raised in a political family. I'm as qualified as anybody else to give an opinion.'

I turned to Weschler, asked him how he felt about that – in particular as a former three-star general.

He reclined and spread his arms on the back of the couch, and I got the impression he'd prepared for this. 'A general doesn't deserve his stars if he doesn't take advice from those who know him best.'

That was well and good, but I wasn't gonna let him off so easy. So I said, 'What do you say to critics who claim your wife wears the pants? That you're tied to her apron strings?'

He made a guffaw that was a little too hearty to be genuine. 'In the US Army I commanded a corps of more than 30,000 personnel – all of them trained to kill. So anybody who thinks I'm some sort of hen-pecked husband better think again.' He leaned forward, as if realising he needed to qualify what he just said. 'By the same token, I'm not a some domestic dictator. I'm one half of an equal partnership.' He glanced at Paula. 'Am I right, dear?'

'You're right,' she said.

This was the part where I had to address the subject of Paula's family funding Weschler's run for office.

I glanced from her to him, then back to her. 'Paula, I know you weren't happy with the *New York Examiner* story about the finance Heck's campaign has received from your family. You told me you wanted an opportunity to have your say. This is it.'

She set down her coffee cup. 'It wasn't so much the facts of that story as its tone. Yes, my family is helping to finance Hector's campaign. And yes, this involves significant sums of money. But to portray it as some sort of gift from a devoted wife to a deserving husband is ridiculous.' She sat on the edge of the couch and looked at me with angry eyes. 'I mean, you'd have to be mentally ill to think of the presidency – with the pressure it entails and the commitment is demands – as some sort of present. As you know, Wat, my father was a senator for 20 years and my brother a congressman for over ten. My dad died in office of a heart attack and my brother survived an assassination attempt. I know from personal experience that public office is not something to be bought and sold, still less enjoyed. It's a heavy burden, a solemn duty. And you give much more than you ever take.'

She looked at Weschler, who was nodding his approval, and continued. 'For these reasons, I've spent considerably more time trying to persuade Hector against running for president than encouraging him to do so. Being raised in a political family meant I didn't want this for my husband. But once he'd made his mind up, once I realized it was the right thing for him to do, then I knew I had to back him to the hilt – including financially.'

This was good stuff. I scribbled away, hoping I'd be able to read back my fast shorthand outlines.

'Clearly you're a woman with political insight and knowledge, Paula. Ever think of running for office yourself?'

'Sure. Maybe the senate or the house. But not for a long while yet.'

'How about running for president?'

She laughed at that, so did Weschler.

When she realized I wasn't laughing along, that it was a serious question, she gave me a studious look. 'That's not something I'd ever want to do. But maybe one woman will, one day.'

# THIRTY-SIX

If Bobby Delacroix had any worries about our meeting, he wasn't showing them.

I slid into a seat opposite him at O'Donnell's Grille in the 1220 block of E Street NW. The lunch hour rush was over and the place half empty.

'You eating, Wat?' The giraffe man didn't look up from his bowl of gumbo. 'I can recommend the fresh-shucked oysters. Best I ever ate.'

O'Donnell's specialized in seafood and although I could have used a bite to eat, I didn't want food getting in the way of what I had to say. So I said I'd get something later.

He loaded his spoon with prawns and bell peppers. 'So what do you want to see me about that's so urgent?'

First I showed him the *Tribune* clip with the picture of him with Christine Zetchik and some other guys at the State Department long-service award presentation.

He squinted. 'Is that me at the back of the room there, Wat?'

'You know it is.'

'Wow, and Christine Zetchik. What a coincidence.'

'You know it isn't.'

Even now, his breezy confidence didn't show any sign of a dent. 'What's your point, Wat? Looking at the date, that picture was taken nearly six years ago and there are at least ten other people in it besides Mrs Zetchik and me.'

'But you knew her, didn't you, Bobby? You worked with her on some narcotics importation scam. And then she started shaking you down.'

He scooped another mouthful of gumbo and peered at me over the spoon with his teacher-like focus. 'That's a very serious allegation, Wat. I hope you got better evidence than a grainy old newspaper picture.'

'Wouldn't be here otherwise.' I produced the bank statements showing six deposits of $19,871 from Meridian Pacific in the summer and fall of 1968.

'Where the fuck did you get those?' Gumbo juice dripped off one side of his spoon.

No reason to hold back so I told him about the fishing hut on the shoreline at Earlstown. I concluded in a sympathetic tone. 'It wasn't actually on the property, which is probably why you missed it.'

He chewed more gumbo. 'Still doesn't prove anything.'

I gave him a get-real look. 'You figure you can explain how you came by $120,000 in a way your boss will find remotely credible? It says Meridian Pacific on the records, but there's no such business, or any other organisation of that name. It was a front outfit, wasn't it, Bobby?'

He gazed down at his bowl, stirring the stew with his spoon.

I leaned forward. 'There was more money where that came from, wasn't there? How much more?'

He looked up with a doleful expression. 'Not that much.

I realized I was getting played for a sucker early the next year and told her I wanted out.'

'Christine kept the bank records, though. Was that part of the deal?'

He nodded. 'It was her insurance policy. So I couldn't rat her out at a later date. But I never thought she'd use that stuff to shake me down.'

'I also know there was no narcotics stakeout at Earlstown.'

'That was a smokescreen. I wanted you and the spook off my back.'

'And the tale you told me about Kim's family, was that part of your smokescreen too? You figured making me suspicious of Kim would throw an extra wrench in the works?'

'That was the idea, sure. But the story was true solid.' He spoke somewhat defensively, as if I might give him credit for not being a complete bullshitter.

'Yeah, I guess it was.' I gave him a weary look. 'But you know this is the end of the line, don't you Bobby? Maybe you can work something out with your boss. Maybe you can plea-bargain with the DA. Strangling Christine, though, that's gotta have consequences.'

He dropped his spoon. It splashed flecks of stew on the table top. 'You think *I* killed her?'

His reaction surprised me.

I took out the photo of him and Le Nguyen Chau outside the accounting firm office, then the shot of Chau in bondage gear.

His turn to look surprised.

'So you don't know anything about the murder of this guy? Le Nguyen Chau, aka DC's *Man in a Suitcase*. Or rather two suitcases.'

'No I don't.' He sounded panicky. 'And I certainly don't know about that S&M shit. I only met the guy once.'

'I found these pictures with your bank records in the fishing hut. You think Christine was blackmailing Chau too?'

He looked again at the bondage picture and winced. 'I'd say that's pretty damned certain. But I had nothing to do with that kinky sex scene.'

I put the pictures away. 'Okay, Bobby, so tell me your version of events. Maybe I can help you.'

He shoved long bony fingers through his hair. 'You couldn't print it because you can't prove any of it. Fuck, man, *I* can't prove any of it. And you sure as hell can't help me. So I got no reason to tell you anything.'

'I wouldn't be so sure. Every story has more than one side. I could tell yours. And even if I couldn't run the piece, I'd be hip to what went down. You know as well as I do how big federal organisations with reputations to protect can bury embarrassing truths, make folks disappear. I could be your insurance policy.'

'Yeah, you could be my fucking undertaker too.'

He got up, started to leave.

Then he froze. I sensed frantic calculations whirring in his head.

He seemed to reach a decision and sat back down.

# THIRTY-SEVEN

'If I *did* tell you. If you *could* make the story stand up, maybe I could be the whistle-blower.'

Seemed he was looking at me as a potential get-out-of-jail-free card. I was cool with that if it got me the information I needed. How it might play with various law enforcement authorities was another matter.

I took out my notebook. 'All right, Bobby, shoot.'

He waited while a waitress cleared his unfinished gumbo. Then he started talking. 'I came across Christine Zetchik in '66 when she was at the State Department over in Foggy Bottom. Our paths crossed on various initiatives, like the Narcotics Liaison Committee. Two years later she was posted to the US Embassy in Saigon. Couple of months after that, she came back to DC on leave and asked for a meet-up. Seemed she'd gotten involved in a heroin importation racket and they needed protection for people bringing weight into the USA – service personnel, low-level State Department officials, even reporters. Back then I was at the Bureau of Narcotics, working liaison with the military, so I was the ideal guy.'

He paused as a party of boozy conventioneers hovered around our table, arguing about who should pay their check.

At last they moved away and Bobby continued. 'I said no at first, even though the work was high dollar, low risk. Then I discovered this sort of racket was going on all over the country. Other people had their snouts in the feedbag, why not me? I was still mulling it over when I got scapegoated in an anti-corruption investigation that was 100 per cent bullshit. Christine offered to hook me up with a guy who knew a guy who could make it go away – but only if I cooperated.'

He broke the eye-contact and stared at the gumbo-splashed table top. 'Back then I didn't seem to have any good choices. So I went along with what she wanted.'

'How did the scam operate?'

'Real easy. Christine told me who would be arriving, and where. I had them picked up at the point of entry and was waiting to search their baggage. I simply turned a blind eye to what they were carrying and sent them on their way.'

'So what went wrong?'

Bobby shrugged. He really did look miserable. 'Dunno, man. Attack of conscience, loss of nerve. By early '69 I'd had enough and we did the deal that gave me an out, with Christine hanging onto that bank stuff as insurance.'

'Then what?'

'Then nothing. Not until last year. Christine's gravy train hit the buffers when we pulled out of Vietnam in '73. She had a rainy day stash, but the trouble was she'd acquired some very expensive tastes during the years of plenty. Her rainy day soon turned into a shitstorm and her money ran out at the end of '74. That was when she started to rack up big debts. She became unbalanced, hit the sauce. Then she hit on the idea of blackmailing me.'

'How come you didn't threaten to blackmail her back?'

He made a hangdog smile. 'I had nothing on her.'

'How did the Chau thing come about?'

'Not entirely sure about the details. She told me she found out about Chau's laundering activities after going through her husband's stuff. She knew Chau was mixed up in some illicit wealth importation scam run by an ex-ARVN general named Pham Tan Giang. They were looking for an accounting firm that wouldn't ask questions and could keep the IRS at bay.'

I guessed what was coming next.

'The bitch set me up by asking me to introduce Chau to the people I'd used to handle my kickbacks back in '68 and '69. Like I said, I only met Chau that one time – when I took him to meet Gerry Hawthorne and Phil Zeiss.' He rolled his eyes to the ceiling. 'Fuck, man, I even told Christine which day we were going. That gave her all the information she needed. She hired a private investigator to snap the pair of us outside the office.'

He made bitter laugh. 'Clearly those shots implicated me in whatever shit was going down with Chau and Giang. That gave her extra leverage and meant she could turn the screw even tighter. Trouble was, the tighter she turned, the less I could pay.'

'That why you went to the Zetchik place? Because you couldn't give her what she was asking for?'

He nodded. 'She'd squeezed me dry, man. I went out there to ask for some more time. But she was dead when I arrived.'

I lit a Camel. It was easy to imagine how Christine wound up that way.

She probably used the same private detective to investigate Chau and soon enough discovered his sexual proclivities. Then she'd have procured the S&M photos to blackmail Chau into skimming funds off the companies whose books he was cooking. If she went to the authorities with the intel she had on Chau she could shut down Giang's entire operation. But it backfired because she put herself in Giang's crosshairs. Maybe she underestimated him. Maybe she was too used to calling the shots with Vietnamese nationals after her time in Saigon. Maybe she was drinking way more than Bobby suspected. And maybe it was a mix of all three. But I figured Giang was behind Christine's murder as well as Chau's.

I said as much to Bobby. He didn't disagree.

I said, 'Poor Chau ended up in pieces in the C&O Canal. Think you could be in danger?'

He shook his head. 'I'm a DEA officer. Giang would never come after me. Besides, he doesn't know who I am.'

'I wouldn't be so sure – '

'Wow!' Bobby jack-knifed, grabbing his gut. 'Think I'm gonna throw up.'

He came to his feet and stumbled at a half-crouch toward the rest room, one hand still clutching his belly, the other over his mouth.

Seafood could do that to you, though it was just as likely a reaction to having gotten nailed dead to rights.

While he was gone I thought about the heroin importation scam run by Colonel Thanh and the MACV officer codenamed Bootstrap. There were a lot of heroin rackets in Saigon that ended in 1973 when the USA pulled out of Vietnam. All the same, I wondered if Bobby had been involved in the early stages of the one I ended up investigating.

Last time I saw Quan Quy Linh alive was in the little presbytery on Cong Ly where I recruited her.

*I'm back there now.*

*Linh is approaching her seventeenth birthday but has the bearing of someone ten years older.*

*We drink black tea that she's poured from an indigo pot and wait for the French priest who operates the safe house to leave the room.*

*'You all right?' I ask.*

*'I'm fine.' She senses my concern. 'There's nothing to worry about. Thanh really likes me. He likes me in a way I don't like. But Madame knows what he's up to and she's always one step ahead of him.'*

*I'm not reassured by this, even though Thanh's fondness for teenage girls is the main reason Linh was signed up in the first place.*

*'Nothing more on the heroin refinery on Pasteur?'*

*She shakes her head.*

*'Bootstrap?'*

*She shakes her head again. 'They had another meeting in Thanh's summer house. I can get there easily enough from my room, but I just can't get a clear view of the guy. And Thanh always does most of the talking.'*

*She seems frustrated, angry with herself. I'd asked her to step it up after talking to Chuck Shaughnessy and she's come back with zip.*

*'It's not your fault, Linh.'*

*'I need to do better.'*

*'No you don't. No more risky stuff.' I look at her hard. 'Understand?'*

*She nods, but I can tell from her expression that she doesn't mean it.*

*We finish our tea, then she says. 'There was something about Bootstrap. Just a little thing.'*

*'Big pictures are made of small detail,' I say. 'What you got?'*

*'I heard him telling Thanh that he flies stateside whenever he can, to see the chiefs.'*

*I place my empty tea cup on the wicker table between us. Like the Pall Mall cigarettes Bootstrap smokes, and the old-time squeeze box music he likes, it isn't much. But not much is better than nothing at all.*

*I chew on it. Returning stateside for meetings with the chiefs of staff will make him a senior officer, at least a bird colonel. But there are plenty of full colonels as well as one, two and three-star generals at MACV headquarters in Saigon – or Pentagon East as it gets called. Yet we already know Bootstrap is a high-ranking officer, so again, this intel doesn't tell us anything new.*

*I try to sound upbeat. 'It confirms what we know from other sources. Good job, Linh.'*

*She isn't fooled. 'I'll do better. Next time I'll have something real good for you.'*

*I want to tell her* not *to do better,* not *to take any chances,* not *to get anything real good. But of course she's an asset and I'm her handler. So I say nothing.*

The presence of a waitress at my elbow hauled me back to O'Donnell's Grille.

She asked if she could get me anything and I said no, I was just waiting for my buddy in the rest room.

The waitress went away and I glanced at my watch.

Bobby must have gotten real sick. I decided to go check on him.

But the rest room was empty and a wide-open window above the urinals told me the giraffe man had left the building.

# THIRTY-EIGHT

I'd just gotten home from Reggie's place. She was in a surprisingly upbeat mood, no doubt on account of having scored some goofballs or nose candy, or whatever shit she'd been able to get her hands on. I was dishing out a can of dog food for Sherman when the phone rang.

Gotta say I was surprised when I heard Paula Weschler's voice on the other end of the line, and even more surprised when I heard what she wanted: A meet up in Mr Chester's, a discreet little bar in Georgetown.

I arrived shortly after 7.00pm, a little late for after-work drinkers and a little early for Friday night booze crews.

I spotted Paula through a veil of cigarette smoke. She was sitting on a tall stool at the end of the counter, wearing a sharp skirt suit with black nylons and expensive shoes. Somewhat formal for the venue, but every bit of classy. Her dark red hair was pinned up and her complexion was fresh and outdoorsy, giving the impression she wasn't wearing make-up, even though she was. Pale green eyes met mine as I moved toward her.

'Thanks for coming.' She showed her teeth. 'Especially at such short notice.'

I asked what she was drinking. She said vodka tonic and I got the same.

When the bartender had brought the drinks I gave her a searching look. 'So what was it you wanted to see me about?'

She took a large swallow from her glass and looked at me full on. 'Hector says he trusts you absolutely. Question is, can I?'

I said sure she could trust me.

This was a weird situation though, and it made me wonder if *I* could trust *her*. We looked for all the world like a couple on a date. Or having an affair. She wasn't exactly low profile and even I sometimes got recognized. Compared to New York City, DC was a village. Last thing either of us needed was a gossip column appearance.

'Does your husband know you're here?'

She helped herself to the pack of Camels I'd placed on the counter and waited for me to give her a light. 'Do you think I need his permission?'

'No I don't.'

I flipped my Zippo and watched her dip the cigarette in the flame.

'Does he know what this is about?'

This provoked a short, slightly shrill laugh. That was when I realized she'd already had a few to drink. Not so that she was drunk, but enough to off-load an inhibition or two. 'Yes, Hector knows what this is about.'

I lit a cigarette of my own. 'So are you gonna tell me?'

'It's not for print. I want your word as an officer.'

'I'm not an officer. Haven't been for five years.'

'I want your word anyway.'

By now I sensed what she really wanted was to tell me what was on her mind. But unless I agreed to her terms, she wouldn't spill. Besides, 'not for print' was usually negotiable. So I said she had my word.

She pinned me through a squiggle of cigarette smoke and said, 'Do you think I'm attractive?'

If she meant to shock me, she succeeded. Kept my shit together though. 'Of course I do. You're not difficult to look at. But you already know that.'

Her stare intensified. 'I don't mean in the physical sense.'

I hesitated. Whatever I said, there were all sorts of ways it could go bad. So I picked my words carefully. 'You're smart, witty, insightful and determined. What's not to like?'

'All those things.'

'I don't get you.'

'Some men see women like me as their worst nightmare.'

'Some men, maybe. But not Heck. And he's the only man who really matters, surely?'

'I never much liked women's libbers.' There was a calculated bluntness to her switch of subject – as if she wanted to underscore a point. 'I was raised to believe a woman's place was in the home. Even with a college education, I used to think it was just how things were – men were the breadwinners, the decision-makers.'

The way she used the phrase *used to* told me she'd changed her mind.

'And now?'

She paused, drank more vodka tonic. 'Now I'm not so sure men are as good as they like to think.'

'You think women can do a better job?'

'Given the opportunity and the right circumstances,

yes I do. And I know you agree because I know about your relationship with Maggie Call. I've been reading her opinion columns since she was on the *New York Examiner* in the 50s. Back then I thought her ideas were crazy and dangerous. Latterly, I've come to think an awful lot of what she says makes an awful lot of sense.'

'That why you wanted to get so involved in your husband's tilt at the White House?'

She nodded and finished her drink, then placed the glass on the counter in a way that told me she wanted another. Seemed her take on gender equality didn't extend to paying her way in a bar, but then I'd known plenty of guys – including Johnny Tedstone – who were happy to let somebody else buy their drinks all night. So I obliged and also got another one for myself.

She drank from the recharged glass with a ruminative expression. 'I've read political thinkers from Machiavelli to Marx. Modern stuff too – Robert Dahl in particular. There's very little I haven't read. But none of it ever mentions the two golden rules.'

I raised an eyebrow. 'Which are?'

'Number one: Keep your dick in your pants. And number two: If you can't do that, don't get caught.' She made a sardonic laugh. 'Of course that presupposes we're talking about men, not women, which is usually a pretty safe presupposition.'

I gave her a long, puzzled look. Did she mean what I thought she meant? That Heck Weschler was fucking around?

'He's not a philanderer.' She covered her mouth and laughed. 'Gosh, that sounds so old fashioned. But he really isn't.'

'But there is a problem, isn't there? Otherwise, why are we having this conversation?'

'Not for print? I got your word?'

'Yes you do.'

Still, she hesitated.

I realized she needed a more solid kind of assurance. I said, 'Look, unless I was recording this – which I'm clearly not – I couldn't publish the information I think you're going to give me unless I could prove it was true. It wouldn't get past Maggie Call to start with, because she'd know the *Tribune* would cop libel damages that would sink the paper.'

She took another drink and seemed to make up her mind. 'He's been having an affair. She's much younger than him. Much younger than me. But then, aren't they always?'

'How long has this been going on?'

'Some years.'

'How long have you known?'

'Some years.'

She looked down at her glass, as if it might contain a solution. 'Thing is, it never bothered me like it does now. I guess that's because there was never so much riding on it. The media attention is invasive on a level I'd never have imagined.'

She kept her gaze on the vodka tonic. 'That makes me sound like a real cold bitch. But I'm not. It's always bothered me. I've always hated it. I just learned to live with it. He was always discreet and he always made sure I knew he'd never leave me.'

I thought about her family wealth. Was that the reason Weschler had gone to such lengths to reassure her?

She said, 'I know what you're thinking.'

I said, 'It's only logical.'

She made a weary sigh. 'You could be right.'

The silence played awkward.

I lit a cigarette for each of us.

She took hers, then a long pull on the filter tip. 'I sometimes wonder what it was I couldn't give him – apart from reducing my age by 20 years.'

She looked defeated, ashamed. And things that hadn't added up a few days ago started to. Like the time she nailed me after my second interview with Weschler and asked me to report her side of that *New York Examiner* story implying she was buying the presidency for her husband. I'd sensed vulnerability then – except it was more like low self-esteem. And again, a few days later, in the interview with her and her husband. What was it he said? *If a marriage can survive an army career, it can survive anything.* She'd smiled at that but said nothing. At the time I thought this was a little odd, but put it down to her wanting to avoid stating the obvious, or coming out with some corny platitude. I couldn't have been more wrong.

I thought carefully about what I was going to say next. 'He's the only person who could say why he did what he did. But this is on him. One hundred per cent. He made the wrong decision, not you.'

'You think?'

'I know.' I stabbed out my cigarette. 'Woman like you – strong, intelligence, righteous – he's gotta be mad.'

'You're being kind.'

I looked at her hard. 'I'm being honest.'

'What should I do?'

That put me in a hell of a difficult position. 'Not for me to say.'

'Very well, let me put it hypothetically: What would you do in my shoes?' Her tone told me she wasn't gonna give it up until I told her what I thought.

And after all that deceit, she deserved a little frankness. So I said, 'Tell him to end it. If he wants to be president, or secretary of state, or whatever, he has no choice. Ten or 15 years ago, he might have gotten away with it. But after Watergate and Vietnam, the press is less deferential than ever. Like you say, the scrutiny is already intense and high office would make it much worse. Sooner or later this affair would get out. I hate to imagine what the headline writers would do with a story like that, but HECK WRECK has a solid tabloid ring.'

She gripped my hand. 'Thank you, Wat. I can't ever repay you.'

'You really don't need to.'

She shuffled off the stool and started to leave.

I caught her arm and tugged her back, close enough to whisper. 'He can't find out we had this conversation.'

'He won't hear it from me.'

At that time, I believed she meant it.

# THIRTY-NINE

It was the eve of America's 200th birthday but Kim didn't seem to have partying in mind when she arrived on my doorstep in an olive drab jacket, dark blue jeans and hiking boots.

That wasn't to say she didn't look sexy. And in a punky kind of way she'd have fit right in at the Cellar Door, or Crazy Horse or any edgy Georgetown nightspot.

I hadn't heard from her since we broke into the accounting firm and found evidence of Giang's wealth importation activities. On one level, I wondered if this had given the CIA enough to shut down the scam. On another level, I thought not, and I was right.

I showed her into my living room where she was greeted by Sherman. I couldn't tell her about my meeting with Joseph Tedstone without breaking my promise to keep Reggie out of this. So I said I was looking after the dog for someone I knew, which was true enough. Kim and I were meant to be cooperating, though, so I shot her the works on Bobby Delacroix and his claims about Christine Zetchik's blackmailing racket.

Kim rubbed Sherman's neck just behind his ear, which he clearly liked. Without taking her eyes off of the dog, she said, 'That ties in with our latest intelligence. Giang's operations are far more advanced than we suspected and any interference wouldn't have been tolerated. He wouldn't have thought twice about killing Christine Zetchik and Chau.'

Given the sadomasochistic stuff that Christine had on Chau, I figured his boss Giang would have thought a lot more than twice about killing the poor bastard – in particular about how his death could be made as long and painful as possible.

But I got what Kim meant. And something else was playing on my mind. 'This latest intel – does it have anything to do with your turning up at my place at 3.00pm on a Saturday?'

Now she did look up at me. 'That depends on you.'

'How so?'

She leaned forward. 'Giang is renting farmland, including buildings and a substantial acreage of cornfields and woodland in rural Maryland – not too far from Earlstown. Our information suggests he's using it as a Stateside training and logistics base for a guerrilla campaign in Vietnam.'

'Why not get the FBI to go in?'

'They couldn't show probable cause.'

I leaned forward too. 'Let me guess, that's where we come in?'

She smiled. 'You up for a recon patrol?'

'I'm a reporter these days, remember?'

'I'm sure you haven't lost your edge.'

I gave her a dubious glance. 'This is a freelance gig, isn't it?'

'My chief can't know. He's a stickler for the law prohibiting the CIA operating on US soil.'

I made a knowing smile. 'That never stopped the Agency in the past.'

'That was then; now is now.'

She reached out and gripped my hand. And although I knew she was playing me, it felt nice anyway. Besides, there was a national exclusive up for grabs.

So I said, 'When do you wanna do this?'

She said, 'How about right now?'

*

We took US50 past Earlstown and across Chesapeake Bay, then cut south and east across country to within a few miles of the Maryland/Delaware state line. The countryside was lush with fields of corn and wheat. Every so often the road entered heavily wooded areas that went on for miles. I could see why Giang would want to locate his base here. It sure wasn't Vietnam, but the mix of forest, arable land and creeks made it ideal terrain for the sort of exercises he'd need to carry out.

She turned onto a side road flanked by woods and, after a couple of miles, parked her Hornet on the shoulder near a galvanized metal gate. On the other side, a dirt track ran off through the trees, quickly vanishing in the dim light under the canopy.

Grabbing her rucksack, she headed off along the trail.

I followed, feeling somewhat naked without a weapon or any sort of kit. Sure, I wasn't in the military any more, but given what we were doing here, it sure felt that way.

I thought of anti-personnel landmines, giant centipedes and toe-popper traps. We were entering the back yard of the people who were almost certainly behind those things.

Which meant they had likely rigged all sorts of unpleasant surprises to keep curious hikers at bay. I'd never gotten spooked by Charlie's dirty tricks, but that wasn't to say I was blasé, and this was no different. So I watched the trail ahead with special focus.

We moved quietly through an interesting mix of trees – white oak, red maple, loblolly and Virginia pine, eastern hemlock and American sycamore and species I didn't recognize. I said as much to Kim and she looked at me like I was a little peculiar.

I shrugged. 'Spend as much time as I did in the boonies, you get to know the plants and trees around you. I got to be something of an amateur botanist and that didn't end when I rode the liftbird out.'

We reached the treeline after a half hour hike and found ourselves peering across a grassy slope overlooking an extensive collection of agricultural buildings. Kim took off her rucksack and fished out a pair of field glasses. She surveyed the scene below, then handed the glasses to me.

There was a big hip-roof farmhouse set apart from a water tower, grain silo, and a row of open-fronted cinderblock outbuildings with rusty tin roofs where tractors, trailers and other machinery was kept. Behind the house was a large metal-frame barn and a half dozen prefabricated arch buildings that looked a lot like World War II barracks. People moved about in small groups. Most were Asians, although there was a significant number of white folk. It would make sense for Giang to use American mercenaries, who would also help to keep up appearances for curious neighbours. Nobody appeared to be carrying weapons, but a lot of those people would be packing handguns.

A crackle of gunfire south of the buildings turned our attention to a meadow set up as a firing range. Beyond that, I clocked an assault course comprising the usual collection of obstacles for climbing, crawling, running and jumping. I guessed most of Giang's recruits would be ARVN veterans, but many would have gotten out of shape so this set-up would be an effective first step on the road back to combat readiness.

I glanced sideways. 'What do you think?'

'It's on a larger scale than I expected.' From her rucksack she produced an SLR camera fitted with a telephoto lens and started snapping. 'What I'm really interested in, though, is that big barn behind the house.'

'You think it could be Giang's arsenal?'

'Quite possibly.' She finished with the camera. 'We need to find out.'

'Going down there would be high risk. Especially in daylight.'

She pulled on the rucksack. 'We need evidence and that means pictures. Which are tricky to take in the dark, wouldn't you say?'

'We also need to get out alive.'

'What happened to the audacious A-team commander?' She gave me a bold grin – the type that reminded me of Linh – and my reservations about her plan began to wilt.

'Also, think about your national exclusive.'

I thought about it and my reservations vanished.

I pointed to a cornfield north of the buildings. Apparently *Knee high by the fourth of July* signified a healthy crop, but the corn in this field was more like chest-height and that would give us excellent cover. One side of the field ran parallel to the barn at a distance of perhaps 100 hundred yards. Between them was a belt of open hardscrabble. That would be the risky part. But either we went the cornfield route, or straight through the buildings.

I suggested the cornfield and she agreed.

So we went back into the trees and skirted the buildings, emerging well to the north and maybe fifty yards from the cornfield.

The corn was great cover, though the crop was dense. A machete would have come in handy, but instead we had to force a path west, then south. This was noisy and slow as we wrestled our way through the tough corn stalks. But at last we emerged on the southern edge of the cornfield. The big barn was farther away than I'd anticipated – more like 200 yards than 100. On the positive side, there was some unexpected cover in the form of busted and rusted machinery dumped behind the building. We scurried to an ancient John Deer tractor, then to a wrecked fertilizer-spreader, and on to a corroded chain harrow that looked like a wreck from the Dust Bowl area. Finally we reach some old oil drums peppered with large calibre bullet holes that must have been used as target practice for heavy machine-gunners.

The barn was just 20 yards away. At this distance, its maroon flanks loomed high, blotting out the sun. Dry, rocky earth crunched under our boots as we moved toward a side-door. Not surprisingly it was locked. Kim went to work with a set of lock picks and had it open in less than a minute.

We stepped inside. The place was illuminated by fluorescent strip lamps. Their grainy radiance wouldn't be ideal for photos, but Kim's SLR would have a slow enough shutter speed so we could get what we needed without using a flashgun. As for the evidence we came looking for, there seemed to be no shortage. The place was filled to the roof with wood and metal crates of the kind used by Uncle Sam to pack military equipment. They were organized in long rows with wide corridors running between so fork-lift trucks could easily move stuff in and out. Three of these vehicles were parked near the main doors, along with a dozen crates that must have recently arrived, or been prepared for despatch.

We moved quietly along the side of the building, although nobody appeared to be around.

The crate nearest us had been left open, with the top removed. Inside I counted sixteen M16A1 assault rifles with integral grenade launchers.

Resting on the crate next to it was the jemmy bar that must have been used to open the crate. It seemed logical to assume that someone had started to inspect the consignment, but had gotten called away part way through the task.

Kim voiced my thoughts, 'We need to see what's in the others.'

I used the jemmy on the second create. Inside were six M60 machine guns.

Over my shoulder I heard Kim snapping away with her camera.

I moved to the next crate, levered off the top and found myself looking down at rows of neatly packed fragmentation grenades. The fourth crate was filled with claymore mines, the fifth with anti-tank mines and the sixth was brimming with Swedish K submachine-guns.

I called over my shoulder, 'You getting this?'

But it wasn't Kim's voice that replied.

# FORTY

It was a male voice, and that was a worry. It was also one I recognized. And that was even more of a worry.

'Hands in the air, both of you. Where I can see 'em.'

In my haste to get the tops of the crates, and hers to get the pictures, we hadn't heard the guard approaching. That was downright sloppy. What were we thinking?

But I did like the guy said and Kim followed suit.

'Now, turn around. Real slow.'

We did that too.

The recognition on the guard's face mirrored mine.

I was standing opposite the big swarthy guy with the Alice Cooper tattoo on his forearm – the leader of the trio who attacked me and Johnny outside the Bayou. What was his name? Rhyme Dillard's words came back to me: Duane Henry, aged 28, a Southeast DC bruiser who pulled time for assault and battery and other violent offences.

He'd been a great deal lighter on his feet now than on that night two weeks ago. But then I guessed he was a great deal less juiced. And he looked just as brick shithouse-like – six-three and maybe 250 pounds.

His mouth stretched in a diagonal grin. 'Ain't it a small world?'

'Ain't it just?' I went along with the taunting banter to buy a little time so I could evaluate the situation, look for a way out, maybe even glean a little information. 'But the cops had you down as a city boy. Strange you and me meeting back on your home turf.'

His brow corrugated. 'How do you know that?'

'General Giang didn't employ you for your military skills. Local knowledge and a white face, those have gotta be your only tradeable assets.'

'Fuck you, Snake-eater!'

Kim took a step toward him – and to his left. She said, 'Listen, I'm sure we can talk about this.'

'Shut your face and stay put, Missy Gook.' He pointed the M16 barrel at her, then back at me.

'You're the motherfucker, Duane.' I kept my voice level and my hands up. But at the same time I followed Kim's tactic of stepping to one side, widening his arc of fire. 'You call the shots.'

Problem was we were running out of time and options.

Duane chuckled, savouring the situation. 'Don't you just love payback, Snake-eater?' He said it like he was really getting his rocks off. I sensed him itching to pull the trigger.

So I said the only thing I could think of that would stop him. 'Shoot us now, Duane, and Giang's gonna be real pissed.'

I saw my reasoning register, sensed his excitement subside slightly.

This was a breathing space, but that was all. Duane still had an M16 on us at a range of less than 12 feet. That sort of distance, it was significantly harder to miss than hit.

Only it wasn't. Duane was holding the weapon at the hip, like they did in the movies. But assault rifles were designed to be fired from the shoulder. See, shooting from the hip sacrificed direct line of sight and weakened your grip because the recoil came into your waist – your body's rotation pivot. If you got ambushed and had to fire from the hip, it was crucial to push the stock tight against your pelvis and lock the elbow of the hand holding the barrel so as to increase stability. Duane was doing none of these things.

I glanced at Kim and we exchanged brief nods. She had no way of telling what I was planning, but at least she knew I was planning something.

I took a step forward, smiling. 'You ever fired an M16 before, Duane?'

Nothing back.

'Back in the early years of Vietnam, the grunts called it the Jammin' Jenny. Highly unreliable in a hostile environment like jungle.'

Another step. Six feet from the muzzle.

'Rifle jams with Charlie coming at you, that's a real bad deal.'

'What the fuck you talking about?'

'They improved later models and the grunts revised their opinion. Trouble is, Duane, that's an early model M16 you got there. Lots of design flaws – especially if you don't maintain it properly. You ever cleaned that gun, Duane?'

And another step. Now I was standing three feet from the end of the muzzle. That close, he couldn't miss.

Unless –

I went at him fast. He opened fire. But his muzzle was already behind my body so there was no way could he hit me. I wrapped my right arm tight around the barrel. Duane clung to the rifle with both hands and that gave me a clean shot. I drove the heel of my left hand hard under his chin. His head snapped back, he let go of the gun, and went down in a heap.

I stooped to pick up the M16.

Before I could reach it the two other guys from the Bayou incident – Arty and Drake McDonagh – burst into the barn, each with an M16.

They saw me instantly and rushed forward. But they didn't see Kim. She'd anticipated their arrival and positioned herself on their right flank. Arty – the one with the droopy moustache – saw Kim, but he was too late. She stepped across his path, gripping his shoulders and pitching him backward over the foot she'd placed behind him. He hit the ground hard, instinctively releasing his grip on the rifle. She took it away, smashing the butt into the face of the younger brother, Drake, before he could get a shot off. He followed Duane and Arty on the barn floor.

A quick survey of the scene showed that Duane and Drake were out cold while Arty was badly winded after Kim's body slam. But Duane and the McDonagh boys were the least of our worries. The sound of gunfire would bring everyone on the farm down on us. Sure, we were armed, but a firefight would only ever go one way.

'There's a bulldozer out back,' she said. 'The loader bucket is elevated so it will shield the cabin from gunfire. It's our best shot.'

There was no time for a debate. I didn't know what exactly she had in mind, but I trusted her judgment. So I nodded, grabbed some extra M16 magazines from one of the crates, and followed her back through the side door.

I saw what she meant about the bulldozer. The steering

position would be protected by the big steel bucket that was raised off the ground.

We were half way there when a group of ten, maybe 12 Asian guys with M16s rounded the side of the barn. They took one look and opened fire.

Their rounds threw up spouts of earth as we sprinted for the bulldozer. My rifle was set to automatic and I gave them a short burst of supressing fire without breaking stride. I had no chance of hitting them but they weren't expecting us to shoot back, and the realisation threw them into confusion.

That was all we needed. Kim climbed into the driving seat and I jumped onto the side of the hull beside her. 'You ever driven one of these things?'

'Not for a long time. But it's like riding a bike. Well, I hope it is.' She hit start and the engine came alive with a throaty growl. Then she began wrestling with the control levers and the big machine lurched backwards, away from the barn in the direction of the woodland.

We'd barely moved when bullets rang and pinged off the steel bucket. Leaning out on the footplate, I fired a half dozen rounds at the figures coming after us. None of them went down, but I sent them running for cover.

I looked back at her. 'What's the plan?'

'Plan? Are you kidding?'

'All right, where are you aiming to go with this thing?'

'The treeline. Then we can use the cover the wood to get away. Maybe reach the road. Maybe even get to my car.'

'How fast can bulldozers go?'

She shrugged. 'Not fast. Maybe five or six miles an hour forward and seven or eight backward. Which is a little weird. But whatever way we go, it's better than going on foot.'

She was right there. The treeline was about 300 yards away, and most of that was up a steep incline. Benefit of that, I guessed, was that they couldn't use two-wheel drive vehicles to come after us.

She said, 'I need you to keep our flanks clear. Can you do that?'

I slapped the stock of my M16. 'Not much ammo, but I'll do what I can.'

The going was slow, but the bucket did its job. Those guys might as well have been shooting at tank armour. Every so often, shadowy figures would appear around one side of the cab. Each time I fired two or three rounds close enough to drive them back.

We were less than half way to the treeline when I heard another engine, higher pitched than the wheezy grumble of the bulldozer's.

This couldn't be good. I braced myself for whatever was coming.

A jeep mounting a .50 cal Browning machine-gun appeared on our left side.

Kim saw it at the same time and we exchanged grim looks. If the jeep flanked us we'd be hamburger.

She gave me a worried glance. 'Can you hit the gunner?'

I slotted a fresh magazine into my M16. 'We better hope so.'

# FORTY-ONE

Leaning out on the footplate, I took aim. It wasn't easy with bullets fizzing around me but I stayed focused. One of the few upsides of attachment disorder was not getting scared. I was aware of danger, sure, but it didn't panic me and I didn't OD on adrenaline. I took my time.

The jeep began to draw level, engine whining, tyres spinning as the gradient got steeper.

I saw the machine-gunner swivelling the heavy .50 cal.

Kept my grip firm. Waited, waited.

'You gonna shoot or what?' Kim sounded more pissed than frightened.

I said nothing, focused on the machine-gunner as the jeep bounced and skidded on the bumpy surface.

I fired three times. A scarlet plume spouted from the gunner's chest and he fell backward. My next volley took out the driver. He slumped sideways across the steering wheel. The jeep veered away and turned over, rolling back down the hill, scattering our pursuers like a misshapen bowling ball.

I turned to Kim with a thumbs up sign, but she was concentrating on the steering gear. I soon discovered why.

I grabbed the side of the cab and braced for impact as the bulldozer ploughed into the treeline.

She killed the engine and jumped from the bulldozer. 'Coming?'

I followed her into the forest and we headed east in the direction of the road.

Behind us, I heard a lot of shouting but the shooting stopped as our pursuers lost their line of sight. We crashed through the undergrowth, stumbling over tree roots and moss-covered rocks. At one point we were on dry, dusty high ground. Next, we were wading knee-deep through a black mouldy pool. Then more high ground, and more muddy wetland. There was no time to stop and figure out if we were still headed in the right direction. Our only guide was the sun, which was starting to set behind us.

We came to a broad clearing and had a decision to make. Skirt around and lose time; or break cover and risk being seen.

She gave me a stern look and said, 'Straight on.'

We entered the clearing and immediately drew fire. Rounds ricocheted off rocks and thwacked into trees trunks, gouging out blond wood shards. But we made the far side of the clearing without getting hit.

We forged ahead.

Branches scraped my face, my foot snagged in a tree root and my ankle twisted. Kim tripped, fell sideways, forced herself up again.

We didn't stop.

At last we emerged from the treeline onto the country road.

Just 50 yards to our left a county sheriff's cruiser was

pulled over behind Kim's Hornet, red light flashing. A deputy was standing between the two vehicles.

Kim said to me, 'We gotta ditch the guns.'

I got where she was coming from. If the deputy saw we were armed he'd be less easy to deal with. I tossed my M16 into the undergrowth and Kim did the same.

Realising he was no longer alone, the deputy turned to face us. He didn't look any part of pleased.

As the lawman started toward us, five guys with M16s followed us onto the road. Their leader – a black bearded Hispanic dude – saw the deputy and came to a halt so fast the others bumped into one another like this was some Keystone Cops comedy routine.

Blackbeard looked at the deputy and the deputy looked at Blackbeard. It was the strangest standoff I ever saw.

Blackbeard seemed to reach a decision: A confrontation with the law was not worth the risk. He turned away and led his heavily armed group back into the forest before the deputy could get close enough to ask any questions.

The deputy was heavy-built and late-middle aged, with a weathered face. 'Who were those people?'

'We really don't know, deputy.' Kim shrugged like she was as confused as the lawman. 'Me and my boyfriend were taking a walk in the woods and they seemed real unhappy to see us.'

Kim clearly didn't want local law enforcement getting involved at this stage, and I could dig why.

The deputy didn't sound at all sympathetic. 'Ever thought you might have been trespassing, ma'am?'

'You're probably right, deputy. But they didn't give us any opportunity to explain.'

The lawman frowned. 'Was all that shooting on account of you two?'

Kim shrugged. 'Not sure. We were walking through the woods and heard gunfire. Then we saw those guys coming toward us and headed back to our car real fast. '

'You could still make a complaint.' He made a pensive frown. 'Can't have folks getting shot at just for straying onto private property. Not in this county.'

She shook her head. 'Thank you, deputy, but we'd just as soon be on our way.'

We moved toward the car doors.

'Hold up, there.' The deputy clearly wasn't done with us. He followed Kim down the driver's side of the car and consulted his notebook. 'Did you know you're illegally parked, ma'am?'

She made a tight smile. 'No, sir, I didn't know that.'

'Technically you're obstructing the free vehicular passage of the roadway, contrary to state law.'

Kim apologized.

The deputy explained that she'd left too much of the car on the road. He conceded that there was plenty room for other cars to get by. But what if a big truck came along? A skilled teamster might just squeeze through, but it would be touch and go.

Kim apologized again. She saw the folly of her ways and promised never – *ever* – to commit another parking violation in this or any other Maryland county.

It was the right approach. Argue with a guy like this, that's the surest way to cop a fine or worse. Throw yourself on his mercy, he just might show you a little.

Which was exactly what happened. He closed his notebook and returned it to his breast pocket. 'I guess I could overlook the infraction on this particular occasion,' he said. 'You've had a bad enough day already. But remember ... '

Driving back to the state highway, Kim finally vented. 'That deputy – what an officious asshole.'

I gave her a curious look. 'Asshole? Or the guy who just saved our asses?'

'Maybe he did. But it wasn't like he meant to.'

I glanced at her. 'You all right?'

'Cuts and bruises. You?'

'Same. You get the pictures?'

'I got *some* pictures. Whether I got enough to convince my chief is another matter.'

I understood her problem. The only evidence we had was photos of a dozen crates of various munitions. We assumed the barn contained enough hardware to equip a significant fighting force. But that was all it was, assumption. Similar logic applied to them shooting at us. Like the deputy said, we were trespassing. We busted into the barn. And it was possible that Giang was legitimately storing whatever was in there. He had powerful friends in the Pentagon and Congress and Kim's chief would be acutely aware of that. My predicament as a reporter was similar. I didn't have enough hard facts to make a news story stand up.

I said, 'What will you do next?'

'Talk to my chief, ask for more time. We need to know who's backing Giang. Operation on that scale, he's gotta have some real big hitters behind him.'

I agreed. Like her, I needed this information before I could even think about writing my piece.

We didn't talk much for the rest of the ride back to DC and it was dusk when she parked outside my place.

I invited her in for a drink and she said yeah, that would be nice.

Sherman was real pleased to see us. It wasn't a good idea leaving him alone for such a long time, but what choice did I have? And besides, it was better than what Holy Joe had had in mind.

I poured two big whiskies and brought the bottle over to the couch where she was sitting. We drank the liquor straight, then two more and another two.

We were still a little jacked on adrenaline and there was also the gravitational pull of unfinished business. These things upped the voltage, but sex with Kim was always gonna be flat out and full on. I'd wanted it since the day I first saw her and this time I'd make damn sure there were no interruptions. We half undressed on the couch, finished the job in my room, and got into bed. We went to it fast but not furious. We stayed hot but never burned out. And right there, right then, there was no other place I'd sooner have been.

When we were done, we lay still, wrapped around one another, just breathing.

\*

I must have drifted off because sometime later I opened my eyes and saw Kim lying on her side, looking at me with a focused expression.

She said, 'You okay?'

I cradled the back of her head in my palm and pulled her close enough to kiss. 'Sure I am. You?'

She made a quirky smile. 'Fine – apart from looking a mess.'

'Not from here.' I pushed away a strand of hair that had fallen across her brow.

She made that ambivalent smile that made me think of Linh. 'We made a great team back there on the farm.'

'Yes, we did.' I smiled back. 'Can I ask you a personal question, though?'

She looked a shade apprehensive. 'Go on.'

'Where the hell did you learn to drive a bulldozer?'

She laughed and tossed back her head and in that moment I thought she was the hottest and coolest woman in DC.

'In North Vietnam, when I was a double agent. Women did all sorts of heavy manual work. I drove a bulldozer to clear up neighbourhoods in Hanoi after they'd gotten flattened by B52s.'

I said, 'That can't have been a good deal.'

She shrugged. 'It wasn't. Sometimes I uncovered dead people, rarely in one piece. I could handle that. It was war, after all. But bodies and body parts of little kids, that was a whole other deal. It made me think of my village when Zetchik's boys had done with it.'

'We did some bad stuff.'

'*You* didn't.'

But I did. We all did, both sides.

I didn't want to spoil the mood though, so I let it go.

Besides, there was other stuff she needed to hear.

After what went down in Maryland, if we were really going to work as a team, I had to come clean about my involvement with Reggie, her belief that Joseph Tedstone was trying to kill her – and my latest meeting with Holy Joe. I felt bad about breaking my promise to Reggie, but this was about survival – specifically hers. And it was becoming increasingly clear that whatever was trouble Reggie was in, Kim would be a help not a hindrance.

When I was done she asked, 'So who do you believe?'

'Honestly, I don't know.'

'One of them must be lying – Tedstone or Acheson. Her word against his.'

'Not necessarily. More like her perception and his perception. But I suspect they're running on separate tracks, looking at different things from different angles. And they're both unbalanced and desperate to the point of crazy.'

'Could Joseph Tedstone be involved in Giang's operation?'

'It's possible. But not if his arch enemy Keith Zetchik was involved, which is the more likely.'

She nodded. 'One thing we agree on is the near certainty that Giang is at the centre of it all. And that we need more information.'

'There's nothing we can do right now, though.' I tugged her mouth close to mine and felt her breath warm on my face.

She pressed her body against mine. 'In the meantime I'm sure we can keep each other amused.'

# FORTY-TWO

Even the Nazis showed up late – and that said a lot about America's 200th birthday party.

Sure, the city resembled a state fairground as I walked along the downtown streets. Vendors peddled street food, candy and all sorts of gimcrack souvenirs. Among the more offbeat stuff were bicentennial toilet seats, star-spangled whoopee cushions and red, white and blue dentures. There was lots of fun and festivity, no argument there. And a spectacular firework display was slated for the evening. Yet everything seemed a little underwhelming and half-assed. Problem was Vietnam, Watergate and other problems had left the country in two minds about itself. A leftist anti-corporate protest rally, for example, drew fewer than 20,000 people to the Capitol steps, compared to 200,000 the organizers had hoped for. The American Nazi Party's counter-protest in Lafayette Park, across the street from the White House, was not only tardy but even more poorly attended. A dozen Adolf Hitler groupies loitered around the statue of Andrew Jackson in the middle of the park. It was the most unNazi-like event I could imagine. I took a quote from them anyways. Meanwhile, Native American reporter Beverly Badhorse wrote from a Cheyenne perspective about a victory dance marking the centennial of George Custer's defeat at the Little Big Horn. Many black communities took a similarly jaundiced view of the 200th birthday scene. I got a quote from their representatives too. Maggie wanted an atmosphere piece for the next day's paper and I got the impression the owners wouldn't much like what I was gonna write. Then again, if they wanted puff, they shouldn't have sent me.

I made a fleeting visit to see Reggie shortly after noon. She seemed more bored than scared and had nothing to tell me except what she'd been watching on the TV. I promised to come back as soon as I could.

Then I met up with Kim at the statue of General William Tecumseh Sherman, namesake of the red setter I was dog-sitting. She'd gone into Langley that morning to make some calls. Upshot was that her chief wanted her to find out more about Giang's backers, and that she'd gotten hold of Bobby Delacroix's home address in Bethesda.

We found the place easily enough. It was a modest duplex on a leafy suburban street. A beat-up Pontiac Tempest stood on the driveway.

I pressed the door buzzer three times before I heard movement in the hallway. The door opened a few inches and Bobby peered at me bleary eyed. He took a few seconds to figure out who I was. When he did, he started to shut the door.

I was expecting this and pushed my way inside.

'What the fuck, man?' Bobby was half cut, his lower face fuzzy under ginger stubble, sandy hair dishevelled. He was wearing old jeans and a beige T-shirt with food and booze stains down the front. He did not look in a good way. It was just five days since I saw him at O'Donnell's Grille and he'd gone a long way downhill in that time. Then he'd been the professor; now he was the dropout.

I said, 'We need to talk, Bobby.'

The air reeked of tobacco and booze and body odour. I went into his living room and wasn't surprised to find it in a mess.

He gave Kim a sour look. 'You two working together now? Spook and a hack, that's not a common combo.'

Kim said, 'We won't take up much of your time.'

Bobby belched beer-breath. 'I got nothing to say to either of you.'

We sat down on his couch regardless.

I said, 'You're in deep serious shit, Bobby.'

'Don't I fucking know it.' He sat opposite and stared at the rug.

'I can help you, remember? I can be your insurance policy.'

'I'm uninsurable, man.'

'Not if you play the whistle-blower. Tell us everything you know and we'll help you.'

He made a hollow laugh. 'No such thing as a get-out-of-jail-free card.'

'But there *is* getting out of jail.' Kim spoke softly. 'You may have to serve some time, but you could still have a life when this is over. Help us to bring down Giang and the CIA will do everything it can on your behalf. Wat will run a story too, isn't that right, Wat?'

Bobby popped a can of Budweiser. 'You're both bullshitters. But I got nothing to lose so telling you the rest can't do any harm. Not that there's much to tell.'

Kim said, 'Tell us anyway, Bobby.'

He chugged some beer, then more, and more still.

I decided he needed a prompt – before he got too juiced to make sense. 'What do you know about Christine Zetchik's activities back in Vietnam? Did she mention any contacts over there?'

He thought about this for a long minute. I was about to give him another nudge when he said, 'There was an ARVN colonel. I forget his name, but it reminded me of commercial vehicles … Truck … Van … something.'

'Thanh?' I sat forward. 'Was his name Truc Van Thanh?'

'Might've been.' He poured more Bud down his neck. It didn't seem to touch the sides. 'Yeah it was, come to think of it. Big cheese up in the central highlands where he controlled some poppy farms. Also in Saigon. He had a production operation there. He and Christine worked with some high ranking officer at MACV, conveniently located at Tan Son Nhut airbase. They shipped the weight direct from there.'

That made my radar ping. 'This guy at MACV, did he have a name?'

'Just a codename.'

Kim spoke softly yet insistently. 'Try to remember, Bobby. This could be really important.'

He screwed up his face, like he was trying to wring the information from his groggy brain. 'Bootcamp … Bootlace … I forget.'

My radar went to red alert. 'Bootstrap?'

Bobby looked at me like I was some sort of mind-reader. 'How the fuck did you know that?'

I took out a Camel and handed it to Bobby in the hope that smoking it would slow down his boozing. 'You meet this guy?'

'Never. He was always in Vietnam and I was always in the States.' He put the cigarette in his mouth and I gave him a light.

'Can you remember anything about him? Rank? Unit? Where he was from Stateside? Anything at all?'

Bobby shook his head. 'That's all I got. Just the codename.'

Even so, this was a major break. It tied Thanh and Bootstrap – and my teenage agent Linh – directly to Christine Zetchik. Directly to here, directly to now.

Kim asked, 'When Christine started extorting you and Chau, did she ever say why she didn't also put the squeeze on this guy Bootstrap?'

Bobby drained his can, opened another. 'I asked her once. She just laughed at me, said he was way outta reach.'

'What do you think she meant by that?'

He made a how-should-I-know? expression. 'I didn't ask.'

I had to press him on this – but not too hard. 'Think, Bobby. This could be a big deal.'

He stubbed out the cigarette. 'Could be she was referring to him being so high up the food chain he was untouchable. Also, she may not have had any dirt on him, whereas she had plenty on me and the sicko accountant. Then again, she could have been referring to him being dead. I mean you can't get more outta reach than that. I dunno … '

There was nothing more to be gained from watching Bobby get more drunk so we came away and headed back to my place.

First thing she asked was why I was so interested in Thanh and Bootstrap. I saw no reason to hold back, so I told her about my black op for SOG in 1971.

We rode the rest of the way in silence and I sensed she was processing the information I just gave her.

Back home I fed Sherman and made a pot of coffee.

She said, 'You think the activities of Bootstrap and Thanh are connected to Giang's enterprise?'

'Unlikely.' I drank some coffee. 'Thanh and Bootstrap were producing and exporting heroin to the US for financial gain. Giang, on the other hand, has no involvement in drugs and is *im*porting wealth to fund a continuation of the war. Their aims and operations are entirely different – even contradictory. That said, circumstances change, people adapt. I never found out exactly what happened to Bootstrap. He just disappeared. Like Bobby said, he could still be around and he could be dead.'

'When you say around, you mean here in DC?'

'Improbable.'

'But not impossible. You think he could have hooked up with Giang?'

'That would be even more of a stretch. But strange shit happens.'

She sipped her coffee. 'And Christine Zetchik is a link.'

'For sure – one we need to look into. On the face of it, her connection to Giang was unfortunate happenstance. She tried to blackmail Chau, thereby threatening Giang's wider operation, thereby bringing about her own demise. But there may have been more to it.'

She leaned closer. 'Go on.'

'Maybe we should look at Keith Zetchik in a different light. According to Bobby, Christine got hip to Giang's operations by sneaking a look at confidential material in her husband's possession. But Bobby's perspective is narrow and not too reliable. I wonder if Keith and Christine could have been involved as a husband and wife enterprise in this and other scams.'

She looked at me hard. 'You think Keith Zetchik was Bootstrap?'

I drank more coffee. 'Again, improbable.'

'But you can't rule it out. Tell me what you're thinking.'

I told her, 'He was never posted to MACV, but he did report there regularly. Also, Christine had an office at the US Embassy in Saigon so he spent a lot of time in the city. And he *did* serve in the central highlands where the poppy farms were located.'

The more I thought about it, the more plausible it seemed. Or did it?

I combed my fingers through my hair. 'Keith Zetchik was mean enough. But I'm not sure he was smart enough.'

My mind explored other possibilities.

I said, 'Joseph Tedstone, on the other hand, is smart but not mean.'

She made a dubious frown. 'You sure? How do you know the Christianity stuff isn't a smokescreen?' She paused, as if considering the implications of her question. 'In fact, how do you know Joseph Tedstone isn't Bootstrap?'

It was an outlandish idea but I ran through what I knew. 'He served at MACV after leaving Weschler's command, so that put him in the right place at the right time. And I'm sure there's stuff he isn't telling us or the cops. All things considered, though, I just can't see him as Bootstrap.'

She wasn't convinced. 'That could be the whole idea. You just said he's a clever guy. What if Christine got some dirt on him that meant he was no longer outta reach, as Bobby put it? If she tried to shake him down it would have been in his direct interest to eliminate her and her husband. After all, both would be in the way of him and that two-star job at the Pentagon.'

I thought about it some more. Tedstone was already in the frame for Keith Zetchik's murder, although he had an alibi for Christine's. Perhaps he got someone else to kill her. But how did Johnny fit in? Could he have found out something about his dad's activities in Vietnam that he shouldn't have? Perhaps Holy Joe really was trying to kill Reggie.

And perhaps I was overcooking this …

I said, 'I think we should keep an open mind.'

We both went quiet.

At length Kim said, 'So what next?'

I set my coffee cup down. 'I want to talk to Joseph Tedstone again. Like Giang, he's at the centre of this – either as a perpetrator or a victim.'

I looked at her. 'How about you?'

'I agree about Giang. I'll carry on digging at Langley. I also want to take a closer look at Christine Zetchik's activities in Saigon.'

That made a lot of sense. But we were at risk of thinking in circles. She suggested shelving the subject until the next day and I thought this was a good idea.

Besides, we had other stuff to do. The bicentennial fireworks kept us up late, but not as late as the fireworks that went off when we got into bed.

I woke in the small hours, with abrupt and absolute clarity. My mind was making me think the thoughts I'd kept buried for five years. Some part of my subconscious must have woken me because even nightmares were too soft-focused for the shit I had battened down in my head. Only full-on consciousness could do it justice.

*I'm driving fast along Hong Thap Tu in Saigon, in the direction of Thanh's mansion.*

*Linh hasn't responded to my messages. She hasn't shown up at our rendezvous.*

*I just spoke to Chuck Shaughnessy. He advised caution. I told him to fuck off.*

*I reach Thanh's house and bang on the front door. A maid opens it and tells me the colonel isn't at home.*

*I search the place anyway. Nobody tries to stop me.*

*I find her in the summer house. They've stripped her and tied her down on a table and raped her and cut her in ways and in places that – for all my emotional paralysis – make me sick with despair and rage and, more than anything, guilt.*

*I put her into that place. I didn't get her out. Not alive. Not unharmed.*

*I might be crazy, but I'm sure this is Bootstrap's way of taunting me.*

# FORTY-THREE

First thing next morning I called Rhyme Dillard to check on progress in the Tedstone/Zetchik case. He didn't have anything to tell me except he was up to his eyeballs in Joseph Tedstone's grand jury appearance. This was good because the homicide chief was less likely to hear about the incident at the farm in western Maryland 48 hours earlier, which would really piss him off.

Next I went to see Reggie. She was in surprisingly good spirits. Maybe she just got her fix, though she didn't appear high or spaced. Just the opposite. It was as if she'd gotten used to her life of solitude. She was half way through Erica Jong's *Fear of Flying* and I left her to it.

My luck continued to hold when I arrived at the Weschler place for my fourth and final interview. Leading me through to his study, Weschler told me Paula was in New York visiting her sister. Knowing that he was cheating on her made me feel uneasy, but not as uneasy as I'd have felt if she'd been there in the house. Her revelation had put me in a difficult position personally and professionally, so I focused on my job and we whizzed through the interview in short order. We talked about the future and how American family values would be at the centre of his domestic agenda. I thought this was rich coming from a guy who was in an extra-marital relationship with a woman young enough to be his daughter. But I reminded myself not to judge. He wasn't the first and wouldn't be the last. And I sure as hell wasn't a saint.

The idea hit me at the end of the interview. 'When you were in Vietnam, did you ever come across an ARVN colonel name of Truc Van Thanh?'

He pursed his lips and shook his head. 'Doesn't ring any bells. What sort of context we talking about?'

'He commanded an infantry battalion in the Central Highlands and was later posted to Saigon. Also operated a major heroin racket.'

He made a sardonic smile. 'The last piece of information doesn't narrow the field all that much.'

I knew what he meant. Corruption was widespread in the Nasty, not least among senior South Vietnamese officers. 'Thanh was unusual in that he was running poppy farms, refining the heroin and then exporting it Stateside. What you might call an end-to-end operation.'

Weschler's frown gave his brow a few extra furrows. 'He'd have needed the active collusion of some high-up Americans to pull off something on that scale.'

'That's exactly what he had.' I didn't want to put him on the spot, but I'd started asking these questions so I needed to see them through. 'Look, sir, I know you avoided visiting MACV, that you served mainly in the field, where it mattered most. But did you ever hear of Pentagon East brass getting involved in anything like this? Allegations, rumours, even O-Club scuttlebutt?'

He gave me a penetrating stare. 'You got a personal stake in this?'

I nodded. 'I was on detached duty with SOG, running an agent in Saigon. Op turned sour, my asset got burned real bad.'

'I'm sorry to hear that, Wat. Any idea of this guy's rank? Service branch? Timescale? Anything at all?'

'He'd have been active from the fall of '68 to the spring of '71, when he seemed to vanish off the face of the planet. All I ever got was a codename: Bootstrap.'

He thought about it, then shook his head. 'Sorry, pal, can't help you there. May I ask, though, why are you asking me now? Has this guy resurfaced?'

'No he hasn't. I thought there could be a remote possibility. But the more I go into it, the more I realize I'm chasing shadows.' Much as I respected Weschler and valued his advice, I wanted to play Bobby Delacroix's disclosure close to my chest. Especially because I really was chasing shadows. I was pursuing a lead based on Bobby's memory of what a dead woman told him about a guy he never met.

I needed to forget the past and focus on the present.

*

I called Joseph Tedstone and asked if he was ready to take Sherman back. In truth I'd enjoyed looking after the dog, but I needed a reason to talk to Holy Joe and this was a good one.

He said sure, bring him round right away, and sounded like he meant it.

Fifteen minutes later I arrived at the Tedstone place

in Kalorama and the red setter bounded up to his master, overjoyed in the way only dogs can be.

Tedstone showed me into his living room. It was much tidier since my last visit and he'd picked up the papers that had been scattered on the floor and put in orderly piles, held in place by improvised paperweights. Among them was an M19 smoke grenade, which I thought looked kinda whacky. He'd also cleaned himself up and I was relieved when he offered me a drink and didn't include a booze option. He said he had some homemade lemonade and I said that sounded cool.

He brought the drinks on a tray and laid it on a table between two armchairs by the big bay window. I was seated in the one Johnny died in, possibly at the hands of the man opposite.

'Your phone call was nothing if not providential, Mr Tyler. I was about to contact you myself.' The manic man I encountered six days ago had gone, leaving the thoughtful guy in control and this was a big boost.

He said, 'Firstly, I must apologize for my behaviour when you were last here. I was at a point of personal crisis and should not have burdened you in the way I did.'

I settled back in the chair and braced myself for an elongated explanation that included the harrowing nature of the last two weeks and finding the Lord despite, indeed because of, adversity.

I got none of that.

He said, 'When I've done telling you how I came to be that way, I think you'll understand. You see, I know who killed Johnny and Keith Zetchik. I've known all along. Before I wasn't ready to tell anyone. Now I am.'

He took a drink of lemonade, placed the glass on the coffee table, and looked at me hard. 'The guilty man is Heck Weschler.'

# FORTY-FOUR

Didn't see that coming.

Tedstone must have gathered as much from my drop-jaw expression. 'I realize it sounds like a wild and incredible claim.'

That was exactly how it sounded. Especially because Heck Weschler was the reason I talked to Holy Joe in the first place. It was Weschler who asked me to carry out a fair and impartial investigation. He claimed his former comrade was innocent and thought I would uncover evidence to prove it. Why would he have done this if he was behind the killing of Johnny and Zetchik?

'Do you have any evidence, sir?'

He looked wretched. 'It was stolen the night Johnny and Zetchik died. Obtaining that evidence was Weschler's objective.'

I started writing shorthand notes. Whatever he had to say couldn't be printed without proof – assuming whatever he had to say was true. But I needed a complete record whichever way this went.

'What exactly was stolen?'

'A cassette tape recording of Heck Weschler ordering

Zetchik and me to carry out atrocities that would certainly have qualified as war-crimes – even by the standards of the time.'

I looked up from my notebook. 'How did this tape-recording come about?'

He drank more lemonade. 'I'd been on bad terms with Zetchik since '66, but as a commanding officer, Weschler didn't give me any real problems until the spring of '69. That was when he decided to enhance his promotion prospects by taking a ground-breaking approach to boosting our brigade's body count.'

Body count was Uncle Sam's way of measuring progress against an enemy who fought almost entirely in territory we occupied. In the absence of conventional battle lines, the logic was that if we killed North Vietnamese combatants faster than they could be replaced, they'd give up the fight. And what Tedstone said about promotion was spot on. This led to two things. First, body count numbers got massively exaggerated. And second, since Charlie operated within the general population, unarmed civilians were frequently counted as enemy combatants. *If it's dead and Vietnamese, it's VC* was a widely accepted reason for killing innocent people.

Like Zetchik did at Kim's village.

'You remember the stink about Operation Speedy Express and Julian Ewell, the two-star commanding 9th Infantry Division?'

'Difficult to forget.' In late-1968 and early 1969 Ewell's unit was responsible for industrial scale slaughter in the Mekong Delta. I heard first hand from a chopper pilot that civilians running toward US forces were gunned down as hostiles, and civilians running away were also gunned down as hostiles. Talk about fucked up. A whistle-blower wrote to MACV, pleading for an investigation. But the high-ups made sure that didn't happen.

Tedstone looked through the bay window at the smooth lawn where Sherman was trotting around, sniffing for scents. 'You may recall that Ewell's boys racked up a body count of 11,000 during Speedy Express, but captured fewer than 750 weapons. That didn't look good from a public relations perspective and this was not lost on Heck Weschler. So he shipped in weapons already captured from Charlie – handguns, AK-47s, light machine-guns, stick-grenades, mines, machetes and more. Then he had Zetchik and me distribute them among our people so they could be planted on the bodies of dead civilians and 'discovered' later – especially by units with embedded news correspondents.'

'How many of these weapons were planted?'

'I didn't have chance to count. They arrived by the truckload. Certainly, many hundreds. I went along with it at first, but I couldn't keep it up. It was the most dishonourable, despicable and unchristian act I have ever committed.'

He leaned forward and put his head in his hands, massaging his skull as if it was in danger of detonating. After some time, he sat back up and carried on talking in a brisker, more businesslike tone. 'Weschler liked to come around to Zetchik's battalion HQ and mine to brief us. He would alternate. Next time one of these briefings happened at my place, I recorded it. I got everything: The body count he expected; his assertion that civilians and combatants were one and the same; his disregard for the gender or age of the folks we killed; and the type of weapons he wanted us to plant.'

I wrote this down. I'd heard of weapons being arranged in this way for window-dressing purposes. But nothing approaching this scale, or on the orders of such a high ranking officer. Weschler would have been a brigadier general at that time, soon to pick up his second star as a major general.

Tedstone seemed to read my thoughts. 'As I'm sure you can imagine, the deception worked. We were hailed as a crack unit because most of the bodies in our count were actually armed. Or so it seemed. All three of us got promoted in fairly short order.'

I stopped writing and looked up from my pad. 'Why didn't you bring the tape to the attention of the authorities?'

He continued watching Sherman patrolling the back yard. 'It is to my enduring shame that I did not. If I'm being brutally honest, I recorded the tape out of self-preservation rather than any noble intention to use it. If the affair ever came to light, I could fall back on a chain-of-command defence. It wouldn't have saved my career but it might have kept me out of Leavenworth.'

I took out my cigarette pack and asked if he minded me smoking.

He said he didn't and pushed an ashtray toward me. 'I'd always been enough of a realist to accept that the system was flawed, yet enough of an optimist to believe it was fixable. But not when we were committing a Mai Lai massacre twice, sometimes three times a week. And not when Weschler was falsifying our body count reports by making the civilians we murdered look like armed combatants. I refused to serve with either him or Zetchik – whose only objection was that we weren't going far enough. I demanded a transfer and spent the remainder of the war on General Abrams' staff at MACV.'

Again I returned to the fundamental contradiction at work here: If Tedstone and Weschler parted company on such bad terms, why did Weschler ask me to carry out an investigation that he hoped would establish Tedstone's innocence? I thought about making Tedstone aware of this but decided to keep quiet, at least for now. I had to keep in mind that Tedstone was due to appear before the grand jury for good reasons. And there was no evidence that this incriminating tape existed.

Something else hit me, something that brought this still closer to home.

# FORTY-FIVE

I said, 'Do you recall a search and destroy mission by one of Zetchik's companies at a village named An Bai in Quang Duc province?'

He nodded. 'Tuesday, May 6th, 1969.'

I was impressed by his recall. Kim's family and just about everybody she grew up with got slaughtered on that day. Not many folks remembered it, but Joseph Tedstone did.

He said, 'Zetchik's body count was 247 on that day, but neither he nor Weschler got the credit they thought they deserved because hardly any weapons were found. Zetchik hunted up a few kitchen knives and machetes of the type you'd find in any rural community, but it still didn't look good. There was no outright criticism from II Corps HQ or MACV, but nor was there any praise. In Weschler's view, that was almost as bad. An Bai was like Operation Speedy Express in miniature, but it also became Weschler's eureka moment. He was determined never to find himself in that position again. That was when he hit on the idea of using captured arms caches to falsely validate his body counts and steer clear of any Speedy Express-type allegations.'

Kim had never mentioned Weschler when she told me what happened at An Bai, but she could easily have found out that Zetchik's battalion was under Weschler's command. Maybe she thought the buck stopped with Zetchik, the guy – literally – with the smoking gun. But I also wondered what she thought of Weschler – and his tilt at the White House.

Tedstone drained his glass of lemonade. 'I never saw Weschler after I transferred out of his brigade in June '69. Not, that is, until last July when I read a newspaper report touting him as a presidential candidate. He'd recently retired as a three-star and was making a name for himself as an outspoken independent. What he was saying played well – centre ground stuff that could appeal to working people as well as corporate America ...'

He broke off and indicated my pack of cigarettes. 'May I have one?'

I nudged the pack and my lighter in his direction and he helped himself.

'I haven't smoked for nearly ten years.' He took a long pull and made a so-what? smile, then returned to his narrative. 'More newspaper and TV reports followed and it soon became clear that he was building up a head of steam. He was making no secret of his ambition for high office – secretary of state, defence, national security adviser, even president.'

He gave me an anguished look. 'Knowing what I did, Mr Tyler, I simply couldn't stand by and witness a power grab by that duplicitous monster. I still had the cassette tape, which gave me some leverage. I approached him directly and told him I'd make the tape public if he ever ran for, or was appointed to high office.'

'How did he react?'

'With astonishing composure. He agreed without much of an argument and I was naive enough to think that was the end of the matter.'

He sucked in another lungful of tobacco fumes. 'Then, in April he announced plans to run for president. I repeated my demands again and again – and he prevaricated, again and again. He knew I was loathe to destroy the career of a brother officer and he exploited that. He thought my resolve would weaken with every bluff he called – particularly after he formally threw his hat into the ring as a presidential candidate.'

He extinguished his cigarette, folding the butt in two and crushing it flat. 'He was wrong there. I talked to the Lord. And, for the first time in a long time, the Lord talked back. He spoke to me through the Gospel of St Matthew, chapter 5, verse 6: *Blessed are they which do hunger and thirst after righteousness, for they shall be filled.* Two weeks ago, I gave him two weeks to pull out of the presidential race, or I would go public with the tape. This time I meant it and he must have finally believed me. I say this because it can't have been a coincidence that Johnny and Keith Zetchik were murdered and the tape was stolen on the same night, 48 hours before my ultimatum was due to expire.'

He went quiet and I filled in the blanks, 'Leaving you unable to expose him, and in the frame for the murder of Johnny and Zetchik?'

He kept quiet, took another cigarette from my pack. Ten years without a smoke and it seemed like he was making up for lost time.

'Sir, you need to tell me exactly what happened on that night.'

'I already went through this with Captain Dillard.'

'Go through it again.'

'He didn't believe me. Why would you?'

'I might not. But if you don't try me, neither of us will know.'

He turned back to look out through the window. Sherman was lying on his side, basking in the sunshine.

'I went for my regular five mile run that evening. I do the same run around Rock Creek Park every Friday, Monday and Wednesday evening. I leave the house at 8.45pm sharp and return at 9.30pm, give or take.' He made a self-deprecating laugh. 'I'm a creature of habit, utterly predictable, and must have made myself an absurdly easy target. Not exactly what they taught us at West Point, was it?'

'I never went to West Point, general.'

I wasn't embarrassed, but Tedstone clearly was. 'Of course. Do forgive me. You were commissioned in the field. Well, all the more strength to your arm my boy. But my point remains the same. Anyone watching me would have known my movements in and out of the house, down to the minute.'

'Did you notice anything unusual on your run? When you left the house? In the park? When you got back?'

He shook his head. 'I returned to the house at 9.35 and saw nothing untoward. Not that I was looking. I took a shower and got changed. I knew Johnny was out for the night – as it happened, with you – and wouldn't be back until late. So I had the house to myself. I fixed myself a drink and went back to a book I was reading.

'Soon after 10.30 I received a telephone call from Keith Zetchik. We hadn't spoken in seven years, so you can imagine my surprise. But I recognized his voice instantly.

He asked me if I knew my tape was missing yet. He said he had it and wanted to make a deal. If I went around to his apartment right away, we could discuss terms. I said I didn't know what he was talking about and he told me to go check it out.'

He laughed at himself again. 'What I fool I was. Zetchik held the line while I went to my study and opened the safe where I kept the tape. He was right. It wasn't there. And there was no sign of the safe having been tampered with. I didn't see that I had any alternative so I told Zetchik I'd be at his place in ten minutes. You'll know the remainder of what I told the police: I arrived to find Zetchik dead. I realized I'd been framed and drove around town trying to think of a way out of what was clearly an impossible situation.'

Sherman started barking at a cat perched on the garden wall and Tedstone went to fetch him back into the house.

I took the opportunity to process what he told me and my thoughts only went in one direction.

When he returned, I said, 'You say the safe hadn't been tampered with. Did that also apply to the display cabinet with the Mauser in it? And the desk drawer where you kept the cyanide pills?'

He nodded yes.

'So whoever set you up knew the combination for the safe as well as where the keys to the gun cabinet and your desk drawer were kept. And they were able to get into the house without leaving any sign of a break-in. That could only have been down to Johnny.'

He shook his head. 'But Johnny was with you at the material times. At some point between 9.00 and 9.30, somebody came into this house and got hold of the tape, the Mauser and the cyanide pills. But it couldn't have been Johnny.'

I thought again about what Weschler told me in regard to volatile people like Johnny using their own suicides to punish others. I thought again about my own experience of combat-fatigued grunts walking into enemy fire after giving out on how bad their folks would feel when they arrived home in a body bag. It was telling, too, that Maggie had refused to rule out a put up job by Johnny. And I thought again about his love of drama and spectacle. Could he have staged suicide as theatre?

I had to ask Tedstone the question I was asking myself, 'Is it possible that Johnny colluded with others – maybe Weschler's people – to frame you for killing him as well as Keith Zetchik?'

He shook his head. He shook it over and over, as if the act of denial would make the idea untrue. If he was innocent, I could sympathise. If he wasn't, fuck, he was the finest actor on the planet.

I pressed my point. 'You must admit, general, that Johnny had mental health problems stemming from drug abuse. He was suggestible and unstable.'

He said nothing.

I recalled something. It had been bothering me for some time and I decided now was the time to brace him. 'You haven't been entirely straight with me about Johnny's medical history, have you?'

He gave me a sharp look. 'What do you mean?'

'Why didn't you tell me Johnny was in a psychiatric hospital two years ago?'

He frowned. 'Because he wasn't. Johnny hasn't been in a psychiatric clinic since he was 18 – in 1969.'

I frowned back. 'Are you absolutely certain about that, sir? Could he have taken treatment without you knowing?'

By now he was on his fourth cigarette. 'I pay the health insurance that would have funded it, so I would certainly have known. Why do you ask?'

'Reggie Acheson told me she first met Johnny two years ago in a psychiatric clinic.'

He rested his cigarette in the ashtray. 'This is the young woman friend of Johnny's who is convinced I'm trying to kill her, but refuses to go to the police? The one who suffers from schizophrenia and has a narcotics habit?'

The way he put it made Reggie sound crazy and unreliable. But wasn't this exactly what she was? If Johnny was capable of killing Keith Zetchik and committing suicide to frame his dad, he could also have persuaded Reggie to make sure I got the murder weapon – with Tedstone Senior's prints all over it. If this was the case, Johnny and Reggie could have produced a cover story about when and where they met. But Reggie was never supposed to be questioned by me, or the cops, or anyone else investigating the double homicide. So why devise a backstory that would never be needed? It could be that the explanation was more straightforward: Reggie was a hopeless junkie and had gotten mixed up over dates, like she had over other a whole bunch of other stuff.

I told Tedstone he was right about Reggie's mental condition, that she was probably just confused over where she met Johnny. Then I said I needed to be someplace else.

He walked with me to the front door and opened it. As I walked onto the doorstep, he said, 'What do you think about what I've told you? Do you believe me?' For the first time since I arrived, there was a note of desperation in his voice.

I looked him in the eye and told him the truth as I saw it. 'I think you've given me a lot to think about, General. I'll make some enquiries and we'll talk again soon.'

# FORTY-SIX

Back at the *Tribune* newsroom I learned Bobby Delacroix died after throwing himself under a subway train. Tragic as this was, there were no suspicious circumstances. Scores of commuters watched him fall into the path of the train as it entered Judiciary Square Metro station. He'd been standing alone at one end of the platform, like suicides did to avoid the risk of some good Samaritan hauling them back from the edge. I could only guess at his reasons, although the prospect of doing significant jail time as a former federal law enforcement officer would probably have been a factor. Did I feel any sympathy? Well, a little. Bobby didn't strike me as evil or greedy or cruel. He just made some bad choices at a time when making bad choices was the national pastime. Did I feel guilty for putting him under pressure? Maybe. But when he asked me to meet him at the National Gallery of Art, he was playing me, not the other way round.

Besides, I had other things on my mind, especially Joseph Tedstone and Pham Tan Giang.

Tedstone's allegations against Weschler were downright mystifying. I called Kim and ran them by her. She didn't sound as surprised as I expected and I wondered if she knew something I didn't. But we didn't have the time to go into it and she said she'd get back to me later with her thoughts. Then I told Maggie and she agreed with my assessment that Tedstone's claims didn't amount to much without evidence. She did, though, suggest taking a look into the activities of Weschler's brigade in early '69.

And she went along with my theory that Holy Joe and Giang were pivotal to what really went down and why. I'd just talked with Tedstone, and Maggie thought it would be a good idea to confront Giang – not at his miniature army base in Maryland, but at the grocery store where he worked.

So I drove out to the shabby mom and pop place on the 1100 block of U Street NW. It was open for business but there was no sign of Giang, or mom and pop, or anybody.

I waited at the counter. Nobody showed.

After a couple of minutes I went to a heavy door, presumably leading to the storeroom. It was six inches ajar.

I pushed it a little farther open, 'Hello? Anyone there?'

No reply.

I gave it a few seconds, called out again.

Still nothing.

I pushed the door open wide. The dimly lit corridor on the other side was deserted.

Something wasn't right.

Could be Giang was using the toilet.

Could be he saw me coming and was waiting with a gun at the other end of the corridor.

So I went ahead carefully. A half dozen paces took me to the storeroom, a modest space crammed floor to ceiling with boxes and cartons of merchandise. Like the corridor, it was illuminated by an unshaded electric bulb. I looked left.

No sign of life.

I looked right. I nailed Giang sitting in an old armchair. He was looking right at me.

But there was still no sign of life.

*

Rhyme Dillard wasn't happy, but then the homicide chief seldom was. Giang had been killed by a single bullet to the head. Nobody in the neighbourhood had heard a gunshot and Dillard figured the killer used a suppressor. Combined with an untouched cash register, this suggested a professional hit. Dillard refused to be drawn on this, though he did concede that the murders of Chau and Giang were probably linked. This, at least gave me a strong follow-up piece to the *Man-in-a-Suitcase* story.

I met Kim for coffee at Roy Rogers on G Street NW.

I told her what happened to Bobby and Giang.

She stirred creamer into her coffee. 'Not a good day if you're name's Bobby Delacroix or Pham Tan Giang. Bobby I can understand. Giang, he's more of a puzzle.'

'You think he was killed as a punishment for what we did out in Maryland?'

'More likely to keep him quiet.'

'By the same people who killed the Zetchiks and Chau and Johnny Tedstone?'

'Chau for sure,' she said. 'Even Dillard's agreed on that. And very likely the Zetchiks. Keith was an associate of Giang's and Christine was shaking down his money man. So that would make sense. As for Johnny Tedstone, he's still a mystery.'

'Unless you believe his dad.'

She gave me a searching look. 'Do you?'

'I really don't know.' I lit a Camel. 'Did you get anything at Langley?'

She produced a manila envelope and pushed it across the table.

It contained four ten-by-eight inch black and white photographs.

I glanced at the top one, then looked again more closely. It showed Heck Weschler with Christine Zetchik and another woman of a similar age. They were sitting in some bar or club in Vietnam with bottles and glasses of booze arrayed on the table in front of them. They were clearly partying. Weschler was decked out in casual civvies and his arms were draped around the bare shoulders of the women.

I looked at the other pictures. There was one of Christine kissing Weschler on the mouth, another of the second woman doing the same, and another still of the two women kissing each other while Weschler watched. Mouth action like that was not platonic, no argument there.

I took a long pull on my cigarette. Was I shocked? Yes and no. I knew Christine had gotten involved in all sorts of far-out shit in Saigon, so a three-way sex deal shouldn't have surprised me. And I knew Weschler had been cheating on his wife for many years, so why not back in Vietnam? But I wouldn't have put Weschler and Christine together. After all, she was the wife of his friend and one of his senior officers. Then again, the boss screwing the glamorous wife of a junior colleague was hardly uncommon. Paula Weschler was 10,000 miles away and it seemed Keith Zetchik wasn't giving Christine what she wanted – whatever that was.

I pushed the pictures back toward her. 'Why were they taken?'

She returned them to the envelope. 'The agency had been keeping Christine under surveillance for some time in late 1970 and early '71. She'd developed some dubious contacts and started moving in circles known for the type of promiscuous activity that could leave her open to blackmail.'

'What about Weschler?'

'He got caught by accident. By then he was a two-star general and a hero in a war not noted for heroes. MACV was as surprised as we were when he showed up in the pictures and further surveillance got canned.'

I said, '*I'm* not surprised about Weschler. I would've been back then. Not now though.'

She looked at me with an unspoken question.

So I told her what Paula told me about Weschler's affair with a much younger woman. I felt bad in the same way as I'd felt bad about shooting the works on Reggie. But Weschler had clearly made a career of cheating on his wife and Kim needed to know.

When I was done, she took a little time to think. Then she said, 'So what do you think about Heck Weschler in view of all this?'

I said, 'Let's focus on what we actually know about the guy. We know he was getting it on with Christine Zetchik and this other woman – both of them apparently bisexual. We know he's been having an affair with a woman young enough to be his daughter for some years. So he has a history of extramarital activity. Also, we know – but can't prove – that Joseph Tedstone is alleging complicity in atrocities against civilians that would amount to war crimes. And we know he's running for president, with offers of high office from both Ford and Carter. What conclusions can we draw?'

She drained her coffee cup. 'He isn't the man we thought he was, or that the American public consider him to be. And he could be vulnerable to blackmail for either or both his sexual adventures, or the alleged atrocities.'

'You got anything on the second woman in the pictures?'

She took out a typed report. 'Name's Deborah Kinsley. She was a middle-ranking State Department official who worked in the same section as Christine Zetchik. Served three years out there – '68 to '71.'

'Any idea where she is now?'

'Portland, Oregon. I got an address.'

I said, 'We need to get there fast – before anybody else does.'

'Agreed.' She came to her feet. 'The plane takes off in an hour.'

# FORTY-SEVEN

We landed in Portland early the following morning. I hadn't slept much on the four-hour flight and felt tired and grubby. Unlike Kim, I hadn't had time to grab an overnight bag. So I bought a disposable razor and some shaving foam from an airport store and cleaned up as best I could in a rest room. After a decent breakfast with lots of coffee, I felt halfway human again.

We rented a car and drove through downtown Portland to King's Heights, a well-to-do neighbourhood on the city's west side.

The woman we were there to see lived in a large ranch house with sweeping views across the Williamette and Columbia rivers to the Cascade mountains. You'd need a high dollar income to live in a place like this and she'd made sure of that when she left the State Department to marry a successful tax lawyer.

Deborah Kinsley was standing on the porch as we walk up the driveway and I recognized her brown wavy hair and sculpted good looks from the photos Kim had showed me. We followed her into a spacious living room.

She gave Kim a flinty look. 'Don't you people ever leave folks alone?'

'Look, Deborah – '

But Deborah wasn't done. 'I know your kind too.' She looked at me like I was something on the sole of her shoe. 'Raking up muck, printing sensationalist trash – '

'I was about to say you aren't the subject of our enquiry.' Kim's voice took on a hard edge. 'But that could change if you want to make things difficult.'

Deborah made an okay-you-win shrug and gestured for us to take a seat on a beige leather couch.

She sat down opposite. She looked distracted and distraught. In all fairness, I couldn't blame her. Kim's call late last night would have come as a nasty shock.

She turned to Kim. 'I'm not sure what you want from me, but what you said on the phone sounded an awful lot like blackmail.'

'That wasn't the impression I intended.' Kim made a tight smile. 'But I did need to make you aware of the seriousness of the situation we're looking into.'

'You said you had some photos.'

Kim took out the envelope and handed it to Deborah. She shuffled through the pictures then dropped them on the coffee table. 'These could wreck my marriage, my life … '

I leaned forward. 'It doesn't need to come to that, Deborah. You weren't the subject of the surveillance operation in Saigon and, like Kim just said, you're not the subject of our investigation now. All we want is a little information, then we'll be gone – along with these pictures.'

'You could print them anyway. Jeez, they could leave Heck Weschler's political ambitions in a smouldering heap.'

I kept my tone amiable. 'The pictures are classified CIA material, so my paper – or any other – couldn't publish them.

But you should believe me when I tell you they're the least of Heck Weschler's problems.'

Deborah looked with a frustrated frown from me to Kim and back again. 'I saw on the TV news that Keith and Christine Zetchik were murdered a couple of weeks ago. Is that why you're here? You think Heck Weschler was involved?'

'Maybe,' I said. 'But we'll have a better idea if you answer our questions.'

She sat back and folded her arms. 'Okay, shoot.'

Kim said, 'What was the arrangement between you and Christine and Weschler?'

Deborah made a slightly hysterical laugh. 'Arrangement? That isn't the word I'd have picked. I mean, nothing was ever that organized. Christine and I were colleagues in a faraway place and we became friends. But she was always so much more of a free spirit than me. Wild and reckless in a way that I envied. She took me to a lot of parties and night spots, and I met a lot of interesting people. She introduced me to various men and I ended up sleeping with some of them. But I was young, free and single and Saigon back then was a crazy place, right?'

She opened the onyx cigarette case on the coffee table, took out a cigarette and lit it using the matching onyx lighter.

I noticed her hand trembling slightly. I said, 'We're not judging you, Deborah. Kim and I were in Vietnam. We saw stuff go down that folks back home wouldn't believe. I did things I'm not proud of. A lot of us did.'

Kim asked, 'Did you meet Weschler through Christine?'

She nodded and made a sour smile. 'She said she knew this hunk of a general who had a thing about three-in-a-bed sex. I was hesitant at first, but I thought 'what the hell?' and gave it a shot. At first it was exciting. We had a lot of fun that was even more fun because we weren't supposed to be doing it. Heck took us out on the town – lavish bashes and exclusive clubs and swish restaurants. Then we'd go back to an expensive hotel room. After a few weeks, Weschler persuaded Christine and me to get it on. He watched at first, then joined in. But we weren't lesbians. For me the whole scene was a heady mix of booze, coke and curiosity.'

She went quiet, like she needed to draw breath. Kim and I swapped a knowing glance and let the silence play a while.

At length I said, 'Did you ever come across an ARVN general named Pham Tan Giang?'

She shook her head.

'Did Christine ever mention him?'

Again, no.

I asked the same questions about Colonel Truc Van Thanh and got the same response.

I tried a long shot. 'Does the name Bootstrap mean anything?'

Deborah seemed puzzled. 'Should it?'

I said, 'No, I guess not.'

Kim picked up the questioning. 'What about Keith Zetchik? Did you ever meet him?'

Deborah sucked on her cigarette. 'A few times, sure. He came to Saigon a lot. Sometimes he came alone, other times with Heck Weschler.'

Kim persisted. 'Did Keith have any idea what was going on with you and Christine and Weschler?'

Deborah laughed again, but this time it was less on-the-edge. 'He had absolutely no idea. That was what turned

Christine on. She saw screwing her husband's boss as a way of getting back at him without him knowing.'

I leaned forward. 'How so?'

'Back then Christine would have been in her mid-thirties, but she was still way too old for Keith's tastes. She'd been a teen bride – sixteen when they tied the knot – but their sex life didn't last much beyond her eighteenth birthday. You see, Keith liked girls. The younger, the better.'

I asked; 'How young?'

'I never saw any of them. But from what Christine told me, early to mid-teens.'

I said, 'And there were plenty in Saigon, especially if you were a senior American officer.'

Deborah nodded. 'Christine wasn't happy about this. She wasn't normally racist, but she was when it came to her husband screwing fourteen-year-old Vietnamese girls. She called them gook sluts and much worse.'

This got me thinking. Truc had a thing for teenage girls. That was why my CIA liaison Chuck Shaughnessy identified Linh as an ideal asset. Maybe Truc and Keith Zetchik were perverts-in-arms. I already thought Keith Zetchik could have been Bootstrap. Given this shared interest in sex with adolescents, that possibility would be much more likely.

This got me thinking some more. I looked at Deborah. 'Was Christine resentful enough to threaten Keith?'

'Like with a gun?' She shook her head no. 'I was never sure about his background, but he was her cash generator. She had expensive tastes and a State Department salary wouldn't have begun to cover them. Sure, she despised Keith, but she'd have tolerated almost anything to maintain the lifestyle he was paying for.'

I pressed my line of questions, 'But what if his money dried up when they got back stateside? And what if Keith continued to chase young girls?'

'Yeah, under those circumstances, I guess she might do something to hurt him. She wasn't a crazy person but she did some crazy stuff. And she could be mean too when the mood took her.'

'Mean enough to kill?'

'I guess.'

'Mean enough to make dangerous enemies?'

'Yeah. Yeah, in theory.'

There was an elongated silence. Deborah looked away and I saw her expression switch as she wrestled with this unpleasant confrontation with the past. Eventually she looked back at me. '*I* wasn't that sort of person. I thought I'd left all that crap in Vietnam and made a new life out here. Please don't wreck it.'

I resisted a cynical smile. Nobody thought of themselves as that sort of person. But we had been that sort of person and an 8,000 mile ride back to the USA didn't make us better or different people.

I said, 'You shouldn't worry, Deborah. You're not in anyone's crosshairs. Forget we were here.'

# FORTY-EIGHT

We drove back to the airport without talking and I sensed Kim, like me, was processing the information we just acquired.

As we entered downtown Portland, she said, 'You think Christine Zetchik could have killed her husband? Could the contempt Deborah talked about have finally overridden her need for his money?'

I was thinking along similar lines. 'Also, if Keith Zetchik was Bootstrap, that would explain why Christine's money dried up so fast when the US pulled out of Vietnam.'

Kim kept her eyes on the road ahead. 'All right, let's assume Christine shot Keith out of desperation or rage. That would have given Giang two motives for eliminating her. She'd murdered one of his main supporters in DC, and on top of that, she was shaking down his money man, Chau.'

'Stacks up,' I said. 'But we're still left with the question of who killed Giang? And why? And how does any of this relate to the death of Johnny Tedstone? And to Joseph Tedstone and Heck Weschler? Or doesn't it?'

'We need to look deeper into Joseph Tedstone's allegations. Fact is, we've travelled nearly two and half thousand miles to learn what we already knew: Heck Weschler is a sexual adventurer. But that doesn't make him guilty of war crimes and it doesn't make him guilty of murder.'

I thought of one man who was guilty of both: Truc Van Thanh.

As we nudged through the traffic on West Burnside Street I remembered the last time I saw him. Again, I was in Saigon five years ago.

*I've gotten intelligence from Shaughnessy that Thanh is holed up in a safe house on Nguyen Dinh Chieu. By the time I get there, his guys have seen which way the wind is blowing and skied out.*

*Thanh is waiting for me in the living room, a big globe of brandy in one hand, a Walther P38 in the other.*

*I raise my Colt Commander and take aim, but he knows I'm not gonna shoot. He knows I want to know who did those things to Linh. He knows I want Bootstrap.*

*Even so, I keep my gun levelled at his chest.*

*'I was wondering when you'd show, Captain Tyler.' He sounds calm, at peace.*

*I try to figure out how he knows my name. Linh couldn't have told him because she never knew it – not my real one. So it must have come from somebody in the CIA or at MACV, probably Bootstrap himself.*

*'The girl had to die.' He sips his brandy. 'But not like that.'*
*'Bootstrap?'*

*He says nothing, just makes a who-else? expression.*

*'Why should I believe you?'*

*'Because I have absolutely nothing to lose.' He smiles, and just for an instant I see an ordinary man, a family man, a man of insight and wit.*

*Then he places the P38 under his jaw and pulls the trigger. In that moment I realize I'm never going to get Bootstrap.*

\*

Kim dropped me off at my place early evening. We'd been in the air or on the road for 24 hours without proper sleep and were both dead beat. I kissed her on the mouth and said I'd see her next morning.

My house seemed a little empty without Sherman to come and greet me. Odd how dogs get under your skin so quick.

I headed toward the kitchen in search of a cold drink.

And stopped.

My brain was flashing red alert. There was no obvious threat, but I knew to trust my gut.

Directly ahead, the kitchen door was wide open so you could see straight through from the hallway.

Usually I closed it when I went out.

Something else: A dish towel near the edge of the kitchen counter facing me.

Had I left it like that? I didn't think so.

I thought about the fake landmine, the giant centipede, the toe-popper trap.

I looked at my feet. I was six inches from the tripwire. One more step and …

I stepped over it, moving slowly along one side of the hallway toward the counter.

When I was on the other side of the dish towel, I lifted it real gentle.

I found myself looking at a home-made single shot pistol.

It had been bolted to the counter with the barrel aimed at chest height and the trigger rigged to the tripwire. The gun was crude and easy to disarm. I had no doubt, though, that the .36 calibre cartridge in the chamber could have killed me if I'd taken one step farther.

Grabbing a dining chair I looked at the motion-activated camera my buddy had installed over the kitchen door. As I expected, it went off when the intruder came into the hallway.

I removed the film and drove to the *Tribune* office. Hank, one of the dark room printers, was pulling a late shift and I gave him five bucks to develop it on the spot.

I waited at my desk and drank a cup of vending machine coffee while I waited.

At last Hank brought the prints over and laid them down in front of me.

What I saw made no sense. It made all kinds of sense.

# FORTY-NINE

I recognized Reggie Acheson instantly – and yet I didn't.

The firm set of her jaw, the purposeful way she moved from frame to frame, this was no scared-shitless junky-hippie. Whoever Reggie really was, she was one cool operator.

I thought about the implications. If she'd fitted the home-made pistol to my kitchen counter, she must also have set the toe-popper trap and pushed the venomous centipede through my mail slot, and rigged the fake landmine.

But why? Where was the sense in any of that?

One thing was for certain: She'd been playing me all along. The way she pulled my strings was every bit of elaborate, subtle and, more than anything, professional. I should have smelled a rat when I discovered her cocaine was baking soda. At the time I'd imagined some hustler had seen her coming. That wasn't true. Reggie had seen *me* coming. Ten million miles off.

I thought, too, about the Led Zeppelin gig she said she went to at Oakland Coliseum last year – the one that never happened because Robert Plant got hurt in a road accident. Plus her use of army slang. Fubar was a word a hippie girl with an officer dad might know, but she absolutely wouldn't have used it as part of her own vocabulary. Yet again, I'd nailed the inconsistency but explained it away in a manner that made me feel particularly obtuse.

Then there was Joseph Tedstone's assertion that Johnny wasn't in a psychiatric clinic two years ago, when Reggie said she met him.

I should have smelled a whole bunch of rats. But Reggie and her Hollywood-standard production unit were good, I had to admit.

I lit a Camel and turned my attention to the two attempted hits – the shooting and the knife-attack. It was clear now that they'd been staged for my benefit. The action in both incidents had been perfectly choreographed and planned with military precision. This was a cliché I usually avoided, but in this case I had no doubt it was factually correct. I hadn't been duped by some amateur con-artist, I was the subject of a meticulously executed secret ops mission. Its objective could only have been to convince me that Reggie was in danger of her life, with Joseph Tedstone lurking in the shadows. But what did this mean? What was its effect?

And who was she working for?

The answer was staring right at me, but even so I was strangely reluctant to accept it.

The arrival of the foolscap envelope gave me no choice.

It was placed on my desk by one of the night shift copy boys. It had been hand-delivered and was labelled *Private and confidential – For the personal attention of Wat Tyler only.*

Inside was a photocopied military personnel file, or 201 file. I flipped to the opening page and saw a blurry but clearly identifiable photo of Reggie Acheson. Her real name was Regina McLintock, so at least her first name was correct. I wasn't at all surprised to read that she was a Women's Army Corps captain until the summer of last year. I was even less surprised to learn that she joined the staff of Lieutenant General Hector Weschler as a first lieutenant when he returned from Vietnam in 1971. She went on to serve with him in Europe, where she received US Army Intelligence Agency training. She was the daughter of Major General Bernard McLintock, so the military dad part was true too. At the back of the document I found a separate, unofficial report, apparently typed for my benefit, referring to a number of off-the-books assignments she'd carried out for Weschler, as well as on detached duty with the Army Intelligence Agency. There were no specifics but judging by the language, terms of reference and knowledge of intelligence work, I guessed the source was a high-up insider at the Pentagon.

What did it all mean? Some of it was obvious, some of it not so much.

Just as crucially, who sent it?

And where was Reggie now?

But I was dead beat and my brain was overloaded, so I headed home. Funny, how your mind sometimes works better when you stop thinking. In the 15 minutes it took me to drive back to my place, I hadn't gotten the whole picture, but big sections began sliding into place, acquiring context and dimension.

I went into the living room and poured myself a large bourbon.

'Aren't you going to offer me one?'

Reggie was sitting on the couch with a suppressed Browning Hi-Power pointed right at me.

# FIFTY

She said, 'I know you know who I work for.'

I made a tired smile. 'Why else would you be sitting there with a gun on me?'

She'd caught me unawares for sure, though I gotten surprised so often lately that surprises were becoming somewhat unsurprising.

So I poured her a bourbon and walked toward her with the glass.

'That's close enough.' She raised the gun, indicating that she wanted it set down on the opposite end of the coffee table.

I did as she asked and backed off.

'You here to kill me, Reggie – sorry, I should have said Captain McLintock.'

'You can still call me Reggie.' She drank some whiskey. 'As for shooting you, that depends on how this conversation plays out. It's not my primary intention though.'

I gave her a curious look. In some ways she appeared very different to the junkie-hippie she'd played so well. More assured, aware, focused. And yet she remained on edge and nervy and I sensed the vulnerability wasn't entirely an act.

'Maggie Call knows everything I do,' I said. 'And she has a copy of your 201 file. You kill me, Rhyme Dillard will know it was you doing Weschler's bidding.' This was a lie, of course, but a plausible one.

She seemed not to hear me and picked up one of three ornamental snow globes that she'd taken from my bookshelf and arranged on the coffee table.

'These are kitschy-cool. I dig how they're all places where it never snows.'

The globe she was holding contained a Sydney Opera House scene. There was also an Egyptian pyramids setting and Taj Mahal tableau.

Without taking her eyes off the snow globe, she said, 'Heck Weschler has no idea I'm here.'

This puzzled me.

'It's all over.' She spoke as if I should have understood what she meant.

All I could manage was a blank gaze.

'It's all over *because of you.*'

Realisation punched me in the head real hard. In that instant I understood exactly where she was coming from: Reggie was the younger woman Weschler had been screwing. The one Paula had come to me about. Here was something else I never saw coming, something else that made no sense and perfect sense.

She said, 'In one way I should hate you. You've destroyed everything I had going with Heck. In another way, I guess I should be grateful. You made me open my eyes.'

There was no point bullshitting, so I told the truth, 'Gotta say, Reggie, I have no clue how I came to do that.'

She shook the Sydney Opera House globe, watched the

tiny white particles drift and swirl across a place where snow never happened.

I thought about rushing her while she was distracted but quickly canned the idea. According to my reckoning she'd killed four people in the last two weeks and could make me the fifth in no time at all.

Besides, she'd just told me she hadn't come here with that in mind. And for some reason I believed her.

She waited until the snowstorm over Sydney Harbour subsided, then turned her attention back to me. 'Until you interfered, Heck and I had a future. He was gonna give me a staff job in whichever department he got – state, defense, national security advisor, whatever. Our relationship would have carried on and everything would have been peachy. *Until ...*'

She stared at me, fiery-eyed, but her words seemed to dry up.

I waited. This wasn't something I wanted to hurry.

She coughed and took a swallow of whiskey. ' ... Until I discovered Heck's bitch of a wife has forbidden any contact with me after the election campaign. He'll toss me aside like the others.'

'Tell me what happened.'

She drank more bourbon. 'I loved Heck, but I never trusted him. Well, you couldn't, could you?' She looked at me as if she thought I was on exactly the same wavelength.

I told her something I did know, 'He always has his own agenda.'

'Of course he does. And it always has Heck right at the top. So I bugged the phone in his office. Earlier tonight I listened in on a call he made to his sister-in-law's place in New York City, where Paula is visiting.'

This time I could see cliff edge approaching. Nothing I could do about it though.

'I heard Paula tell Heck she'd talked to you about the affair he was having with me. Of course she assured him she hadn't identified me, but that was by the by. She said you'd strongly advised her to force the issue and make him ditch me.'

I thought, *Oh shit.*

Paula had sworn never to reveal our conversation. Not only had she gone back on her word, she'd disclosed my advice to the younger woman Weschler had been having an affair with – who just happened to be his private assassin, and who was pointing a 9mm pistol at my chest.

I couldn't blame Paula. She wasn't to know Reggie would be listening in. But it was a clusterfuck of broken trust, bad luck and coincidence.

'I had no idea you were the other woman in Heck's life.' It sounded lame, but it was the best I could manage.

'Would it have made any difference if you *had*?'

'No it wouldn't.' I reminded myself that if she'd come here to kill me I'd be dead already, and told her the truth. 'Fact is that if Heck is given any of those cabinet jobs, the media will be all over him. He'll instantly become the hot favourite for next president and his personal life will go under a microscope. That being so, sooner or later, the affair would have come out and that would be the end of his political ambitions.'

She picked up the snow globe with the Egyptian pyramids scene. It depicted a caravan of camels at the base of the great structures. She shook it hard and suddenly a blizzard was sweeping across the Land of the Pharaohs.

There was a stretched out quiet. The longer it went on, the more I realized it needed filling. So I said, 'Do you believe it would have worked out any different if I hadn't had that conversation with Paula? That she wouldn't have forced the issue anyway? And even if she didn't, that he wouldn't have looked at his agenda and decided there was no room on it for an extra-marital relationship?'

The snowflakes settled on the pyramid scene and she looked right at me. She seemed angry, betrayed and hurt – but more than any of these, scared.

'You're right, Wat. You're always right.' A remote forlornness entered her tone. 'Even Reggie the junkie knew that.'

For all her complicated neediness, I'd grown fond of Reggie the junkie. Even though she'd duped me, I shared the sadness of her passing. 'So where do we go from here? You said Heck didn't know you were here. You don't need me to tell you he won't be happy when he finds out.'

She hesitated, then went straight to it, 'I want to make a deal.'

# FIFTY-ONE

Once more I was mystified. 'What sort of deal?'

'Pour me another of these and I'll tell you.' She shoved the whiskey glass along the coffee table. I fixed her a drink and got one for myself.

She took a sip and looked at me straight. 'The moment Heck agreed to ditch me I became one of his loose ends. And I know what happens to Heck's loose ends. I spent the past two weeks tying them up.'

Now I understood why she was scared. Weschler would never allow Reggie to roam free with all his murky secrets and a real big grudge against him. At some stage, he'd have her eliminated.

She drank more whiskey. 'So here's the deal: I give you all I got on Heck and you bring him down so he can never come after me. Also, you give me enough time to get on a plane for someplace that doesn't have an extradition treaty with the USA.'

I was not in a strong bargaining position, but I felt I needed to give the alternative a shot. 'There's a better way out of this. You could turn state's evidence. Take Weschler down that way. The DA would offer a generous plea bargain.'

She threw me a halfway amused look. 'Get real, Wat. I killed Keith and Christine Zetchik, Johnny Tedstone, and Pham Tan Giang. You really think there could be any sort of plea deal that doesn't involve me going to jail and never coming out?'

She was right. I didn't push it.

I said, 'Very well, tell me what you got and I'll do everything I can to make sure Heck gets what's coming.'

She started talking. Her words came fast, as if she really needed to get this out of the way. 'I guess it doesn't matter anymore, but for what it's worth, I'm not a psychopathic killer. I got carried along by the thrill and the pace of it all. You know how persuasive Heck can be. He made grand promises about changing the world and how I could be a part of it and I was dumb enough to believe him. And I was in love. Maybe I still am. You can't flip from love to hate that fast.'

She glugged the rest of her whiskey but didn't ask for more.

I thought she needed a little reassurance. I said, 'I get where you're at, Reggie. We all make mistakes. We all get taken in by people.'

'Even you?'

'Sure. You took me in, didn't you?'

'Junkie Reggie did.' She made a rueful laugh. 'I liked junkie Reggie more than real Reggie. I liked what you and I had – even if it was bogus.'

'I did too,' I said, and it wasn't a lie. 'We were good friends, weren't we?'

She nodded and there was a trace of regret in her voice. 'While it lasted.'

Then she went back to business, back to laying down what she knew quickly, efficiently. 'All I can give you is information relating to my own activities. I was never made aware of the bigger picture because we treated the whole thing like a black ops mission. I got my orders, I executed them, I got debriefed, and that was that. No explanations, no questions, no justification.'

She looked at me, is if seeking approval, or at least acceptance, and I told her I dug why Weschler would want to work in that way, whether he was in the army or not.

'Okay,' she said. 'The overview of my mission was to obtain a cassette tape that Joseph Tedstone had been using to threaten Heck. I never knew exactly what was on it, but Heck told me it related to atrocities in Vietnam committed by Tedstone's unit. According to Heck, Tedstone was trying to pin this shit on him in order to destroy his political career. The operation meant recruiting and eventually eliminating Johnny, then zapping Zetchik and his wife – and finally, taking out Giang. But there were a lot of hiccups and sidesteps and improvisations in between. Stuff didn't go to plan. I had to react fast, think on my feet. That's the way of it, though, isn't it?'

I nodded. 'No plan survives first contact with the enemy, right?'

She made a tight smile. 'Right.'

'So how did you get Johnny to play ball?'

She ran her fingertip around the rim her empty whiskey glass. 'You know from my 201 file that I'd done a considerable amount of off-the-books stuff for Heck. I gotta say recruiting Johnny was the opposite of challenging. I knew he hated his dad. I knew he had a narcotics habit. And I knew he had mental health problems. I was also aware of his anti-establishment politics. So I engineered a meeting shortly after Christmas and presented myself as a kindred spirit. Very soon he was giving out on how his dad had wrecked his life and forced him to have electroshock therapy because he was gay.'

This was Johnny to a T. He told me the same stuff. He told anyone who'd listen.

Reggie continued. She was in her stride now and her tone became a little more relaxed. 'Later, I asked him if he ever thought about getting his own back and he said sure he had, but he wasn't prepared to serve time for murder. He told me his dad kept some cyanide kill pills in his desk drawer and how he'd fantasise about lacing his old man's food or drink. Then he talked about his dad's antique guns cabinet. In another revenge scenario, he'd thought of getting one of those old pieces and blowing his dad's brains out.'

She paused, smiling, like we were reminiscing about a mutual friend, rather than one of the folks she'd recently murdered. 'Johnny was the ultimate in suggestibility. The kill pills didn't interest me – not then. But I said if he could get me a gun from the cabinet, I could kill one of his dad's enemies and Johnny could watch his old man take the fall. I said it as a sick joke, but he jumped at it. Can you believe that?'

I said, yes, absolutely I could believe that.

'Johnny was so into the idea that he suggested smoking Keith Zetchik. That saved me a great deal of trouble introducing the idea. In fact I had to rein Johnny in. He wanted to do it there and then, but I explained how we need to take our time, plan it properly.'

This, too, was Johnny all over. The way it had unfolded, Weschler must have been purring.

Reggie carried on in her easy-going tone. 'First, though, I needed to get hold of the cassette tape. Heck was certain there was only one copy and knew Joseph Tedstone kept it someplace in the house. So I told Johnny I was ex-Army Intelligence – which, of course, was partly true – and had it on good authority that his old man was behind horrible war crimes in Vietnam. Then I mentioned that his dad had this tape recording that could incriminate him and a bunch of other high-ups. I knew Johnny had a hard on for the peace movement. I thought this would be a big turn-on and I was right.'

She made a pensive frown and her voice became less chatty. 'At the time I thought it was so damn exciting, how brilliant I was at manipulating him, what a shit-hot handler I was. In truth, Johnny was a self-recruiting asset. I didn't pull his strings, he pulled his own. He knew his old man had a safe where he kept valuables. He said he could find out the combination. After a couple of weeks he'd done this – and more. He'd also located the keys to the gun cabinet and his dad's desk, where he kept the cyanide pills. This made me think again and I realized they could be used after all – though not on Tedstone Senior. But first I had to report back to Heck.'

'He must have been on cloud nine.'

She nodded, without seeming to notice my sarcasm. 'But we still needed to be sure the tape was in there, so four weeks ago we did a dummy run. Johnny's dad went for his jog, we opened the safe, and bingo. It was a very long recording so I got the first thirty seconds on a miniature recorder, then another thirty seconds half way through, and a third section toward the end. Without any context it was difficult to understand what was being said, but I heard Heck's voice and Joseph Tedstone's and another guy, who I assumed was Zetchik. I took these excerpts to Heck and he green-lit the operation.'

'It must have been tricky to set up,' I said. 'Lots of moving parts.'

She made a maybe/maybe-not shrug. 'You must remember that Heck was in touch with Zetchik so it was fairly straightforward to get a date when he knew Zetchik and his wife would be at their apartment. Once this was fixed, I briefed Johnny. As soon as his dad left the house, we'd grab the tape and the Mauser. Next, Johnny was to act drunk in a public place and broadcast that his dad was gonna kill Keith Zetchik that night. The more witnesses, the better. As you know, Johnny excelled at running his mouth while under the influence. But the challenge was to do it sober. He practised over and over. Gotta say, his dedication was incredible. In the end I couldn't tell when he was out-of-it and when he was clean. He also hit on the idea of using props, like a plastic mouthpiece that made his face look out of shape.'

I recalled how Johnny's face looked like it was sliding off his head at the Ramones gig. It wasn't down to drink and drugs, it was a joke-store trick.

'When Johnny mentioned that he was going out with you that particular night, Heck got really, really excited.' She looked at me with an appreciative smile that I didn't appreciate one bit. 'He explained that he served with you in Vietnam and how getting you involved as a Washington-based crime reporter would be a massive bonus.'

# FIFTY-TWO

I smiled. 'Glad I was able to help.'

Again, she didn't pay any attention to my irony.

One thing confused me, though. I said, 'When Johnny did his routine at the Bayou, he didn't mention Christine Zetchik at all. Was that deliberate or did he just mess up?'

'Deliberate.' Reggie was upbeat and focused. This might have been some slick corporate presentation. 'But also, as it turned out, fortuitous. You see, Joseph Tedstone had a very powerful motive to murder Keith Zetchik, but none whatsoever to kill Christine. Heck wanted them both gone, but the idea was to make Christine's death look like collateral. As it happened, she wasn't at the apartment when I got there, so I had to improvise. In the end, though, it worked in our favour.'

I poured myself another bourbon. She shook her head when I offered her a refill. 'So tell me how it went down.'

'You already know most of it. Tedstone Senior went for his five-mile run at 8.45 on the dot. Five minutes later, Johnny let me into the house. We opened the safe and I got the tape, then we went to the display case and I took out the Mauser. Next, when Johnny was out of the room, I used the key to his dad's desk drawer, took out a kill pill, and re-locked the drawer.'

'That was smart.' This time I wasn't being sarcastic. 'The homicide detectives found Johnny poisoned and the cyanide locked in the desk drawer, so they dismissed suicide on the basis that Johnny wouldn't have had the time or inclination to return the bottle to the drawer, then lock it all up again nice and tidy. And that placed his dad front and centre of the frame.'

'It was smart, wasn't it?' Reggie was still so excited about reliving the operation that the cost in human life wasn't an issue. She carried on in the same, positive tone. 'A few minutes after 9.30 Johnny left to meet you in Georgetown and I waited outside the Zetchiks' apartment until they arrived home from a social function. Except Christine never showed. I called Weschler from a pay phone and he told me to proceed anyway. This would have been a little before 10.30.'

She went quiet, as if the wind had suddenly fallen from her sails, and started examining the third snow dome – the one of the Taj Mahal scene.

I decided she needed a nudge, 'So, what? You went up to the apartment and told Keith Zetchik you had an urgent message from Heck Weschler? Zetchik let you in, you pulled the Mauser and forced him to call Tedstone. Zetchik said he had the tape and wanted to make a deal. Tedstone had no choice, so he agreed to come. You waited until you saw Tedstone's car approaching, then you shot Zetchik dead and skied out. Am I wrong?'

She didn't look away from the snow dome, though I knew she still had me covered with the Hi-Power. At last she said, 'You're not wrong.'

'Then what?'

'I waited outside, saw Joseph Tedstone go into the apartment, come straight out, and drive away.' Now she sounded tired, even bored. 'I'd expected him to call the cops. But he seemed to have sensed a trap. I had no idea where he went, but I stuck to the plan and met Johnny back at the family home. That would have been around 11.15. Apparently his dad wasn't coming home any time soon, but that didn't matter. After all, I had the kill pill and I was gonna be alone with Johnny when he swallowed it. So we went inside. I suggested we have a drink to celebrate. We had a glass of whiskey each and he downed his in one. I offered to get him another and dropped the pill as I poured the drink.'

She shook the dome and the Taj Mahal was at the centre of a snowstorm. 'You know the rest. When I was sure Johnny was dead, I beat it.'

I said, 'But you still had the loose end of Christine to deal with?'

She watched the white flakes settle on the unlikely scene. 'Yes I did. But, as I said, it worked out for the best.'

'Not so much for Christine.'

She looked up from the snow dome with a so-what? expression. 'She'd had a fight with her husband and stayed at a friend's, then went to the place in Earlstown next morning. Meantime, Heck discovered Joseph Tedstone had been at his sister's place from midnight until the following morning, when he was arrested. This meant he was untouchable as far as Christine was concerned. We needed to improvise so I drove over to Earlstown and dealt with her.'

She said this with a blasé air, like she'd sorted out a parking fine. I was struck by her transition from enthusiasm to lethargy to indifference, and I wondered what might be next. These mood swings were somewhat concerning because she was still pointing the Hi-Power at me. On the other hand, I needed more information. I said, 'Heck wanted someone else in the frame, though, didn't he? And Giang was an ideal substitute for Tedstone Senior.'

She nodded, her expression unreadable.

'Did Heck tell you Christine had been shaking down Giang's money man?'

'All I knew was that she'd been interfering in Giang's activities. When she died, Heck wanted you and the cops to start looking in Giang's direction.'

'But I needed a little help, didn't I? Heck deliberately fed me information about Giang and the grocery store where he worked in his day job. Then, of course, there were the Vietnam-themed booby traps.'

This seemed to pique her interest. The earlier keenness returned to her voice. 'They seemed to be working too. I mean, who else would be targeting you in that very specific manner?'

'For a while I thought it might have been Kim.'

'She was our backstop. But you buddied up with her pretty quickly.'

'So all that Viet Cong stuff was just an amusing distraction?' I was pissed off and didn't try to hide it. 'The fake landmine, the giant centipede, the toe-popper trap, the tripwire and pistol? I didn't find any of those things particularly amusing.'

She seemed unconcerned. 'I took the work seriously but it never occurred to me that you might get hurt. You're way too smart.'

I guess I was supposed to be flattered, but I said nothing and she picked up her story.

'Problem was that Giang started to panic after you and

Kim infiltrated his place in Maryland. Heck thought there was a risk of him talking to the wrong sort of folks at the Pentagon and I was sent to shut him up. That way, you, the CIA and the cops would continue to think Giang killed Christine. It wasn't the neat tie-up we wanted because the cops would never find out who did it. But unsolved murders in DC are a dime a dozen and under the circumstances Heck said it would have to do.'

I could see the end of this conversation approaching fast, which meant I needed to tackle the aspect that was bothering me most. 'Why did Heck want you to develop a relationship with me?'

She made a sad smile. 'I don't know exactly. But once he decided to get you involved, you became central to his planning. He asked me to carry on playing the role of Johnny's junkie-hippie friend and win your trust. He said junkie Reggie's version of events would lead you to believe Joseph Tedstone was vindictive as well as guilty. Also, Heck wanted me to feed back to him on how you were thinking so he could make adjustments, as and when necessary. I guess he didn't trust you to be incompetent.'

I shook my head. 'Man, that's the most backhanded compliment I ever heard. But I gotta say, the two attempted hits were convincing.'

'He brought in ex-special ops guys. The drive-by shooting and the knife attacked were works of art. Timing was vital. Everyone had to know their part down to the last detail. Even the beat cop who handled the guy with the knife was working for Heck.'

'He was good,' I said. 'He added a ring of authenticity.'

She went quiet again and the silence hung strange. I

could tell she was mulling something over, conducting some internal debate.

Finally she appeared to reach a decision. 'The more I think about it, the more I believe Heck was doing a set-up job on me. Maybe Paula had been dropping hints. Maybe, as you said, he could see there was no long term future for me in his plans. I mean, if there were two failed hits and then a third one succeeded, you and the cops would have naturally concluded that the drug pushers junkie Reggie owed money to had finally got to her.'

'Figures,' I said. 'What about next of kin?'

'The real Regina Acheson didn't have any. She was an only child killed in a plane crash three years after her mom and dad died in a house fire. They were not a lucky family. That was why we used her identity. The cops would've been looking at a junkie with no family. If Joseph Tedstone could be implicated, well and good. If not, my death would be put down to being in hock to drug dealers. Whichever way it went, Heck would be free of me and in the clear.'

She smiled faintly. 'You know what's worst? I can't change my feelings for him. He had me setting the stage for my own death and I still can't hate him.'

I gave her a sympathetic look. 'You just gotta give it some time.'

'Yeah, sure.' She stood up, keeping the Hi-Power pointed at my chest.

I began to think her talk of a deal was bullshit, that she was gonna shoot me right there.

She said, 'Come on, Wat. Time to go.'

# FIFTY-THREE

I was not at all convinced she wasn't planning to leave me face down in a ditch.

'Where are we going?'

'You'll find out when we get there.' She picked up my car keys and tossed them to me. 'You drive.'

I gave her a wary look.

'You're gonna have to trust me, Wat.'

'I've been trusting you for two weeks, Reggie, and it hadn't gone so well for me.'

But I had no other options so I followed the directions she gave me. We headed out of town and crossed the Potomac on I-66 into Virginia. We drove west to Haymarket, then took US15 south, eventually exiting left. We drove in no great hurry along a series of country lanes. Last place name I saw was Casanova, which had to be the sexiest place name on the planet. Whether it was a sexy place to live, I never got to find out. We were deep in the sticks, and we went deeper still into dark and featureless countryside.

I guessed we'd been driving two hours when she said, 'Pull over here.'

She must have been reading my thoughts. 'I'm not gonna shoot you, Wat. But I am gonna leave you.'

I could guess why. She didn't trust me to give her time to disappear.

So I got out the car with the engine running and stood back while she walked around the trunk and slid into the driver's seat.

She looked at me over the barrel of the pistol. 'Remember, Wat, I'm counting on you to bring him down. I don't wanna be looking over my shoulder for the rest of my days.'

'What you gonna do?'

'Who knows.'

I gave her a solicitous look. 'Still not too late to cut a deal with the DA.'

'Never happen, Wat. Me going to jail won't bring any of those people back. Besides, the Zetchiks and Giang were assholes and the world's a better place without them.'

'That what Heck told you?'

'Was he wrong?'

I thought about it. 'About those three, probably not.'

She said, 'I'm sorry about Johnny. But he was fucked up real bad. Maybe he's better off out of it.'

'We're all fucked up, Reggie, one way or another.'

She gave me a whimsical smile. 'Can't argue there.'

I looked one way along the pale band of starlit road, then the other. 'So where do we go from here?'

'I'm going the way this car is pointed. You can go whichever way you want.' She pulled an apologetic face. 'As far as I can tell, the nearest habitation is ten miles away. It's gone midnight so the chances of you flagging down a passing vehicle aren't great. You might get lucky, but I figure I'll have at least an hour's head start. Plenty of time to vanish.'

This was an under-estimate. I hadn't slept for 36 hours or eaten for 12. I was dead beat and disoriented. I wasn't gonna start running blind through dark countryside in hopes of coming across a farm or isolated dwelling.

So I set off walking along the road with the main aim of staying awake long enough to find someplace with a phone.

Over my shoulder I heard her gun the engine, then watched her accelerate past me, tail-lights fading fast into the gloomy night.

*

I reached a farmhouse a little after 1.30am.

The folks living there were understandably suspicious. Stranger appears out of nowhere in the middle of the night and starts banging on your front door, you're not gonna throw it open and welcome him inside. So I spent 15 minutes on the wrong end of a shotgun persuading the elderly farmer in pyjamas to let me use his phone.

I reached Dillard at home and spent another few minutes getting my ear chewed off for getting him out of bed. When I'd finally explained the situation, he grudgingly accepted I'd done the right thing. He said he'd put an APB out on Reggie, but we both knew she'd have switched cars already, probably her identity too. An MPD cruiser came to pick me up and took me to Dillard's office, where he was waiting in a sweat-shirt and jogger bottoms. We went through Reggie's revelations in detail, but at the end of it all, we didn't have jack shit on Weschler. The only witness to the deaths of Johnny, the Zetchiks and Giang was Reggie herself. Even if she had turned state's evidence, it would have been her word against Weschler's.

'You should have told me about this Reggie Acheson, or McLintock, or whatever she's called earlier.' Dillard gave me an exasperated look.

'I'm sorry. I thought I was protecting a source.'

'And you realize we can't even think about going after Weschler? Not yet. Not on what we got.'

'I'll get more.'

'No, Tyler, you won't. *I'll* get more. That's my job, not yours. Same goes for your CIA pal. From here on in, this is police business, nobody else's.'

I said yeah sure, without meaning it, and accepted his offer of a ride home in the cruiser that brought me back from the Virginia farmhouse.

I arrived at my place not long after 3.30 and called Kim at home. She didn't pick up, and that wasn't surprising, so I left a message on her answering machine to contact me urgently. Then, on the off chance, I tried her at Langley. The duty guy said she wasn't there and I left the same message.

Then I ate a huge bowl of cereal and allowed myself four hours' sleep.

By 8.00 Kim hadn't returned my calls. It could be something, could be nothing. I phoned her again at home and at Langley. Same result.

My stomach was feeling hollow again, so I made myself a breakfast of bacon, eggs and waffles and washed it down with a big jug of coffee.

Feeling a little more human, I took my last cup through to the living room and lit a cigarette. I'd left an old copy of the *Tribune* on the floor near the couch. It was folded open at my first interview with Weschler. The page was dominated by a picture of the man in his Alexandria office, looking statesmanlike yet approachable.

I'd seen the photo before. It was a thoroughly professional job, but there was nothing special about it – nothing to make you look twice.

But it *was* making me look twice.

I looked closer.

Closer still.

Even closer than that.

Deep in my mind, distant memories reframed themselves, perceptions realigned. Comments of no consequence started taking on huge significance. And old certainties started to dissolve and flow into new realities.

How had I missed it? How had I failed to make these connections?

Everything was there, had been from day one. I just hadn't seen it.

I forced myself to slow right down, go through five-year-old thought processes one step at a time.

I recalled what I knew about Bootstrap from Linh. She'd told me Bootstrap flew stateside to see the chiefs whenever he could. She'd heard him say he loved old accordion music. At that time I assumed the chiefs were the chiefs of staff and Bootstrap liked traditional folk or country music. I mean, what else would I have thought? Later, Linh said Bootstrap mentioned his family roots. She'd caught the first word: Northern, but not the second. She thought it might have been Ireland or Iceland. She also learned Bootstrap smoked Pall Mall cigarettes and my CIA liaison Chuck Shaughnessy laughed that off because it was one of America's most popular brands.

I looked yet again at the newspaper picture in front of me. I looked at the shelf of framed photos in Weschler's office: Weschler with Paula and their two daughters; Weschler with General Creighton Abrams, and Weschler with Len Dawson, Kansas City Chiefs' star quarterback. And I looked at the bottle of Scotch on the drinks cabinet behind his desk. My mind went back to that first interview two weeks ago. He'd picked up the bottle and poured two drinks. 'Old Orcadian single malt.' He'd sipped the whiskey and smiled. 'Distilled in the Scottish Orkney islands, where my mom's family is from.'

I made myself go through the evolution of my thinking again, even slower.

But it stayed clear – in fact it got clearer still.

When Bootstrap flew stateside to see the chiefs, he was watching the Kansas City Chiefs play in the National Football League.

Bootstrap didn't love old accordion tunes, he loved Old Orcadian single malt Scotch.

And his maternal family wasn't from Northern Iceland or Northern Ireland. They were from the Northern Isles of Scotland – specifically Orkney.

There was even a pack of Pall Mall pictured on Weschler desk.

I dropped the paper and sat back in the couch.

Bootstrap was Heck Weschler.

And I was back in Saigon, in the deserted heroin refinery on Pasteur. With Colonel Thanh dead, his people had scattered and it hadn't been difficult to locate the production facility. I searched every corner, every inch of that place. But I couldn't find any leads on Bootstrap. His trail ran cold.

Until now.

# FIFTY-FOUR

I sat there, staring into space for a long time. I wasn't sure how much time, but it was a lot of time.

Talking to Deborah Kinsley convinced me Keith Zetchik was the best match for the information I had on Bootstrap. And if not Zetchik, then some MACV bigshot I had no chance of tracing. Now, though, I had zero doubts that Weschler was the guy. More I thought about it, the more certain I became.

And the upshot? One phone call from Gerald Ford or Jimmy Carter could put the most unsuitable man in US history into one of its most powerful political positions. If he wasn't stopped he might even make president. All that stood between Weschler and high office were unprovable allegations from Joseph Tedstone, who was facing a grand jury; an outlandish story from Reggie, who was almost certainly out of the country; and my deductions, based on verbal intelligence from a sixteen-year-old asset who died five years ago.

And Kim. Wherever she was.

My emotions went in a cycle of worry, anger, and frustration. At least I was experiencing emotions. For a guy like me, feelings like these were rare. But of course this didn't help anybody in any practical sense.

The phone rang. I snatched it up, hoping to hear Kim's voice.

I wasn't surprised, though, when I heard Weschler's.

He said, 'We need to talk. There's a disused paper mill near Naylor Road and Alabama Avenue SE.'

I knew where he meant.

'Come alone, Wat. First sign of law enforcement, I'm gone. You understand?'

I said I did and he gave me until 11.00am.

I didn't have a car after Reggie drove off in my Maverick so I took a cab to the *Tribune* office. I told Maggie everything, real fast. She said we should leave it to Dillard. I said fuck that. This was my story and Weschler specifically told me he'd bug out at the first sniff of cops. Maggie was worried. And rightly so. But knew me too well. No way was I staying away from the confrontation I'd been craving since 1971.

I took one of the reporters' pool cars and drove out to Joseph Tedstone's place. He more than anyone deserved an explanation and I had just enough time to give him one.

He didn't seem surprised to see me and I soon found out why: Tedstone had sent me Reggie's 201 file. He'd contacted a buddy at the Pentagon with the photo of Reggie I'd left with him. The friend came back with a photocopy of her file – plus the addendum about her off-the-books activities – and Tedstone hand-delivered the package to me at the *Tribune* office.

I told him the whole story and he listened without a word.

When I was done he said, 'I have to confess I'd have thought I was guilty too. As to Weschler's activities with Zetchik's wife and this Deborah Kinsley, we all knew that sort of thing went on. I simply never imagined that a man with as much to lose as Weschler would have gotten involved.'

I said, 'That's his weakness. He's always seen himself as invulnerable.'

'Then we should exploit it. Do you have a plan?'

I shrugged. 'Apart from showing up, no I don't. But I'll think of something.'

'I wish I shared your confidence.'

'I wish I had some to share.'

He was too polite not to smile at my bad joke. 'Let me come with you. I know Weschler. I could persuade him of the futility of persisting in this wickedness.'

I shook my head. 'Thanks for the offer, sir, but it would be playing into his hands. He already has all he needs from you – the tape. And from his point of view, the situation isn't futile. Just the opposite. He's all too aware of the gulf between what we know and what we can prove.'

He stood back and made a resigned expression. 'At least tell me you're armed.'

I showed him the Heckler & Koch P9 in the pocket of my windbreaker.

Then he showed me to the door. On the way I remembered something I'd noticed when I last visited his place and asked to borrow it. He gave me a curious look but said nothing as he went to bring it.

On the doorstep, he extended his hand. 'Please take care of yourself, Captain Tyler.'

'You too, sir.'

The traffic from Kalorama to South East DC was light and I arrived with ten minutes to spare.

The former paper mill was the only remaining structure

on an old industrial site slated for redevelopment. Tall brick walls were mired in soot and colonized by outcrops of weed that had taken root in the crumbling mortar. All the windows low enough to throw rocks at had had been broken, giving the impression of a blinded derelict.

I climbed over the chain-link fence that bounded the site and hustled across the broken ground to the mill. Weschler was expecting me so I went in through the front entrance and found myself in a spacious lobby. A big crescent-shaped reception desk was still in place, though it was covered in fallen plasterwork and shattered glass. A framed portrait of a guy sporting a frock-coat and a handlebar moustache had been left hanging on the wall behind. I guessed he was one of the mill's founding fathers. He gazed like a melancholy ghost at the ruinous scene and I sure couldn't blame him.

'Wat – good to see you.'

Weschler as standing by an open door to my right. He was wearing a sharp business suit and tie, as if this place had never shut down and he was still the boss.

'Do come through.'

I went through the doorway and into an office. Like the lobby, it had once been a grand affair, with Victorian tiled flooring and dark wood walls. There was even a long boardroom table. Like the front desk in the lobby it was coated in debris. A perished leather chair had been left at one end. It was occupied by a soft toy rabbit made of pink fabric. With shiny button eyes and a goofy smile, it looked much more spooky than the dude in the picture frame.

We faced one another from opposite sides of the table.

'So, I finally get to meet Bootstrap.' I spoke the name out

loud, as if physically connecting it to its owner would make this situation less surreal.

He threw up his hand in mock surrender and made a toothy grin. 'You got me, Wat.'

'Gotta say, Heck, I never thought this moment would ever happen.'

'You better make the most of it. I'm not that guy any longer. Haven't been for a good long while.'

'You'll always be that guy.'

'And you'll never learn to quit. You never caught me. But you did force me out of Vietnam. You should have taken that as a win.'

'But it wasn't was it? The racket carried on another two years until Uncle Sam pulled out. I shut down some of the poppy farms and the refinery on Pasteur, but Thanh's associates just relocated. Pretty soon it was business as usual.'

'I can't take too much credit for what went on after I went to Europe. Christine acted as my proxy, but I was no longer involved at an operational level.'

'Why did you cut Linh?' I gave him a fierce stare.

He looked at the pink bunny and picked it up off the chair. 'I didn't. Not personally.'

He walked around the table so he was on the same side as me. 'I did fuck her, though. That was something I did do personally. She was very good.'

He must have clocked the look on my face.

'Shucks, I just realized she never told you. She came back for more too. She thought she was going to nail me as Bootstrap that very night, but I was one step ahead. I'm also pretty sure she came back because she enjoyed spreading for me.'

I ignored the taunt. Attachment disorder was more

a problem than a solution, but it did allow me to keep my emotions in check. Times like this, that was an advantage. I was gonna make Weschler pay, but only when he'd given me what I needed.

I went back to my earlier line of questioning, 'Why did you have one of your goons cut her?'

'You sure you want me to answer that?'

I said nothing.

He stroked the bunny's head between its ears. 'It was for your benefit. I wanted to screw with your head, throw you off balance. And it worked. First time I ever saw you lose it. I sat back and watched you charging around Saigon like a bear with a wasp up its ass.'

I failed to keep the incredulity from my voice. 'You had a sixteen-year-old girl raped and mutilated to send me a message?'

'Like I said, it did the trick.' He held out the bunny and wiggled it playfully. 'All that commotion, I got away home free.'

'Until now.'

'And isn't fate a curious thing? Who'd have thought you and I would cross swords again five years later, having swapped Saigon for DC?'

'It's not a fucking game, Heck.'

He raised an eyebrow. 'Isn't it, Wat? I suspect we're more alike than you think. We're both natural competitors.'

I laughed at that. 'You're running for president and I'm a newspaper hack. We couldn't be less alike.'

'You shouldn't sell yourself short.' He held the pink bunny by its ears, swinging it back and forth. 'You ran me to earth, didn't you?'

'I guess.' I held his gaze. 'But I still haven't joined all the dots.'

'You've gotten close enough to figure it out.'

'Indulge me.'

'Okay, why not?'

# FIFTY-FIVE

He sat on a corner of the long table and placed the bunny at his side. 'I needed three people dead, or permanently silenced. First there was Joseph Tedstone. As you know, he was threatening to expose my body-count enhancement methods, including my creative approach to armed resistance verification.'

He talked about the mass slaughter of civilians like it was some commercial process. For him, I guessed it was.

'Then I had to handle Zet. He was becoming dangerously vocal about supporting Giang and his group of generals. In country they were a necessary evil. Back here, they were a volatile liability. Anyone with half a brain knows getting out of Vietnam was the USA's top priority; that there's no possibility whatsoever of us funding a continuation of the war. Problem was, Zet didn't have half a brain. Maybe a quarter.' He made a quirky smile, as if amused by his own off-the-cuff quip. 'Maybe less than that.'

'He'd got no brain at all after you had Reggie put a bullet through it.'

He made a long philosophical sigh, as if so say Keith Zetchik was simply too dumb to live. 'Zet presented an additional problem. Like Joe Tedstone, he knew about my body-count augmentation techniques. Zet would never have threatened me – fuck, he was proud of what we did. But he may well have run his mouth in the wrong company. And the more he mixed with Giang's people, the more talkative he became.'

He picked up the pink rabbit again. 'Next, there was the issue of Christine – the only person alive who knew I was Bootstrap. When the heroin racket came to an end in '73 her income stream started to dry up and she became increasingly desperate. It was only a matter of time before she tried to blackmail me. So I devised the plan to eliminate Zetchik and have Tedstone take the fall. Christine would get hit at the same time in what would seem like a wrong-time/wrong-place tragedy.'

I made a crooked smile. 'Except Christine didn't play to the script and Reggie had to kill her separately.'

'Give the man a cigar.' He gave me a condescending look. 'I knew about Giang's activities through Zet. I also knew Christine had been shaking down Giang's money guy Chau, all of which made Giang a great patsy.'

'Hence the Vietnam booby traps? I gather they were your idea.'

He gave me a playful wink. 'Did you like 'em?'

'Loved 'em.' I decided it was time to stick a pin in his balloon. 'But then it all started to go wrong, didn't it? What were the odds of Paula confiding in me about your affair with Reggie, and Reggie finding out about it by bugging your phone?'

He gripped one of the bunny's ears and jerked it hard, ripping it from the head.

'I must admit that was a contingency I hadn't anticipated. And Reggie had done so well up to that point.'

I could tell he was pissed and I wasn't gonna let up. 'That wouldn't have stopped you getting rid of Reggie though, would it? A third, successful hit wouldn't have surprised anyone, including me.'

'You know me, Wat. Thorough to the last. I was fond of Reggie, sure.' He tore off the rabbit's other ear and tossed the disfigured toy onto the table. 'But there's no room for sentiment in this business.'

I continued to press him. 'You got a little sentimental when you found out I was in town though, didn't you?'

He made a you-got-me grin. 'Maybe a little. But there were significant practical benefits to getting you involved. If you believed Tedstone was guilty – which was almost certain – that would give me a big advantage. The cops *and* DC's top crime reporter reaching the same conclusion? Nobody would question that.'

He paused, is if to allow me time to appreciate his tactical brilliance. 'Bringing you onto the scene also meant I could keep tabs on Tedstone, and even influence your thinking, while appearing to be on his side. Then there was our CIA friend Kim. I fed you that intel on her because I wanted you to suspect her, or at least put some doubt in your mind. That way, I thought you'd do me a favour and maybe throw a wrench in her works.' He gave me a disappointed look, like I'd let him down. 'But that didn't work out too well because you ended up fucking her.'

I recalled our meeting at the Botanic Garden. He'd planted the idea that Johnny could have staged his own suicide to frame his old man. Then he suggested Kim was looking into

Keith Zetchik's relationship with Giang. And he put forward the notion that Langley sent her to recover something from Keith Zetchik's apartment, that she zapped Zetchik when he disturbed her search, then went to Earlstown and killed Christine because she also got in the way. And finally, Weschler gave me Giang's workplace address. At the time I thought he was being helpful. He was a smart bastard, I had to admit. Maybe too smart.

He gave me a sidelong glance. 'There was another reason I wanted to bring you into the game.'

'I'm all ears.'

'As I said, you and I, we're competitive guys. I saw an opportunity to get the better of the best Special Forces operator I ever knew. I watched your attempts to track me down in '71. There were times when you came close without realising it. You handled your asset real well.'

I thought: *Not well enough.* But I kept that to myself.

'Then I saw your byline in the *Tribune*, and realized the perfect symmetry of it all. The prospect of another head to head with Wat Tyler was too good to pass up.' He looked at me straight. 'Shame you had to lose.'

'Who said I lost?'

'You did when you agreed to meet up with me.' He indicated a door at the back of the room. 'Come on, I'll show you.'

The negative vibe I picked up when I agreed to come here got a whole lot worse. Of course I knew this meeting was high risk, but until now I was confident I'd find a way to make it work in my favour. Now I wasn't so sure. There was a smugness in his manner that suggested the outcome was a done deal. I'd just told Tedstone Weschler's Achilles' heel was his overconfidence. Maybe that was *my* weakness.

We went through the door and entered the main production area.

First thing I saw was Kim. She was gagged with a strip of duct tape and tied to a chair in the middle of the cavernous industrial space. She didn't seem to have been harmed. She wasn't naked. And she wasn't spread out on a table. But seeing her like that made me think of Linh and gave me an awful sense of déjà vu.

With its high walls and arched windows, the manufacturing hall resembled the bombed out Catholic churches I saw in Vietnam. There were smells of industrial lubricant and mildew and damp plaster. The place had been gutted of its heavy paper-making machinery, but the steel stairs, platforms and gantries that had been used to operate the equipment were still in place.

Four guys, two toting AK-47s and two with hand guns, were positioned on the stairs. One pair were on the first level, maybe 20 feet up, the other two on the highest platform 40 feet higher. Between them they had the place covered.

I recognized the two on the lower level as the seasoned beat cop and the knife-guy from the staged stabbing. The two up top I presumed were the guys who faked the drive-by shooting. Ex-special ops, Reggie had said. That didn't necessarily mean Special Forces, but it did mean they'd know how to handle themselves.

And in any case this would be like shooting fish in a barrel.

# FIFTY-SIX

'The good news is she's fine.' Weschler walked slowly around the back of Kim and returned to stand opposite me. 'Bad news is she won't be for too much longer.'

I glanced at her, but the duct tape prevented any facial expression and her eyes were unreadable.

Weschler was talking again. 'My guys are up there on the stairs because I don't want them to hear what I'm gonna tell you. But they won't hesitate to drop you on the spot if you make any sort of wrong move. You dig, Wat?'

I dug.

'That being so, I'd be grateful if you'd hand me the gun I assume you have in your possession. Take it out real slow, place it on the floor and kick it over.'

I didn't have any good options – I didn't even have any bad ones – so I did as he asked. He picked it up and placed it in the pocket of his suit coat.

Then he gave me a supercilious smirk. 'You know what Kim here has in common with your other Vietnamese girl?'

I kept my mouth shut. There was nothing I could do to spoil his moment of triumph, but I wasn't going to add to it.

After a few seconds he broke the silence, 'Keeping important stuff from you, that's what.'

He knew he had me hooked and was obviously savouring the moment.

'Linh, well she never told you she spread for me, then came back for more. She was only sixteen so maybe you can make allowances. Kim, on the other hand, is 36 and her secret is much more egregious.'

He glanced across at Kim. 'Should I tell him what you are, Kimmy?'

She tried to talk but all I heard was a sequence of muffled grunts.

Weschler turned back to me. 'Kim, here isn't a double agent. She went one better. She's a triple. She's really working for the People's Public Security Forces of Vietnam. Has been since 1970. We turned her in '68, but they turned her back two years later. All that turning, it's enough to make your head spin.'

Weschler looked for some expression of shock or bewilderment on my face, but the truth was I wasn't shocked and I wasn't bewildered.

He went on anyways. 'To some extent her CIA mission overlapped with her Hanoi mission – to stop the campaign by Zetchik and Giang to continue fighting in Vietnam. But Hanoi sent extra, top priority orders. She's here in DC to prevent me getting any of the top cabinet posts by exposing my bodycount augmentation methods. But she failed. Silly girl went rogue and took it upon herself to take me out personally. Can you believe that, Wat?'

'Yes I can, Heck.' I recalled my thoughts about Kim's motives. She'd never mentioned Weschler when she told me what happened at An Bai, but she must have known Zetchik's battalion was part of Weschler's brigade. For her, this wasn't about the CIA or the People's Public Security Forces of Vietnam. It was about finding justice for her mom and dad and her people. I looked straight at Kim. 'In her place, I'd have done just the same.'

He seemed to find this amusing. 'Loyal to the last. Honour among enemies – isn't that sweet? But it's too bad that's not the way this story will play out.'

He went to stand immediately behind Kim, looked down and stroked her hair.

I saw her flinch but she kept her eyes on me. I made a faint smile, as if to say *Don't worry, I got this covered.* But I hadn't.

Then I thought about the item I borrowed from Tedstone.

Weschler looked directly at me and started talking again. 'Here's how it's gonna go down, Wat. I'll kill you – or one of my boys will – using Kim's gun. We took it from her when she turned Lone Ranger and came looking for me at my place this morning. Next, I'll have one of my guys shoot Kim with *your* gun. As with most of my plans, there's a real cool element of symmetry to this. I do like symmetry.'

He paused, as if to reflect on the aesthetics of his strategizing. Then went back to full throttle. 'Next, I'll tip off the cops – and, of course your colleagues in the media – that Kim was a Hanoi agent. This will, of course, also be true. Your body and hers will be arranged here in the mill to suggest a gunfight in which you shot one another. Yet again, Wat, you'll be hailed a hero. Unfortunately, though this time you'll be a dead one.'

I thought some more about the item I borrowed from Tedstone.

I needed to buy time, so I said, 'You got it wrong, Heck. You have too much to cover up. Rhyme Dillard, head of MPD Homicide, knows the whole story. So does my city editor Maggie Call, not to mention Joseph Tedstone. This plan of yours might seem perfectly symmetrical, but in reality it's bent and busted. It just won't wash.'

He laughed. 'It already has. There's no evidence linking me to anything incriminating, now or in Vietnam – especially with you and Kim gone. I already destroyed Joe Tedstone's tape and the Zetchiks are dead.'

'What about the photos of you and Christine and Deborah Kinsley?' I was grasping at straws, but I still needed more time. 'They would turn Paula against you, wreck your marriage and ruin your political career.'

More laughter. He was totally getting his rocks off. 'Deborah called me soon after you left. She told me all about those pictures and exactly what you said to her.'

That was unexpected. Or was it? We went after Deborah and threatened the new life she'd made in Portland. People under that sort of pressure can do all sorts of unpredictable shit. Maybe she panicked, maybe she saw an opportunity.

He must have read my expression because he went on chuckling. 'I wouldn't be too hard on her. She was trying to play both ends against the middle. But ultimately, she has every reason to want those photos kept under wraps.'

I said, 'It won't be up to Deborah.'

He moved away from Kim and came back toward me. 'Doesn't really matter. As you told Deborah, those photos are classified CIA material. And I know people at Langley who'd be desperate to make them vanish. Don't forget they were obtained by a communist agent who infiltrated Langley.

And she obtained them specifically to bring down a US presidential candidate. If the CIA high-ups did anything except destroy those pictures, they'd effectively be doing the bidding of Uncle Sam's sworn enemies.'

I thought again about the item I borrowed from Tedstone. And again about Weschler's weakness. Maybe it was overconfidence after all – or, more specifically, blind faith in his own planning skills.

The immediate upshot of this was he didn't have a gun on me. True, he had my Heckler & Koch, but that was in his pocket. He was relying on the shooters on the stairs.

And now he was standing nine feet in front of me. Not as close as I'd have liked, but close enough.

I took a breath. I looked at Kim and tilted my head ever so slowly, ever so slightly.

She blinked several times in quick succession and I knew she was on my frequency. Of course she had no idea what I had in mind, but she knew I had something.

I glanced up at the shooters, then across the shop floor, then back at Weschler. 'You sure your boys got every angle covered?'

'Of course I am.'

I didn't say anything. I hadn't actually been looking for a blind spot – that wasn't part of my plan. But I spotted one. Weird how you sometimes see stuff when you're not really looking. Right then this knowledge couldn't help us, but I hung onto it all the same.

A few seconds went by. More, then more still. But Weschler wasn't buying.

It seemed my ruse had failed.

Then he took my bait. He half turned and looked up. Like a lot of meticulous people, he couldn't resist a quick check.

# FIFTY-SEVEN

I moved the moment Weschler did.

His shooters hesitated. They should have opened fire. Instead they were wondering why their boss was looking up at them.

I closed the distance before they could react.

I tackled Weschler side-on and got my right forearm around his neck, twisting him through 90 degrees so I was directly behind him. Next, I hauled him to the ground on top of me, using him as a shield. He wriggled and twisted, but that only made target acquisition even more difficult for the shooters.

They were shouting among themselves. They were confused. Just what I wanted.

I kept my right arm locked tight around Weschler's throat and used my free hand to reach into my wind breaker pocket for the item I'd borrowed from Tedstone – the M18 smoke grenade he'd been using as a paperweight. Weschler was still struggling but he couldn't get any leverage. He must have thought I was trying to strangle him because he put all his efforts into trying to prise my arm from his throat.

More shouting up above told me his boys didn't know what to do. Maybe they thought I had a gun in his back, or a knife.

I placed the smoke grenade ring between my teeth pulled the pin. Dense violet fumes came fizzing out of the canister, billowing fast into the industrial space. When I was sure we were covered I grabbed my Heckler & Koch from Weschler's pocket and shoved him away into the purple fog. Ripping the duct tape from Kim's mouth, I took out my pocket knife and set to work cutting her wrists free.

Over her shoulder, she said, 'Why didn't you shoot the bastard? Or at least hang onto him?'

I carried on sawing the nylon cord. 'I couldn't hang onto him *and* cut you free. Which would you have preferred?'

The smoke was still getting thicker, but I knew it would start to subside in 60 seconds or less. Weschler's voice carried through the psychedelic mist. He was telling his guys to come get us.

Seconds later feet were clanging on the steel stairs, louder and louder.

It was difficult to tell how many. I thought I counted two sets of footfalls.

The cord binding Kim's wrists parted and I gave her the knife so she could free her feet.

I looked around and saw the knife guy appear through the smoke holding a snub-nose revolver in two hands.

I was used to working in smoke and nailed him before he saw me. I veered left and went at him from the side, driving the heel of my hand into the side of his face. There was a muted crack and he went down mid-stride.

My advantage vanished when the guy who played the

beat cop emerged from the smoke with an automatic pistol pointed right at me at a range of three feet.

I braced myself.

I saw him smile.

It got wiped clean off his face when Kim loomed behind him and smashed the chair she'd been tied to over his shoulders. He went down on all fours. She sent a knee-height karate kick to his head and it was good night from him.

There was more movement on the stairs. But the footsteps weren't coming toward us. I guessed Weschler was regrouping, waiting for the smoke to clear, which was starting to happen.

So we grabbed the guns from the beat cop and knife guy and headed for the cover I'd spotted by accident a few seconds earlier – the cylinder head of an old steam engine. It wasn't ideal. We had to crouch low and flush against the rusty metal. We couldn't even stretch our legs without getting our feet shot off. But the smoke was fading fast and the block of old machinery was a damn sight better than nothing.

I glanced at her. 'You all right?'

She nodded and asked the same of me and I nodded back.

I made a grim smile. 'Never thought I'd end up fighting alongside Charlie against an American three-star.'

She racked the Berretta she'd taken from the knife guy and gave me that bold smile that reminded me so much of Linh. 'Strange world we live in.'

# FIFTY-EIGHT

We carried out a quick inventory of our ammunition and the outcome wasn't encouraging. I had nine rounds in my Heckler & Koch and there were eight rounds in the Beretta, plus six in the Smith & Wesson snub-nose. Against this, Weschler had two AK-47s, each holding 30 rounds and possibly more, depending on the magazine type. And this was assuming they didn't have spare magazines or other weapons.

If we stayed in our present position we'd run out of ammunition long before they did. Just as importantly, those assault rifles were much more accurate than our handguns.

Making a run for the main doors across 50 yards of open ground was out of the question. Closing the range was almost as problematic. If we went after them we'd be exposed on the stairs, while they'd have the cover of the elevated steel platforms.

We leaned back against the cylinder head and tucked our knees to our chests.

After some time she said, 'Any ideas?'

'No. You?'

'We need to think. We can't just sit here.'

So we sat there, thinking.

At last I came up a plan. Of sorts.

I pointed to the nearest of a sequence of rectangular iron columns that flanked both sides of the main mill structure. Each one comprised two parallel shafts reinforced by diagonal latticework. 'If I can get up top, I'll be level with the highest platform. Then we'll have a fighting chance.'

She gave me a sceptical look. 'If they spot you halfway, that old ironwork won't give you much protection. You'll have nowhere to go and they could pick you off in fairly short order.'

I mustered a smile. 'Better make sure I don't get spotted.'

In the absence of anything better, she agreed.

She kept the Beretta and snub-nose and I took my Heckler & Koch. The plan was for her to fire at prolonged intervals, giving the impression that both of us were still pinned down behind the cylinder block.

My first challenge was reaching the iron column. It stood thirty yards away, close to the wall opposite the one Weschler and his guys occupied. Unless I could get there undetected, the whole plan would turn to shit.

On my mark, she fired three rounds. The idea wasn't to hit Weschler or his guys, just to keep their heads down as I broke cover.

I set off at a crouch across the uneven concrete floor. I had to move fast, but just as importantly, quiet. The ground underfoot was covered in all sorts of trash – broken booze bottles, crushed soda cans, candy wrappers – so I was extra careful where I put my feet. Kim laid down four more rounds of suppressing fire, spaced out at intervals of five or ten seconds. Whenever she fired I increased my pace, using the gunshots to drown out any noise I made.

By the time I reached the base of the column I'd counted seven shots from Kim – more than half of her 13 rounds. Weschler's boys had returned fire with two or three short bursts that struck the cylinder head and went whining away into the empty mill. That would have reduced their ammunition too, though I was sure they had a lot more to spare than we did.

Close up, the column was much bigger than I first thought. And badly corroded. Some of the wrought iron flaked away in my fingers. I looked up at the 60 foot climb. I didn't have a lot of confidence, but then I didn't have a lot of choice. So I started my ascent, using the diagonal lattice ties and horizontal members as hand and footholds.

I made the first 20 feet without a hitch. The column ran parallel to the main mill wall, which was only two feet away. I had hoped to brace my back against it as extra support, but the brickwork was slick with moss and rivulets of water so I ditched the idea and pressed on.

I was a little over 30 feet up when a diagonal section of latticework came away in one hand. I swung outward, holding on with other. A shower of rusty fragments fell to the ground, but made no sound.

I glanced across the mill. I was level with the guy on the lower platform. He was lying prone, aiming his AK at the cylinder block. Kim was crouched behind it, a pistol in each hand. Atop the second flight of stairs, Weschler and the other shooter seemed to be standing on the highest platform. I could see their heads and shoulders but I needed more elevation to get a clean shot at them.

I had to carry on moving. First, though, I had to work out what to do with the chunk of iron that had sheared away in my hand. If I tossed it to the ground it would make a resounding clatter. So I tucked it inside my shirt and continued to climb. It was heavy and chafed my skin, though I guessed worse things could have happened.

Fifty feet up, one of them did.

I heard the critters before I saw them. At first I thought the noise came from old electrical wiring that was somehow carrying a current. Then a hornet buzzed me, and another and another. Within seconds they were all around me, blurring my vision, fizzing in my ears.

I pressed on, reminding myself that I was invading their turf, not the other way round. Trouble was, these guys didn't get that I was just passing through. Their nest would be close by and as far as they were concerned I was threatening it. One landed on the back of my neck, a second on my forehead, others on my hands. I'd been stung before by bigger hornets than these, so that didn't bother me. Multiple stings, though, was something else. That might affect my coordination and make me fall. I also knew some hornet species could squirt venom in the eyes of intruders, causing temporary blindness. Ordinarily I'd have shut my eyes, but I couldn't carry on climbing without looking where I was going. All I could do was hope these hornets weren't squirters and move up the column as fast as possible.

A few feet higher, I came across their nest. It resembled a misshapen papier-mâché basketball crammed into a wall cavity. Scores of hornets were swarming in and out of the entrance, but most seemed to be coming out – and heading right at me.

I pressed on, groping up through the blizzard of wings. After another ten feet their attention started to wane. Ten feet higher than that, they vanished, apart from one or two that had gotten caught up in my windbreaker. I gave them a few seconds to find their way out. Then I pressed on.

Soon after that, I reached my objective. This was a steel beam that ran horizontally from one side of the mill to the other, linking the column I just climbed to the platform where Weschler and one of his guys were positioned. Weschler was holding the second assault rifle and the other dude didn't seem to be armed.

At last, Kim and I were in a position to engage them on more equal terms. The accuracy of the AKs would still give them the edge, but from this elevation I had a good chance of hitting them. And I had the element of surprise.

I looked down and gave her a thumbs-up sign. She returned it and prepared to fire.

Taking out the Heckler & Koch, I aimed at the guy on the lower platform. I fired two rounds at his head. A pink feather of blood spurted from his skull and he went limp.

Weschler and the other guy reacted fast. I got two shots away before ducking behind the column. A burst of automatic fire pinged and snapped against the iron latticing. Somehow the ancient shafts and ties kept me safe.

I looked over and saw Weschler moving along the platform, trying to get a better line on me. The other guy was racing down the stairs to retrieve the other assault rifle from his dead buddy.

Kim stepped out from behind the cylinder head, took aim with the Beretta and fired four times. The guy cried out and grabbed his thigh. He was bleeding heavily, but he didn't stop. He went tumbling down the bottom few steps, rolled across the lower platform and snatched the AK from the hands of his compadre. Anticipating what was going to happen, Kim threw herself back behind the cylinder head. The same instant, it was hit by a long burst of automatic fire.

I craned forward and fired two rounds into the wounded man's back. He twitched and rolled sideways, still firing. Then he dropped the gun and slumped forward.

On the upper platform opposite, Weschler had gotten distracted by the action below. But he quickly returned his attention to me and took aim with his AK.

I had three rounds left and no time to do anything except shoot in his general direction. I must have gotten lucky. One of my shots ricocheted off the handrail near to where he was standing. It didn't hurt him, but it did spoil his aim and his volley struck the brickwork behind me.

In my peripheral vision I saw Kim running up the lower stairs. She snatched up the second AK, leaned out over the safety rail and fired a short burst at Weschler. He threw himself backward as the rounds hit the steelwork around him.

He looked at me, then back at Kim. I could see the frustration on his face. He knew I was out of ammunition and wanted more than anything to finish me off. But he couldn't ignore the threat from Kim. I was effectively unarmed and going nowhere, so dealing with her had to take priority.

She'd started to climb the steps to the higher platform with her back pressed against the wall. Weschler saw this and fired three short bursts. She pressed herself flat on the stairs. Bullets flew over her, hitting the flaky brickwork and showering her in a cloud of red dust. She picked herself up, shooting back as she continued her climb. She fired once, twice, three times and ... a hollow click.

She was out of ammunition. Game over.

# FIFTY-NINE

I shouted, 'Kim, get out now!'

She hesitated.

Weschler didn't. He shouldered his AK and aimed at me.

'Plenty of time to bag the pair of you. You first, though, Wat.'

I wasn't interested in his gloating. 'Kim, for God's sake, go!'

Weschler was loving this. 'Isn't that touching? Such devotion, such selflessness.'

Kim moved up a step. Maybe she thought she could rush him, but she wouldn't even get close before he put her down.

To me, he said, 'I got you in my sights now, Wat. It's been a blast going up against you, it really has. But this is one fight you're not gonna walk away from.'

I continued to ignore him. 'Kim, unless you get out right now, no one will know what went down. Not the truth, anyways. Please, just – '

The rest of my sentence was cut off when Weschler opened fire.

The bullet ripped through my left deltoid, ricocheting off the wall behind me. I twisted under the impact, felt blood ooze warm and sticky down my arm.

That was his screwing around shot. The next would be for real.

If he went for a head shot I'd know nothing about it. But I was certain he wouldn't. That would end the fun way too soon. He'd want to watch me suffer. I guessed he'd put a bullet in my upper body, then two, then more. And he'd pause at intervals to watch me checking out, savouring the moment, the sense of hard-won victory.

I steeled myself. I'd been close to death too many times to fear it. My overwhelming feeling was exasperation at not having nailed Bootstrap. And concern for what he'd do to Kim if she didn't do what I'd told her.

Weschler was riding me again. 'This is it, Wat. Ready to field a big one?'

I said nothing. Refusing to play along was the only weapon I had.

I looked him right in the eyes. I waited for the inevitable and –

Another click echoed across the space between us.

He pulled the trigger again, with the same result. He looked at the gun, as if it was to blame for the lack of bullets.

In those few seconds, the whole fight turned on its head.

I stepped out onto the steel beam connecting the iron column to the platform he was standing on. The beam was 12-inches wide and the surface was flat but smooth.

I started walking toward Weschler, still looking at his rifle. Blood continued to run from my shoulder to my fingertips, dripping down into the void and slapping on the concrete floor 60 feet below.

Weschler sensed what I was doing. He looked up at me.

He looked over his should at Kim, who had appeared on the platform maybe 20 feet from him.

He seemed angry and confused, as if this couldn't be happening.

The way I saw it, he had three choices: Stay put and take on Kim and me; try to get past Kim; or try to get past me.

I knew what he was gonna do before he stepped onto the beam and headed in my direction.

He'd brought the assault rifle and I figured he was planning on clubbing me with it, or using it to poke me off of the beam.

He started out with confidence, striding out with only me in mind.

By the time he was 20 yards out, though, he seemed to become aware of his surroundings. He hesitated, stopped, and looked back at the platform.

'You could always turn around and go back, Heck.'

'Fuck you, Wat.'

I kept on walking. Seven years in Special Forces meant I was used to operating at height. Just as vitally, my attachment disorder meant I had zero anxiety. I'd learned before my first birthday that there was no such thing as a safe haven. I calibrated my emotions accordingly. This wasn't to say I was reckless or stupid. I knew as well as Weschler did that I'd die if I fell. For me, though, the solution was real simple: Don't fall. That beam might as well have been six inches off the ground as sixty feet.

I kept on walking. I crossed the midway point.

Weschler stayed where he was. There was less than five yards between us.

'You're losing blood fast, Wat.'

'Plenty more where that came from, Heck. You should have shot me properly instead of messing around.'

He turned the assault rifle through 180 degrees so he was holding the barrel in both hands.

Then he came at me swinging it like a club.

I stood my ground, watching the arc of the wooden stock, and ducked as it swept across the centre of the beam.

Weschler wobbled, slowly regaining his balance.

He switched the rifle again so the barrel was pointed at me. Of course there was no bayonet, but he lunged at me as if there was, trying to shove me off of the beam. I feinted left and he jabbed the barrel under my right arm. I grabbed it with both hands and tugged. My footing was sure, his was all over the place. He could either let go of the rifle or go over the edge. He let go. The AK was of no interest to me so I let it fall.

'Just you and me now, Heck. The White House looks a long way off now, wouldn't you say?'

'Depends on your perspective, Wat. I get past you and the girl, the big prize is still waiting.'

'Think you can do it, Heck?'

He made a wistful smile. In that moment I recalled the guy I'd fought with deep inside Charlie country. The guy I'd liked, the guy I'd trusted.

'You're a poetry geek, Wat. You recall those lines Montgomery quoted to Allied troops on the eve of D-Day?'

I nodded. 'From James Graham, Marquis of Montrose. *My Dear and Only Love.* Nice verse.'

'What was it? *He either fears his fate too much, or his deserts are small, who dare not put it to the touch, to win or lose it all.* Just as appropriate here and now, wouldn't you say?'

'Yeah,' I said. 'Pretty appropriate.'

He glanced down at the ground. For a moment he seemed panicky. By the time he looked back at me, though, his expression was determined. He was gonna win or lose it all.

He shuffled forward, jabbing left, then right. I titled one way and the other and watched his punches go wide. Then I caught him under the jaw with right fist. He staggered back, almost fell, but somehow stabilized. I hadn't hit him hard, but the blow had the intended effect. I could see fresh rage burning in his eyes. He came at me again, this time without any sense of caution. I stepped back from one roundhouse punch, and another and another. Gotta say I was impressed that he could do all that crazy shit and still remain on the beam. It was only when he tried to kick my kneecap that his self-defeat came to fruition. I saw it unfold in slo-mo. As his right foot came up, his left ankle buckled. He keeled over backward and sideways, smashing his pelvis against the sharp edge of the beam. I heard a muffled crack of bone, a faint wince, and he went tumbling.

Didn't make a sound as he fell. I supposed that was his final *fuck you* to me, to Kim, to the world. He hit the ground and lay real still, a scarlet halo seeping around the circumference of his head.

# SIXTY

I crossed to the platform where Kim was waiting. She hugged me tight and close for a long time. But we both knew whatever there was between us died with Weschler's revelation that she was working for Hanoi. She didn't deny it, I didn't press it. But we both knew the deal.

At last she said, 'We've won.'

'*You've* won.'

She looked at me, mystified. 'Surely we've finally gotten justice – for my family, for Linh, for Johnny. For thousands of innocent people who got chewed up and spit out by Weschler's bodycount machine.'

I made a sorry smile. 'True enough. Weschler's dead and won't get anywhere near high office this side of hell. But we still don't have any evidence. We can't prove any of the stuff he did actually happened.'

'You can still run a story. You can quote Joseph Tedstone. I can get you those photos of Weschler with Christine and Deborah Kinsley. And you can write what you like about Weschler because you can't libel the dead.'

'Nor can they answer back, which dilutes the credibility of the story. As for quoting Tedstone, he's still under indictment for the murders of Johnny and Keith Zetchik. And those pictures are well and good, but they don't directly incriminate Weschler of anything except playing away in Vietnam.'

I hated pissing on her parade, but this wasn't the victory she imagined and there was no good pretending otherwise.

We went down to the shop floor and examined the carnage. Weschler had died instantly. The two guys on the stairs were also dead, and the two on the ground still unconscious. The one I hit had a badly broken jaw and had bit clean through his tongue, part of which was lying nearby. The one Kim kicked in the head was barely breathing. Clearly, they needed urgent medical attention.

'We gotta call an ambulance,' I said. 'And we gotta call Dillard.'

# SIXTY-ONE

The homicide chief was disturbingly calm all the way back to MPD headquarters. He asked Kim to wait in the reception area and showed me into his office. When I was seated, he tore a strip off me. I didn't blame him. I'd trampled all over his investigation, along with all sorts of law enforcement jurisdictions and federal agency protocols. I was a reporter, so none of that bothered me, but I understood why it bothered Dillard. He was left with a dead presidential candidate and two other bodies, plus two guys out cold with head injuries in the hospital. This was not to mention a series of high level and highly complex conspiracy allegations going back to 1968.

When he was done riding me, he and a sergeant took separate statements from me and Kim. She and I had agreed what we were gonna say before calling the cops and I told Dillard the whole story, leaving out her Hanoi connection.

By early afternoon we were both free to leave the cop shop, although Dillard insisted we stay inside the beltway. I went to talk to Maggie and Kim went back to Langley.

Maggie wanted a two-paragraph holding story and some time to think about what we should publish in the next day's paper. Then she sent me home under strict instructions to get some rest.

The rain had started to come down by the time I opened my front door. I opened a beer, made a cheese sandwich and went into the living room. Four hours' sleep in the last 48 left me dead beat and I had no intention of ignoring Maggie's orders. I finished the beer and sandwich and headed for the stairs.

Half way across the living room I notice the flashing light on my telephone answering machine. Probably nothing, but I checked anyways. The first message was from Maggie. She said she was calling at 1.00pm and wanted to know where I was. I'd arrived back in the newsroom shortly after, which made the message redundant.

My eyes were stinging, my brain barely functioning as I played the second message.

Reggie's voice filled the room.

I was wide awake.

'Hello again, Wat. I hope you got back from the Virginia boonies without too much trouble.'

There was an apologetic note in her voice, and, I thought, forlorn longing. I stared at the answering machine as if she was actually there – that she'd somehow squeezed inside it.

'As you've no doubt gathered, I'm out of the country. I don't think you'd come after me. Not worth your while. But it's not a chance I can take, so I'm not going to tell you where I am. I just hope you got him and I can find some sort of peace. I guess I'll find out soon enough. That sort of news will be on the front pages the world over.'

She paused. I heard hollow electronic popping and

sizzling, a background babble of conversation, but it was way too faint to tell which language.

For a few seconds I started to think she was done. End of message.

Then she was talking again. 'I suppose you're wondering what I'm rambling on about. Truth is I'm deeply sorry about all this. I really regret what I did. But, like I said, spending the rest of my days behind bars won't change any of that.'

More hesitation. In the echoey fizzing I picked up some sort of public announcement. Again, though, it was too distant and distorted to pick out any words. She'd no doubt made the call at an airport or train station. I thought about where she might be. She'd ditched me in the Virginia countryside just after midnight and left this telephone message sometime after the one from Maggie at 1.00pm. That would have given her at least 13 hours to disappear. And she'd have had her escape route carefully planned. By now she could be anywhere – Mexico, Canada, South America, someplace in the Caribbean, even Europe.

Suddenly she was talking again. 'One thing I can do, though, is give you something by way of atonement. I couldn't have done this any sooner because I wanted to be out of reach – specifically *his* reach. But here's my parting gift: I made a copy of Joseph Tedstone's cassette tape, as well as a recording of Heck briefing me on the elimination of Johnny and the Zetchiks.'

She broke off yet again. She must have been using a public pay phone and I figured she was waiting for passers-by to move away. I started to worry she'd run out of change, or we'd get cut off before she could complete the message. I pictured more travellers milling around that pay phone, stopping her from talking: *Move you fuckers, move!* The silence continued.

How much change did she have?

How much space was there left on my answering machine tape?

Then she came back. 'You can find everything you need in my old apartment in Adams Morgan. Guy like you will find it easily enough, but you may need to get that front page story written fast, so here's a clue to help you. Remember the EP we listened to the second night you stayed over? Think about the second part of the title.'

I thought about that night, and about the record she played: *Hot and Cool* by the Slickee Boys.

'I'm gonna sign off now, Wat. Goodbye and God bless. I don't deserve it, but if you can find it within yourself, wish me luck.'

She hung up. She was right, she didn't deserve it. She'd killed four people in cold blood and whether any of them had it coming was irrelevant. But she had seen the error of her ways and she had given me Weschler. And, weirdly, our fake friendship had felt somehow genuine. So I wished her luck anyways.

With my tiredness forgotten, I picked up the keys to the pool car parked outside and drove over to her place on Columbia Road NW. I used my lock picks to open the door and went inside. The place was oddly neat and tidy, like the Reggie I knew had never lived here.

I stood in the middle of the living room and thought about the clue she gave me. She could have been using the second part of the *Hot and Cool* record title literally or colloquially. I considered the former more likely and looked around the little apartment for something cold where she might have placed the recordings. The refrigerator was the most obvious option. I opened the door and found myself looking at a Tupperware container. Taking it out, I placed it on the counter and took off the lid. Inside were two cassette tapes. One was labelled *Heck Weschler briefing*, the other *Joseph Tedstone, Vietnam*.

I inserted one cassette in the tape deck Reggie had left in the living room and played it, then the other. Then I grabbed the phone and called Maggie.

I said, 'We got our story.'

# SIXTY-TWO

Next morning I walked to work despite the heavy rain – or more accurately, because of it. I'd slept 12 hours straight but still felt a little groggy and there was a comforting illusion of cleansing as I moved through the downpour.

I hadn't planned on making the detour. That came later when I realized I was being tailed. All those umbrellas in the wet fuzzy air made it difficult to tell. But after turning left, left and left again I was sure of my instincts. I wasn't worried, but I was curious.

I headed south along 17th Street NW, past the Executive Office building and Constitution Hall, then out toward the Tidal Basin. By the time I reached the west end of the Reflecting Pool the crowds of sodden pedestrians had thinned and I waited for my tail to catch up.

To my right, the mid-section of the Washington Monument was obscured by a strand of cloud, as if somebody with a pencil eraser had cut it in two. Over to the left, at the far end of the Reflecting Pool, the white marble of the Lincoln Memorial was weirdly luminous in the haze.

I heard her footsteps on the sidewalk behind me.

She said, 'What are you doing out here in the rain?'

I folded my umbrella as the downpour gave way to drizzle. 'What are you doing tailing me?'

I turned to face her. She looked outasight lovely in a shaft of watery sunlight that found its way through the rain. And even more like Linh.

'I didn't want any witnesses to this conversation.'

I smiled. 'Who's to say *you* weren't tailed?'

'See anyone watching?'

I took her point and told her about the phone message from Reggie.

She seemed pleased. She'd been a reporter and understood why it was important not just to bring down Weschler, but also to get the story out.

She came closer. 'Happy with your piece?'

'It's not my piece. Maggie said I was too much a part of the story to write it myself. It was the right call, no argument there. I went in yesterday and did an interview with Neil Dickinson, the White House correspondent, so it's his byline.'

'Still your scoop. Everyone will know that.'

'I guess.'

I told her I'd talked to Joseph Tedstone, that the charges against him had been dropped. And that I'd called Paula Weschler before the story hit the streets. She sounded composed and dignified and I got the impression she wasn't done with the political game.

Kim said, 'You did right by Joe Tedstone and Paula.'

There was a dragged-out quiet – a lot of things I wanted to say, and a lot of reasons not to say them. I didn't want to make this any more difficult than it already was for both of us.

At last she said, 'You know this is goodbye?'

'That's why I came out here. It's a good spot for farewells.'

'I have no choice, Wat.'

I looked away from her, along the Reflecting Pool. 'You think I'd rat you out, Kim? After all we've been through? Fuck the politics. Fuck it all.'

She gripped my arm, turned me to face her. '*You* wouldn't betray me. But someone else would. Weschler got that information from somebody at Langley. They might not have solid evidence yet, but they will sooner or later.'

She was right. Of course she was.

She moved a little nearer. 'Besides, how would you feel, knowing I was a communist agent operating on US soil?'

I said, 'I could live with it.' I knew I couldn't though. Up until now our loyalties hadn't been tested. But that might change. It would change.

'Take good care of yourself, Wat.' She leaned toward me and her lips touched mine. The kiss was delicate and brief, like the brush of a butterfly wing, yet somehow this added to its intensity.

We stood very close without touching. For a time I was lost in her fuzzy warmth. Then she took a step back and turned, walking away into the misty morning.

I stood and watched and thought.

I'd left part of myself in Vietnam and that was okay. I'd also *lost* part of myself, and that had never been okay. Kim came to DC and gave me back some of what had gone missing in action five years ago. She hadn't made what I lost okay. No one ever could. But she *had* levelled the score.

I glanced skyward as the rain came on again, heavier now. When I looked back, she'd vanished.

Where next for me? I had no clue. There was always work

for a hot metal hobo on the *Anywhere Times*. This was where I'd wind up, never mind the location or the job or the pay. For most folks there was no place like home. For me, though, there was no home like a place somewhere else. This was where you could always find me.